Sweet Life

Sweet Life

MIA KING

BERKLEY BOOKS, NEW YORK

THE BERKLEY PUBLISHING GROUP
Published by the Penguin Group
Penguin Group (USA) Inc.
375 Hudson Street, New York, New York 10014, USA
Penguin Group (Canada), 90 Eglinton Avenue East, Suite 700, Toronto, Ontario M4P 2Y3, Canada
(a division of Pearson Penguin Canada Inc.)
Penguin Books Ltd., 80 Strand, London WC2R 0RL, England
Penguin Group Ireland, 25 St. Stephen's Green, Dublin 2, Ireland (a division of Penguin Books Ltd.)
Penguin Group (Australia), 250 Camberwell Road, Camberwell, Victoria 3124, Australia
(a division of Pearson Australia Group Pty. Ltd.)
Penguin Books India Pvt. Ltd., 11 Community Centre, Panchsheel Park, New Delhi—110 017, India
Penguin Group (NZ), 67 Apollo Drive, Rosedale, North Shore 0632, New Zealand
(a division of Pearson New Zealand Ltd.)
Penguin Books (South Africa) (Pty.) Ltd., 24 Sturdee Avenue, Rosebank, Johannesburg 2196,
South Africa

Penguin Books Ltd., Registered Offices: 80 Strand, London WC2R 0RL, England

This is a work of fiction. Names, characters, places, and incidents either are the product of the author's imagination or are used fictitiously, and any resemblance to actual persons, living or dead, business establishments, events, or locales is entirely coincidental. The publisher does not have any control over and does not assume any responsibility for author or third-party websites or their content.

The recipes contained in this book are to be followed exactly as written. The publisher is not responsible for your specific health or allergy needs that may require medical supervision.

ISBN-13: 978-1-60751-084-0

PRINTED IN THE UNITED STATES OF AMERICA

Dedicated to my husband, Darrin

acknowledgments

This is always the easiest and the hardest part of writing a book.

In the course of writing *Sweet Life*, I learned to surrender more than once. My heartfelt thanks to my dear friend Nancy Martin, who read early drafts of the novel and offered words of wisdom whenever I felt stuck or at an impasse. To loosely paraphrase Byron Katie: *It is what is because it is, so you may as well enjoy it.*

To the readers of my first novel, *Good Things*, who took the time to tell me how much they enjoyed the book, and shared their contagious enthusiasm with others—thank you. Hugs to Marie Fellenstein Hale, Debbie Davis, Jamal Cuellar, and Patricia Wood, my Hawaii contingent who cheerleaded the book upon its release and told everyone to buy a copy. To my friends at the Thelma Parker Memorial Library, who at times saw me more than my own family and who love books and reading as much as I do—you'll always be the best home away from home.

I was fortunate enough to include recipes from some of my favorite local chefs and purveyors—thank you for being so good at what you do and for giving the book a true Hawaiian flavor.

Much aloha and gratitude to my agent, Jenny Bent, and her assistant, Victoria Horn, who are my lifeline to New York and always available whenever I need them. My editor, Wendy McCurdy and editorial assistant Allison Brandau, at Penguin Group and copyeditor Denise Barricklow all deserve a big thank-you for helping me craft a better story. Thank you.

And last, but never least, to my family, who have shown me how sweet life can be regardless of what life might throw your way: to my children, Maya and Eric, who put up with a preoccupied and distracted mother for the past few months, and especially to my husband, Darrin Gee, who was unwavering in his encouragement and support, and to whom this novel is dedicated.

We are full of paradise without knowing it.

THOMAS MERTON
(1915–1968)

prologue

"What am I doing here?"

Marissa Price, forty-one, was sitting in the driver's seat of her Audi SUV, staring at a house they paid too much for, watching her husband, Paul, from across the street. He was in the bedroom, moving around frantically, packing as if he had only five minutes to spare.

Four, actually.

Their daughter, Pansy, was still at a classmate's house, a random fourth-grader whose parent Marissa had seized in the parking lot of Pansy's new school, jockeying for an evening playdate so she and Paul could celebrate Valentine's Day with a romantic dinner out. It was their first time dining without Pansy since they had moved to Hawaii from New York last December, where they left behind a freezing ice storm, their nanny, and a killer three-bedroom apartment on East 72nd and Lexington.

The Waimea rain was coming down sideways, pelting the windshield with the force of a frenzied drummer at a rock concert. Marissa didn't bother to turn on the wipers—this way she couldn't tell if it was the rain or her tears that were obscuring her vision.

Three minutes to go.

In the not-so-far distance, a cow mooed. Another joined in. Marissa knew that it would only be a matter of time before the whole herd of cattle behind their house would join in the chorus. After about an hour of bellowing off-key, they would fall off to sleep, one by one, snoring loudly as if they all had bad colds and were terribly congested.

Which was ridiculous, of course. First, she had never heard of a cow catching cold, and second, it was seventy-six degrees outside.

Marissa saw Paul move rapidly through the house, from their bedroom down the hallway past the living room. He went out the side door to the small guesthouse that served as his study, where he spent the next couple minutes gathering the last of his things.

One minute to go.

The front door opened and Paul stood in the doorway, the light framing his body as he looked out into the night. Marissa's heart gave a kick of hope. Then she realized that he wasn't looking for her, but checking to see if he could make it to the garage without getting wet.

I should run him over right now, Marissa thought bitterly as she blinked back the tears. *Happy Valentine's Day, Paul!*

Instead, she turned on the headlights and maneuvered the car back into the street to get Pansy. Paul would be gone by the time they returned, and Marissa could probably get through the night without having to give her an explanation. Which was good, because Marissa had no idea what to tell their eight-year-old daughter.

How did this happen? Marissa supposed she was still in a state of shock. They had just moved to Hawaii. They had been celebrating Valentine's Day, for pete's sake! They were supposed to be toasting their new life in paradise.

The rain came down harder, making it difficult for Marissa to see into the night. Frustrated, but with no other choice, she wiped her eyes and slowed down, keeping her eyes fastened on the immediate stretch of road in front of her.

PART I

Paradise Calls

He ‘e‘epa ke aloha, he kula‘ilua.

Love is peculiar; it pushes in opposite directions.

'ekahi | one

When Marissa first heard the news last November, it was almost too good to be true. Leave New York city for Hawaii? *And* get paid for it?

"Just think," her husband said as he broke the news over dinner at La Pacifica. His name was Paul. "White sand beaches, balmy tropical breezes, swimming with the dolphins . . ."

"I know, Paul, I know. I was with you on our honeymoon, remember?" Marissa sipped her champagne, trying to appear nonchalant, but inside she was ready to burst.

"Of course. But that was Maui, honey. This is Hawaii."

Marissa gave a small laugh. "I heard you the first time, Paul. And if I remember correctly, Maui is *in* Hawaii, is it not?"

"Maui is in the *state* of Hawaii. The offer is to move to the *island* of Hawaii, which is also in the state of Hawaii." As if on cue, Paul pulled out a pocket map. "See? Flowing volcano, telescope observatories, Kona coffee . . . I'll be working on the coast, so we can either live here"—he pointed to some obscure point on the map—"or here." Another obscure point.

Marissa peered at the map, taking in the squiggles of blue and red. "Where are the schools?"

"The ones closest to where I'll be working are up here, in the town of Waimea. It's old cowboy country, about twenty-five-hundred feet up from sea level. It's supposedly cool in the evenings, but only twenty minutes to the beaches or the resort."

"Good. Because Pansy needs to be in whatever top school they have." Their daughter, Elizabeth "Pansy" Price, was eight and already a straight-A fourth grader at the prestigious L'Ecole Jardinière. She had skipped the second grade and still managed to be at the top of her class.

Paul glanced up from the map, a confident look on his face. "I'm sure they have excellent schools there. After all, this is Hawaii—all the dot com kids are probably out there lounging on the beach with their thirtysomething retired parents."

"Really?" She considered this.

"Supposedly." He grinned, knowing he had her attention now. "Michael Dell bought one of the resorts down the coast and is building a home nearby."

"Do you think his kids go to school there?"

"I don't know, I . . ."

"We should find out. Can you have Evelyn call around?" Evelyn was Paul's secretary at Fallon.

Paul sighed. "Just mellow out about it, Marissa, okay?"

"Okay, okay. I was just asking." Marissa picked up her fork and gave it a little wave before stabbing a spear of asparagus; she could do mellow.

"So Sam is proposing that we fly out for a short visit. I have a couple of meetings, but other than that we can check things out, see what the housing is like, visit the schools, soak in some sun . . ."

"That's a great idea." A winter tan . . . ha! Kate, her best friend, would be completely envious. "When?"

Paul didn't miss a beat. "How does this weekend sound? We could fly out on Friday. Shall I have Evelyn arrange it?"

Friday? Marissa stared at him, incredulous. "You mean *this* weekend?"

Paul was unfazed as he cut another piece of his guava-grilled rib eye steak. "Sure, why not? We'll fly out Friday. Catch a flight back late Monday evening, back by Tuesday. You'll be out of the office for a couple of days. Couldn't be easier."

Yeah, if you don't have a major deal closing and two more projects breathing down your neck. "Paul, I have the Schumann deal closing this week. Plus I need to start reviewing the feasibility studies for the Macomber project in London." She reached for her water, shaking her head in disbelief. *Friday!*

"But you don't need to be there to do that, do you? I mean, you can take your work with you—we do it all the time." Paul polished off his steak. "You fly out at a moment's notice whenever a client has a problem and still manage to juggle your other projects while you're on the road. This will be a hell of a lot easier. You can respond to e-mails and your clients won't have a clue if you're sitting at your desk or lying on the beach."

"Point taken, but this is not a good week for me to leave . . ."

"Marissa, it's not my call. The company wants us to go out before we say yes, to make sure you won't have any second thoughts. They've had a run of bad luck with general managers at this property and they need to know that if I say yes, my spouse is on board."

"On board?" Marissa felt herself stiffen. "But you *just* told me about the offer, Paul!"

"Well, they just told *me*. These things move fast, Marissa, you know that. Fallon needs a GM now—they need to know now who's going to be steering the ship this busy season." Paul's company, Fallon Resort Properties, LLP, was an upscale international hotel and resort chain. He had never considered a position on any of the properties, preferring to stay in New York at the home office, but this opportunity, along with a hefty raise, seemed to have changed his mind.

"The busy season? Wait a minute." Marissa frowned and did the math in her head. "If Fallon needs a GM on property by the busy season, which is traditionally November-December . . ."

Paul busied himself with buttering a roll.

"Then you need to be there . . . *now*." She stared at him in disbelief. It was already the beginning of November.

"Three weeks, to be exact," he said. "Maybe four. Now before you say anything else . . ."

"Paul, are you crazy? There's no way we can move that fast!" The calendar for the next month scrolled before her eyes. "Pansy has semester finals. I'd barely have time to give notice and wrap up my work. And what about the apartment?" They lived in a highly coveted three-bedroom apartment on 72nd and Lexington.

Paul wasn't concerned. "Fallon will back us up as best they can—help us sell our old place, help us get a new one, pay any penalties for pulling Pansy out of school—this sort of thing happens all of the time. The current GM will be gone by mid-December and they need someone to be there. So why not me? Us?"

"Why not? Because we need time to plan." Marissa's mind swirled with all the things that would need to be done. Work, Pansy's school, the apartment, their things . . .

it was overwhelming. How could they just walk away from the life they had? "Because these things take time, Paul."

"And sometimes these things just happen." Paul leaned forward and looked at her earnestly, taking her hand in his. "Marissa, this is a great opportunity . . . you know it is. You always talk about quitting and getting out of the rat race. Now, with my bump in pay, you can. And we'll be in Hawaii, of all places. It couldn't be better than if we had planned it this way."

That part was certainly true: they had been talking off and on for the past few years about Marissa resigning from her position as a director for Paradigm Management, a boutique management consulting firm, so that she could have more time with Pansy. They had been paying Consuelo, the nanny, overtime for the past year and a half and the idea of spending more time with their only daughter had its appeal.

Still, being a dual-income family had its advantages: they liked the extra money and it kept Marissa well-dressed with a few choice designer pieces. Plus, there was always some new deal coming up that Marissa wanted to be involved in ("Probably the last one," she always said). Work could be a pain in the ass but it also gave her a rush of adrenaline that she couldn't find anywhere else.

In the past, whenever there was an opportunity for her to leave Paradigm, it just never seemed to make sense. Pansy was busy with school and with all of her extra-curricular activities, and Marissa would basically be a chauffeur, so what was the point? But now, with this offer to move to Hawaii and a sizable raise, it certainly wasn't something to ignore. Just the same, Marissa couldn't help but feel a little uneasy.

The waiter began to clear their table. "Would you like dessert this evening?"

Marissa shook her head just as Paul said, "Definitely." She

fidgeted while Paul made his selection. How could he think about dessert right now?

Paul turned back to her, his face eager. "Okay, here's what I'm thinking: we fly out this weekend for a few days. It'll be great, like a second honeymoon. We'll take Pansy, bring Consuelo . . . I'm sure Fallon will be more than happy to pay for two rooms if it means they might have a new GM in place soon."

Marissa hedged; everything was moving so fast. She brushed away some stray crumbs the waiter had missed. "I just . . . I don't know. I don't want Pansy to fall behind in her studies."

Paul rolled his eyes. "She's in the fourth grade, Marissa, not some post-doctorate program. She'll miss a couple of days of school—oh no! What's the worst that could happen? She gets an A instead of an A plus?"

He was teasing her now. Marissa pulled a face and looked away. "Very funny."

Pansy's education had always been more important to Marissa than Paul, due in large part to the fact that she had struggled through both college and business school—financially, not academically. Her parents had worked union jobs and couldn't afford to send her to anything other than a state school, so Marissa made up for it by holding one, and sometimes two, jobs while juggling a full-course load. In retrospect, she wouldn't have changed anything because it primed her for the business world she was now so successful in, but it also made Marissa committed to Pansy's education.

She had explained to Paul, over and over again, why a good education from a highly respected institution was one of the best things they could do for Pansy, especially since she was a girl. But Paul was used to having things happen so effortlessly that he didn't believe her. He got into the schools he wanted, his family had enough money to pay for it, and in the end he got offers from the companies of his choice. Maybe he was right, maybe he wasn't, but Marissa didn't want to take that chance. Now, not wanting to rehash it all again in the middle of dinner, she simply said, "Pansy's such a smart kid. I just want her to have every opportunity."

"And living in Hawaii is one of those opportunities," Paul pointed out. He settled back in his chair, feigning resignation. "I'm not going to beg you to move to Hawaii. If you want to stay in New York, we'll stay in New York."

"Paul, that's not what I'm . . ."

"I'm fine passing on the promotion and pay raise. It'll be fun, both of us working until retirement. You and me, honey—I can see it now!" He put up his hands, framing the future, then he looked over at her and grinned.

Despite herself, Marissa smiled. He had her and she knew it. *Oh, what the hell!* They never did anything spontaneous anymore and the city was already gearing up for another cold winter. A short break in the sun would be nice. "Okay, fine. You win. If they need me at work, they can always conference me in. We'll fly out this weekend to take a look. And if it goes well . . ."

". . . then it's paradise for us!" Paul was beaming. "I have a feeling about this, Marissa. Like it's *really* going to change things for us." He leaned forward and gave her a deep kiss, catching her off guard, then settled back in his chair, beaming.

With her lips tingling from the warmth of her husband's kiss, Marissa felt a surge of hope. Maybe Paul was right: this move could be exactly what they needed. No more late night arguments or days of silent treatment. Sex might even become a reality again.

Paul gave her a broad smile as he reached for his dessert fork and dipped it into the coconut tiramisu. He closed his eyes in exaggerated ecstasy. "Oh, this is amazing. You have to try this, Marissa." He pushed a forkful toward her.

She took a bite, not used to having Paul feed her. Wow, it *was* good. Why did things always taste better in a restaurant? Not that she could have made this at home, but still. She motioned for him to give her another bite, enjoying the moment. "How long is the assignment for again?"

"Three years."

Three years. In three years, Marissa would be forty-four, Paul would be forty-seven, Pansy eleven. It seemed like a long time but she knew it would fly by.

"Well," she said, sighing, "I'm probably due for a midlife crisis, so I may as well do it on the beach."

Paul pointed his fork at her, suddenly serious. "You saw me through mine, honey, I'll see you through yours. Although I'm sure it will be more fun with a couple of mai tais in hand, of course."

Marissa bit her lip, not wanting to ruin a good moment. A few years back, Paul had been passed over for a major promotion and, both disappointed and stressed out, had gained fifteen pounds in the span of two months, which then threw him into a mild depression. His waistline had expanded two sizes and Marissa had to order him new pants online since he was too embarrassed to go shopping. Not exactly her definition of a midlife crisis, but Marissa stood by him as he went to therapy (and where she took her fair share of potshots from Paul, who claimed she "wore him down" with all the arguing and was "demanding" and "unromantic"). But they got through it. Paul started exercising again, had regained his trim figure and, along with it, his confidence.

Now he was leaning across the table to give her another kiss. "This is going to be great, I just know it." He was almost giddy.

Marissa gestured for the waiter. If they were going to do this, she was going to need reinforcements after all.

The waiter appeared. "Yes?"

"Do you have any Kona coffee?"

"We do. Handpicked, estate-roasted. It's not a blend, so you should be prepared. It's pretty strong."

"That sounds great. Oh, and bring whatever dessert has the most chocolate."

"That would be our signature chocolate lava cake, served warm with vanilla bean ice cream and fresh raspberries."

Marissa checked the time: 9:45 P.M. She'd be working late tonight, that much was clear. "Perfect."

"You're going where? Why? *When?*" Marissa's best friend, Kate Porter, was staring at her dumbstruck from across the table at their favorite restaurant, Euphrates, on 51st and Broadway.

"The island of Hawaii. They call it the Big Island." Marissa let this sink in for a moment before continuing. "Fallon made Paul an offer that'll be pretty hard to refuse. We'll go out this weekend to take a look. There are a lot of factors to take into consideration, Kate. It's a big decision."

"Mm hmm, yeah." Kate nodded her head impatiently. "So if you say yes, how soon before you go?"

Marissa took a deep breath. "*If* we say yes, then we'll be out there by December."

"December? That's next month! I can't believe you're telling me all this now . . . you may as well just have sent a postcard!" Kate was glaring at her. At forty, Kate was single and the owner of a successful art gallery in Tribeca. She and Marissa had been best friends for the past decade and a half.

Marissa gave her friend an apologetic look. "I'm sorry, but Paul just told me last night. I had five minutes to process the news and then it was crazy when we got home." She would tell Kate later how they ended up having the best sex she'd had all year as soon as they walked through the door. "And then there was a mini-crisis at work and I had to spend the morning assuring Arthur that I wouldn't drop the Schumann deal in the toilet." Arthur Mesker was the managing partner of Paradigm Management.

"Oh, please," Kate scoffed. "When have you ever dropped anything in the toilet? That man is a bloodhound—he knows something's up. And, of course, he'd be right." Her Stephen Dweck dangle earrings swayed indignantly, the topaz gemstones glittering at Marissa. "I mean, you do realize that you'll be in a *completely* different time zone, right?"

Marissa passed a plate of marinated olives to her girlfriend, who accepted it sullenly. "Come on, Kate. If it's any consolation, you trumped my daughter—we haven't even told Pansy yet. We plan on telling her tonight."

That seemed to mollify Kate somewhat. She smoothed the napkin in her lap. "So . . . you're okay to just quit your job and move to Hawaii? Just . . . quit?"

Marissa felt a twinge of discomfort. She was still working through that part of the deal. "I'm . . . getting there. Like I said, there are a lot of factors to consider. My job, Pansy's school, our apartment. There are pros and cons either way."

"Pro: you won't look so pasty white anymore. Con: you'd be away from me and the most amazing city on earth. Pro: they have great coffee. Con: we have the Yankees. Pro—"

Marissa laughed. "I get it. But it's not just that, even though those are all excellent reasons. We both know that I've been burning out this past year. Hawaii might be a nice change of pace."

"Sure, if you're retired."

"Kate!"

"What?" Her friend gave her an innocent look, then relented, her features softening. "Okay, I'm sorry. I'm still absorbing the news."

"You and me both."

Kate clucked her tongue. "So does this mean that you and Paul are doing okay?" Kate had her poker face on, which meant that, despite Marissa's answer, Kate was convinced that things were still *not* okay.

Marissa sipped her tea. "Actually, things are going great." There was last night, of course, and then this morning Paul surprised her with a long kiss and one of his deep, soulful looks before Marissa headed out the door.

Okay, so she wasn't a fan of the deep, soulful looks, which seemed more needy than loving, but it was a heck of a lot better than their regular parting routine: him grabbing the *Wall Street Journal* and filling his travel mug with what was left of the French-pressed coffee Consuelo had prepared for Marissa. Sometimes there would be a nod and, if she was lucky, a wave. More often than not, his parting words would be, "I won't be home for dinner," unless, of course, Marissa said it first.

"Then again, it's hardly been twenty-four hours," Kate noted as she popped an olive into her mouth.

Marissa shot her an exasperated look. The problem with telling your friends everything was that, well, they knew everything. "Look, I know we've been on the rocks for some time now, but I'm just feeling hopeful about this whole thing. Paul is convinced that it's going to change things for us. A new place—it's Hawaii, for pete's sake! The promotion, the pay raise, a chance for me to take a break . . . We'd be crazy not to give it a try. Right?"

Kate was silent for a moment, then finally sighed. "Right. And I'm sure you know that I'm not so much angry as I am jealous. Why do you get to move to Hawaii and live the sweet life while I'm stuck here?"

Marissa smiled. "Kate, you wouldn't leave the city if I paid you a million dollars." Kate was fiercely loyal to New York.

"True. And lucky for you I have tons of anytime minutes." Kate refilled their teacups and held hers up in a toast. "To Marissa . . . may your travels this weekend enlighten and illuminate, and may the promise of paradise be fulfilled."

The women clinked teacups.

Kate downed her tea in one sip and tapped her cup on the table for Marissa to pour her some more. "And, if it doesn't, could you please remember to bring back some chocolate-covered macadamia nuts?"

Marissa and Paul decided to break the news of their Hawaiian weekend to Pansy over dinner.

"We're having dinner?" Pansy was instantly suspicious as she looked between her two parents who had come home early from work. She was still dressed in her green-and-white plaid school uniform, playing Nintendo at the breakfast bar in the kitchen. She set the game console aside and waited for a response. *"Together?"*

"Yes, is that such a surprise?" Marissa had given Consuelo the night off and was pretending to sort through the mail, as if coming home before 6:00 P.M. on a weekday was the norm.

"Are you *cooking?*" Pansy looked up at her mother in disbelief.

"Of course not." It was no secret that Marissa was a lousy cook. "Dad got takeout."

"Yeah, what's the matter? You don't want to have dinner with us old folks?" Paul held up two plastic bags filled with food. "And it's not just any dinner, Pansy. It's Beggar's Chicken from New Canton!"

"Really?" Pansy's eyes grew large as she sniffed the air. She loved the fragrant stuffed chicken wrapped in lotus leaves and clay. "Wow." She plucked a paper menu from the bag as Paul started to bring out containers of food. Her fingers began working the paper, folding and creasing, her eyes cast down. "Are you going to give me some bad news or something?" There was a slight tremble in her voice.

Marissa and Paul froze, staring at their daughter. A few seconds passed before Marissa finally gave a little laugh. "No. It's good news, actually." Her voice caught in her throat and she forced herself to swallow.

"Really good news," Paul added quickly.

Pansy looked relieved, and then her face lit up. "Are you going to have a baby?"

"No, no. Not *that* kind of good news." Marissa glanced hastily at Paul, who nodded for her to continue. "We're thinking about moving to Hawaii and Dad's company is going to fly us out this weekend so we can go take a look."

"What?" Pansy gaped at them.

Nervous, Marissa licked her lips. "It'll just be for a few days. You'll miss some school next week but I'll clear it with your teachers and your ballet instructor at the ABT . . ."

Pansy's mouth was still open in disbelief. "Are you serious?" she finally managed.

"We won't move if you don't want to," Marissa tried to reassure her, just as Paul shot her an exasperated *who's-the-parent-here?* kind of look. Marissa ignored him and focused on her daughter. "It'll be a family decision. This trip is just a look-see. A mini vacation. We can bring your homework with us if you're worried about falling behind . . ."

"Are you kidding? We're going to Hawaii! And I get to miss school!" A look of pure elation crossed Pansy's face. "*And* we have Beggar's Chicken!" Pansy gave a whoop before handing Marissa a perfectly folded crane. "I'm going to go wash my hands. Don't start without me!" She jumped off the stool and ran to the bathroom.

Paul started to set the table. "See?" he said cheerfully, the awkwardness of a few moments earlier already forgotten. "I told you it wouldn't be a problem." He peered into one of the containers. "Ooh, and they threw in some of those steamed scallion rolls that you love." He held one out to her. "It's a sign, Marissa."

Marissa's iPhone strummed with a new e-mail message. She hesitated, seduced for a moment by the inviting scent of green onions, sesame oil, and black pepper, but then her iPhone strummed again and she shook her head. Pansy came bounding back from the bathroom and settled herself eagerly at the table, a scallion roll already in hand. "In a minute," Marissa said, and stepped away to check her messages.

'elua | two

Marissa sat next to Paul in first class, listening to the gentle hum of the airplane as her husband talked on the Airfone, absently swirling his Scotch on the rocks. They had been in the air for a couple of short hours, with many more to go, and Marissa wasn't in the mood to work. She was tired, actually, having pulled several late nights in order to clear her desk before leaving, but it was done, and there was a smug satisfaction with that. "Super Woman" is what her managing partner, Arthur, had called her. Marissa had smiled modestly, blithely waving the compliment away. But the minute he was gone, she dropped into her chair like a rag doll, her mind frozen in exhaustion. The idea of being able to quit her job was becoming more appealing by the second.

Paul's company had agreed to fly them first class but the flight had been fully booked with only two first class seats available, which meant that Pansy and Consuelo were sitting in coach. Paul had cheerfully proposed that they play musical chairs for the flight, specifically at the times when the Häagen-Dazs ice cream sundaes were being served, which seemed to suit everyone just fine.

It was lucky, too, that Consuelo had been willing to leave her fifteen-year-old son, Manuel, to join them for the long weekend. It would be a busy few days as they explored the island and looked at housing and schools, but Marissa also hoped to have some serious downtime at the beach or in the spa. Paul had mentioned a sunset cruise, a helicopter ride over the volcano, a luau. Marissa's head was swimming with all of the things they could do. If the offer was to move to any other place, Marissa doubted they would have seriously considered it. It just didn't make sense. New York was New York. There was no comparison. Everyone knew that.

But Hawaii . . . award-winning resorts and world-class beaches, not to mention palm trees and balmy, year-round perfect weather—it was like getting an overseas assignment but better. No language barrier. Same currency. They could easily roll the gain from the sale of their apartment into a house. Marissa saw herself lounging on the beach, could hear the sounds of crashing waves. Sunsets. Dolphins. Humpback whales. Hikes through the rain forest. No need for tanning beds or bronzer. She would take on a sun-kissed look that would make everyone back home envious.

Marissa scanned the spacious first-class cabin, flipped through a selection of magazines, then scanned the cabin again. She was restless. She picked up the Airfone on the seatback in front of her, slid her credit card through and called the office.

"Hi," she said, smiling brightly when her secretary, Robin, picked up. "Any messages?"

"No, everything's quiet here," Robin said. "Everyone went out to celebrate the close of the Shattuck project. Oh, wait, there was one message . . . hold on . . . here it is. Consuelo's son wants her to call home as soon as she can."

"Oh. Okay. Anything else?"

"No. I've already FedEx'd your mail to your hotel; it should be there tomorrow by ten A.M. I didn't see anything urgent. And there was a fax from Jay Schumann but Arthur said he would take care of it. Something about a typo on the final contract. I faxed a copy of it to you at the hotel."

"That's it?" Marissa tried to hide her disappointment.

"That's it."

Weird. On any other day Marissa would be swamped with voice mail and last-minute requests, small fires that needed to be put out. "Well, okay," she said reluctantly. "If anything comes up, you know where to reach me."

"Got the numbers memorized."

"Bye, Robin."

"Bye. And don't forget to tell Consuelo to call her son. It sounded urgent."

Marissa hung up and glanced at her husband. He was still on the phone and, by the look of it, wasn't planning on getting off anytime soon. The plane hit a small air pocket as Marissa stood up, causing her to wobble uncertainly. She caught her balance, then slowly made her way back toward coach.

She found Consuelo and Pansy playing video games and laughing. They looked up, clearly surprised to see Marissa standing in front of them.

Pansy's fingers were still tapping the buttons on her Nintendo. "I thought that was you."

"It's me," Marissa said with a smile. It felt awkward standing there, hovering over them, but every seat in coach was taken. She noticed a few people glancing her way, curious, including a mother with dirty blond dreadlocks who was nursing her child. How old was that child? Two? Three? And the woman was definitely giving Marissa the stink eye. Marissa cut a glance to the woman's shoes . . . Birkenstocks, no surprise there. She turned her attention back to her daughter and Consuelo, who were looking at her expectantly.

"Consuelo, Manuel called the office. He wants you to call him when you can."

"Oh." Consuelo looked worried. She fumbled with the video game as she tried to check her watch. "Did he say if anything was wrong?"

"I don't know, but Robin said it sounded important. You can use the airplane phone." Marissa had brought her credit card and swiped it for Consuelo, then handed her the Air-fone.

Consuelo gripped the phone nervously. "Thank you, Mrs. Price." Her forgotten video game made a dying sound.

"So how are you doing so far?" Marissa asked her daughter, who was now flipping through the in-flight magazine.

"Fine."

"You didn't want the window seat?"

Pansy shook her head. "No, not really."

Marissa was surprised. "I thought you told Dad that you couldn't wait to look out the window during takeoff and landing."

Pansy shrugged indifferently. "Well, Consuelo was feeling a little sick and I thought that being near the window might make her feel better." She carefully tore out an advertisement for shoe lifts and began creasing the paper.

Marissa smiled fondly at her daughter. "They're going to show a movie later."

Pansy focused on her folding. "I know. I already saw it."

"I think there are at least three movies between here and Hawaii."

"Four. I've seen them all anyway."

Really? Marissa wondered. *When?* She couldn't remember the last time she had seen a movie, much less with Pansy. When would Pansy have seen them? Were they already on HBO?

Consuelo was speaking in Spanish, the Airfone pressed to her ear, her voice rushed and worried. Pansy looked at her, concerned, and Marissa suddenly felt apprehensive.

"Is everything all right?" she asked when Consuelo hung up.

"Manuel burst an appendix. They operated on him and my neighbor is with him at the hospital. He's okay now but . . ." Consuelo shook her head, her eyes filling with tears. She fumbled through her purse for a tissue.

Marissa checked her watch. They were due to land in L.A. in about three hours. "We'll get the airline to get you on the next flight back to New York," she promised, her mind racing as she thought about what would need to be done. "Don't worry."

Marissa had dreaded the layover at LAX, but now she was stressing that they weren't going to make their connection to Hawaii. It had taken longer than they thought to get Consuelo's ticket changed, and they had walked her to the gate to make sure she boarded without a problem.

Pansy seemed panicked as they waved good-bye, looking behind her as Paul and Marissa hurried her toward their terminal in the opposite direction. The ticketing agent had called ahead to the gate but said she couldn't make any promises.

"Come on, Pansy, move!" Marissa's heels clicked against the terminal floor.

Pansy was dragging her feet, still glancing behind her. "Who's going to sit with me now?" she asked.

"Your mother or I will," Paul called over his shoulder. He was a few steps ahead of them. Over the PA system they could hear the final boarding call for Kona. "Come on!"

They made it to the gate, breathless. Paul straightened his tie and fished for their boarding passes, as Marissa gave the gate attendant an apologetic but grateful smile.

"Who?" Pansy planted herself by the door, her thin arms crossed. "I want to know who's going to sit with me."

Paul glanced at his daughter, and then at Marissa.

"I will," he said, reaching over to give his daughter a tickle. The once-solemn Pansy, caught off guard, burst into laughter, the intensity gone. Paul glanced up at Marissa. "We can switch later." Paul placed his hands on Pansy's shoulders and steered her down the jetway, then looked back at his wife and gave her a warm smile.

It could've been PMS, but Marissa felt a surge of elation. For a moment she was taken back to the Paul she remembered, the easygoing Midwesterner who wanted a family, the one who talked about kids before they were even officially dating. Marissa knew that Paul loved Pansy, but it was rare for him to take the lead in doing things with their daughter. He had to be coaxed to step away from his busy schedule and—who was she kidding?—Marissa wasn't much better. In fact, having a family had been the last thing on Marissa's mind. It was Paul who showed her that life could include many things, among them a husband and partner for life.

They had both been in their last year of business school, having met at a recruiting dinner hosted by Bank of America. Marissa had been listening halfheartedly to the animated pitch and smiling politely to the B of A associate at their table who was actively trying to recruit her for a position in their global fixed-income division. Marissa couldn't think of anything more boring. Then Paul leaned over and said under his breath, "Doesn't it make you wonder if there's more to life than OTC derivatives and securitized products?" It was all she could do not to burst out laughing.

Afterward, they grabbed a cup of coffee and compared recruiting schedules: she had six offers, he had three. Marissa was leaning toward management consulting and Paul was drawn to the hospitality and tourism sector. She was worried about making the right decision; he wasn't.

His background was quick and simple—born and raised in Michigan, football scholarship, state school. Three girlfriends, one serious, a handful of flings and one-night stands. Parents were still in Grand Rapids, retired and avid golfers. Like her, he was an only child. He came to New York on a whim, thinking it would be fun to see what life in the big city was like.

He wanted to know everything about her. Marissa willingly obliged as she recounted her past: growing up in Bethpage, winning a partial scholarship to a small college, working at the local copy shop, waiting tables, graduating, and accepting a grueling sales position with PepsiCo, Inc., where she became a leading sales analyst. Her father passed away from a heart attack while she was in high school, and when Marissa was accepted into Columbia Business School, her mother had taken the money from her pension and assumed full-time residency as an art student in Chile. Marissa knew that while her mother grieved the loss of her father, she had also discovered a new life for herself. At Columbia, Marissa felt the same way—that's when she felt her life finally begin to change. She was only one of a handful of women in a class that was predominantly male. She expected Paul to acknowledge this somehow, as most in her peer group did, but instead Paul asked if Marissa ever planned to get married or have kids.

With anyone else, she would have been steaming with indignation. But Paul asked so directly, so earnestly, that Marissa didn't feel defensive or have a problem answering. Definitely one, she had said. Maybe even two. If pressed, she could see herself with a child, still working and climbing the corporate ladder. But marriage? Marissa knew there were lots of good things in store for her, but she'd been in enough relationships to know that it might just be easier to forgo the whole marriage thing altogether. When she told Paul this, he shook his head.

"Oh, you don't want to do that," he said adamantly, his face serious.

"I don't?"

"Nope."

Marissa suppressed a smile, keeping her tone solemn as well. "And why is that?"

"Because if you do that, you'll miss out on someone to share all those good things with." And gently he took her hand and held it in his.

That was the moment when she started falling for Paul Price.

Their courtship lasted a year before they decided to move in together; they were married two years later. Paul wanted to start trying for a family but Marissa kept putting it off— work was always too demanding and her travel schedule too hectic. Just the same, Pansy was born five years later. They cooed and played with her little toes and then took her home swaddled in a Vera Wang receiving blanket.

After six weeks, they hired Consuelo and were both back at work. It was as if nothing had happened. Life in the city kept them busy, and once Pansy was old enough to go to preschool, *her* life became busy, too. They saw less and less of each other. Somehow they had become like three ships passing in the night, each sailing its own course.

Now, Pansy was giving Marissa a quick hug as they separated at the split in the jetway corridor—first class and business to the left, coach to the right.

Paul called to Marissa, "Tell them I want my filet mignon delivered to coach!"

"Me, too!" Pansy sounded gleeful.

Marissa's heart swelled with affection as she watched her husband and her daughter wave good-bye, just as the stewardess closed the door behind them with a slam.

Marissa stretched out luxuriously, slid off her stilettos and accepted another glass of champagne. A fresh orchid flower had been placed on a dish of dark chocolate–covered macadamia nuts that sat on the armrest table. Marissa looked placidly out of the window as the plane took off down the runway, eating one piece of chocolate at a time, savoring it. She was in heaven.

When they were in the air, Marissa reached for the first-class toiletry bag and found a scented eye mask. She lowered the window shade and slipped it on. *Ahhhh . . .* lavender. She sighed heavily and the muscles in her shoulders began to relax. She felt herself drift to sleep.

"Honey?"

The edge of her eye mask was lifted and Marissa stared, one-eyed and drowsy, at her husband.

"Pansy needs you."

Marissa was suddenly awake. "What? Is she okay?"

"Yeah, yeah. I think she just needs her mother."

The stewardess came up behind him. "Sir, I'm sorry, but you need to be seated with your seat belt fastened until we reach cruising altitude. The captain will make an announcement when it's safe to move about the cabin."

"Oh, sorry." Paul slid into the seat next to Marissa. "I'll have a Scotch on the rocks," he told the stewardess.

"Certainly, sir."

Marissa stared at him. "Paul, you left her back there by herself?" She pulled off the eye mask.

"Only for a minute, Marissa. It's not as if she's going to get lost. Were there chocolates on this plate?"

"Paul, she's *eight*." Marissa slipped her heels back on and unbuckled her seat belt.

"The stewardess said to wait until . . ."

"Oh, give it a rest." Holding firmly on to the tops of the seats, Marissa made her way back to coach despite the protests of the stewardesses along the way.

When she reached Pansy's row, Marissa saw that her daughter was finally sitting by the window, her ear buds on as she played her Nintendo. She looked small in the seat with no one next to her.

Marissa sat down and buckled her seat belt, then turned to face her daughter. She gently pulled one of the buds out of Pansy's ear. "Hey."

"Hi."

"So . . . what's up?"

Pansy's braids were loose as a result of their mad dash to the gate. Marissa reached over and tucked some stray strands of hair behind her daughter's ear.

Pansy looked back down at her game. "Nothing."

"Nothing?"

Pansy's eyes didn't leave the screen. "Well, I'm about to top the high score."

Marissa forced a chuckle. "Dad said you needed me."

"Oh." Pansy looked perplexed, and then she remembered. "I wondered if Consuelo gave you her game console before she flew back to New York."

Marissa shook her head. "No, Pansy, I don't think getting back her Nintendo was foremost on our mind when we were trying to get her home. I'm sorry."

Pansy shrugged. "I didn't think so. That's okay." She put the game in her backpack, then fiddled with the seat pocket in front of her. "Hey, I know where all of the emergency exits are. Want to know?"

"Sure."

As Pansy pointed them out, Marissa shifted in the narrow coach seat and looked longingly up the aisle. The curtains were drawn, separating first class and coach. Here, she was surrounded by boisterous families and honeymooning couples. Marissa longed for the peaceful serenity of first class.

A line formed by the bathrooms as soon as the captain announced that they could move around the cabin.

"Excuse me, miss," a stewardess said briskly as she pushed the beverage cart past their row, almost clipping Marissa's stilettos. No smile, no eye contact, no apology. Marissa sighed.

Pansy was still talking, something about evacuating in the event of a water landing. She was animated, and her hair continued to slip out of its braids.

Marissa reached toward her daughter and pulled the elastic bands out of her hair. She motioned for Pansy's backpack and fished around until she found a hairbrush.

"Pigtails?" Marissa asked. "Or should we try something more glamorous?" She kicked off her shoes, then pushed them gently under the seat, out of harm's way.

Pansy seemed uncertain. "Something more glamorous?" she finally ventured.

Marissa pretended to think. "I'm thinking Audrey Hepburn in *Breakfast at Tiffany's* . . ."

"Who's Audrey Hepburn?"

Marissa smiled. "Never mind. Turn around and face the window, Pansy."

As Pansy turned obediently, Marissa began to brush her daughter's hair in slow, long strokes, wondering why she never noticed how it had begun to turn from dark chocolate brown to a lighter chestnut color. Pansy's hair was soft and clean, emitting the healthy shine of young hair. Marissa found herself leaning forward, inhaling her daughter's scent, when Pansy jerked around.

"What are you doing?"

"Nothing," Marissa said hastily. "Nothing! Now turn around."

"Okay," Pansy said suspiciously, and turned back around.

Why am I embarrassed? Marissa wondered as she pulled Pansy's fine hair into an upsweep and attempted, unsuccessfully, to pin it in place. She let Pansy's hair fall back to her shoulders, and tried again. *I'm her mother, for God's sake. Can't I smell my own daughter's hair?*

"Mom?" Pansy strained to turn around as Marissa tried to hold the upsweep in place.

"Yes?"

"It's too tight. You're pulling on my scalp."

"Oh, sorry." Marissa released Pansy's hair again. "I think I'm going to have to try something different. Maybe something else, like a French twist?"

"I don't know what you're talking about, but okay." Pansy turned back around and tilted her head back slightly, as if offering it to her mother. Marissa was touched.

"I'm not sure either, but I'm willing to give it a try," said Marissa, brushing her daughter's hair again, this time more gently. "Okay, let's give it a whirl."

The plane started its descent, waking Marissa with a gentle jolt. She had fallen asleep with Pansy's head in her lap, her fingers still entwined in her daughter's hair. Marissa smoothed Pansy's hair, then felt for her shoes and slipped them on.

Paul was coming down the aisle, an apologetic look on his face.

"I'm sorry—" he started, then lowered his voice when Marissa nodded to their sleeping daughter. "I'm sorry," he said again. "I fell asleep."

"That's okay. We did, too."

"We'll sit together on the way back. Meet you when we land?"

Marissa nodded and accepted a peck on the cheek as a stewardess motioned for Paul to return to his seat. He gave Marissa one last grin before heading back to first class.

"Honey?" Marissa said gently, rubbing Pansy's shoulders. "We're almost here. Hawaii!"

Pansy stirred, opening one eye and then the other. "We're here?" Her voice was scratchy from the dry cabin air.

"Almost. I thought you might want to see us land, check out the palm trees and everything." Marissa felt a frisson of exhilaration.

Pansy sat up, groggy, and leaned toward the window. "I just see black rock," she reported, before settling back into her chair. She rubbed her eyes and yawned.

Confused, Marissa peered over Pansy's head. Fields of ropey black lava rock, hard and shiny in the sun, flashed in front of her eyes as they approached the runway. Where were the white sandy beaches? The palm trees? The waterfalls? It looked more like a desolate wasteland.

The stewardess announced their arrival in Hawaii. Melodic strains of a ukulele played over the PA. Even though the plane was still moving, there was a chorus of seat belts unbuckling. People stood up, reaching for the overhead compartments or jostling into the aisles, ready for their Hawaiian adventures to begin.

Pansy and Marissa remained seated and looked out the window, doubtful.

"Is that the airport?" Pansy pointed to a weathered, open-air quadrangle.

Marissa strained to look through the window. "I'm not sure," she said.

"I thought you said it would look all green and tropical."

"Well, Maui was," Marissa confessed. "I suppose the Big Island is different. But it definitely looks tropical. See? There are palm trees."

"Where's the gate?"

"Um . . ." Marissa cast a furtive look out the window as the plane slowed to a stop on the tarmac. "I don't think they have gates exactly."

They watched as a moveable stairway was pushed toward the plane. Marissa chewed her lip uncertainly.

"Wow." Pansy started gathering her things. "I haven't tried this before. And look, there's Dad!" She pointed out the window.

Sure enough, Paul was one of the first passengers off the plane, his jacket slung casually over his shoulder, sunglasses on. He stood at the bottom of the stairway, his hand shielding his eyes from the sun. She watched him as he nodded and laughed easily with the other first-class passengers who were leisurely walking across the tarmac while the rest of the plane waited impatiently to disembark.

"This line isn't moving," Pansy pouted. The man in the aisle next to them grunted in agreement and then moved forward an inch. Pansy sat back down and let out a noisy exhalation.

Marissa turned her attention to the stalled line next to her seat. The nursing mother had wedged her way into the aisle as she slipped on a brightly colored fabric baby sling.

"I've never seen anything like that before," Marissa couldn't resist commenting. "Is that for your child?"

The woman answered by picking up her child and putting her inside the sling so that she rested snugly against her mother's hip. The child stared back at Marissa with huge blue eyes, her long golden locks curling around her shoulders.

"Yes," the woman said curtly, clearly uninterested in having a conversation with Marissa.

"Did you make it yourself?" Marissa asked. She tried not to look appalled when the child began groping for her mother's breast, wanting to nurse.

The woman seemed to be gritting her teeth. "I got it from a company in California."

"Really? Is it safe? Because it looks like your child could slip out. I mean, I'm just curious. I'd hate for her to fall."

"It's perfectly safe," the woman retorted, tightening the strap and pulling the child closer to her. "And he's a *boy*." She turned her back to Marissa.

Marissa winced and tried to apologize. "Oh, I'm sorry. I must have been distracted by the curls. But you know, if you really want a good carrier, I had the Björn, and it was wonderful—"

The woman held up a hand before Marissa could continue. "Let me guess. L.A.?"

"What?"

"You're from Los Angeles. Am I right?"

"No." Marissa was clearly offended.

"New York?"

Marissa said nothing.

A haughty look crossed the woman's face. "I thought so. Well, have a nice vacation." She moved down the aisle, bouncing the baby on one hip as she lugged a huge army duffel bag behind her.

Marissa was speechless as she watched the woman's retreating back. It wasn't like her to get into a disagreement with a total stranger, and quite frankly it made her feel like crap. Pansy gave her sleeve a tug, and Marissa forced herself to snap out of it. She quickly gathered their things, cutting in line and nodding for Pansy to step in front of her. "Let's go," she said, still a bit irritated.

They met Paul in the waiting area. He looked rested and refreshed, which was more than Marissa could say for herself. He tousled Pansy's hair, which was finally down after she and Marissa had tried every hair style they knew. "Can you believe it? We're in paradise now!"

Pansy was bouncing with excitement. "Dad, can I get money for a cart?" she asked as they headed toward the baggage carousel.

"The hotel should have sent someone, Pansy. They'll take care of the bags." Paul scanned the greeters who were holding signs. "Ah, there we are." He waved.

A young tanned woman holding a sign that read PRICE FAMILY smiled and walked over, speaking into a walkie-talkie before introducing herself. "I'm Leilani. Welcome to the Big Island of Hawaii." She gave them each a kiss on the cheek as she placed an orchid lei over each of their heads. When she was finished, she was still holding one lei. She checked her clipboard. "There are only three of you?"

"Oh, our nanny had to go back to New York," Marissa explained, inhaling the fragrance of the flowers. The lei was cool against her neck.

"Then I guess this means you get two." Leilani draped the extra lei over Pansy's head, who beamed. "The car is waiting for you at the curb. If you'll give me your claim tickets, I'll have Keoni pick up your bags and bring them to the hotel."

They followed Leilani to the curb and Pansy immediately exclaimed, "Wow, a limo!" Even Marissa was impressed. She fished in her purse for her sunglasses, then turned to glance back at the baggage claim.

Keoni was already plucking their bags off the carousel. As Marissa was about to turn away, she spotted the nursing mother. The woman wore a smug look on her face as she bounced her son on one hip, pointedly glaring at Marissa. She looked considerably shorter, though just as formidable, as she stood by the baggage carousel in her worn Birken-stocks.

Go grow some hemp, or whatever it is you do! Marissa wanted to yell. Instead, she narrowed her eyes and slid on her sunglasses, then stepped into the waiting limo.

'ekolu | three

The Kohala Bay Resort was a finely manicured, lush luxury resort set on the cusp of a beautiful white sand beach surrounded by the island's signature black lava rock. It had a thirty-six-hole championship golf course, tennis courts, two swimming pools, and a spa. Fallon Resort Properties had bought the resort during a distress sale from a Japanese holding company the year before. They installed a new general manager and watched sales fluctuate and eventually plummet. The GM had resigned, complaining that his wife and children suffered from "island fever," and that the stress of trying to produce occupancy numbers equivalent to pre-9/11 was near impossible, especially given the competition with new and refurbished hotels and time-shares along the coastline.

They were greeted by name by Duke, the head bellhop, who had another lei waiting for them plus a candy lei for Pansy. Pansy's eyes were wide as Leilani guided them into the marbled lobby, flanked on both sides by orchids and glistening koi ponds. A balmy breeze met them as they headed toward the VIP line of the front desk.

"Aloha, Mr. and Mrs. Price. Welcome to the Kohala Bay Resort." The front desk clerk gave them a bright smile. A fresh hibiscus was tucked behind her ear. "Leilani called ahead and told us of your change in plans. We have your suite all ready, including the roll-away for your daughter in the living room."

"Excellent," Paul said, signing his name with flourish. Marissa had to hand it to him; when he wanted to turn it on, he definitely had a presence about him.

"Mom, look!" Pansy pointed to the lagoon swimming pool overlooking the ocean. Finally, the sandy white beaches and aquamarine ocean she had been looking for. Lounge chairs and cabanas. Pool attendants strolling around with tropical-looking drinks, most likely alcoholic. A small sigh escaped Marissa. This was more like it.

"Okay, I've got our keys. Let's go." Paul handed Marissa a card key. "I want to get out of this suit . . ."

". . . and into the pool?" Pansy asked, her voice hopeful.

". . . and into the shower," Paul said with a smile. "Mom will go with you to the pool."

"Actually, I was hoping to take a nap," Marissa interjected quickly. "I didn't get much sleep on the plane and I was up all night clearing my desk for this trip."

Pansy looked at both of her parents, waiting.

"Well, they're expecting me at the office . . ." Paul started.

Pansy turned to Marissa. "Mom? Pool? Please? Or the beach? It's right here!"

"Pansy, I . . ." Marissa looked to Paul for help but he only shrugged.

"It's up to you," he said. Then he turned to Pansy, "Mom needs to get some rest, honey . . ."

Pansy looked so crestfallen that Marissa caved in. "Fine, we'll go," she said. "And then I'm finding a hammock somewhere!"

Pansy gave her mother a grateful hug and Marissa, despite feeling tired and crabby, softened.

"You're the best," Paul confirmed, slipping the card key into the slot. He pushed open the door and kept a firm hold on Pansy's shoulder, nodding for Marissa to step inside. "Welcome to Hawaii."

The suite was huge and luxurious, the sliding door to the lanai already open, the sheer white curtains waving in the breeze. On the paneled console by the door rested a huge arrangement of tropical flowers. The scent of tuberose tickled Marissa's nose. A three-tiered arrangement of fresh fruit and cheese rested nearby, along with a generous pot of chocolate fondue with several unlit tea lights underneath. A bottle of champagne was chilling in a silver ice bucket, as well as a bottle of sparkling cider for Pansy. Three champagne flutes were on the table. A pink card with her name rested against the flowers.

Inside, she found a beautiful handmade card. *May we always find ourselves in Paradise,* it read. A gift certificate for an oceanside massage and spa treatment was tucked inside.

Marissa turned around and faced her husband, who had walked up behind her. "Thank you," she murmured, wrapping her arms around his neck.

"You're welcome," Paul said, kissing her. "I'm sorry I have to run, but when I get back in a couple of hours, you can rest or do your massage. It's up to you." He quickly changed into some fresh clothes and was gone.

Pansy bounced on the roll-away bed that had been brought in for her, mussing the pristine bedding. She flopped down with her arms spread and stared up at the ceiling, beaming. Marissa slipped off her shoes, sighing happily as her tired feet sunk into the plush carpet, then turned to give her daughter a smile. "Get your swimsuit on," she told her. "We're heading to the beach!"

"I could live here forever," Pansy declared at lunch the following day. They were poolside, Marissa under the shade of a cabana and Pansy struggling with a floatable beach chair. Half-eaten Hawaiian-style crispy dumplings with a tangy ginger-chili sauce rested on shiny green banana leaves. Marissa took a sip of her lemongrass iced tea as Pansy tossed the beach chair into the water and jumped on top of it.

"Here in Hawaii or here at the hotel?" Marissa was reading through the thirty-four-page list of things to do that Paul's secretary, Evelyn, had compiled for them.

"The hotel."

Marissa jotted something down. "I don't think anyone would disagree with you there."

"Well, that's because I haven't really seen Hawaii yet," Pansy said reasonably, paddling along the side of the pool. Her arms were stark white and slathered with sun block.

Marissa held up the sheath of papers. "You're in luck . . . you'll have *plenty* of opportunity to see Hawaii the next couple of days."

Pansy whooped gleefully, her hands making little fists as they punched the air.

Marissa gave her daughter a smile. They were managing just fine without Consuelo, and Marissa couldn't help but feel a little proud. She had been worried about what it would be like to be on their own. Consuelo had been with them since Pansy was a baby, and it had been a while since they had taken any kind of a trip as a family. Not that Marissa couldn't handle it. She could. Really. How hard could it be? "So after lunch our real estate agent, Jenny

Olsen, is picking us up to show us some houses. Then we have a luau for dinner at one of the other hotels. That should be fun, Pansy."

Pansy rolled off the beach chair and swam underneath it.

"Then tomorrow . . . ooh, Pansy, you'll like this." Marissa held up a brochure with a helicopter hovering over a volcano spewing lava. "A morning helicopter ride to see the volcano. Then we'll take the afternoon to look at more houses, maybe even visit some coffee farms." Marissa circled this on the calendar with a red pen and wrote GIFTS!!! in the margin. "Then, on Monday, an interview and tour with Hawaii Day School first, and then the Kohala Academy for the Arts. Then we have lunch, get a little more beach time and catch our flight back to New York that evening."

Pansy dove under the beach chair once again, just as Marissa spotted Paul striding across the lawn toward the pool.

Marissa warmed at the sight of him, remembering the previous night. With Pansy asleep, Paul had pressed up against Marissa as they stood on the balcony, burying his face in her hair and brushing his lips against her neck. Maybe it was the warm breeze or the full moon, but Marissa had turned around to kiss him passionately, and then led him back into their bedroom, quietly closing the set of French doors that separated their room from the living room, where Pansy was fast asleep.

Now, as Paul headed toward her, she admired how good he looked in his silk shirt and khaki slacks. *Really* good, in fact. He was tall and fit, with an air of relaxed confidence surrounding him. A few women looked at him with interest as he walked by them, then turned away when they saw him bend down and give Marissa a kiss.

"Where's Pansy?" he asked.

Marissa pointed to the empty beach chair floating nearby. "She would be the skinny shadow hiding beneath that."

Pansy popped back up to the surface for air. "Dad!" she called. She swam to the edge of the pool.

"Hi, Pansy," he said affectionately, leaning over to chuck her under the chin.

Marissa knew Pansy was thrilled to have so much time with her parents, a rarity back home. They were usually all out the door between 6:30 and 7:00 in the morning, and Pansy was back by 4:30 or 5:00 P.M. where she spent the remaining afternoon and evening with Consuelo. Marissa and Paul rarely made it home for dinner except on weekends, unless they had plans to go to the opera. Paul often played golf out in Westchester County on Saturdays before making his way back into the city by late afternoon. Family time had been reduced to frenzied breakfasts, good-night kisses, and weekends filled with errands.

Paul straightened up and clapped his hands together. "Who's up for some lunch before we check out some houses? I'm starving!"

Marissa and Pansy exchanged a guilty look, and Marissa furtively covered the dumplings with her wide-brimmed straw hat. "Er, we are," they both replied in unison.

"Great! I have to make a couple of calls. Why don't I meet you at the Beach House in ten minutes?" Paul's cell phone rang and he cupped it against his chest, giving them a wave as he walked away.

"I love Hawaii!" Pansy did a happy dance as an amused Marissa started to gather their things. "Do you think we'll need binoculars to see the whales?"

"I don't know. We can ask. I'm sure they have them at the front desk." She stood up, looking for a place to dump their trash. A trash can was on the other side of the pool, so

Marissa walked over. Paul was there, facing the ocean. He was still on the phone, and he was laughing. At that moment he turned and spotted Marissa, and quickly covered the mouthpiece with his hand.

"Be there in a minute," he whispered, giving her a wink. He walked a few steps away from Marissa and turned to face the ocean, his back to her.

"I am famished!" Paul declared jovially when he finally joined them at the table. Marissa and Pansy had been waiting twenty minutes. It hadn't been too bad, because every table had a set of binoculars and they had already spotted six whales.

"Dad, look through here." Pansy held up the binoculars. "If you see any white water, it could be a whale coming to the surface."

"Okay, hold on. Let me get some food in my stomach first." He picked up the menu. Pansy had already asked for an ice cream sundae, to which Marissa had said yes. Marissa wasn't really hungry, but maybe she could share something with Paul. She turned to ask him what he would be getting.

His gaze was elsewhere. "Oh, look," he said offhandedly to no one in particular. "Here comes Malia." He turned to Marissa and explained, "Malia's the executive secretary for the office. I don't believe you've met her before. She's been out to New York a few times."

The name wasn't familiar. "No, I don't think so," Marissa answered, but Paul was already standing, tossing his napkin onto the table. Marissa turned to see a young woman approach the table.

She wore a silk Hawaiian sundress, a floral pineapple motif set against red silk. It fell modestly to the woman's calves but didn't do much to hide her lean but otherwise voluptuous figure. Her face was evenly tanned, and she had long, bronzed locks that seemed to fall in just the right place. A white plumeria was tucked behind her right ear. As Malia brushed a strand of hair away from her face, Marissa saw that her nails were long but nicely manicured.

The woman smiled, revealing perfect teeth that matched her perfect body. "Hi," Malia said, smiling at Pansy and Marissa. She held out her hand. "I'm Malia Fox."

"Malia's the executive secretary for the office," Paul repeated. "My right-hand man when I'm here." He gave a chuckle.

"Oh, hardly," Malia said modestly.

"It's nice to meet you," Marissa said. She introduced her daughter, keeping a possessive hand on Pansy's shoulder. "This is our daughter, Pansy."

Malia crouched down so she was eye level with Pansy. She took the plumeria out of her hair and tucked it behind Pansy's ear. "Hello, Pansy. I'm Malia."

"Hi," Pansy said, a bit in awe.

"Would you like to join us?" Marissa asked, gesturing to the empty chair across from her.

Malia cut her eyes quickly toward Paul, then back at Marissa. "Oh, I'd love to, but I actually just came to tell Paul that New York sent a couple of faxes that need his signature. They want them back by the end of the day." She looked sincerely apologetic.

"I guess New York isn't on island time." Paul gave an exaggerated sigh. "Order me the fish tacos, honey," he said, standing up. "Mild salsa. My stomach's been acting up since yesterday. I'll be right back."

"It was nice meeting you," Malia said as she turned away. "If you need anything, just give me a call. I'm always in the office or you can reach me by cell. Paul has the number." She gave them a little wave, then turned to stroll alongside Paul as they headed for the office.

Marissa stared after them, unable to pull her eyes away. Paul said something out of earshot, and Malia laughed. When they reached the building, he opened the door, placing his hand in the small of Malia's back to usher her in. It was an innocent gesture, completely harmless, but for some reason Marissa found herself electrified.

Pansy had removed the plumeria from her hair and was twirling it underneath Marissa's nose. "Mom, smell. It smells nice, doesn't it?"

Marissa shook her head and waved the flower away. "Not now, Pansy." Her stomach was in knots. Malia and Paul were already inside the building but Marissa continued to stare at the closed door, her mind cloudy with irrational thoughts. She forced herself to snap out of it, then settled down to the business at hand of ordering her family some lunch.

The afternoon was spent driving around the northwest coast of the island and up into the lush green hills of Waimea, which Paul had determined would be the best place for them to live.

"Close to work, close to the schools," he was saying. "Plus, it's got personality."

"Lots," confirmed Jenny Olsen, their Realtor from Aloha Nui Realty. She was in her fifties, stick thin, sun spots dotting her arms. She reminded Marissa of a bird by the way she tipped her head to one side when talking. "Waimea is *loaded* with charm!"

Pansy was peering excitedly out the window, her face pressed against the glass. "Wow, it sure is green."

"Yes, isn't it gorgeous?" Jenny gushed. "Waimea gets just enough rain to keep it lush. And look at those hills! It's like an oil painting, except that it's real. Remarkable!"

Pansy gave a start. "Mom, there's cows! I've never seen so many cows before!"

"Cows?" Marissa looked up from her iPhone, where she was idly checking her messages. Sure enough, a herd of cattle stared at them indifferently as they drove by. They had gone from balmy beach to cow country in less than twenty minutes. Marissa patted Paul's shoulder and shot him a questionable look.

Sensing some dissention in the ranks, Jenny craned her neck to look at Marissa, who was sitting in the back of the car with Pansy. "Waimea is a *highly* desirable place to live," she insisted. "It's *so* difficult to find a good listing, and when you do, it's gone. Just like that!"

"Really," Marissa said, not bothering to mask her disbelief as they passed a couple of gas stations.

"Well, let's just take a look first before we make any decisions," Paul suggested, sensing Marissa's skepticism. "You never know."

"That's right!" Jenny crowed, beaming at Paul. "You never know where you'll find that gem of a house!"

Marissa had to admit that the idea of actually living in a house, instead of an apartment, was a bit thrilling. She had lived in the city all of her adult life and was accustomed to efficient living spaces. She would miss their doorman, Frank, and the pristine elevator that shot them up to the twenty-first floor where they lived, but the privacy would be nice, and having an exterior that they could paint or landscape or do whatever it is you do when you have an exterior, was exciting. Pansy was gunning for a yard. Paul was looking forward to a garage, maybe even a toolshed.

With her neck obviously tired from having to turn around, Jenny gave Marissa a final, polite smile in the rearview mirror before looking at Paul and turning on the charm full blast. "So, how long have you worked with the hotels?" Marissa, sitting in the back with Pansy, was no longer a part of the conversation.

Pansy continued to gaze out the window. "I've never lived in the country before," she said longingly.

Marissa gave her daughter a smile as she strained to hear the conversation between Paul and Jenny. From the way Jenny looked positively riveted, it was clear that she had determined that Paul was some sort of hotshot. Marissa was longing for some adult conversation, but Paul and Jenny were in their own little world, talking about the tourism market, housing, and golf, with Jenny agreeing vehemently to whatever Paul was saying.

Pansy had settled back into her seat and was looking through a selection of activity brochures she had picked up from the lobby of the hotel. "I think I might want to try surfing sometime," Pansy was saying. "Just once, in case I don't like it. Can I?"

"We'll see."

Pansy waved a brochure for a trail ride. "What about horses? Can I try riding a horse?"

"Sure," Marissa said absently. She glanced back down at her phone and skimmed her e-mail messages. Nothing important other than an upbeat message from Robin telling her that all was (unusually) quiet in the office, and an enigmatic message from Kate that read "Be still my beating heart—more later!" Marissa thought of sending back an e-mail, but, feeling a bit carsick, decided to wait until later.

"Oh," Jenny said, glancing in her rearview mirror at Marissa. "I forgot to tell you that there are some great shops just down the road from Waikoloa, called the Waikoloa Kings' Shops and Queens' Marketplace, in case you want to do some shopping later. A lot of the ladies love to go there, and there's a boat and a tram at the Hilton Waikoloa Village for your daughter." She turned back to Paul. "So, what were you saying about the Japanese market?"

"Mom, can we go?" Pansy looked at her hopefully.

Marissa sighed, acutely aware of her rapidly receding role as corporate executive to the not-so-glamorous role of corporate wife and mother.

Sunday morning, 8:00 A.M. Hawaii Standard Time, 1:00 P.M. Eastern Standard Time. Pansy was up like a ray of light, dragging the heavy curtains aside to reveal another sunny day in paradise. *Too sunny,* Marissa decided groggily, covering her head with a pillow.

They had been here a couple of days, but Marissa still hadn't felt like she'd had much of a vacation. Plus she had spent every waking moment with Pansy, with Paul being called to the office for one reason or another. Not that she minded, but Marissa needed a break. If they said yes to the move, then she would probably become a full-time mom like she and Paul had discussed a while back, and that was fine. After all, other people did it and they seemed happy, and Pansy was their only child. It's just that Marissa wasn't ready to start being a full-time mom *right this instant.*

The space next to her was empty, a nest of rumpled sheets with the occasional gray hair, more evidence of aging. Paul, not her. At least not yet.

"Mom, get up! We have to get ready for the helicopter ride." Pansy was already tugging on a tank top and shorts.

"Pansy, just five more minutes . . ." Last night's luau, which included an open bar and maybe one too many mai tais, still pounded in her head. "Where's your father?"

"Gym. He said he would be back with some breakfast and that we needed to be ready to go." Pansy disappeared into the bathroom.

Again? Paul had gone to the gym every day since they arrived. What kind of vacation included the gym? "What time?"

"He said he'd be back by eight fifteen."

Marissa squinted at the clock. Damn. She pushed herself up wearily with a sigh and yawned. She swung one leg over the side of the bed and stared at her foot. Was she retaining water? Great.

The sound of a card in the key slot triggered Pansy into a near frenzy. "It's Dad!" she told Marissa, running from the bathroom to the door, hairbrush in hand. Marissa had never seen Pansy as energetic as she was on this trip. Back in New York, Pansy was considerably more reserved, enthusiastic about a few things, but otherwise keeping to herself and spending most of her time in her room, organizing things or on the computer. Come to think of it, Pansy had not played her Nintendo once since they had landed.

"Good morning!" Paul sang. He had a tray filled with croissants, sliced papaya and pineapple, white rice, Portuguese sausage, and assorted jams and jellies. And coffee. Thank God.

"I am *so* hungry," Pansy announced as Paul gave Marissa a kiss and handed her a steaming cup. Both of her parents looked at her in amazement. She had definitely eaten their money's worth last night, including something called *poi,* a starchy, gelatinous purple-colored paste made from the taro plant.

Pansy had loved it, as well as most of the items on the overstocked buffet, and still found the energy to get on stage with the hula dancers and other guests to learn the "Hukilau," a hula celebrating a fishing festival in a village. Paul and Marissa watched in amusement as their daughter earnestly tried to imitate the pulling in of fishing nets while bumping into other guests, most of whom were older and slightly drunk.

"Looks like she's found her alter ego," Paul had murmured, pulling Marissa close to him. The music was loud and buoyant, and Marissa, still spinning from the drinks and food, let herself relax in his arms. She felt happy. *Really* happy.

"Well, fill up that bottomless pit and let's get going," Paul was saying now. "They're sending a car at nine o'clock to take us to the heliport. I'm going to take a quick shower." He turned quickly toward the bathroom, peeling off his T-shirt as he walked.

"How was the gym?" Marissa called after him, taking a bite of the croissant.

"Fine. They need to wipe down the machines more often." He had turned on the shower and his voice was muffled.

Back in New York, Paul worked out occasionally but oftentimes his busy schedule precluded him from establishing any sort of routine. Now, however, it seemed as if he was intent on making it a regular part of his schedule. If he wanted to work out, she shouldn't complain. She'd seen him heavier, and it wasn't a pretty sight. Plus he seemed happier, more self-assured. What wasn't to like?

Marissa dressed, abandoning a Tory Burch turquoise tank top for a Rebecca Taylor short-sleeved knit top. They were going to look at more houses after the helicopter ride and the temperature in Waimea was definitely cooler than the resort. The idea of living in a small, ranching town ("up-country," Jenny liked to remind them) was starting to grow on her, but they had yet to find a place to live.

Marissa walked into the steamy bathroom to wash her face and brush her teeth. Paul emerged from the shower, towel-less, with a part of him very happy to see her. He grinned as he closed the bathroom door.

"Paul, we're late," Marissa protested, giggling as he caught her in a wet hug. "Stop! I'm all dressed and I don't want to change again."

Paul gave her a quick kiss before releasing her. "Your loss," he said, then sauntered into the closet to look for something to wear.

Marissa prided herself on being able to handle most situations, and it certainly wasn't her first time in a helicopter. Still, despite being in the island's "premiere" six-passenger helicopter, Marissa was feeling both claustrophobic and cramped. She was hardly ten minutes into the trip before she felt her stomach pitch and she wished they were back on solid ground.

"Need this?" the pilot asked into the microphone, offering Marissa a barf bag. *Great.* The other three passengers, along with Paul and Pansy, glanced warily at Marissa. If Marissa threw up, it would be a long two hours before they were back at the heliport in Waikoloa.

Marissa shook her head. She had never been sick before, and she wasn't going to start today. She just prayed her body knew that as well.

"Okay, people. First stop, Kilauea," the pilot was saying. "She was flowing pretty heavily yesterday and throughout the night, so there's a good chance you'll be seeing some lava today. Make sure your camera has plenty of film."

A small cheer went around the helicopter but since it was almost impossible to hear one another even with the microphones and Bose headphones, the group settled for a half-hearted semisalute.

Marissa gazed out the window, keeping her eye on the horizon. While she was momentarily stunned to see how small the island really was (it seemed so much bigger in the car), she kept looking back to check the digital clock on the instrument panel that was timing the trip. What had the pilot said—fifteen more minutes before they reached Volcanoes National Park?

Despite her queasiness, Marissa was looking forward to seeing the lava flow. All the other volcanoes Marissa had ever visited—in Greece, in Bali, on Maui—were either dead, dormant, or just not flowing. Marissa wanted to have her *National Geographic* moment and see the lava up close, have a story to tell back at Paradigm.

"We're approaching Volcanoes National Park, home of Pele, goddess of the volcano." The pilot did a sharp turn for effect, making Marissa's stomach lurch. "Having traveled for many miles in search of a suitable home for her fire and family, Pele settled in the crater of Halema'uma'u at the summit of Kilauea. Pele is volcanism in all its many forms. Her Hawaiian name means 'the woman who devours the land.' When her molten body moves, the land trembles and the sky is afire with a crimson glow. Those present whisper in awe, '*Ae, aia la 'o Pele;* there is Pele.' "

A sense of reverence overtook the helicopter and, for a moment, Marissa forgot about her motion sickness. She looked with anticipation at the steam rising up ahead. Cameras and video cameras were poised and ready.

The pilot continued. "Since the 1983 eruption, more than five hundred fifty acres of new land have been added to the Big Island. We are one of the few land masses that continues to grow. The park's active volcanoes, Kilauea and Mauna Loa, continue the island-building process that formed the thirty-five-hundred mile Emperor Seamount–Hawaiian Island chain."

The pilot put his hand to the ear of his headphone, obviously receiving a message of some sort. He glanced back at the passengers and then at the approaching volcano, clearing his throat. "Well, folks, it seems that Pele is keeping to herself today. I just heard from one of our other birds that the lava flow has just gone underground. But there is a sky-light, an opening, right above one of the lava tubes, and hopefully you can take some good pictures of that."

A collective groan of disappointment filled the helicop-ter. What had been the point of coming out? Marissa could have bought a postcard in the gift shop and been done with it.

The helicopter hovered above a square of glowing lava. Inside the lava tube, Marissa could make out a river of lava through the five-by-five-foot skylight. Paul snapped a cou-ple of pictures on the digital camera and then looked at Marissa and shrugged.

The pilot tried to cheer them up. "It's not uncommon for much of the lava coming out of Kilauea to flow steadily be-neath the surface of the lava fields and empty into the ocean. We'll go there next, and you should be able to get a shot of the lava hitting the ocean and forming new land."

He circled around so they could see the lava dripping slowly into the ocean, resulting in huge plumes of steam. A few seconds later, the pilot turned the helicopter away. "Now we're heading to the lush rain forests and waterfalls of the Hamakua coast . . ."

Marissa glanced at the timer. *Twenty-three minutes to go. And counting.* She licked her lips and tried to focus on other things, like being back in New York where, if they had a volcano and promised a lava flow, you'd get a lava flow, no excuses.

Malia was waiting for them in the lobby, a sweet smile on her face. Marissa might need that barf bag after all. "So how'd it go?"

"The flow went underground," Paul reported. "Marissa was disappointed. And she also had a bit of motion sickness . . ."

"What?" Marissa cut him off with a quick laugh. "I wasn't sick, Paul, I was just feeling queasy. Plus we were *all* a little disappointed that we didn't get to see anything. Right, Pansy?"

Pansy shrugged. "I still thought it was pretty cool."

"That it was," Paul agreed. "You could just *feel* the intensity of the lava, even if you couldn't see it."

Malia was nodding intently, her luminous brown eyes fixed on Paul. "You're so in tune with the island, Paul."

Oh, give me a break, thought Marissa. She placed her arms around Paul and Pansy and attempted to steer them out of the lobby. "Well, it was lovely to see you, Malia, but we're meeting the Realtor in a few minutes . . ."

"Oh," Paul said, snapping his fingers. "I forgot to tell you. Pansy and I are meeting the Realtor. You get the afternoon off so you can finally get your massage."

"But don't you want me with you in case you see something good?"

Paul rolled his eyes. "The housing market is pretty tight right now. I'm not expecting much, but if there's something good, we'll arrange to have Jenny take you before we leave tomorrow night. Go and enjoy yourself, Marissa. You deserve it." He leaned over to give her a kiss, just as Malia thrust a small packet at Marissa, jabbing her sharply in the ribs.

"Oh, Mrs. Price, I *am* sorry about that!" Malia said, looking genuinely flustered. "Are you all right?"

"I'm fine," Marissa said, giving Paul a look that said, *Can you believe her?* But he didn't seem to have noticed.

Malia fastened on a bright smile. "Okay, well, your appointment is at one o'clock. I've booked you with our top massage therapist; she does all of our celebrity clients. If you leave now, you'll have time to sit in our famous lava rock sauna."

"It's almost as good as being in the volcano with Madam Pele," Paul joked.

Malia laughed merrily along with him, making Marissa wish that they were near the volcano so she could give Malia a gentle push in.

The moment Marissa stepped into the Kohala Bay Spa, she was in heaven. She forgot about Malia, forgot about how she wasn't ready to be a full-time mom, forgot about how there wasn't a volcano flow for her to rave about when she returned to New York. Marissa felt her shoulders begin to relax and wished she could collapse into a puddle right there. Soothing and tranquil music played in the waiting area, and a wonderful, warm fragrance filled the air.

"It's nice, isn't it?" the woman behind the spa counter said. She pointed to a small aromatherapy burner on the countertop. "Organic ginger, sandalwood, and ylang ylang. It's one of our most popular blends."

Marissa picked up the small bottle of essential oil as the woman typed something into the computer. "Avalon Aloha," the bottle read.

"Do you make it here or this is a private label?"

"Oh no, this is definitely one of our own. Kavena, your masseuse, does all of our proprietary blends in-house." The woman handed her a spa pass and locker key. "An attendant will meet you at the entrance of the women's locker room and then take you out to the massage *hale,* your private outdoor massage cabana. Enjoy your afternoon, Mrs. Price."

"Thank you," Marissa said gratefully. She walked through tables of tastefully displayed merchandise, mentally choosing gifts for Kate and Robin.

In the locker room, Marissa put her things away and changed into a robe and slippers. She followed the attendant outdoors to the massage *hale*, which was a small hut with bamboo thatch walls. Marissa could see the ocean only a few feet away and could hear the sound of waves crashing gently against the rocky shore. The *hale* was pleasantly infused with the Avalon Aloha scent.

Bliss.

"Kavena will be with you in a moment. Go ahead and lie facedown on the table, between the blankets. Have a wonderful massage."

"Thank you."

The attendant closed the door behind her and Marissa took off her robe and slid between the warm blankets, facedown. It was like sinking into a cushion. She lowered her face into the face cradle and saw three pink plumerias floating in a silver bowl of water resting on the floor directly beneath her. Now that made sense. If you were going to spend half an hour on your stomach, you may as well have something nice to look at. Not that Marissa intended to keep her eyes open for very long.

She was almost asleep when she heard the door to the *hale* open and then close.

"Mrs. Price?" a voice said softly. "Aloha, I'm Kavena. I'll be doing your massage today. Are you comfortable?" A comforting, heavy hand smoothed the blanket over Marissa's back. She wanted to purr.

"Wonderful," Marissa murmured drowsily, her eyes still closed.

"Just relax. Any health issues you'd like me to be aware of?"

Marissa managed to grunt a no.

"Okay, let me get ready and then I'll do a blessing before we begin."

Kavena padded softly around the *hale*. Marissa heard the

sound of Kavena quietly chanting in Hawaiian, and then felt warm, oiled hands on her shoulders and back. With the sound of the ocean right outside of the *hale*, Marissa drifted to sleep.

"Mrs. Price?" A voice gently roused her and Marissa could feel a hand rubbing her back. "I'll need you to turn over onto your back now."

Marissa slowly opened her eyes, the bowl of plumerias slowly coming into focus. How long had she been asleep? Her body felt soft and warm, like jelly. She didn't want to move . . . ever. She could easily lie here forever.

"I'll step outside for a moment. Take your time; there's no need to rush." Kavena walked around the table and Marissa saw her step into a pair of worn, tan Birkenstocks before going out the door.

Birkenstocks?

Marissa lifted her face out of the face cradle, and stared at the closed door. It couldn't be . . . no, that was crazy. There were plenty of people who wore Birkenstocks. Not in New York, true, but this was Hawaii. And this Kavena person was a masseuse, a masseuse who blended essential oils on the side. Of course she would wear Birkenstocks—she couldn't very well do her job in a pair of Lanvin flats, could she?

Besides, Kavena had to be a local woman, probably a large woman given her heavy healing hands and the way she had gently kneaded Marissa's body into a blob of Play-Doh. Not a petite, slightly chunky, nursing mother with dirty blond dreadlocks . . .

There was a tap on the door as it slowly opened. "Mrs. Price? Are you ready . . ." The voice trailed off. The voice, that is, belonging to a petite, slightly chunky, nursing mother with dirty blond dreadlocks and Birkenstocks who was staring at Marissa as if she'd seen a ghost.

Marissa, who had yet to flip over onto her back, was frozen with her head craned in the direction of the door. She opened her mouth but nothing came out.

"Well." Kavena was the first to speak. She stepped into the *hale* and closed the door behind her. "It's a Big Island, small world after all." She cleared her throat several times, then crossed the room to pour herself a glass of water. She took a couple of deep breaths with her eyes closed. Then she reached for a clean glass and poured some water for Marissa and held it out, waiting.

Marissa didn't move. To be honest, she wasn't exactly sure what to do or say.

"Go on, take it," Kavena said, somewhat exasperated. Now she was sounding like the woman Marissa had met on the plane, which oddly made Marissa feel slightly more at ease. She knew how to work with the irritable Kavena more than the peaceful one. "Just a sip. You need to start moving the toxins out of your body. Plus it will help with the shock."

Marissa warily accepted the glass. "Thanks," she finally managed. She pushed herself up on her elbows and took a sip. It did help. She handed the glass back to Kavena, who looked as uncertain as Marissa about what to do next.

Marissa gathered the blankets around her and sat up. "Look," she said. "Maybe we can ask them if there's another masseuse that's available . . ."

Kavena had her back to Marissa, busying herself with putting the caps on her lotions and massage oils. "There isn't. We're fully booked—it's the start of the high season."

"Well, maybe I can go right into my facial . . ."

"You still have almost an hour left. Malia booked you for

a deluxe massage. The aestheticians are fully booked as well, so you'd have to wait." Kavena was lighting the end of something and Marissa sat up, frowning, as she saw the flicker of a large flame.

"What's that?"

"White sage." The flame subsided to a red glow at the tip of what seemed to be a bundle of silver leaves. "I thought it might be good to clear the energy in the room before we continue." Kavena began waving it through the air, walking around the *hale*.

The smell was somewhat overpowering and Marissa began to cough. "Don't you think that's kind of ambitious, given that we're in a hut made of dry grass and bamboo?"

Kavena gave Marissa an annoyed look before dropping the small bundle of leaves into a bowl and covering it. "I think I know what I'm doing. I have done this before, after all."

Marissa waved a hand in front of her face. "It's just that the smell is kind of strong and there are all these reports about second-hand smoke. As 'the best' masseuse . . ." Marissa tried to use air quotes but almost lost her blanket, "this resort has to offer I assume you would know . . ."

"Stop." Kavena closed her eyes and held up a hand. "I suggest you stop while you're ahead," she said, "and before you say something you're going to regret later." Kavena went to the head of the table and pulled off the face cradle. "Come on, let's get you on your back."

"What are you doing?"

Kavena looked at her steadily. "I'm finishing this massage. It just so happens that I am 'the best' this resort, or any resort on the coast, has to offer. And I didn't hear you complaining before." She patted the table. "Come on." She unfolded a fresh blanket and held it up as a drape so Marissa could adjust herself and lie down in privacy. Marissa could hear Kavena breathing deeply on the other side, and some mumbling, like she was repeating a mantra.

"All right," Marissa finally said, turning over and lying on her back. "But I think you owe me an apology."

The drape snapped down. *What?!*" So much for the deep breathing.

"You were *completely* rude to me on the airplane," Marissa reminded her. "I was just trying to help."

Kavena's mouth dropped open. "Excuse me, but you were unbelievably *condescending*! You don't think I know what's best for my son?"

"I was just trying to be helpful. I have a daughter, you know, and I raised her . . ."

"You *raised* your daughter?" Kavena asked sarcastically, arching an eyebrow. "Was that her grandmother sitting across the aisle from me when we took off from New York? Because I could smell nanny a mile away!"

"I work!" Marissa said hotly. But then her voice seemed to stick in her throat when she realized how everything was still in flux. "I mean, it might change if we move but we haven't decided that yet, so it just made sense that we bring Consuelo along, and anyway, she had to fly back to be with her son so it's just been me—"

"Please." Kavena was angrily folding the blanket drape. "Maybe you're right. Maybe this isn't going to work. I can call the front desk and have them give you a refund. You can sit in the sauna until it's time for the rest of your spa treatments." She started to gather her things.

Marissa sat up, holding the blanket in front of her. "Now who's being condescending? And, by the way, it's not like I see your son here, hanging on to you like a koala. It looks like you need to work, too."

Kavena raised her chin stubbornly. "That's different."

"How? Where is your son, anyway?"

Kavena was silent. Then she let out a long breath. "At Keiki Make the World Go Round Day Care. *Keiki* means children in Hawaiian." Her voice seemed to catch, and Kavena looked away. She started to fuss with something on the table.

An ocean breeze blew gently through the *hale,* dissipating the smoky white sage and somehow taking the charge of the room with it. Marissa felt suddenly deflated, no longer interested in fighting with this woman she didn't even know. And, she supposed it really wasn't any of her business how Kavena raised her son. God knew Marissa felt enough pressure about raising Pansy, about what she should or shouldn't do.

Kavena still hadn't turned around. "Look," Marissa finally said, clearing her throat. "I'm sorry to have butted into your business. I'm a consultant, I tend to do that. It's my nature." She tried a small laugh but it died when Kavena didn't respond. Marissa tried a different approach. "Well, I'm sure your son is having a great time at that *keiki* daycare place. He's probably learning a lot."

Kavena spun around, distraught. "But he's not!" she wailed, then buried her face in her hands. It took Marissa a moment to get over her shock before spotting a box of tissues. She quickly handed one to Kavena.

Kavena sniffed. "He hates it. But they're the only school that I can afford."

"Even as the top masseuse for the resort? With tips and everything?"

"Do you know what rents are like here? It's insane! All these people from the mainland come over and buy up property like it's candy, and then charge us locals an arm and a leg!" Kavena pulled more tissues from the box, blowing her nose and dabbing at her eyes. "And groceries—and gas! It's unreal."

"I'm sorry," Marissa said. "I guess we'll be in that same boat soon, too."

"What?" Kavena clutched at her tissues and stared at Marissa. "Are you *joking*?"

Marissa noticed dryly that Kavena didn't seem so distraught anymore. She straightened up on the table. "What do you mean? I'm sure you know by now that my husband has been tapped as the next GM, and we're just trying to decide whether or not to make the move."

"I know, but I didn't think you would seriously consider it." Kavena tossed her tissues away, then went to wash her hands. "I mean, I heard the rumor but now that I know it's . . . you . . . I mean, really!" Kavena waved the thought away, chuckling.

Now it was Marissa's turn to look indignant. "I don't get what's so funny," she said stiffly.

Kavena stopped chuckling enough to realize that Marissa was serious. "Oh, it's just that . . ." She cleared her throat, suddenly ill at ease. "I'm sorry, it's just that . . . if I can be honest . . . I just don't see you here."

Marissa didn't know why, but it felt like a slap in the face. "Why not?"

"Well, you're a big-city girl, a corporate woman who probably likes designer brands and eating in fancy restaurants. I can see you in Honolulu—*maybe*—but the Big Island?" Kavena scoffed. "You'd be bored and out of here in a week!"

Marissa started to protest. "I find that a bit presumptuous, seeing how you don't even know me . . ."

"I know, I know, and maybe you're the exception"— Kavena rolled her eyes to indicate that she didn't think Marissa was—"but I've seen countless people come from the mainland, all starry-eyed and excited, only to turn around and leave within the year. Pele's Slingshot never misses."

"Pele's what?"

"Pele's Slingshot." Kavena refilled Marissa's water glass and handed it to her. "The island either welcomes you or it doesn't. And if it doesn't, the goddess Pele will send you right back to the mainland, just as fast as you came."

Marissa felt a shiver run up her spine. "Come on, that's just some kind of urban legend."

Kavena narrowed her eyes. "Oh yeah? Well, why do you think the current GM is leaving? By my count, it's been exactly eleven months and a week. And he's not the first."

"Well, maybe the problem rests more with HR and executive recruitment than anything else," Marissa said stubbornly.

"Sure. Maybe." Kavena didn't sound convinced. "All I'm saying is, this island is a very special place. There's a lot of energy here—we have five volcanoes, two that are active, another two that are dormant, and one that's extinct. All this on an island the size of Connecticut." Kavena closed her eyes reverently and breathed deeply.

Now it was Marissa's turn to roll her eyes. She didn't doubt anything that Kavena was saying, but it was a little off-putting since, in her opinion, Kavena didn't necessarily look like she fit in any more than Marissa did. "Okay, so let me ask you: you consider yourself a 'local'—how long have you been here?"

Kavena lifted her chin defensively. "I've been here for a while."

"Are you Hawaiian?"

A pause. "It depends on what you mean by Hawaiian. It's like asking someone if they're *American*. What constitutes being American?"

Sheesh. "Okay. Well, is Kavena your real name?"

Kavena raised herself up. "It's my Hawaiian name," she

said haughtily. "I was given it by my *kumu*, my spiritual teacher."

"Uh-huh. Well, what was your name before?"

"That *is* my name," Kavena insisted adamantly.

Marissa persisted, enjoying that the shoe was finally on the other foot. "Is it your legal name? Do you have a last name?"

Kavena poured some water for herself and sipped it silently.

Marissa sighed. "I'm genuinely curious," she said, because she was. "Besides, I'm sitting here naked under this blanket with an hour to kill before my next appointment. Consider it an opportunity to educate a naïve New Yorker about"—Marissa struggled to keep a straight face—"*your* ways on the island."

Kavena sighed. "It's Jones."

"Jones?"

"Margaret Jones. Margaret Annabelle Jones. *That's* my legal name." Kavena made a face.

"Well, I think it's a nice name," Marissa said graciously.

From the look on Kavena's face, it was obvious that she wasn't surprised that someone like Marissa would like that name.

"But I definitely think Kavena suits you," Marissa added quickly.

Kavena sighed. "Thanks." She put down her glass. "Okay, enough small talk. Let's get you back on your back."

"Why?"

"I'm going to finish this massage. I don't like to do things halfway . . . That's *my* nature." She patted the table.

Marissa smiled. "Touché." She lay back down on the massage table and adjusted her blanket.

Kavena walked around the table, straightening Marissa's

blanket and breathing deeply. "**All** right, I'm going to do a new blessing and then **we'll get star**ted." She placed a cool eye mask over Marissa's **eyes. Maris**sa couldn't place the fragrance, but Kavena was a step ahead of her. "It's *maile*, by the way, which is used in the most sacred of celebrations. It's a native vine." Kavena touched Marissa's shoulders and, as if by command, Marissa felt her shoulders relax.

Kavena began to chant quietly. The scent of *maile* was intoxicating. And before she could think another thought, Marissa drifted off to sleep again.

Time seemed to stretch over the next couple of days. Marissa was amazed at how much they were able to do in a single day. Their lives in New York were full and busy, there was no question about that, but sometimes at the end of the day Marissa wasn't quite sure what she had actually accomplished. Here, they seemed to be able to cover the island—looking at houses, visiting Pansy's prospective schools, a coffee farm, a snorkel cruise—and still have time to lounge on the beach or by the pool.

Pansy had turned on the charm full blast during her school interviews, doing her best to win over the admissions directors. On top of Pansy's references and amazing test results, the schools were completely taken with her, so Pansy's perfect-child performance really wasn't necessary. But Marissa knew that Pansy had fallen in love with the Big Island, for whatever reason, and was doing what she could to make sure they could move here.

The other challenge was finding a place to live.

"Slim pickings," Paul had muttered as they walked out of another house.

"You only need to find one!" Jenny had chortled as she bustled them into the car. "And I would be happy to send you any new listings as they become available. Going online to my website is sometimes best because things come and go *so* quickly, but I'm *very* good at keeping it updated daily. You just never know when that perfect house will reveal itself!"

"If nothing reveals itself in the next couple of weeks, we're renting," Paul told her.

Jenny's eyes narrowed—she wasn't ready to lose a sale. "I know of at least two pocket listings coming up next week," she said, lowering her voice conspiratorially even though there was no one else but them in the car. "I'm not sure where they are exactly, but once I find out, I'll send you pictures."

But now, as their visit came to a close, Marissa was thinking about what Kavena had said—all cows and lava flows. And, technically speaking, Marissa didn't even get to see the lava flow. She had been so excited by the initial thought of moving to Hawaii that she hadn't really thought it out. No decent shopping. No theater, no opera, no ballet. And she would miss Kate, no doubt about that. Marissa didn't know anybody in Hawaii.

"I'm having a slight panic attack," Marissa told Paul the night before they were due to return home. A warm ocean breeze wafted through the room, and Pansy was already asleep in her bed, a content look on her face.

"Why?" Paul was stretched out on the bed, his eyes on the TV screen.

"It's all happening so fast," she said. "What if this doesn't work out? If I walk away from Paradigm now, I may as well kiss my career good-bye. It will be harder than hell for me to jump back in three years later."

"It'll be fine. Don't worry." He idly reached into the bag of pretzels he had taken from the minibar.

"Paul, I'm serious." Marissa picked up the remote and turned the TV off. Paul sighed and turned to face her.

"But I thought you **wanted to** quit," he said. "Remember how you used to talk **about staying** home with Pansy, maybe even working from home or starting your own company?"

Marissa was annoyed. "That was in *theory*," she snapped.

"Well, now you have a chance to make it a reality. No pain, no gain. You gotta take a risk sometime." He poured the remaining contents of the pretzel bag into his mouth.

"Easy for you to say—*you'll* still have your job. What am I supposed to do while you're at work and Pansy's at school?"

Paul started laughing. "Marissa, I am not about to tell you what to do. It hasn't worked before. I'm sure it's not going to work now."

"Everything's just moving so fast," she grumbled. "I don't see how we can make the move so quickly. I just wish there was a way that we had more time to decide . . ."

"Well, we don't," Paul said, his mood shifting. "What are you saying, Marissa—that you *don't* want to move to Hawaii?"

"I'm just saying that I don't know. I want to, but I'd be giving up a lot. I worked really hard to get to where I am, Paul. I don't want to just throw it away."

"Marissa . . ." Paul rubbed his temples.

"What?"

"I told Fallon this morning that we would take the assignment." He dropped his hands and looked at her, almost angry.

"*You what?*" Marissa stared at him in disbelief. "Paul, how could you? I haven't made up my mind yet, and I thought we were going to decide as a family!"

"I thought we had! You and Pansy seem so happy here, and I was feeling good about everything—I figured that it was just a matter of time before we had the conversation. Fallon was hinting that there was someone lined up behind me if I said no, and I just didn't want to lose any leverage." He kicked the side of the bed. "If I tell them that we need more time, we may as well forget about it."

"You should have thought about that before you gave them an answer." Marissa felt panic well up inside her. "It's been barely a week since you first told me the news, Paul. What do they expect?"

"Marissa, they flip through GMs on this property like it's nobody's business. But here's the thing: I think I can make a difference—in fact, I *know* I can. If I hesitate, they're going to go to the next guy. I'm sorry I didn't check with you first, but I honestly thought we were on the same page. I had to make a split-second decision and I didn't want to lose it— this is an amazing opportunity."

"For you." Marissa let the words sink in. She had more to lose—that was clear to her. Why wasn't it clear to him? "Paul, I can't believe you did that. I just can't make the decision while I'm here. I need to get back home and think about it some more. I just don't think a decision as big as this should rest with one person."

He looked at her steadily before striding to the bathroom. "Funny. It sure seems like that's what's happening now."

And the door closed behind him with a slam.

They had returned to New York amidst a thunderstorm and freezing rain. By the time they reached their apartment, they were wet and jet-lagged, utterly exhausted from the flight. Just the same, Marissa was up early the next day, eager to head into the office and to avoid a confrontation with Paul. A flurry of meetings had kept her busy all day and she quickly lost track of time, grateful for the familiar rhythm of her workday. For once she was actually grateful for the pile of work on her desk.

She was surprised when her secretary, Robin, appeared in the doorway of her office, bundled up with her purse slung across her body.

Robin looked at Marissa's cluttered desk. "Storm front is heading our way," she said. "Are you heading home soon?"

Marissa shook her head. She and Paul were barely talking, and even Pansy seemed to deflate once they stepped into their apartment. Staying in the office would definitely be easier. "I need to catch up on some work."

"Well, don't get stranded. But if you do, I have powdered donuts in my bottom drawer." Robin gave her a friendly wave good-bye just as Marissa's computer beeped to tell her that she had mail.

She opened an e-mail from Jenny, the Realtor. YOUR HOME, read the subject line, and then several pictures immediately appeared on the screen.

Marissa scrolled through the e-mail, looking at the pictures and reading Jenny's narrative.

It was a huge house, five bedrooms with four bathrooms. There was also a separate one-bedroom, one-bath guest house with a small kitchen. "It's called an *ohana* unit," Jenny wrote. "It's like a mother-in-law unit; a place for extended family to stay. The previous owners used the house as a bed-and-breakfast. It's spacious, has an amazing view, and backs into a pasture, so it'll feel like you have some acreage, too. It will probably be sold before the end of the business day—places like this don't stay on the market for long!"

Marissa halfheartedly clicked on the images and found herself becoming more and more interested with each picture. The house looked nice. The price was steep, but everything over there was. If they moved, they would have to sell their apartment in New York in order to take on a new mortgage.

Marissa sighed and turned back to her work. How did all those other women do it? The city was filled with them—working mothers and wives. How did they manage to keep it all together?

She worked steadily, moving through her work quickly but efficiently, determined not to bring any of it home tonight. The office emptied one by one, until only Marissa was left. After a couple of hours, she gave in and raided Robin's drawers, munching through the donuts as she signed off on two more projects. Outside, the sky had turned a menacing gray.

Her phone rang and she picked it up without thinking. "Marissa Price."

"Weather Channel says a storm front's heading in," Paul said shortly by way of greeting. Marissa could hear the familiar tightness in his voice.

"I know. Robin told me."

"Well, I've sent Consuelo home already and I'm here with Pansy. I think you should come home before it gets worse."

Marissa looked at her nearly cleared desk. "I'm almost done here."

There was a long pause. "Marissa," Paul started, and his voice was no longer defensive, but gentle. "I want to apologize. I shouldn't have accepted the assignment without checking with you first. I just got caught up in the moment."

Marissa softened with the apology. "I know."

"I'll call around and see who's still delivering. Can you make it back for dinner and we can talk about it some more? Whatever we decide, I'll tell Fallon tomorrow."

She glanced out the window and caught her breath. The rain was coming down in sheets, the sky dark and foreboding. Thunder rumbled and there was a flash of lightning. "I'll leave now . . ." she started, but then the lights flickered and the phone went dead.

Power came back on almost immediately, but Marissa found herself staring at the handset. New York was in the middle of a storm, and here she was, the lone person in the office while her family was tucked away safely at home. What was the matter with her? Why on earth wasn't she tucked away with them?

At lunchtime, she had gone to an ATM to withdraw money and couldn't help but notice the colorful posters lining the windows of the bank. There were various shots of a family dressed in their bathing suits and playing on the beach. The words HAWAII were printed across the bottom in large, colorful letters. Bright, warm colors. It was the bank's annual winter giveaway, one free entry with every new six-month CD that was opened. Marissa always scoffed at such contests. Really, what were the odds? It was probably worse than the lottery.

But Paul, Pansy, and Marissa had hit the jackpot—an all-expenses paid "trip" to Hawaii for three years. What were the odds of that?

Hawaii. The promise of paradise. A small smile slowly spread across her face.

Marissa dialed home. Paul answered on the first ring. "Are you all right?" he asked.

"I'm fine," she said, and felt a rush of exhilaration.

"Are you coming home?"

"Not yet, I need a few more minutes . . ."

Paul sounded frustrated again. "Marissa, I really think the storm's just going to get worse . . ."

". . . to draft my letter of resignation."

There was a pause. Then Paul asked carefully, "Don't you want to talk about it first? Are you sure about this?"

Marissa's fingers were flying over the keys. The letter she had dreamed about writing for the past couple of years spilled onto the screen. "I'm sure," she said, with more certainty than she'd felt in days. "I'll hang up so you can call Sam. And Jenny. It's still early there—she can put in an offer on that house. I know you saw the e-mail."

"I did." She could tell he was grinning through the phone. "Pansy and I love it. So what are you saying—it's paradise for us?"

Marissa smiled as her printer hummed to life. "It's paradise for us."

'eha | four

"So are we going straight to the house?" Pansy was pressed against the glass of the rental car, excited. Their Audi SUV and BMW sedan were on the boat from the mainland and wouldn't arrive for a couple more days.

"Of course. What's the point of buying a house if we're not going to use it?" Paul grinned at his daughter in the rearview mirror before taking Marissa's hand and raising it to his lips for a kiss. "Did Jenny say everything would be all set?"

Marissa nodded and gave his hand a squeeze. "All set."

Jenny Olsen had turned out to be more resourceful than Marissa had originally given her credit for. Their offer had been accepted and Jenny had pushed for a twenty-one-day close, taking care of the inspection and all the other buyer's details. Marissa concentrated on getting everything taken care of in New York and enrolling Pansy at Hawaii Day School. Everything they would need was coming by container, scheduled to arrive later in the week.

Kate had balked at the news of the move, but still came over to help Marissa pack. She snapped at movers and appropriated a few choice pieces of clothing that Marissa had planned to donate, even though Kate was almost two sizes smaller than Marissa ("Is this from Barneys? You're donating a $450 quilted vest from Barneys to the Salvation Army? It'll go right on the rack next to fleece jackets from the Gap!"). Paul's parents had bemoaned the distance to Hawaii, ignoring the fact that they rarely ever made the trip to New York from Michigan, having seen Pansy twice in the past five years. Marissa's mother, still in Chile, had murmured her assent while noting that the fresh air would be good for Pansy.

Paul pulled into the driveway and cut the engine. "This is it!" he announced, his hands still gripping the steering wheel.

The Price family sat in the car, staring at their new home.

"Are you sure?" Marissa finally asked, looking at the printouts in her hand. She tried to ignore the creeping sense of dread that was overtaking her.

"Of course I'm sure," Paul answered, though he didn't sound convinced.

"It looks different in real life," Pansy noted. "A bit more . . ." Her voice trailed off.

They all stared at the house in silence.

"So there's some wear and tear," Paul finally said. He forced a bright grin. "Jenny left the garage door opener in the house. I'm going to go get it. Coming?"

Marissa tried to swallow the lump in her throat. What had they done? "In a minute," she finally managed.

Pansy jumped out of the car alongside Paul. "Can I look around?"

Paul nodded, his enthusiasm forced. "Go for it!"

Marissa watched as Paul struggled to open the front door

by pushing his weight against it. The house was large, all right—it was a rambling eyesore, to be precise. Peeling paint, dirty windows, and a garden gone wild . . . It looked nothing like the pictures. They traded their shiny apartment in New York for this?

Panic took over. This house, which was now *their* house, was clearly a fixer-upper. They had rolled the gain from the sale of their apartment into this house and had used their savings to pay off their debt. They were starting with a clean slate, but didn't have any money left over for renovations. Marissa fished in her purse for her phone to call Jenny.

"Aloha!" Jenny gushed. "Welcome to Hawaii! How is the house?"

"Great, except that someone clearly Photoshopped the pictures you sent us. This place is—"

"Full of possibilities, I agree! It's a one-in-a-million; I knew you'd love it. When I saw it, I *instantly* thought of your family. A little TLC, it'll look as good as new!"

"Jenny . . ."

"Both Home Depot and Lowe's are on the island—so many choices! Now, I have to run but I'll be by at four o'clock to say hello. I'll see you then. Aloha!" Jenny hung up before Marissa could get another word in.

Paul returned to the car, his face sour. "Go on inside," he told Marissa. "I'll grab our bags."

"Don't you want to put the car in the garage?" she asked.

"Jenny left a note. Garage door isn't working. She'll have someone out to fix it soon."

Marissa got out of the car and walked to the front of the house. It had been sunny in Kona and on their drive to Waimea, but Marissa could see gray clouds rolling toward them from the east side. A cool breeze tickled her arms, along with a wet mist.

Pansy was climbing the oak tree in the front yard. Her

daughter, climbing a tree. This was a first. "Pansy, let's go inside," Marissa called.

Paul was still bringing in their suitcases when fat drops of rain began to fall. Inside, the house was bare except for a couple of folding chairs and a card table Jenny had loaned them until their furniture arrived, along with a couple of mattresses. Pansy was quick to choose her room, and even Paul seemed cheered by his claim of the *ohana* unit, which he would use as a home office.

"I love it," decided Pansy as Paul chased two cockroaches out of the living room. "It's absolutely perfect." She was beaming, a look of contentment on her face.

Paul and Marissa exchanged a bemused glance. That made one of them, anyway. Paul finally shrugged. "Well, I guess it could be worse. For example"—he gestured toward a corner in the living room that Marissa hadn't noticed—"if that extra dryer vent wasn't there, we'd never have the option of doing laundry in the living room." A lone dryer vent pipe hung listlessly out of the wall.

"What the . . ." Marissa couldn't believe it. "Well, Jenny's coming at four o'clock. We can tell her then."

"What's she going to do? Tear out the wall? Install a washer and dryer?" Paul shook his head. "Besides, I'm pretty sure she knows. I'm going to unpack. Coming?"

Marissa shook her head as she sat on a folding chair. She wished now that she had taken up Paul's suggestion that they stay in the hotel for the first couple of nights. They had been so excited about the house that it had seemed apropos that they sleep there the first night.

Jenny arrived at 4:45, her arms full of plastic shopping bags. "The Price family!" she said exuberantly. Her hair was wet and pasted flat against her head. "Looks like we got a bit of that Waimea rain today. That's good luck in Hawaii, you know."

"Really?" It was difficult for Marissa to hide her dismay. She'd had a couple of hours to stew on things a bit, pacing on the creaky hardwood floors and frayed carpet. The house was a mishmash, a white elephant. "Jenny, this house . . . You said it was a bed-and-breakfast before?"

Jenny nodded vigorously. "Yes, that's right. That's why there are three separate entrances into the home and, of course, the *ohana* unit. What a find! They are *so* hard to come by and *everyone* wants one. Wonderful rental income potential!" She went into the kitchen and deposited the bags on the counter.

"Yes, well, we're not planning to rent anything out—we bought this home to live in. I had no idea from the information you sent us that it was so . . . unusual."

"Isn't it? Truly one of a kind! And did you see the view?" Jenny swept past her to the large bay window that overlooked a deck and the pasture behind the house. "Breathtaking! This view of Mauna Kea alone is worth it!" Jenny almost looked faint.

The view was indeed breathtaking. Pansy had read the in-flight magazine aloud on the airplane, informing Paul and Marissa that Mauna Kea was a dormant volcano and considered the tallest mountain in the world when measured from its base on the sea floor. Its name in the Hawaiian language meant "white mountain," since snowfalls left the top of the mountain snow-capped in wintertime. The mountain appeared to Marissa to be both stately and quiet, impressive in its solid stature as it dominated the sky and earth in front of her.

"It is lovely but . . ." Marissa stopped and squinted. "What's that?" she asked, her eyes narrowing as she pointed to the pasture a hundred feet or so beyond their backyard.

Jenny didn't blink. "It looks like a few cows."

"A few? There's got to be a dozen at least!"

"Yes, possibly. What a bonus! It's like you're ranchers without all of the day-to-day responsibilities! Your friends back home will be so jealous!"

Marissa stared at her in amazement. The woman was a piece of work. "Jenny, those cows are practically in our backyard. And that fence—it's practically falling down! Are you sure they can't break through that fence?"

Jenny paused as she leaned toward the window to peer closer. "Oh no," she said cheerfully. "They could *definitely* break through that fence."

"*What?!*"

Jenny was nodding vigorously. "I would definitely have someone come out and fix that. Is Paul handy?"

"No!"

"Hmmm." Jenny turned to give Marissa a bright smile. "Well, who knows. It's lasted this long and I don't see any cows in your yard. Do you?"

"Well, no, but—"

"Paul!" Jenny spotted Paul as he entered the living room and scurried toward him. "Aloha! And where's your darling daughter, Patsy?"

"Pansy," Paul corrected. He jerked his thumb down the hallway. "She's choosing her bedroom as we speak, and I couldn't help but notice that—"

Jenny looped her arm through his and gave him a maternal pat. "Isn't it wonderful? So many choices! Did you see the view?"

It was hopeless. Marissa left Paul to fend for himself and escaped to the bedroom to unpack.

It had been a rough couple of weeks, but now that their cars and things had arrived, Marissa no longer felt like they had made the worst mistake of their lives.

Not exactly, anyway.

There was the first night, which Paul had dubbed their "initiation" to the Big Island. They had fallen asleep, exhausted, only to wake up shivering a few hours later. Marissa had bought them all matching pajamas in celebration of the move, soft brushed cotton shorts with a matching short-sleeved top in a cheerful pineapple and hula girl motif. Perfect if your home was right on the beach, but at a couple thousand feet above sea level, the Prices may as well have been sleeping in their underwear.

The temperature in the house had to be in the mid-fifties. They had ended up layering almost all of their casual clothes on top of their pajamas before falling back asleep, all three of them as round as the Pillsbury Doughboy.

Then it had stopped raining and the clouds parted to reveal a starry sky and full moon, which sent what seemed like three hundred watts of brilliant moonlight through the skylights in the bedroom and right into their faces. ("Skylights in the bedroom!" Jenny had crowed on the phone to them when they put in their offer. "Your window to the universe!") It was as if someone had flipped on a light switch or pointed a turbo-charged flashlight at them. The room was fully lit. Marissa felt her corneas pinch and threw a layered arm over her eyes.

"Oh, my God," Paul moaned, covering his head with a pillow.

Eventually, he and Marissa got up and managed to drag the bed to a corner of the bedroom that was the least lit up, and promptly fell back asleep, exhausted.

They slept for another hour before a mysterious braying woke Marissa with a start. She shook Paul awake, who clutched the sheets as he listened intently, eyes wide. Her heart pounding in her chest, Marissa flipped through a number of scenarios—someone was in a great deal of pain and camped out on their patio, the house was haunted (which would actually explain a lot), they were about to be attacked by aliens from outer space—until Paul got up and padded to the window in his four pairs of socks.

"Be careful!" Marissa whispered urgently.

Paul put a finger to his lips as he tentatively looked outside the window. She saw his shoulders relax, at first in relief, and then, in defeat.

"It's the cows," he said flatly, returning to the bed.

"The cows?"

"They're asleep. I think they're snoring."

Marissa was speechless as she listened to the eerie sound. "Cows snore?" she finally asked.

Paul pulled the covers over his head. "These do," he said, and fell back asleep.

They had tossed and turned for the rest of the night, and then Marissa and Pansy had driven Paul to work in the rental car so they could have it for the rest of the day. It didn't help that Malia happened to be walking past the entrance of the lobby, looking fresh and perky (Marissa, on the other hand, hadn't even showered, her hair twisted up and fastened with a clip). Malia had leaned over to give Marissa a polite kiss on the cheek, offering a quick view of the top of her ample breasts. Damn, and she smelled nice, too. Pansy waved sleepily from the backseat, and Malia once again removed a flower from behind her ear. The small cluster of *pikake*, or jasmine, blooms instantly filled the car with its heady fragrance, which Marissa had to smell for twenty minutes as they drove back to the house.

Marissa, who had at one time been expecting to awaken to the sound of waves lapping on the beach, was instead greeted each morning with nonstop rain pelting their roof. Pansy had found the first leak in one of the guest rooms, then Paul reported another one in the master bath, along the seam of yet another skylight. On one particularly wet morning, Marissa walked into their closet and saw a small puddle in her favorite pair of Chloe flats.

Their fix-it list was growing alarmingly long, which Jenny blithely dismissed as the perfect chance for Paul and Marissa to apply those "final touches" that would make the house "theirs." Having bought the house "as-is" ("typical for Hawaii properties," Jenny had told them), they didn't have much choice other than to fix what they could and postpone the rest to later.

"We have plenty of time," Paul had said optimistically one night. That was before the garage door, which had supposedly been fixed, stopped midway as Paul was getting ready to drive to work, leaving him stuck until he figured out how to release the door altogether and eventually drive out, muttering under his breath.

Now, with Paul at work and Pansy in school (and the house efficiently unpacked in a record three days, a feat that impressed Jenny to no end), Marissa found herself sitting at the kitchen table, bored. She jumped online every now and then to check her e-mail or surf, but that only took a few minutes. Now that she was no longer working, her inbox was no longer stuffed with messages from work, just up-dates from Kate, who was uncharacteristically oozing over the latest "totally thoughtful and random" thing her new corporate-attorney boyfriend, Oliver Lawrence, did. (Four dozen roses! Buggy rides in the Park! A last-minute jaunt to California—Rodeo Drive, specifically!) It felt like a subtle betrayal, because in the past, whenever Marissa would talk about a romantic or thoughtful thing Paul did, Kate would just roll her eyes, unimpressed, refusing to give Paul—or anyone, for that matter—any credit. She was the one who used to tease Marissa about Paul's deep, soulful looks, em-barking on a scornful tirade about sensitive men. Kate was particularly suspicious about any man who claimed to be "family-oriented," declaring that she would never have children for that reason alone. "Kate-oriented" was how she liked her men.

Marissa thought she'd spend days at the beach, but instead found herself flipping channels aimlessly, looking for something to watch. She wasn't interested in exploring the island, much less Waimea, and certainly not alone. She napped, but never seemed to be able to doze more than an hour before the cows behind the house started mooing in chorus, as if to make sure Marissa stayed on her toes.

Cooking was the other new thing. Marissa, who felt generally inept in the kitchen, found herself enthralled by the Food Network, and began downloading recipes en masse. She had managed to serve Paul and Pansy two homemade meals so far, and while delicious, in the end had cost the same as five nights' takeout. Really, what was the point? Plus she was exhausted afterward and then there was the cleanup, which Paul gamely volunteered to do, missing the occasional spot that would send Marissa back to the sink. She would vow never to cook another meal, only to have another episode of the Food Network suck her in again.

Today, Marissa was going to try a simple grilled chicken with a pine nut pesto. It looked simple to make and leftovers could easily be converted into sandwiches the next day. She already had the chicken and would only need a couple of ingredients. Enthused (really, how hard could this be?), Marissa made a shopping list and headed to the local grocery store.

But the store didn't have pine nuts, one of the main ingredients for the pesto, and had run out of fresh basil.

"It goes fast," said a clerk who was stacking green onions. "What about dried?"

"Dried won't work," said Marissa, disappointed. She knew that much.

"You could try something else, like spinach," he said. "My aunty does that. Tastes good." He reached over and handed her a bunch of fresh spinach. "Picked today from Nishimura Farms, right down the road. Don't even need to cook it."

Marissa reluctantly placed the spinach in her cart. She wasn't good at winging it with recipes, and while the spinach might work in lieu of basil, she still needed the pine nuts.

Her eyes scanned the shelves. Peanuts, almonds, walnuts, pecans . . . none of these would do. Then her eyes rested on something.

Macadamia nuts.

Why not? she thought as she picked up a small tin. Now that they lived in Hawaii, where mac nuts were in abundance, it would be a good substitute for the pine nuts. Marissa giggled as a thought crossed her mind: *Mac nuts— the other white nut.*

Marissa decided to do a quick sweep of the aisles, grabbing a few more things. *This is me, shopping for my family. This is me, Marissa Price, master chef extraordinaire, picking up a few things for a gourmet home-cooked meal. This is me, Marissa Price, corporate-exec-turned-Martha Stewart, but with better hair and cuter shoes.*

She headed for the checkout line, elated. She might be able to pull off this cooking thing, after all. Marissa tried not to look too shocked as her grocery bill was added up (eight dollars for a box of cereal? Insane!), wishing now that she had paid more attention to the prices before filling her cart. The same amount of money in New York—*New York!*—got her almost twice as many groceries.

In the parking lot, Marissa started her car and then had a niggling feeling that she was forgetting something. She pulled out her receipt and compared it to her shopping list.

Everything looked fine. She checked her lipstick in the rearview mirror, then put the car in reverse and backed out.

There was the crunching sound of metal hitting metal. Marissa slammed on the brakes and saw, to her horror, that she had hit another car that was driving by, looking for a parking space.

"Shit!" Marissa hit the steering wheel with the palm of her hand. She tried to remember if she had notified their insurance company of their move to Hawaii. Marissa put the car in park and cut the engine, then braced herself for the worst as she opened the car door and stepped out.

A small crowd had already started to form outside the grocery store. Marissa ignored them as she made her way to the back of her car.

One of the Audi's rear lights had been smashed, and the bumper of Marissa's SUV had put a noticeable dent in the side of a rusty Toyota station wagon. The owner of the car looked to be in her sixties, her salt-and-pepper hair cut short and slightly spiked, a pair of wire-rimmed glasses hanging from a chain around her neck. The woman was dressed casually in a long-sleeved shirt and shorts, her hands on her hips as she came around to study the damage to her car. Seeing the dent, she shook her head in defeat.

"Crap! This is not my week," the woman muttered. She checked her watch.

"I'm sorry," Marissa apologized to the woman, who looked more resigned than distraught. "It was my fault; I'll have my insurance company cover it." She pulled out her phone to call Paul.

Malia answered. "Office of Paul Price, this is Malia," came the prompt, cheery voice. Frustrated, Marissa hung up. Whenever Paul was busy or in a meeting, he had his phone forwarded to Malia, and Marissa was in no mood to deal with her today.

Another car pulled up behind the Toyota and a uni-
formed police officer stepped out of the car. A small traffic
jam was forming in the parking lot, and Marissa felt a
creeping sense of dread as the officer took his time to assess
the damage.

The police officer stood in front of the two women. "License and registration, please."

"How could you not see me?" the woman asked as they
handed him their information. "I was barely going five
miles per hour!"

"I checked and thought it was clear."

"Well, it wasn't."

Marissa forced a smile. "No, apparently not."

The women stood in silence as the officer wrote down
their information, then walked back to his car.

"So, did you just get here?" the woman asked, nodding at
Marissa's car. "Your license plate says New York."

"Two weeks," Marissa said. "And off to a great start as
you can see." She strained to see what the officer was doing.

The other woman let out a noisy exhalation, then looked
around the parking lot at the small crowd that had gathered to
watch. "With luck we'll make the six o'clock news," she said.
She extended her hand to Marissa. "My name is Jane Crisp."

Marissa shook the woman's hand, grateful that Jane
wasn't irate. "Marissa Price. And again, I am really sorry."

Jane brushed it off with a shrug. "It's just been one of
those weeks."

"I hear you," agreed Marissa wryly. She pulled out her
phone to call Paul again but, remembering that Malia was
on the other end, shoved it back into her purse.

Jane had an amused look on her face. "Honey, you look
like someone who just swallowed a vat of sour lemons."

Marissa bent down to pick up the broken pieces of her
taillight. "It's a long story."

Jane grinned. "I got time." She nodded toward the police officer who was sitting in his car, jotting something down. "Who knows how long this will take?"

Marissa sat on the bumper of her car as Jane leaned against hers. "It's just . . . Oh, forget it." It sounded too petty to admit that she was jealous of her husband's secretary. "It's silly."

"If you could see your face a minute ago, I don't think you'd be saying that. Come on, spill." Jane was looking at her with a grin on her face. "I can smell a good story a mile away."

The police officer was walking back toward them, a stern look on his face.

"Tell you what," Jane said. "When he's finished—unless he has to haul you off to jail for any reason—let me buy you a cup of coffee. My treat."

Marissa hadn't expected this. She knew Waimea wasn't New York, but to have the person whose car you hit invite you out for coffee? She wouldn't have believed it. If she were still in New York, she definitely would have thought it weird and declined.

But in the short time since they'd arrived, Marissa had yet to meet anybody new. Even Kate didn't have time to talk on the phone, now that she was spending all of her free time with Oliver.

"This is partially your fault," Kate had informed Marissa when they spoke last. "If you hadn't left, I wouldn't have been so desperate to find someone to listen to my every rant, which he does very well. Plus there's the sex and the gifts, which are nice, too." There was a pause and Kate reluctantly added in a low voice, "And it just so happens that he's really sweet and I like spending time with him, too."

Paul had told Marissa to go out and make some friends, making it sound like it was the easiest thing in the world to do. "Meet someone for lunch or go to the beach," he said. "Gossip. Do whatever it is you women do—just get out of the house!"

"I don't know anyone here, Paul. What am I supposed to do, stand on the street corner with a sign?"

Paul had started to exercise in the hotel's gym after work, adding another hour and a half before returning home. "You can come and meet me to work out," he suggested.

Marissa declined. Trolling the gym for potential friends would be the ultimate low.

Now, as Jane grinned back at her good-naturedly, Marissa found herself smiling back. She nodded. "Sure," she said. "Why not?" Drops of rain started to dot the cement of the parking lot.

The police officer gave Marissa a stern warning to be more careful and handed both women a copy of the accident report.

"Great." Jane beamed at her before climbing back into her car. She leaned over to roll down the passenger side window. "I'll meet you across the street at Kava Java in five."

Kava Java was a comfortable coffeehouse that seemed to be a cross between Starbucks and a little grass shack. The hardwood floors were covered with tightly woven rugs and runners, rattan settees, and couches with overstuffed cushions. Trendy lamps glowed and dangled from the high ceilings. A smattering of bookshelves were tucked in corners and pressed against the walls, stocked with books as well as an assortment of coffeemakers, espresso machines, mugs, decorative creamers, and spoons. A tasteful selection of Hawaiiana antiques and kitsch adorned the walls, along with several large paneled oil paintings. Ukulele and slack key guitar music strummed through the coffeehouse.

Jane came in right behind her, shaking the rain off her shoulders. "Nothing like the smell of a coffeehouse on a wet day, eh?"

"It's heavenly," Marissa agreed.

"Go grab us some seats by the fireplace," Jane suggested. "I'll get our coffee. You strike me as an espresso kind of gal. Am I wrong?"

"No, you got it." Marissa smiled warmly. This kind of kindness was practically against the law in New York— you'd be scorned and kicked out of the city for life.

"Double?"

"Please."

Marissa watched as Jane headed to the counter. Marissa's smile faltered somewhat when she saw Jane continue *behind* the counter and tie on an apron. She gave a high five to another barista and seemed to be explaining the car accident to a clerk as she prepared their coffee. Jane chose a few pastries and, seeing Marissa watching her, gave a wave.

Oh, God. Why hadn't she thought this through? She was making friends with a barista. A ten-dollar-an-hour glorified coffee waitress who was sixty years old. Marissa should have just gone home while she had the chance and called it a day. Marissa's mind spun as she watched Jane approach, arms full.

"Wow, everything looks wonderful," Marissa said, eager to drink her coffee, eat her croissant, and get the hell out of there.

"We make the pastries fresh in our small commercial kitchen in the back. Here's your double shot of espresso. And this"—Jane handed Marissa a steaming mug—"is a special coffee I've been working on. Let me know what you think."

Marissa took a tentative sip. The coffee was full-bodied, smooth and rich, with a hint of vanilla and something else Marissa couldn't identify. "It's good," she said politely.

Jane didn't look satisfied and dipped a biscotti into her coffee. "It's a work-in-progress," she said, munching a bit sulkily.

"No, it's good . . ." Marissa insisted.

Jane waved the compliment away as she put the mug on an empty table beside them. "I'll get it right eventually," she said. "I always do." She pushed the espresso toward Marissa. "Now . . . let's continue our conversation from the parking lot!"

Marissa's eyes darted nervously to Jane's shiny name tag. "I don't want to keep you from your work."

"Oh, I have ten more minutes before I need to be behind the counter," Jane said. "Come on . . . spill!"

"No, no. What about you? Have you been here long?"

"Me?" Jane laughed. She finished her biscotti and reached for a shortbread cookie. "Let's see: I started in Kauai, right after they had that big hurricane in 1992. The island was completely ravaged; it was terrible. Homes and businesses were devastated. And the people." She shook her head. "There was a lot of hardship. But I had just lost my first husband, Bill, to lung cancer and I was needing some healing myself. The man had never smoked a day in his life—he was as healthy as they came, Marissa. When we got the diagnosis, he was already stage four. He died three months later. I needed to get out of Oregon so I came over with a Red Cross group and never left."

Marissa had stopped trying to figure out how to escape. "Oh, Jane. I'm sorry."

"Yeah, it was pretty heavy stuff. I stayed in Kauai for a few years, worked in a coffee shop there and found out I really liked it. I mean, I was in my late thirties at the time, widowed, and making four-dollar cappuccinos. I didn't graduate high school, so it wasn't like I had all these job opportunities waiting for me. But it wasn't just that—I liked the culture of it, you know? The people. The conversations, the atmosphere. I ate it up, and it really helped me heal. Then the owner decided to retire and I came to the Big Island to get closer to the coffee beans." She gave Marissa a friendly grin as she sipped her coffee. "And I haven't left since."

"Wow."

"Okay, your turn now. I only have five minutes left and I need to get my fix of drama for the day."

"Drama?" Marissa tried to laugh. "There's no drama."

"Oh, honey . . ." Jane looked amused. "It's written all over you. There's a mess of good stories in there."

Marissa frowned. "That didn't sound good."

"It's all good," Jane assured her. "But clearly some drama is going on, and I want in."

"What? No, no, it's nothing like that. It's just, you know, my husband got transferred here and my daughter's in school over at Hawaii Day School, and I'm just . . ." Her voice trailed off.

Jane's eyes were wide and then narrowed in comprehension. "Oh, I get it. You've never been a stay-at-home mom before."

Marissa added some sugar to her coffee and stirred furiously. "I'm not a stay-at-home mom exactly . . ."

Jane guffawed. "Marissa, you are *so* the stay-at-home mom." Her voice lowered as she leaned toward Marissa conspiratorially. "Just look around."

Marissa hadn't paid much attention to the people inside the coffeehouse, but now that she did, she saw that many of them were moms, sitting with other moms, some with baby strollers and others without. Still, they wore their mark of motherhood—cotton clothing, comfortable shoes, very little makeup. Marissa looked down at what she was wearing and groaned. "Oh, God. I *am* a stay-at-home mom. But you have to understand—less than a month ago I was a director at a management consulting firm in the city . . ."

"Oh, I have no doubt. A lot of these women have similar stories. Of course now they're all about soccer games, ballet recitals, soaring tuition bills, and wayward husbands." Jane's eyes narrowed shrewdly for a moment. "A woman's lot—it's a bitch. Unless you're the other woman, of course. And even then, it's still a bitch."

"Well, that's not the case for me," Marissa informed her defensively.

Jane's eyes registered surprised as she focused back on Marissa. "Oh, I know. I didn't mean you," she said. "But thank goodness our lives aren't like that, huh?"

Our lives . . . for some reason it made Marissa nervous to be aligned with Jane already, like on the first day of school. She saw one of the khaki-clad mothers glance over in their direction, a pinched, lofty expression on her face.

"Well, I need to get to work." Jane swept the table crumbs into her hand with a napkin. "Stay as long as you like. Do you want a refill?"

"Oh, I should probably get going, too. Groceries in the car and all . . ."

Jane studied her for a moment before standing up. "Yeah, well, it was nice meeting you. Under the circumstances."

"Right. Again, sorry about that." Marissa quickly gathered her things. "You have the number for my insurance company. I'll let them know it was my fault. And the coffee . . . it was great. Thanks. Really." Marissa stood up.

Jane looked at her awkwardly. "Okay, well. Good-bye." She began to clear the table.

"Good-bye." Marissa offered another smile before hurrying out the door.

Back at her car, Marissa felt guilty relief, then an odd sense of remorse. Marissa had hit the woman's car and Jane had been gracious about the whole thing, even inviting her out for coffee. She was funny and easy to talk to. And talk about life experiences—in five seconds she had shifted Marissa's perception about her own troubles. To have met another woman with whom Marissa felt comfortable with was huge. Yet all Marissa could think was how to get out of there as quickly as possible, and all because Jane was working minimum wage. When had she become such a snob?

Marissa wished she could go back inside, but it would be impossible to pick up where they had left off, and Jane was probably working by now. Anyway, Jane probably had a lot of friends—after all, she said herself that she had been here forever. Marissa doubted Jane would even remember her after today.

'elima | five

Christmas was less than a week away. It was the first time in a long time that the Prices would be celebrating the holiday without snow. Still, despite the sunny days and warm temperatures, Paul was festively decorating the house with snowflakes and snowmen. He'd donned a Santa hat while Pansy pranced alongside him, a pair of felt antlers on her head and jingle bells on her wrists.

"Ho ho ho!" he chortled. He had bought what seemed like a thousand feet of Christmas tree lights and was liberally draping lights everywhere, inside and out.

"Ho ho ho!" Pansy echoed happily. It was a Saturday, and Pansy was thrilled to be out of school for two weeks. She didn't seem particularly challenged in school, but Marissa figured the workload was probably light with the holidays so close—surely things would pick up in the new year. Like Marissa, Pansy hadn't had much luck in making new friends, and it was becoming a chore to get her ready in the mornings. Usually the early bird, Pansy now sat at the breakfast table, yawning.

Marissa watched them work as she did her nails. The resort's annual holiday party was later that night, and she wanted to look good when she met Paul's colleagues and the rest of the staff. Paul was humming as he fiddled with the lights and hammered nails at random.

Paul was looking stronger and leaner, his New York suits and stiff white shirts hanging listlessly in the closet as he opted for new "aloha" businesswear—a short-sleeved silk Tommy Bahama shirt, slacks, wingtips. He was sporting a nice, even tan, which made his sandy-colored hair look almost blond. Marissa found this ironic, since Paul was working and Marissa was not, and she still hadn't made it down to the beach. She was more of a pool person, anyway, but was reluctant to use her privileges at the Kohala Bay Resort, not wanting to deal with Malia. Her days were spent taking Pansy to and from school, figuring out meals, documenting all the things to be fixed in the house and then trying to find someone to fix them.

"This is the life," Paul liked to say, even as Marissa hurried to put a pan under a new leak in the roof or chase cockroaches out the door. The bellowing bovines didn't bother him, and at night he slept like a rock, immobile and solid, while Marissa lay there, annoyed by the moonlight streaming into the bedroom. She still didn't know how to cover the skylights so she could get a decent night's sleep. Paul thought she was making a big deal over nothing.

"You'll get used to it," he said. "Think of how incredible this is—you can see the moon from your bed!" He was starting to sound like Jenny. "When I tell people about it at the office, they're envious."

Marissa stared at him. "You tell people from the office about our bedroom?"

Paul instantly became uncomfortable and tried to laugh it off. "Not about our bedroom exactly," he said. "Everything. The house, Hawaii, our view . . . you know, everything."

Marissa was reminded of a recent phone call from Kate. "Tell me you're still having that great sex," Kate demanded, suspicious.

"What? I'm not going to tell you that!" Marissa retorted. *Especially since I could count the number of times on one hand.* It seemed like once they got to paradise, they went back to their regularly scheduled program of hardly any sex.

"Uh-oh," was all Kate would say before launching into the latest episode from the Kate and Oliver Show.

Now, Marissa was sniffing the air. "Is that a new after-shave?"

"What?" Paul looked over his shoulder at Marissa. He was standing on a ladder.

"I smell something different."

"Oh." Paul gave an uneasy laugh. "We're doing a Secret Santa in the office. It's Burberry. Like it?"

Alarm bells were going off in her head. Marissa pretended to be occupied with blowing her nail polish dry. "I thought you hated cologne."

"I don't *hate* it," Paul said. "Anyway, I just put it on because everyone was watching and now I kind of like it."

"I think it smells nice," chimed in Pansy. She hung a final piece of tinsel on the tree. "Can I go wrap some presents in my room?"

"Sure," Marissa said. She watched Pansy walk down the hallway, then turned her attention back to Paul. "So I take it you have no idea who your Secret Santa is?"

"No, of course not. That's the whole point. Haven't you ever done Secret Santa?"

"Yes, I have, and it's pretty obvious after the first day who your Secret Santa is."

"Well, it's not obvious to me. Anyway, where's your Christmas spirit?"

"I have plenty of Christmas spirit. I'm just not comfortable with you wearing something that another woman gave you."

Paul looked at her, astonished. "You have got to be kidding me, Marissa. Are you telling me you're *jealous*? It's Secret Santa, for God's sake!"

He made it sound as if she had proposed mugging the Salvation Army Santa. Marissa immediately wished she hadn't said anything. "I'm not jealous . . ." she started.

"There are seven people in the executive office, and three of them are women. For all I know it could be Bob who gave me the cologne. In fact, statistically speaking, the odds would be higher that my Secret Santa is a guy."

Marissa tried not to sound exasperated. "Paul, since *you* are one of the four men, that would leave three men, three women as your potential Secret Santa, making the odds fifty-fifty."

Paul shrugged indifferently. "Fine. Whatever."

"And Bob Stewart is *not* your Secret Santa. I met him when I dropped off your briefcase two weeks ago. He talked my ear off for ten minutes about how he's living in a fixer-upper in Waikoloa. He shipped his ten-year-old Jeep from Fort Lauderdale. His shoes look like they have holes in them, and he brings his lunch to work. He's cheaper than hell, Paul. He did *not* buy you a fifty-dollar bottle of cologne."

Paul dropped a handful of lights and stepped down from the ladder. "Maybe not. But he's a damn good CFO."

"Paul . . ." Marissa's voice was tangled in frustration.

Paul moved the ladder across the room. "Marissa." He shook his head before grabbing the bundle of lights again. She watched his back as he climbed the ladder once again.

"You have *way* too much time on your hands. You need to lighten up."

It took every ounce of her not to react to the "lighten up" comment, and after a long shower, Marissa knew what needed to be done. She was going to rise above the petty fighting and show him that she had *just* enough time on her hands, thank you very much. She, of all people, did *not* need to lighten up. At all.

Marissa didn't nag him once all afternoon, not about the nails he had left out or the ladder still splayed open in the hallway. Instead, she had smiled gamely, then spent most of her time in the bathroom where she washed, polished, shaved, and primped, taking time to get her makeup just right for the party.

She was already dressed in an oriental-patterned silk gown that she had bought especially for this occasion, heels in hand. Paul stood in front of the bathroom mirror, fiddling uncertainly with his bow tie. After a moment's hesitation, Marissa came up behind him and, slipping her arms through his, finished tying it for him.

The thin material of her dress brushed against his back and he stiffened. Remembering her vow not to overreact, Marissa dropped her hands and stepped back. "I'll go check on Pansy, see if she's ready."

Paul continued to fuss with his collar, exasperated. "We're going to be late if you take any longer."

Marissa, who had been dressed for the past half hour, hurried out of the bedroom before she said something she would regret.

She found Pansy on her bed, reading a book and eating Oreos. Her Laura Ashley crushed velvet dress was hitched up around her waist and she wore sweat pants and athletic socks underneath.

"Pansy, that's not a good look. Trust me."

Pansy rolled off the bed as she popped another Oreo in her mouth. "I was cold."

"It'll be warmer on the coast." Marissa grabbed the remaining bag of Oreos as her daughter reached for another one. "And we'll be eating when we get there."

Sighing, Pansy stepped out of her sweatpants and socks and into a pair of Mary Janes. She went over to her vanity and brushed her hair, then applied a thin coat of Bonnie Bell lip gloss. She twirled dramatically in front of Marissa, the picture of polished perfection. "How's this?"

"Fabulous. Now let's go before your dad has an aneurysm. It's a big night for him."

In addition to being the resort's annual holiday party, tonight was Paul's official welcome to the Kohala Bay Resort and the Big Island. He had a small speech prepared, written to motivate the staff into a customer-service frenzy. "Our focus as we move into the new year is *ohana*—family," Marissa had heard him rehearsing in the bathroom. "Our staff, our guests, and our vendors are part of the Kohala Bay Resort *ohana*, so let's be sure to treat one another that way. There's nothing more important than *ohana*."

As a native New Yorker and ex-consultant, Marissa had seen her fair share of glamorous parties and balls. This wasn't one of them.

She felt absurdly overdressed. Some people were dressed up, but many wore sun dresses or muumuus, slacks, short-sleeved shirts, even slippers. It was easy to tell the outdoor staff from the indoor staff by their sun-kissed glow and casual attire compared to their paler, more formally dressed counterparts. It was clear that the two groups did not mix, and as expected, the groups had cliques of their own. F&B, beach and pool, admin, sales team, front desk. Paul laughed and shook hands with people as he walked through the crowd, very presidential, his voice deeper than normal.

Pansy sighed. "I knew I should have kept my sweatpants on."

They approached a cluster of people that were clearly the executive team. Marissa recognized Bob Stewart, the CFO, who was dressed in a wrinkled aloha shirt, and Malia, who was wearing a crimson sheath dress that tastefully accentuated the curves of her body. Paul introduced Marissa to the other members of the group—John Scott, head of Operations; Will Brown, Plant and Grounds; Angela Thompson, director of Marketing and Sales; and Carol Digby, Public Relations. Both John and Will looked like mainland transplants as well. Carol was an older, serious woman who radiated a "business-only" energy. Angela had a definite East Coast edge about her but seemed to know how to have fun, her eyes dancing with amusement as she looked around the ballroom.

Marissa introduced Pansy. "Our daughter, Elizabeth," she said. "But she goes by Pansy."

"Hi." Pansy gave a small wave before scanning her eyes around the ballroom.

"We have it on good authority that there's supposed to be a chocolate fountain tonight," Marissa explained as Pansy craned her neck even more and stood up on her tiptoes.

"Now that's a quest I'd love to be a part of," Angela said. "I'll join you. Carol? Malia?"

Carol shook her head, still engaged in a conversation with John.

"Oh, I'll pass, thank you," Malia said, running a hand over her flat stomach.

"Oh, to be young," Angela whispered to Marissa as they walked away. "I'm so glad to finally meet you. Paul always has so many nice things to say about you!"

"Likewise," Marissa said, even though Paul rarely mentioned anybody in the office. "But I never get the good details. Have you been here long?"

"Five long years on the Big Island, eight years with Fallon." Angela let out an exaggerated sigh, smiling wryly. "I keep thinking about moving on, but here I am."

Marissa noticed a handsome platinum wedding band on Angela's finger. "Is your husband here?" she asked as they followed Pansy onto the balcony overlooking the swimming pools.

"What? Oh this." The smile left Angela's face as she studied the ring on her finger, as if noticing it for the first time. "I'm actually going through a divorce," she said. "My son, Chris, just turned thirteen. He lives with me. His dad, my soon-to-be ex, still lives in Chicago."

"I'm sorry," Marissa said automatically.

"Oh, don't be," Angela said with a wave of her hand. "My marriage was over years ago. It just takes a while to wrap up the details."

Pansy suddenly exclaimed, "Wow, cool!"

She pointed to a four-foot chocolate fountain ahead of them that appeared to be carefully guarded by a few women who had their plates full of dipped fruit. A curtain of dark chocolate shimmered as it cascaded down several tiers. Silver trays of cut pineapple, strawberries, dried apricots, and bananas filled the table. Pansy's eyes bugged. "Look!" she gasped, pointing to another table filled with cookies, pretzels, marshmallows, and cakes.

"Looks like they've thought of everything," Angela said with a laugh. "I wish I could have brought Chris."

"He didn't want to come?"

"He's in Chicago with Rich for winter break. That's our arrangement—I get to celebrate the holidays alone. But that's okay. I actually appreciate the downtime. Gives me a chance to get some things done." She looked wistfully at the chocolate fountain. "And right now that chocolate fountain is on the top of my list."

The women were met with suspicion by the chocoholics guarding the fountain.

"Now if we could only get through," Marissa whispered, and they both laughed.

Pansy had filled a plate with fruit and cookies, ready to be dipped. "I'm going in," she announced, and squeezed between two women for prime real estate right in front of the fountain.

Marissa glanced around. "I can't believe how many people are here," she said. "There's got to be at least eight hundred people in this room."

Angela's eyes quickly darted around the balcony and into the ballroom. "More like a thousand, I think, inside and out, since people brought their families. But as you probably know, we do have one of the largest payrolls out of all of the resorts. As the saying goes, it takes a village, and Kohala Bay Resort is one needy child."

"Well, Paul's speech is all about *ohana*, so that would be fitting." Marissa gave a little laugh. "He's been rehearsing all week in front of the bathroom mirror."

Angela was checking the tortoise shell clip that held her sleek red hair up in a twist. Marissa envied hair like that, the obedient kind that seemed to stay in place no matter what you did. "So . . . how are you liking Hawaii? Big change from New York, I bet."

Marissa watched Pansy as she doused a banana in a stream of chocolate. "That's probably the understatement of the year," she said. "We're still getting acclimated. The house needs a lot of work, unfortunately, but we've got a great view and some snoring cows."

Angela laughed, picking up a spear of pineapple and

twirling it on a toothpick. "Sounds wonderful. Are you working here as well?"

"Not here. I was a consultant back in New York, though."

"Oh, right. I think Paul mentioned that. So now you're home with Pansy?"

Marissa nodded. "That's the plan, at least."

"Wow, I'm jealous." Angela actually did look jealous. "If I thought I could pull off the stay-at-home-mom thing, I would, but now I'm the primary breadwinner for our household so that's not an option anymore. My ex is a therapist, and when he's not analyzing me, he's coming up with excuses as to why he can't send his child support payments on time."

"It must be tough."

"Well, what are you going to do?" Angela shrugged. "I did the executive MBA program while I juggled my day job and Chris, who was just a baby at the time. It completely wrecked my marriage. At my last high school reunion I saw all these noncareer moms having a life and not needing to worry about the bills. It made me want to kill Gloria Steinem." The two women watched Pansy as she piled her plate high with chocolate-soaked fruit and cake. "So, shall we dive in? By the way, I *love* your dress. Is it Emilio Pucci?"

It was. Marissa smiled, nodding happily. Finally, someone she could relate to. Marissa reached for the plates and handed one to Angela. "After you."

The night wore on and Marissa found herself having fun. Paul's speech had been well-received, and he was still working the room, chatting and visiting with all of the employees. Pansy stayed by his side, offering a friendly smile to everyone they met, which seemed to break the ice with several employees who still hadn't decided if they liked Paul yet.

That left Marissa alone, but she didn't mind. Angela proved to be good company, filling Marissa in on all the details of the resort and how her marriage had fallen apart.

"Rich is completely unsupportive," Angela was saying as they freshened up in the ladies' room. Marissa listened intently as she applied a fresh coat of lipstick. "That's where you're lucky with Paul."

Marissa was thinking about how to respond when the door opened and Malia walked in. Malia looked startled, but quickly composed herself and gave the women a polite smile.

"Enjoying the evening?" she asked, pausing by the mirror.

"We're having a wonderful time," Angela said. Marissa managed a tight smile and nod in lieu of saying anything. They waited until Malia was finished and had returned to the party before resuming their conversation.

Marissa stared after the closed door. "Okay, I've only seen Malia on a few occasions, but I swear it looks like she's had her breasts done." Marissa didn't mean to sound catty, but she'd had a few drinks and it came out that way anyway.

Angela's lips twisted into a smile. "I think it's the dress. I don't think she's even taken vacation this year, much less taken a leave to get her breasts done. Especially now that Paul's here—they really get along. She's *very* eager to please."

Marissa visibly stiffened. Noticing, Angela laughed. "Not like that," she said. "Don't worry. Malia likes the bad boys."

"Really?"

"Her boyfriend came into the office one time. She was mortified. Big muscles, tattoos, bad attitude. Reeked of cigarette smoke. He was nice to us and all, but you could tell he was a troublemaker. I think she said he was in construction over at one of the developments."

"Hmm." Marissa still wasn't convinced.

Angela snapped her purse shut. "Ready to go back out into the fray? A couple more hours of this and then I'm going home and breaking out a pint of Godiva ice cream and watching *Grey's Anatomy* reruns."

Marissa grinned. Angela was a woman after her own heart.

The next day, Marissa took a final load of last-minute Christmas presents to the post office. Pansy went with her, but seeing the long lines, begged to stay in the car.

Marissa hesitated. "It's not safe, Pansy. Anyway, I think it's against the law to leave your children unattended in the car."

"Mom, this is Waimea. Besides, they'd have to arrest everyone in the parking lot."

Marissa looked around. Sure enough, almost every car had at least one unattended child inside. "I don't know . . ."

"Please? I just want to finish this book. I'll lock the doors, I promise."

Marissa sighed. She knew it was probably a false sense of security, but things did feel safer and easier here. "Fine. But don't open your door under any circumstance."

"Mom, I'm from New York. I haven't gone all soft or anything. Anyway, I still remember some kung fu from my self-defense class." Pansy put her fists up in a kung fu position and grinned.

"That's it. You're going in with me."

"Sorry, sorry! Just let me stay, please."

Marissa glanced at the line, which was now snaking out the door. "Fine. Lock the doors." Marissa gathered the packages and, after hearing Pansy lock the doors, went to stand at the end of the line.

After twenty minutes, her arms tired, it was finally Marissa's turn.

"I'm mailing these packages and I'm also checking on the status of our post office box application." Their house, not even five minutes from the center of town, was on a rural route with no mail delivery service. There was a wait-list for boxes at the post office, and in the meantime all of their mail was being forwarded to the resort.

"A box isn't available yet," the clerk said, checking a clipboard. "Maybe next week." Before Marissa could complain he scanned her packages and pushed some forms across the counter to her. "You'll need to fill these out if you want insurance and delivery confirmation. You can stand to the side there and hand them to me when you're done. Next!"

A tall man in a worn cowboy hat came up behind Marissa. He wore brown leather boots beneath his jeans and work shirt. "Hi, Ely. Got two packages to pick up." He slid a yellow card across the window.

"Be right back." Ely ignored Marissa's glare and disappeared.

The man gave Marissa a friendly smile and took off his hat. His auburn locks were due for a haircut, and his skin was bronzed from being in the sun. He was tall, nicelooking, about her age.

The pen Marissa was using was dry. Marissa dug through her purse to no avail. She looked at the man next to her. "Excuse me, but I don't suppose you have a pen?"

He patted his pockets. "No, sorry." He turned to the postal clerk in the next booth. "Ginny, have you got a pen for this lady?"

"Sure, Tom. Here you go."

He handed the pen to Marissa. "Thanks," she said. She

began filling out the forms, throwing the first one away when she wrote their old New York address as the return address.

"New in town?" he asked.

It was the question of the week. "It's really obvious, isn't it?"

"A little. You have that efficient, mainland air about you."

Marissa didn't look up, but kept writing. "If I were efficient, I'd have had these forms filled out before I got in line." She glanced up before lowering her voice. "And what's up with the P.O. boxes? They won't deliver mail to my house but there's a wait-list for a box! How am I supposed to get my mail?"

Tom leaned against the wall of the window and gave a good-natured shrug. "It is a dilemma," he admitted.

He wasn't making fun of her exactly, but Marissa knew she came across as high maintenance. Which she wasn't. Her friend Kate was high maintenance. Marissa was more like . . . medium maintenance. But either way, it didn't seem to bother him.

He held out his hand. "I'm Tom Oakes."

"Marissa Price." They shook hands. Despite the dirt on his flannel shirt, he smelled clean, like grass.

Ely returned with his packages. "There you go, Tom."

"Thanks, Ely. Nice meeting you, Marissa Price. Welcome to Hawaii." Tom gave her a small wave, gathered his packages, and headed out the door, saying hello to people along the way. He kissed a few women on the cheek by way of greeting. James Dean meets Mr. Popularity.

Marissa completed the forms and sent off her packages. She hurried back to the car where Pansy was still safely inside, her window rolled halfway down.

Marissa was not happy. "Pansy, what is the point of locking the doors if someone can just grab you and drag you out of that window?"

"I know. I'm sorry. But look—horses!" Pansy jutted her chin in the direction of the truck parked next to them. A horse trailer was attached, and two horses stared out at them. "They were looking at me, and I was talking to them, but they couldn't hear me so I rolled down the window." Pansy gazed back at them. "Good horses. You're good horses, aren't you?"

"Okay, now say good-bye," Marissa instructed as she started the car.

Pansy's face was screwed up in intense concentration. "I like the chestnut brown one. His name is Abacus. See that white spot on his back? I like that part best. The black one is named Sirius. They're quarter racers, you know."

"No, I didn't." Marissa eased out of the parking space, careful to keep her distance from the horse trailer, which was caked in red mud and looked like it had seen better days. "How do you know their names?"

"He told me." Pansy pointed out the window, then waved. "Bye, Tom!"

Marissa looked just in time to see Tom wave back and get into the truck. He gave them another friendly smile, then touched the rim of his cowboy hat.

It was just like the movies. There was just something so appealing, so masculine, about a guy in a cowboy hat and boots. Marissa waved back weakly, then said through clenched teeth, "Pansy . . ."

Pansy was contrite. "I know, Mom, I'm sorry. But everyone knows everyone here. If anything happened, there would have been at least ten eyewitnesses, and they all know him anyway. Besides, you can tell he's not a psycho."

"Really? And how's that?"

"Psychos aren't responsible enough to own horses." Pansy made this pronouncement confidently.

Marissa pulled away from the post office, catching one last glimpse of Tom as he turned on his signal light and headed in another direction.

"I can't believe we're actually in Hawaii." Pansy sighed happily, settling into her seat. "New York feels like a million miles away."

They headed home, where a herd of vocal cows awaited their return, no doubt.

"Yeah," Marissa said. "It sure does."

'eono | six

By mid-January, things were definitely starting to look up. The holiday drama had passed, Pansy was back in school, and Marissa was starting to feel less like a stranger in their new town. Paul in particular was in good spirits. The numbers at the resort were strong for the busy season, but more important, presale numbers for the upcoming year were significantly higher than in years past. All of this boded well for Paul, who was so pleased that he upped his hours at the gym. "Strong body, strong mind," he told Marissa. "I'm on a *roll*."

A particularly cold night revealed a surprise in the morning: a snow-capped Mauna Kea, which they could see from their back window. Paul and several others from the office decided to make a trip to the 13,796-foot summit. Malia knew someone who had skis and snowboards they could borrow. Because of the high altitude, it wasn't recommended for children under sixteen years of age. Pansy was crestfallen when she learned that she couldn't join them, so Marissa opted to stay home and cheer her up.

By nightfall, Paul hadn't returned. Marissa started to worry—her calls were going straight to voice mail. It was the same when she finally caved in and tried Malia's number. Pansy, who was in her PJs but still awake, surfed online until she found a website with a ski map and pictures of successful (and unsuccessful) runs down the mountain. It was a challenging terrain studded with lava rock and varying, unreliable conditions. There were no formal ski lifts, no resort or ski lodge. Basically you drove your four-wheel drive to the top, skied down, met a fellow skier at the bottom who then ferried you back up. Skiers were getting hurt, stuck in the snow, sometimes requiring medical care to treat altitude sickness or serious injury. You had to be in top physical condition to ski the summit. The more Marissa read, the more she was convinced that something terrible had happened to Paul.

In all their years of marriage, it had never occurred to her that she could lose him. Even when they had established a living trust with medical directives for both her and Paul in case something should happen, she never expected that anything actually would. For better or worse, they were going to be stuck with each other until they were old and gray, through retirement and grandkids. But now, Marissa felt for the first time how vulnerable life really was.

The night wore on. Pansy fell asleep unexpectedly with her head in Marissa's lap. Marissa was grateful she wasn't alone. If she didn't hear back from Paul within the hour, she was going to call the police.

And then he walked through the door.

"Paul!" Relief flooded her. She gently laid Pansy aside before throwing her arms around him. Then she stood back at arm's length. "What happened? Where were you? Why didn't you call?"

"Sorry, my phone ran out of juice while we were up on the mountain." He dropped a backpack on the floor and stripped off his jacket and shoes before leaning over to give her a quick kiss. "We didn't come down until a few hours ago, and then we went to grab a bite to eat. I lost track of time."

He lost track of time? It was almost midnight. Marissa leaned closer, and noticed that even though he was wearing the same clothes he had left the house in, his hair looked clean and his face was washed. "Did you take a shower?"

He didn't seem fazed. "Yeah. I stopped by the office on the way home to check on some work and decided to stop by the gym for a shower—it got pretty gritty up there." He ran a hand through his hair, and then his face lit up. "You should have seen me, Marissa. *I snowboarded down Mauna Kea*. It was incredible. There were some young guys up there, regulars, and I outlasted them. They couldn't believe it." He chuckled, squaring his shoulders. "It got me thinking that maybe I should start training for a mini-triathlon. Work my way up to the Ironman. I think I could do it."

The Ironman? He had to be kidding. Marissa didn't know how to respond. "Paul," she finally said. "I've been worried sick. I thought something happened to you. You said you'd be back by six."

"I know. I just had no idea it would take so long. But nothing happened to me. See?" He gave her another quick peck on the cheek and headed for the bedroom.

Marissa followed him. "Well, why didn't you call me from the office?"

"What?" His back was to her and she couldn't see his face.

"If your phone was dead and you knew you were running late, why didn't you call me from the office?"

He turned to shake his head. "Honestly? It didn't cross my mind. I was still thinking about Mauna Kea. I felt really in tune with the mountain." He headed for the bathroom. "I still feel a bit grimy—I think I'm going to jump in the shower again."

Marissa stared after him. *Really in tune with the mountain?* That didn't sound like Paul. But it sounded a lot like someone else.

Malia.

This had to be about Malia. Marissa cut him off as he was about to step into the shower. "Are you sleeping with her?" The words came tumbling out of her mouth.

"What?"

"Are you sleeping with Malia?"

"Don't be insane." He stepped past her into the shower. "I cannot believe you would even think that, Marissa. It's late. Let's just wash up and get to bed."

"No." She was shaking now, fueled by relief but also by anger. One phone call meant she could have gone to bed without worry. Instead, she had stayed up and let her mind wander into dark places. And she still wasn't entirely convinced.

Paul turned on the water and stepped under the spray. "Marissa, what do you want me to say? I took a day off and went up Mauna Kea. I asked you to come, if you remember. Not that you would have, but I did invite you."

"You knew I had to stay with Pansy, Paul!"

"Oh, Marissa, come on. You hate the outdoors. We're in this amazing, beautiful place and you find every possible excuse to stay holed up in this house. I'm not going to apologize for wanting to get out and enjoy some fresh air."

That was completely unfair. She watched him through the glass door, her fury building. "What are you talking about? *You* get to leave every day, Paul! *I'm* the one who's stuck here. Has it occurred to you that I haven't had a day off since we got here?"

He vigorously soaped his body. "A day off? *Every* day is a day off for you, Marissa! You're not working, Pansy's in school . . . You can do whatever you want. But that's the irony, because there's nothing you want to do! But why can't I do the things I want to do? Why do you insist on giving me a hard time about everything?"

"I don't give you a hard time," Marissa said, a bit taken aback. *At least not about* everything.

"Oh, really?" Paul rinsed off, then turned off the water. He stood there, dripping and naked, staring at her. "I want to move to Hawaii . . . you throw up every barrier imaginable to sabotage it. I take a day—one day!—to ski down Mauna Kea, one of the most amazing experiences of my life . . . you wait up to badger me and accuse me of sleeping with my secretary. Have you even noticed that I've lost weight? We've been here six weeks and I'm down ten pounds and I've built muscle mass. Everyone else has commented on it. Everyone except you."

Marissa had noticed and didn't want Paul to think that his losing weight made a difference to her. She loved him no matter how much he weighed.

Her indignation grew as she watched him towel off. He was pissed, clearly, but so was she.

"That's not fair," she said vehemently. "Because you know what? I *did* agree to move to Hawaii, I *did* give up my career, and I *am* spending my days in a house that we've sunk all of our money into and, unbelievably, still needs work."

"Fine. I get it, Marissa . . ."

"Do you? Because while *you're* prancing around in your five-star resort having fancy lunches and playing rounds of golf, *I'm* stuck in this cow town with a leaky roof and leftovers for lunch. So I'm sorry if I haven't had time to comment on your muscle tone."

Paul stood there silently, towel wrapped around his waist, his jaw set. *Say something!* Marissa wanted to yell.

Finally he said, "I feel like we're fighting all the time. Hawaii is one of the most romantic places on earth, but it's like we can't stop arguing. We keep wanting different things."

Marissa struggled not to get more upset. "Paul, it's *marriage*. We're human beings with our own thoughts and personalities. We're two different people, after all."

"I guess that's what I'm saying," he said, stepping past her into the closet. "Maybe we're too different."

For the next couple weeks, Marissa did her best to stay on Paul's good side, anticipating (when possible) whatever he would need. She didn't forget to pick up the dry cleaning, she found someone to finally fix the errant garage door, and she didn't say anything when he came through the door late at night.

She even complimented him on his muscle tone. While he had kept a trim figure the past couple of years, you could now actually see his abs. Marissa, on the other hand, had let herself go a little soft.

"You look fine," he assured her one night as she studied herself critically in front of the mirror. He was already in bed, reading a magazine.

"I look my age." Marissa sucked in her gut then let it out again.

"So do something about it," Paul said. "Plenty of women don't look their age. Besides, it's all in your mind—if you think young, you are young."

Marissa tried not to grit her teeth. After their big blowup the night he skied down Mauna Kea, Marissa wanted to keep the peace for as long as possible, to show Paul that they didn't always have to fight.

"You should drink more water," Paul continued. "Water cleans out all of the toxins. How much water did you drink today?"

"I really have no idea. Probably three glasses' worth."

"You should try to drink at least eight glasses' worth," he advised. "If not more."

Marissa kept the smile pasted on her face. "Okay," she said. It was easier to agree than disagree.

But as the days wore on, Marissa was beginning to realize that maybe Paul *was* right. She wasn't exactly a silver-lining sort of person and her practical, sometimes critical, disposition didn't seem to work as well in their marriage as it did in the office. And Hawaii *was* one of the most romantic places on earth. For Paul, ever the romantic, coming here and then having his wife act like they had moved to Siberia was probably more discouraging than she had realized. A little more effort on her part wouldn't kill her.

So for Valentine's Day, she made dinner reservations at one of the top restaurants on the island. Since Pansy claimed that she had yet to make friends in her new school, Marissa scoped out the parking lot for a few days before picking a single mother and cornering her near the water fountain, chatting her up. It took only three more "random" meetings before Marissa asked about an evening playdate on Valentine's Day. The woman said yes, much to Marissa's relief, and Marissa promised to bring dinner for everyone that night. Even though Pansy had vehemently protested, "Mom, that kid is weird—he's even more of an outcast than me," Marissa felt it was a win-win.

She didn't bother to buy a new outfit, but she did get

herself some new underwear. If there was ever a time when she'd want to have some new lingerie, this would be it.

Marissa chose a nice card and took the time to find the perfect gift: heavy-gauge stainless steel wine glass and bottle holders for use at the beach or for a picnic, something Paul would love and Marissa would, hopefully, eventually love. Either way, it would show him that she was looking for more things for them to do together, and if it had to be outdoors, so be it.

Valentine's Day. Marissa woke up minutes before Paul began to stir, quickly throwing on her robe and heading for the kitchen. The sun was already on its way up, and the mountain had a fresh dusting of snow on top.

She had bought heart-shaped toaster-oven waffles, which she sprinkled with powdered sugar and sliced strawberries. The coffee was on, the eggs were scrambled, and she placed a single red rose next to Paul's plate and a pink one next to Pansy's. It was the first time she could think of that she had ever done anything like this, and it felt good. Strike that—it felt great.

Pansy was the first one at the table. Her face brightened when she saw the little foil hearts sprinkled liberally around the plates. So maybe it was a bit much, but Marissa couldn't resist. It was her first time "doing" Valentine's Day for her family, so why not?

Pansy picked up the valentine Marissa had placed near her orange juice, along with a heart-shaped twisty straw and a new tube of lip gloss.

"Mom, thanks!" She gave Marissa a hug. "I have one for you, too." Pansy reached into her book bag and brought out an origami heart for Marissa. There was a note tucked inside a secret compartment: FOR A GREAT MOM, the note read.

"I love it, thank you," Marissa said, reading the note, then giving her daughter a kiss. She put it by her own place setting, feeling buoyant. It was definitely a Hallmark moment.

Paul entered the kitchen in a rush. "I'm late," he said. "I snoozed the alarm too many times." He glanced at the table in surprise. "What's this?"

"Happy Valentine's Day, Dad!" Pansy gave him a kiss and handed him an origami valentine as well.

"Thanks, sweetheart." Paul gave his daughter a hug then leaned over to give Marissa a quick kiss on the lips. "We're on for dinner tonight?"

"Six o'clock, Merriman's," she said. She tried not to look too expectant, but in the past, Marissa would usually arrive at the office to find a dozen roses, chocolate, maybe a CD. They would meet for lunch or dinner, where Marissa would then hand him a card, usually with tickets for a show or whatever else Robin had come up with.

But now, with no office to go to, what would happen?

"Wow, I'm so sorry I can't stay for breakfast," Paul said, looking at his watch. He plucked the strawberries off the plate and ate them, then grabbed a waffle and placed it on a napkin. "Six o'clock tonight. See you there." Another quick cursory kiss and he was gone. It wasn't until his car pulled out of the driveway that Marissa realized he hadn't noticed the Valentine's Day card she got for him, or the gift, which was leaning against his chair, unopened.

Marissa sat the table at Merriman's, feeling self-conscious in her new dress. Okay, so she had given in at the last minute and gone shopping, feeling that she needed—and wanted—to look her best today. Since moving to Hawaii there hadn't been many occasions for her to get dressed up or for Paul to see her dressed up, and she missed that. Getting dolled up was for her as much as it was for Paul.

Paul arrived exactly at six, waving to Marissa from the front of the restaurant as he waited to approach the hostess stand. Marissa straightened up and smiled, happy to see him. He was grinning as he followed the slow glide of the hostess to their table.

"You look great," he said, leaning over to give her a kiss on the cheek. "Is that a new dress?"

Marissa nodded, feeling herself blush. "Thought the occasion warranted a new dress. Happy Valentine's Day."

"Happy Valentine's Day."

There was an awkward pause.

"Do you realize that this is the first time that we've gone out since we've moved here?" Marissa finally asked. "Just the two of us?"

Paul's eyes scanned the restaurant for a waiter. "No, really?"

"Really."

"That's just . . . unbelievable."

"I know." There was a lull in the conversation and Paul looked at the menu. "So, have you decided what you'd like?"

"What? Oh . . ." Marissa picked up the menu. "Well, the panko and Kaffir lime–crusted scallops look good. Maybe with the organic greens and goat cheese salad as a starter?"

Paul nodded. "I think I'll try the wok-charred ahi. Do you want to share the salad and maybe get something else as well, like the miso-steamed clams? Try something new?"

"Sure," Marissa agreed happily. She watched her husband as he motioned for a waiter and then placed their order, along with two glasses of white wine.

"So." Paul settled back in his chair, smiling brightly. "Here we are. It almost seems . . . unreal."

"You mean surreal?" It was so refreshing to have a normal

conversation at last. Their conversations at home were brief, limited to Pansy updates and work on the house. "Because I was sort of thinking the same thing. A year ago today, even three months ago, if you told me we'd be living in Hawaii, I wouldn't have believed you."

"I know." The wine had arrived and Paul held up his glass. "To Hawaii."

"To us." Marissa clinked glasses with him. The wine warmed her throat. "You know, I'm thinking that you're right. We should go out more, do things together. Hire a babysitter for Pansy, go out for dinner once a week. Like the old days."

Paul gave a wry smile. "The old days."

"Yes. I don't miss work, but I miss the structure of my day, of getting up and having someplace to go. I've been feeling kind of useless since we moved here, but you probably figured that out." Marissa took another sip of wine, then went for the bread basket. "God, this is so nice. Bread?"

Paul shook his head. He cleared his throat. "Marissa . . ." he started.

"Yes?" She looked at him, smiling, her butter knife poised in midair.

"There's something I need to tell you." He licked his lips and tried to smile. "You see, it's like this . . ."

The smile faded from her face. Paul was looking visibly uncomfortable now, refusing to make eye contact. Marissa felt the back of her neck prickle.

"Since I've been here—*we've* been here—I've been feeling like something's off track. At first I thought it was the move, the new job, you not working . . . those sorts of changes. And then I realized what it was."

Her mouth was dry but she managed to ask, "What?"

"It's not the things that *have* changed, but the things that *haven't* changed. Like us. You."

"Me? Paul, I have no idea what you're talking about."

"I just . . . I think I need some time to myself." He reached for his wine, took a long drink.

"Some time to yourself?"

"I thought things would be different for us once we moved here, but obviously they're not."

She stared at him in disbelief. "They are for *me*. In fact, I can't even think of one thing that's the same from three months ago!"

"See, like this! We're always arguing, snapping at one another." He shook his head dismally. "I'm tired of all the fighting, Marissa. The disagreements, the bitterness. I mean, if we can't get along in paradise, where can we get along?"

Marissa had no idea how to respond. Was he kidding?

His voice was accusatory. "You're never satisfied. Nothing's ever good enough."

"That's not true . . ." she started to protest.

"A day doesn't pass where you're not complaining about how the house is a dump . . ."

"But the house *is* a dump!"

The look on his face was one of abject consternation. "I feel *alive* here, Marissa. At work, on the mountain, in the water. I love being outdoors—you hate it. Here we are on this gorgeous island, and you can't even be bothered to figure out how to get to the ocean for a swim. You wonder why I don't come home earlier after work? Because it's like you have to drag me down to your level of dissatisfaction. You're half empty, always looking at what's not working rather than what is."

"But isn't that what you're doing now?" Marissa was blinking rapidly, willing herself not to cry. "Looking at what's not working? What about what *is* working?"

"I feel like I'm just going through the motions," Paul

said, a pained expression on his face. "I just think I need to be on my own for a while."

Marissa stared at him, stunned. "What?"

"Just for a little bit. I thought some time apart might do us some good, before things get really bad."

Her chest felt like it was caving in. "Is this about someone else? Malia?" She wanted to jump over the table and shake him, shake the truth out of him.

"God, Marissa, how many times do I have to tell you? No, this is not about anybody else, least of all Malia. This is about you and me. A trial separation, just to see . . ."

"A trial separation? To see what? If you still love me?"

"It's not about that, Marissa." He sighed heavily, as if he were explaining this to a child. "I need to find myself."

Marissa could hear an echo of years prior and it snapped her back to reality. "Paul . . . you *had* your midlife crisis! You're only allowed *one*!" Marissa's voice was wavering as she leaned toward him, her voice hitting a crescendo.

"Marissa, calm down," Paul said, chuckling nervously as he glanced around. A few of the neighboring tables were peering with interest at them. "We're in a restaurant."

"No kidding, Paul! You're telling me this *now* . . . here . . . on *Valentine's Day?* We *just* ordered dinner!"

"I wasn't expecting to talk about this now. Look, let's just have a nice dinner and finish the conversation later . . ."

"Are you insane? You're insane!" Marissa was almost hysterical. "I am *not* having dinner with you if we're going to separate!"

"*Trial* separa—" he began.

She couldn't stand to hear any more. She stood up just as the appetizers arrived, fumbling for her purse and car keys. "I have to go. I have to get Pansy in a couple of hours and when I do, I want you and your stuff out of the house."

"Two hours?" he said, a look of shock on his face. "Where am I supposed to go?"

"Gosh, I don't know. You're the GM of a 435-room resort. You figure it out."

Paul managed an awkward smile at their bewildered waiter, promising he'd be right back as he hurried after Marissa.

In the parking lot, he sounded distraught. "Marissa, don't be rash . . ."

She was being rash? In response, Marissa popped the trunk of the Audi and unceremoniously dumped the Valentine's Day gift she had bought for him in the parking lot. The sound of clashing metal made him start.

"Did you buy me golf clubs?" Paul asked dumbly as Marissa threw him an incredulous look.

She climbed into the car, slamming the door behind her. She started the engine, then rolled down the window. "And whatever's left, I'm taking to the Salvation Army in the morning. So Paul?"

He was looking around the parking lot, as if lost. "Yes?"

"If you need to find yourself, I suggest you get going."

PART II

Paradise Lost

'Ino ka moana ke ahu mōkākī nei
ka puna i uka.

*The sea is rough, for the corals are
strewn on the beach.*

ʻehiku | seven

The day after. The week after. In some ways the difference was impalpable—shuffling Pansy off to school in the mornings, running errands, cleaning the house, fixing dinner, helping Pansy with her homework and then getting her to bed. Marissa would even forget, for a moment, what had happened.

But then there was the empty double sink next to her, void of his toothbrush and razor, his empty half of the medicine cabinet. The long, quiet night interrupted by the occasional bovine snore, but no Paul. There was no blanket-grabbing, no muttering in his sleep, no warm body to press against or push away. Marissa had intentionally moved to the middle of the bed, mussing up all of the sheets and pillows, determined not to be one of those women who left their forsaken husband's side undisturbed.

Then she would wake the next morning and find herself curled up on her side of the bed. What usually followed was a fifteen-minute bout of crying and pillow pounding before she forced herself out of bed to get Pansy ready for school.

Pansy had known immediately that something was awry, but Marissa didn't feel ready to tell her the truth. Her daughter was only eight and was used to Marissa and Paul being gone on business trips when they were in New York. Why should this be any different?

"A business trip?" Pansy had asked when Marissa had picked her up the night Paul moved out. "Where?"

"Um, Florida," Marissa said. She kept her eyes on the road. "Miami. It was a last-minute thing."

"For how long?"

"A week." Marissa figured a week would give her enough time to come up with a game plan.

Except now a week had passed, and she didn't have a game plan. Not even a vague idea of what to do next. She would cheerily drop Pansy off at school and then, despondent, drive around town until it was time to pick Pansy up. On her better days, she would actually park the car and wander past the stores in the small shopping center in town. For some reason it helped to be among people who were going about their day, oblivious to Marissa or her disintegrating marriage.

Marissa even found herself drawn toward Kava Java, each time turning away at the last minute until finally Jane pushed open the door and emerged on the sidewalk.

"So are you going to come in or what? You're wearing down the pavement."

She hadn't seen Jane since the day of the car accident, when Marissa had been mortified to learn that Jane was a simple barista. Now, ashamed, Marissa shook her head. "I'm just walking by."

Jane tucked a dishtowel into her apron. "We know. You've been walking by since Thursday. Come on in; I'll fix you a double espresso."

"Thanks, but you've already been too generous, Jane . . ."

"I'm not paying. You can buy your own coffee this time, Marissa. And leave a tip."

Marissa sat timidly by the fire, sipping her coffee, and dreading the conversation that was sure to ensue. But Jane was busy working, never once wandering over to pry for details. When Marissa finally got up to leave, Jane, who was restocking the muffins, put one in a bag and handed it to Marissa.

"Pineapple and orange rind. Bits of ginger. Toasted coconut. See you tomorrow."

Before Marissa could respond, Jane had turned to help the next customer.

So Marissa returned the next day, and then the next, until a morning stop at Kava Java became her ritual. Jane didn't bother her, but bestowed small acts of kindness—a freshly baked biscotti tucked next to her coffee, pastries to take home, a reassuring pat on the shoulder. It was enough for Marissa, giving her the energy to make it through another day.

Paul had called only once, and that was the hardest. Despite her tough-wife stance, she had hoped for an apology, but the one he offered was not what she expected.

"Marissa, I'm sorry you feel this way," was his response, which just incensed her even more.

"Me?" she had retorted. As if any of this was her idea.

"I had hoped you would have been more supportive of what I'm going through," he said. "But obviously you're not."

Marissa had just stood there in the kitchen, staring at the stained linoleum, a dripping faucet, and two pots under newly found leaks in the roof. No job, no husband. A child under the illusion that her father was at a conference in Florida.

And he wanted *her* to be more supportive.

"Call Pansy tonight," was all she had said before hanging up. "And remember, you're in Florida."

As agreed, Paul called that night. Pansy had answered the phone with an enthusiastic, "Hi Dad! I miss you. How's Miami?"

Marissa, who pretended to be busy washing dishes, tried not to look alarmed when Pansy frowned after the first minute.

"But I thought you were in Miami," Pansy said. "Oh. Fort Lauderdale. Is it nice?"

Damn, Marissa swore to herself. She probably should have worked out the details a bit better with Paul.

"Uh-huh . . . fine . . . I'm fine, Dad . . . school's fine . . . yes, it rained today . . ."

Marissa put the dishes away, then concentrated on scrubbing a stubborn spot on the stove, edging closer to the phone.

"When are you coming back? I can't hear you . . . What? Oh, okay. Here's Mom. I love you, too." Pansy handed the phone to her mother, covering the mouthpiece as she whispered, "He's not in Miami anymore—he's in Fort Lauderdale."

"Oh. That's right." Marissa took the phone with a smile and watched her daughter return to her homework. "Hi," she said brightly.

"Why did you tell her I was in Miami?" Paul asked. "There's nothing in Miami!"

"Great!" Marissa nodded her head vigorously.

"What? Oh, forget it. I told her I'd be back in a couple of days. I don't like your business trip idea and I want to see her. I miss her."

What about me? Marissa wanted to ask. Instead, she said, "Wow! How interesting!"

Paul sighed. "I don't think we should keep the truth from

her, Marissa. We should figure out a way to tell her together."

"Yeah, sure. Maybe later." Pansy looked up and Marissa
gave her a wink. What, exactly, would they be telling her?
"That sounds like fun!"

"Marissa, I also think that maybe after a little time has
passed, maybe we can talk again. Things sort of spun out of
control last week . . ."

"Don't I know it!" Was it her puffy eyes from crying and
the dark circles from lack of sleep that gave it away? Oh,
right, he couldn't see her.

"Maybe we could have dinner, just you and me . . ."

That was the final straw. Dinner? Especially after what
happened the last time they had dinner together? Not
wanting to lose it in front of Pansy, who was clearly listening in on the conversation (like mother like daughter, apparently), Marissa deftly pressed the OFF button on the
phone and finished the conversation to a dial tone. "Great.
I miss you, too."

"Bills, bills, bills," Marissa mumbled from behind her dark
sunglasses. She was sorting through her mail at the post office after her morning stop at Kava Java. "And more bills."

American Express, Visa, MasterCard, Macy's, Neiman
Marcus, Barneys, L.L. Bean, Banana Republic, the Gap. All
that last-minute Christmas shopping was starting to rear its
ugly head. Their car payments (whose idea was it to lease
those cars anyway?), their next mortgage payment. Marissa
stood next to a trash can and unceremoniously dumped all
the junk mail and mail order catalogs, rescuing a water bill
at the last minute. "Can't forget that one," she muttered.

"Talking to yourself?"

Marissa, bent over the trash can, looked up.

It was Tom, the cowboy with the horses. Make that the good-looking cowboy with the horses. He was grinning at Marissa, his arms also full of mail.

Marissa straightened. "Hi," she said. "Tom, right?"

"That's right. And you're Marissa. It's nice to see you again. Congrats on getting your P.O. box, by the way."

"What? Oh, thanks. It was actually the highlight of my month." She tossed a flyer away.

Tom's mouth twisted into an amused smile. "Sun too bright?"

Marissa glanced outside where the slanted Waimea rain lashed against the post office window. The wind was flipping people's umbrellas inside out as they struggled for cover.

She thought of a couple witty retorts, but found herself too tired to banter. Instead, she lowered her sunglasses so he could catch a glimpse of her red-rimmed eyes. The expression on his face immediately changed.

"Oh. Sorry. Everything okay?"

She shrugged, pushing her sunglasses up the bridge of her nose. "Like I said, getting the P.O. box was a high point." She gathered her mail. "I've been better."

The look on his face was pure sympathy, but all he said was, "I don't doubt it."

She checked her watch and reluctantly saw that she needed to go. "I've got to run. I have to go pick up my daughter from school."

Tom shifted his mail from one arm to the other. "Listen, I've got a beginner's clinic starting later this week. I know it's short notice, but if your daughter would like to join in, I'd be happy to make room for her. Friday, three o'clock, Pualani Stables, right past the hardware store."

Marissa thought about the bills. Riding lessons weren't

exactly a part of the budget. "I appreciate that," Marissa said. "But I'm not sure if now's a good time . . ."

"I understand. But there are some nice kids in the group. Your daughter would really enjoy them and I'm betting she'll have fun."

Ouch. He hit her in her soft spot. Pansy still hadn't made any real friends at school. And with everything happening at home, the idea of Pansy having fun was very appealing.

Tom headed toward the door. "Just think about it. I've got to run, but I'll tell you what—come Friday, as my guest. No charge. Just see if you and she like it. We could even get you up on a horse."

"Me?"

"Sure. You seem like someone who would ride. You're probably a natural. See you on Friday." He waved and was gone.

"Wow." Pansy had the awestruck look of a five-year-old in a toy store. But it wasn't a toy store. It was a stable, filled with horses and hay, not to mention a voluminous amount of horse manure. At least it smelled that way.

"Yeah, great," Marissa said, gingerly watching her step. She should have worn different shoes but hadn't thought that far ahead. These days, she couldn't go beyond five minutes before her mind went blank. "Are you sure you want to try this instead of ballet lessons? There's a dance studio in town. It'd be a shame to let all of your training go to waste." She avoided another suspicious-looking mound.

Paul had felt the same way. He didn't care much about Pansy continuing her ballet studies but didn't like the idea of their petite, eight-year-old daughter getting up on a horse.

"I'm not sure how I feel about that," he had said. "It's not safe."

"Well, Pansy's really excited about it. With all that's going on, I think she could use a healthy diversion."

"Oh, so you're doing it out of guilt."

"*I* don't have a reason to feel guilty," she had said acerbically. "Tell you what: as soon as you're back from Fort Lauderdale, we can talk about it. And who knows . . . maybe I'll take some lessons as well."

Paul had snorted. "Marissa, I was with you when we tried to do that trail ride in Colorado, remember? You weren't interested in getting on that horse any more than I was."

She had completely forgotten about Colorado. This was before Pansy had been born, when Marissa and Paul used to travel on a whim. Marissa had heard of a four-day trail ride in Colorado hosted by a premier luxury tour company that boasted "experiential" vacations. It was all-inclusive with four-star accommodations and gourmet meals. It had received rave reviews and people they knew had gone on it and loved it. But one look at the huge beasts they would be riding and Marissa and Paul opted to stay behind. With all their vacation money tied up on the nonrefundable trail ride, they ended up at a nearby Holiday Inn, lounging by the miniscule pool and watching Pay-Per-View movies. And despite bed sheets that felt like sandpaper and paper-thin bath towels, they had fun.

But that was ages ago. And a lot had changed since then.

"It's just one lesson," Marissa had told him before hanging up. "We'll see how it goes."

Now, Pansy slipped her hand into her mother's. "Mom?" she asked.

"Yes?"

Pansy hesitated and then said, "Don't be upset, but I don't really like ballet."

Marissa stopped. "What? Why didn't you tell me that before?" Lessons at the prestigious ballet school hadn't been cheap and Pansy had been taking them since she was five.

The look on her daughter's face was full of patience. "I did," she said.

Marissa was about to disagree when she flashed to a memory—several, actually—where Pansy had told her exactly that. But it had been hard enough getting Pansy *into* the school, so Marissa had brushed it off, hoping that it would eventually grow on her. She felt a stab of regret that she hadn't listened, and felt even worse that her daughter hadn't forgotten.

How was it that Marissa had missed all this? First Paul, and now Pansy. But Pansy wasn't unhappy now; in fact, it was quite the contrary. Her daughter was smiling at her, her hand still holding Marissa's, thrilled by the prospect of riding her first horse.

There was the sound of hooves galloping toward them. They looked up just in time to see Tom arrive atop a handsome brown-speckled horse.

"Good afternoon, ladies," he said. Marissa could feel the excitement bubbling from Pansy. Tom rode his horse into the training ring in the stable and jumped off in one smooth move.

He handed the reins of the horse to a young girl Pansy's age, then strode across the muddy yard to meet them. He didn't seem to mind that he was getting mud and wet grass on his boots and jeans. He grinned when he saw Marissa.

"Glad you could make it," he said. He pulled out a red handkerchief from his back pocket and wiped his hand. "Pansy, I have Abacus all ready for you. Head over to the tack room and Kaui will get you set up. The other kids are already up on their horses and warming up. We'll start in the training ring and then go join them." He pointed the way and Pansy flounced off, beaming.

Tom turned to Marissa. "So . . . are you dropping off or staying?"

"Staying. Definitely staying." Realizing that may have sounded a little too enthusiastic, Marissa quickly corrected herself. "I just want to make sure Pansy's going to be okay. She hasn't really been on a horse before, you know, other than at the fair or at a petting zoo. Not that I don't trust you," she added.

"No worries," Tom said. "I like mothers who care about their kids. Some parents think this is an after-school day care center." The lines around his eyes crinkled in amusement. "Is today a better day?"

What to say? Marissa gave in, not having the energy to come up with a story. "Not really, no. My husband and I are having a trial separation, whatever that means. It's week two, which means that things are still pretty lousy. For me, that is."

"Oh." The look on Tom's face changed to concern. "That's too bad."

"Yeah, it is." She turned to look out at the pasture, where several riders were happily trotting along the perimeter of a larger riding ring. "On the bright side, I now have more room in my closet."

Tom laughed, and despite herself, Marissa did, too. It felt good to laugh—she needed to do more of that.

He began to walk toward the riding ring, beckoning Marissa to follow him. "Come on. I'll get you set up with front row seats."

Front row seats turned out to be a worn wooden bench outside the ring. Tom tossed a thick horse blanket on the bench for her to sit on before heading toward Pansy inside the ring.

"Thanks," she said, sitting down on the bench. It was comfortable, warm and dry. Marissa relaxed and turned her attention to Pansy, who was listening intently to Tom's instructions.

Marissa smiled as she watched Pansy nod her head and then urge the horse to move forward. Tom continued to talk to her, and Marissa couldn't help but smile at that as well. He was completely engrossed in what he was doing, and he was great with children. She could see that Pansy already trusted him.

Her mind drifted to Paul. In all their years of marriage, they had never been apart other than for business. Their arguments rarely escalated into full-blown fights, and even when they did fight it had just seemed like the stuff marriage was made of: peaks and valleys. She had soldiered through Paul's first midlife crisis (which apparently had been a warm-up to the main event) but there had never been talk about anybody moving out or time apart. The possibility of divorce seemed like a reach, the thing that happened to other people, and now it might happen to her.

She was reluctant to hire a lawyer. The whole thing could blow over and then what? No sense in making things worse than they were; maybe she had overplayed the drama card a bit. She thought about Pansy and ballet—clearly she needed to sharpen her listening skills. After all, Paul never said he wanted a divorce; he just wanted a little time to himself. And, practically speaking, it wasn't entirely out in left field. She could reposition this whole thing as a marriage sabbatical. It was certainly the trend, and then nothing drastic would have to happen. If it really was over, then she could get a lawyer and find out what her options were.

Pansy sat on her horse, looking comfortable and self-assured. She was laughing along with the other students at something Tom had said. Without thinking, Marissa fumbled for her iPhone and tapped number one on her speed dial. She watched Pansy join the other riders in the pasture as she waited for Paul to answer the phone.

"Hello?"

Hearing his voice made her miss him, and she forgot about her anger. She cleared her throat, suddenly nervous. "Paul, it's Marissa."

"Oh. Hi." He sounded surprised, even though Marissa knew her name and picture appeared on his cell phone display. "What's up?"

What's up? "Paul, I think we should have dinner and talk about things. You're right: things have gotten so out of control and it's crazy that you're staying at the hotel and . . ."

"I got an apartment." His voice was flat.

Marissa wasn't sure she had heard him correctly. "What?"

"This morning. Just signed a six-month lease. Two bedrooms, so Pansy has a place to stay whenever she wants to visit. I can't keep staying here and thought it would just be better if I got myself settled into a place."

Marissa clenched the phone. "Paul, this doesn't sound like a trial separation anymore. It sounds like you're moving on."

He sighed. "It's just a six-month lease, Marissa. It's a small place in Puako, on the beach . . ."

"On the *beach*?" Property on or near the beach wasn't cheap, which is why they were living in Waimea. "We still have a mortgage! And the house still needs work! And there's Pansy's tuition . . ."

"I know, Marissa. But I think this is for the best."

For you! Marissa wanted to shout, but Tom and Pansy had glanced her way and offered a wave, forcing her to smile and wave back. "Paul, tell me what's going on."

"Marissa . . ." His voice was strained. "I have to go. I have a meeting in five minutes."

"Great, so you have five minutes. If this is it, Paul, I want to know. Tell me, so I'm not acting like a dumb-shit wife waiting around for you!" Tears were stinging her eyes and she blinked rapidly, not wanting to cry.

"You're not a dumb-shit wife . . ." Paul said softly.

Too late. Tears started spilling down her cheeks and Marissa stood up, heading for the car to wait for Pansy there. The last thing she needed was for Tom and a group of kids to see her cry.

"Let's just give ourselves some time to be on our own, think things through," he continued. "I just need some space, Marissa."

"So what am I supposed to do, wait for you?"

There was a long pause before Paul said, "I suppose you should do whatever you feel you have to do."

"Husbands Gone Bad," Kate said. "Paul could star in the first DVD. We'll run infomercials on Lifetime. We could sell millions!"

"I wish." Marissa sat at the kitchen table, staring at their dwindling bank statement.

"Does your mom know yet?" Kate had a stubborn admiration for Marissa's mom, another single woman slinging it out in the art world.

"She told me that she was sorry to hear it, but that she knew I was a smart woman who would make the right choice in the end."

"Ouch. Doesn't give you much room in case you screw up and make the wrong decision, does it?"

"Exactly." Marissa sighed. "Kate, what am I going to do?"

They had hired electricians and contractors to take care of some of the structural and electrical problems, and those problems weren't cheap to fix. And now that they had rent *and* a mortgage, money seemed to go as quickly as it came in. "I'm going to have to get a job. And to think that there was a time when all I wanted to do was work! Now I'm dreading it."

"Can't Paul pay you alimony?"

"Kate, we're not divorced!" Marissa snapped, then instantly regretted it. It wasn't Kate's fault things had gotten to this point.

"Sorry," Kate apologized. "Would it be too callous if I suggested raiding the joint checking account?"

Marissa sighed. She knew Kate was trying to be loyal, but her flippant suggestions weren't helping. "Thanks for the suggestion, but there's nothing to raid, Kate."

"What about calling Paradigm? I bet Arthur would jump at the chance to get you back."

Marissa gazed into the backyard, looking at the pasture beyond and the cows as they stood stock-still, their tails slapping at the flies. "And how would that work? I live here, Kate."

"Maybe you should try to get back to New York. It won't take you very long to get back into the groove of things. Once you're here, I'm sure everything will be fine."

"I can't afford to move back. All our money is tied up with this house." Marissa could hear the desperation in her own voice.

Kate's tone was grave. "Marissa, you're going to have to cut your losses. Put that behemoth on the market, get an attorney, and call it a day."

"Kate, as much as I detest this house, you have to understand something: *I don't want to get a divorce.*"

"I know." There was silence on the other end. "It's just that . . . well, it kind of seems like Paul may have started down that path anyway, you know? It was his idea to separate, his idea to get the apartment. Not yours. It just seems like he's not really thinking about you right now. That's all I'm saying."

The words stung. She knew Kate had a point. The idea of having to take care of the house on her own, with all the things that needed to be fixed, was overwhelming. Marissa knew that it would be tough to get a decent job on the island. Maybe moving back to New York was her best option.

Jenny had tittered sympathetically when Marissa invited her to look at the property.

"Can we list it and see if we get a nibble?" Marissa had asked.

"Of course! You and Paul are the client so whatever you want. I'm at your service." Jenny had nodded feverishly. "But the market has gotten soft in the past couple of months and we'd risk chasing it down. Plus you'd be best tidying up the house and yard a bit before showing it." Jenny's eyes briefly darted around the problem spots of the property. "Did you ever fix that fence out back?"

Marissa shook her head. "We were waiting to finish the electrical and structural problems in the house before we focused on anything cosmetic."

"Well, that needs to be on the list." Jenny tilted her head to one side, considering the house. "You know, I'm surprised to learn that you want to sell. I ran into Paul at the resort and he didn't mention it."

"Well, he probably didn't mention that we've separated, either."

Jenny's eyes grew wide. "Ohhh . . ."

Marissa instantly regretted having told her. Jenny was competing with Malia as head of the Paul Price Fan Club. "Pansy and I may be heading back to New York, which is why I'd like to see if there's any interest in the house."

"I see. Well, under the circumstances I suppose we can always try. If you and Paul want to come in tomorrow and start the paperwork . . ."

"Actually, Jenny, I was hoping we could see if there was an offer on the table first. Paul doesn't want to sell. But I thought if we had a bona fide offer he'd realize . . ."

Jenny shook her head remorsefully. "I can't take on the listing unless you both agree to sell the house. It's in both your names?"

Marissa nodded, already knowing the answer.

"Then unfortunately the best I can do is advise you to get the house fixed up as best you can. Taking out the extra wall in the living room would really bring in the light, don't you think? And then if you and Paul decide to sell, it'll be ready to go." Jenny began to tick off the repairs and renovations that she thought would be necessary to get a good offer and bring up the value of the house.

Afterward, Marissa stared at the two-page list for a long time. It would take a small miracle to pull this off.

"But I just had them dry-cleaned!" Marissa stared in dismay at the limp pile of wrinkled clothes the owner of the local consignment shop, Just As Good As the First Time, had handed back to her. As a last resort, Marissa had rummaged through her closet, pulling out pieces she no longer wore. In New York, it would have easily fetched a couple hundred dollars.

"I'm sorry, but I've had them out for a month and I really need to make more space for all the beachwear that's come in. But a few of your pieces sold. I just cut the checks so let me see if I can find yours." The woman rummaged through a basket by the register. "Ah, here it is! Don't spend it all in one place!" She handed an envelope to Marissa.

Marissa thanked the woman before gathering her clothes

and going outside. Pansy was looking through a display rack of activity brochures.

"Well, hopefully we've got enough for a couple more riding sessions with Tom," Marissa said, waving the envelope. The riding lessons were the highlight of Pansy's week—she was even begging Marissa to take her there early so she could help Kaui Nilsson, another student of Tom's who worked part-time in the stables, set up.

Marissa pulled out the check and stared at it grimly. "Or not." She let out a heavy sigh.

"Mom, look." Pansy thrust a handful of brochures under her nose. "I think we should do this."

"Paragliding?"

"No . . ." Pansy pulled out another brochure. "Look. A bed-and-breakfast."

"You want to go to a bed-and-breakfast?" Marissa was confused.

"No, Mom. *We* should have a bed-and-breakfast. Isn't that what the old owners use to do? We have those two rooms we never use and there's the *ohana* . . ."

Marissa unlocked the doors to the Audi. "Pansy, I don't want strangers coming and going. It's not safe."

"Well, what about renting the rooms? That way you can choose who will be there."

Marissa turned to face her daughter. "Pansy, why are you doing this?"

"Because we need the money."

It had never been Marissa's intention to share her concerns about their financial situation with Pansy, so she shifted uncomfortably as she held the door open. "I don't know what you mean."

Pansy climbed into the car. "Mom, I hear you talking on the phone. Dad has his new apartment, and we're pinching pennies."

"We are *not* pinching pennies. Things are not that bad."
Marissa closed Pansy's door. She got herself settled in the
driver's seat before catching her daughter's stubborn glare in
their rearview mirror. Pansy knew better, and Marissa suddenly wasn't sure if she was being optimistic for Pansy's
sake or for her own. Dinner for the past week had consisted
of simple sandwiches and a couple of Happy Meals from
McDonald's. Marissa had even forgone the taro chips that
Pansy loved—at five dollars a bag for a handful of chips, it
seemed like an extravagance. It was a far cry from the regular weekly sushi takeout Paul used to bring home. "Things
are just . . . up in the air."

"I hear you talking to Aunt Kate about going back to
New York."

"That's one option I'm exploring."

Pansy crossed her arms. "Well, I don't want to go back. I
like it here."

"Well, it costs money to live here, Pansy. There's not a lot
of job opportunities for me here."

"Which is why we should rent rooms." Pansy jutted out
her chin.

Thankfully, Marissa's phone rang before she had to come
up with a response. The display flashed PAUL. Marissa
handed the phone to Pansy, not wanting to talk to him. "It's
your dad."

Eagerly, Pansy reached for the phone. "Hi, Dad!"

Paul's absence at home, while noticeable, had not seemed
to upset their daughter even though Marissa knew Pansy
missed him. Marissa made sure that Pansy had an opportunity to talk to Paul whenever possible and arranged to drop
her off at the resort for some Dad and beach time as often as
she could manage it. Granted, Marissa hadn't done great in
the "not-bashing-Paul-in-front-of-his-daughter" depart-
ment, but she'd done her best. Marissa suspected that Pansy

was coping with all the uncertainty by shifting into problem-solving mode.

Renting rooms . . . the mere thought made Marissa flinch. She coveted her private space. Who knew what would happen if they were suddenly surrounded by strangers?

Besides, the money probably wouldn't be worth the hassle. She had two rooms with separate entrances and private bathrooms, plus the separate *ohana* unit. Marissa stopped at a red light, listening as Pansy chatted about her day.

The day's newspaper was on top of the mail on the passenger seat. Not wanting Pansy to see her, Marissa quickly flipped to the rentals, looking for something similar to what they would have to offer. She took an average and did the math in her head.

Marissa was stunned. Even when the light turned green and the cars behind her started to honk impatiently, Marissa sat at the light, running the numbers through her head once again. It wouldn't make them rich, but it would more than help meet their monthly obligations, which were now strained by Paul's additional expenses.

"Mom, Dad wants to talk with you." Pansy held the phone out to her mother.

Paul sounded irate. "I just ran into Jenny at the bank and she told me you were trying to put the house up for sale. When were you going to tell me?"

Damn that woman. "I just wanted to get her opinion on whether or not the house was sellable. And, in case you're wondering, it's not. At least not until we get some things fixed."

"Well, we don't have the money to fix things right now."

"No. Really?"

Paul sighed. "I thought we were going to lay low for a while, have some time apart to think things through."

Marissa glanced in the rearview mirror at Pansy, who was looking out the window, and lowered her voice. "I'm sorry, but when did *we* decide this?" Two months had passed since Paul had moved out.

She could tell he was flustered. "Look, I didn't think you'd try to sell the house and move back to New York."

"Well, it doesn't make sense for me to stay here, now does it?"

"Marissa . . ."

"Don't worry, Paul. Clearly, we can't sell the house right now unless we want to take a loss, which I don't."

She heard Paul breathe a sigh of relief. "Good, because I think if we hold on to it for the long-term it will appreciate. Real estate always does."

"Paul, I'm going to get the house fixed up and then we— as in you *and* me—are going to put the house on the market so Pansy and I can go back to New York."

"But . . ."

"And in the meantime, you should probably know that I'm going to put an ad in the paper. I'm going to rent out the extra rooms and the *ohana* unit." She heard a triumphant shout from the backseat.

"What? Now you're out of your mind! Marissa, I'm going to have to strongly advise against that . . ."

Marissa pulled into Pualani Stables. The car was barely at a full stop before Pansy jumped out excitedly and headed straight for the tack room. Tom was in the riding ring, holding the reins of a horse that he pointed to before pointing to Marissa with a grin.

"Knock yourself out," she told Paul as she cut the engine. "In the meantime, I've got to go. There's a horse with my name on it."

*   *   *

"Flipping through the want ads?" Jane was standing behind Marissa with a large slice of focaccia bread. It was the first time Jane had struck up a conversation since Marissa had been coming to the coffee shop.

"Just checking on my ad," Marissa said. "I've got some extra rooms in my house and I'm looking to rent them out. I'm not getting much of a response, though."

Jane peered at the paper, reading the circled ad over Marissa's shoulder. "Wow, you must have a big house."

"It's big. But in slight disrepair. I'm hoping the rental income will help me finish with some renovations and give me some discretionary income."

"Are the common areas shared, like the kitchen and living room?"

"Yes, except for the *ohana* unit. It's got its own kitchen and it's pretty spacious. It used to be my husband's study and he barely used a quarter of it."

"Your husband doesn't mind giving it up?"

"Not exactly . . ."

Jane hadn't asked Marissa any personal questions since that first day they had met, and Marissa hadn't offered any details even though it was apparent that something was amiss. But now, after a few weeks of quiet friendship, Marissa felt ready to talk.

Jane must have noticed this, because she raised an eyebrow, then glanced around before slipping into the chair next to Marissa. "I can sit for a minute. Spill."

Marissa was now accustomed to Jane's cut-to-the-chase directives. "Long story short: my husband is having a midlife crisis and needs to find himself. He proposed a trial separation and I freaked out. I was so upset that I kicked him out on the spot. This happened on Valentine's Day."

"Yuck." Jane made a face.

"By the time I calmed down, he had already found an

apartment and signed a lease. He doesn't seem to have an interest in trying to work it out, and I'm feeling like it's time to just let it go. Our finances are really stretched and I need to get some cash flow so we can sell the house and I can return to New York with my daughter." Marissa let out a heavy exhale, then gave Jane a glum look.

Jane patted her arm comfortingly. "What's your daughter's name?"

"Pansy. She put two and two together pretty quickly. Took it like the mature eight-year-old she is. Not choosing sides, still pretty chipper. She was apparently spared the drama gene."

Jane smiled. "She sounds wonderful. Do you have a picture?"

"No, I don't really carry pictures with me. Oh, wait, I think I still have some on my phone." Marissa pulled out her phone and tapped the screen, then scrolled through the pictures.

"Mm hmm." Jane was nodding appreciatively. She pointed to a picture. "You look happy here."

It was their first picture in front of their new house, a *Thelma & Louise* type of shot. Paul had one arm around Marissa and held the camera phone with the other, Pansy tucked in the crook of his arm. They all looked good. Even the house looked good.

"Calm before the storm," Marissa said, staring at the picture. They *did* look happy. How did things get turned upside down so quickly?

Jane squinted, then put on the reading glasses that hung from a chain around her neck. "Is that your husband?"

"Husband or soon to be ex-husband, Paul. I have no idea how I'm supposed to refer to him now."

Jane pressed her lips together as if trying to think. "I've

seen him in here before. Five-eleven, sandy blond hair, snappy dresser?"

"Yes, but I don't think he's ever been here."

"I could be wrong." Jane looked at the picture on the screen again then took off her glasses. "Nope, I'm not. One thing this job's done is keep my mind sharp. I've got a pretty good memory for people and faces." Her voice was resolute.

Marissa shook her head. "It's got to be somebody who looks just like him. His place is down by the beach and his job is on the coast. Why would he be in Waimea except to see Pansy? I think he's only come up once or twice since we separated. The rest of the time I'm driving her back and forth."

Jane seemed reluctant to say anything but finally said, "No, it was him. And he wasn't alone."

"Not alone?" Marissa blinked rapidly. "Oh my God. He told me it wasn't about her! He lied to me! He said it was just about him and me." She stood up, then felt her knees buckle.

Jane grabbed Marissa's sleeve and pulled her back down before she could stumble and fall. "Listen, Marissa, I wasn't paying close attention so I can't say that they were together, as in a couple. Don't go there. Is she a friend?"

"No." Marissa felt her eyes welling up with tears as she clenched her fists. "She's his secretary. I knew it from the start, but he kept denying it. God, I'm an idiot!"

Jane wore a perplexed look on her face. "She didn't really seem like the secretary type. What does his secretary look like?"

"Local girl. Gorgeous. Midtwenties." Marissa added bitterly, "Huge breasts."

"Brown hair?" Jane was frowning.

"Of course. Long. Past her shoulders."

Jane shook her head. "It wasn't the same woman, then."

Marissa was taken aback. "It wasn't?"

"No. This woman was older, with a definite mainland air about her. Savvy. Lousy tipper. Hair like fire. Red hair, not from a bottle."

Angela.

'ewalu | eight

Marissa fell into a deep funk after discovering the news about Angela and Paul. She couldn't shake it for days, managing to get Pansy to school and back but not much else. It would have gone on longer if not for the fact that there hadn't been much interest in her rental ad, and Marissa was now even more determined to fix the house so she could sell it and move back to New York. She needed to find some tenants.

She had ruled out men as housemates since they would be sharing the kitchen and living room. Jane told her that newspapers were not the most effective way to get the news out there. Word of mouth, or the "coconut wireless," would be her best shot at getting the right people. Jane volunteered to tell people at Kava Java, but Marissa knew it wouldn't be enough. She didn't have time to wait for people to trickle in.

It was time to do things the New York way. Marissa made flyers for an open house, inviting people to come and take a look. Pansy would spend the morning at the stables during that time so Marissa could focus on showing the house and interviewing potential applicants, weeding out any suspicious characters.

Marissa awoke on the day of the open house, keyed up and ready to find some renters. It was the first time she could think of when cleaning the house didn't feel like a chore. Whatever was going to help her reach her goal of getting some cash flow was worth it, and Marissa was determined to make this work.

When it was time, Marissa put out a sign on the street. She left the front door open and waited in the living room for people to arrive.

An hour later, nobody serious had come by. Dejected, Marissa had turned on the TV and flipped channels, completely at a loss for what to do next. She jumped when she heard a voice calling out.

"Hello? I'm here about the open house. Is the *ohana* unit still available?"

Marissa straightened up and cleared her throat, then hurried to the front door. She slowed her pace when she saw who was standing there.

It was the masseuse from Paul's resort, Kavena Jones. She stood on the doorstep with her son. She still had her dreadlocks and Birkenstocks, but she was wearing a pressed sundress, clearly wanting to make a good impression. Kavena's eyes quickly took in Marissa's own attire, which Marissa had painstakingly chosen in an effort to look like a landlord with lots of aloha. It was a slight stretch for both of them, and they knew it.

"Come in," Marissa finally said. She was in no position to turn somebody away and was relieved that things between them had ended on a good note. Noticing Kavena's hesitation, Marissa bent down to greet her son. "I have cookies in the kitchen. Would you like one?"

Kavena's son nodded enthusiastically just as Kavena said, "Thanks, but we don't do sugar."

"Well, I have fruit . . ."

"That's okay, we're fine." Kavena glanced around uncertainly, still unwilling to step foot inside the house.

Marissa knew that she had to move quickly or she'd lose her only viable applicant. "It's good to see you," she said sincerely. "Come on, I'll walk you over to the *ohana* unit and you can take a look."

"Wow, it's spacious," Kavena said a few minutes later as they did the walk-through. "But to be honest the rent's a little more than I was hoping to pay."

There was a knock on the door and a man stepped inside. "Hi, I'm here for the open house?" He looked fidgety, his eyes darting around the *ohana* unit. "Wow, it's great. Is it rented yet? I can pay cash. You said it's available immediately?"

Marissa felt her defenses go up. She may have been from New York, but this guy's pushiness was rubbing her the wrong way. He seemed edgy and a bit creepy, too. She didn't want him anywhere near her or Pansy, shared living space or not.

"It is, but I'm sorry," Marissa replied sweetly, batting her eyes quickly at Kavena. "We're just about to sign the lease."

The man looked at Kavena as if noticing her for the first time. "The paper said you have rooms for rent in the house, too?"

"Yes, but I'm only renting those rooms to women." Marissa looked him in the eye.

The man's eyes narrowed. "That's discrimination," he said darkly.

"Not when you're sharing living space with the land-lord," Marissa corrected with a firm smile. She had done her homework.

"All right then," he said, a smirk on his face. He left, much to Marissa's relief.

Marissa waited until she knew he was gone before turning to Kavena. "What can you pay?"

"Probably about seventy-five percent of the rent. That was my budget."

Marissa nodded, doing the calculation in her head. It was better than nothing. "I can do that."

Kavena didn't look convinced. "It'll be weird renting from the GM of the resort I work for. Isn't that some sort of conflict of interest?"

"Not for me," Marissa said. "Paul and I have separated. He doesn't live here anymore. It's just me and Pansy."

"Oh, wow. I mean, I'm sorry about that. You seemed like such a . . . compatible couple. When did this happen?"

"Valentine's Day."

Kavena's brow furrowed as they walked back to the main house. "That was two months ago. Are you sure you're not going to reconcile? I'd hate to move in and then have to move out right after."

"Chances of reconciliation are slim, seeing how it hasn't even come up in conversation. But don't worry. I have every intention of honoring the six-month lease, and it will go month-to-month after that. I'm planning to sell the place once I've done some work on the house." Marissa pointed to different parts of the house that needed work. "I'm not very handy though, so I have no idea how long this will take."

Kavena nodded, deep in thought. "I used to build houses with Habitat for Humanity and I'm pretty good with a hammer. I can pay the seventy-five percent and then make up the rest by helping you with some of your projects. Would that work?"

"Really?" Marissa couldn't believe it. "That would work out . . . amazingly well. And, just so you know, Pansy would probably love to do some occasional babysitting. After her homework's done, of course."

That apparently sealed the deal. "Holy goddess, who would have thunk it?" Kavena muttered, shaking her head in amazement. "How soon can we move in?"

Marissa was floating when she went to pick up Pansy at the stables.

"Good news," she told Tom as Pansy was washing up. "I just rented the *ohana* unit, which means, among other things, that Pansy can continue her horseback riding lessons."

Tom frowned. "I wish you had told me that was a concern," he said. "I had no idea. But now that we're on the subject, I do have something I want to ask you."

He led her off to the side of the barn, away from the prying eyes of the other parents who were picking up or dropping off their kids. His hand felt warm on her arm, and Marissa suddenly felt nervous.

Tom turned to face her, leaning in. Close. Marissa could see that he was even more handsome close up—heavy eyebrows, tanned cheekbones, just enough stubble. His skin was tan from the sun, but his eyes were a clear, gorgeous blue. And his lips . . .

"Tom, I'm not ready to date," Marissa blurted out. "It's just too soon."

Tom's eyebrows shot up. "Date?" he asked. "You're shooting me down before I've even had a chance to ask? *If* that's what I was going to ask."

"That isn't what you were going to ask?" she asked faintly.

"No." He smiled. "But it's good to know where I stand."

Marissa closed her eyes in embarrassment. "God . . ."

"It's okay, Marissa. You have a lot on your plate, plus I'm sure it doesn't help that you're an attractive woman. I figure you're probably spending an inordinate amount of time fending men off."

He thought she was attractive? Marissa gave him a grateful smile and glanced down at her ring finger, which was bare since the afternoon she had learned about Paul and Angela. "So now that I've embarrassed myself, what did you want to ask?"

"Do you still have anything available to rent?"

"I still have the two rooms in the house," said Marissa. "Private baths, separate entrances. But I'm only considering female tenants since it's just me and Pansy."

"No, that's perfect. I have a friend who needs a place to stay. Turns out that she's pregnant and her boyfriend took off. The landlord just gave her notice and she needs a place to stay. She can easily pay the rent; she's got a good job."

"She has family here?"

Tom shook his head. "Her older brother was my best friend; he was hit by a drunk driver ten years ago. Their family is on Oahu but she doesn't want to quit her job or move back there. Her mom passed when she was younger and her dad has some judgment about her having gotten pregnant. I've been trying to get her to go back, even offered her a room in my house, but she won't do it. Too independent."

"It's a short-term lease, Tom," Marissa said, a bit reluctantly. God knew she needed to find another tenant, but she wanted him to know the situation. "Six months, until September. I'd hate for her to move in and then have to move out, especially if she's pregnant."

"Me, too, to be honest. But nothing else is working out and I know I'd feel better if she was around another woman. The baby is due in September, so it'll be close. If you would be willing to lease one of the rooms to her now, then that will give me time to help her find a longer-term arrangement. What do you think?"

At this stage, Marissa was open to anything. Plus, if it would help Tom, she'd be more than willing to see what she could do. "Come by this evening," she offered. "And see if she likes it. Seven o'clock?"

"Great." Tom looked relieved. "I can't tell you how much I appreciate this. And, also, I'd like to comp Pansy's lessons . . ."

Marissa started to protest. "That's not necessary . . ."

Tom held up a hand. ". . . in exchange for an hour's work before and after class. She's been working a lot with Kaui, who has more than she can handle, and I figured she may as well get paid for it. I'm lucky to find two bright girls who handle horses well, so if you're okay with that, I'd be pretty happy, too."

A potential renter and free riding lessons? Marissa couldn't believe her good fortune. "Pansy would love it."

Tom straightened up. "Great. I should get back. People might think you're trying to corral me back here."

"Me?" Marissa gave him an indignant look.

"What can I say . . . I'm an attractive man." And with that he tipped his hat and strode off.

The next day after school, Marissa and Pansy pulled into the driveway of their house. Kavena was already there, taking Isaiah out of his car seat. Pansy immediately went to him, and he bounced excitedly in Kavena's arms, anxious to be set free. Marissa could tell that Kavena was reluctant to let him go.

"Oh, let him play," Marissa said. "Pansy can watch him while you unpack."

Kavena slowly lowered her son to the ground and he went straight to Pansy. Marissa began to unload groceries from the car. "Why don't you and Isaiah come over for dessert tonight, once you're settled in? Pansy and I bought all the fixings for ice cream sundaes. Sugar-free."

"We don't do ice cream," Kavena said, pulling two suit-cases out of her trunk. "We just went vegan. We're dairy-free."

"Come over for tea then. That'll leave more ice cream for me." She headed toward the house as Pansy danced around the driveway with Isaiah.

"And me!" Pansy crowed.

"An' me!" Isaiah echoed. Kavena shot Marissa an annoyed look, but Marissa gave her a *kids-what-can-you-do?* kind of shrug before stepping into the house and breaking into a smile.

Later that evening, there was a knock on the door.

"Come on in," Marissa said as Isaiah barreled past her, making a beeline for Pansy.

"We can't stay long," Kavena said, slipping off her shoes and leaving them outside. "It's past Isaiah's bedtime."

"Really?" Marissa turned to watch Isaiah as he ran from room to room, his face lit up. "Yeah, he really looks tired."

Kavena opened her mouth and Marissa braced herself for a witty retort or reprimand. Instead Kavena's shoulders dropped and she heaved a sigh. "Ah, who am I kidding?" she said. "He probably won't go down for another three hours. He's a total night owl."

"Well, the night is young, so he's in the right place." Marissa led them into the kitchen. "I've already started the tea. I have another potential renter coming to look at one of the rooms in the house tonight. It's a favor for Pansy's riding instructor." Marissa chose a lemon from a white porcelain bowl near the sink and began slicing it up. "She's a friend of his family's. Apparently they gave her notice on the place she's in. She's pregnant and her boyfriend left her."

Kavena wrinkled her nose. "Every time my faith in men is restored, one of them goes off and does something like this." She shook her head in disgust.

The tea kettle was whistling and Marissa went to the stove to turn off the heat. "Well, she's a friend of Tom's, and he's definitely one of the good guys." It came out with a bit more feeling than she had intended.

"Oh, really?" Kavena gave Marissa a meaningful look.

"It's nothing like that," Marissa said, pretending to look appalled.

"If you say so." Kavena shrugged, but Marissa could tell she wasn't convinced.

"I'm so glad Pansy and Isaiah are getting along," Marissa said, turning her attention to the kids. She cocked an ear toward the living room. "It sounds like Pansy is showing him the ropes on her GameCube. She hasn't played that in ages."

"GameCube? What's that?"

"GameCube. You know, video games on the TV. Now, I have Earl Grey, chamomile, green tea . . ."

Kavena was already rushing into the living room. A few seconds later, she heard Isaiah crying. *Uh-oh.* Marissa hurried to the living room, tea boxes still in hand.

Pansy and Isaiah were sitting on the floor, holding on to the game controls. Marissa was relieved to see "Frogger" up on the screen. Kavena was kneeling and trying to coax the game control from Isaiah, who was crying and refusing to let it go.

"Isaiah, come on," she was saying. "No TV, remember? And no video games."

"Kavena, it's just Frogger." Marissa tried to explain. "See? The frog has to cross the road and dodge the cars or . . ."

"Or what?" Kavena asked, eyes narrowed.

Marissa sighed. "Never mind. Pansy, why don't you show Isaiah your room, okay? You can play another time, Isaiah."

Kavena's body language was signaling an *over-my-dead-body!* message. Isaiah continued to cry hysterically until Pansy offered to carry him piggyback style to her bedroom. That seemed to do the trick. The crying stopped immediately and he climbed onto Pansy's back and they were off.

Marissa stared at the television screen before turning it off. "Oh, look—he was about to top the high score," she joked.

"Very funny." Kavena held out a hand and Marissa helped her up. "You know, there was a study on media and childhood development . . ."

"For God's sake, Kavena, we're talking about a couple of rounds of Frogger. It's not a national conspiracy." They walked back to the kitchen and Marissa held out the tea boxes. "Choose your poison."

Kavena still looked defiant but nodded toward one of the boxes. "Chamomile."

"Good choice. I'll have it as well."

Marissa was pouring the hot water into the teapot when the doorbell rang.

"I'll get it," Kavena volunteered.

"Thank you." Marissa set out extra mugs, then checked herself in the mirror before heading to greet Tom and his friend.

As she neared the front door, Marissa heard excited voices and laughter. That had to be a good sign. She felt herself relax as she put a bright smile on her face and stepped up behind Kavena. "Hi, I'm Marissa Price . . ." Her voice trailed off.

Malia Fox, Paul's secretary, stood next to Tom with a look of shock on her face. She visibly stiffened. Kavena frowned and looked between the two women.

Tom also looked perplexed. "Um, I'm sorry we're late. Marissa, this is . . ."

"Excuse me," Malia said, her voice breaking. "But this isn't going to work." She spun on her heel and hurried toward Tom's truck in the driveway.

"Malia?" Tom called after her. He looked back at the two women, bewildered. "I'm not sure what . . . I'm sorry about that. I'll call you later, Marissa." He hurried after her.

"Well," Kavena said dryly as they drove away. "What was that about?"

Marissa closed the door slowly. "Oh . . ." She tried laughing. "Well, it's funny . . ."

Kavena waited impatiently.

"Okay, fine. I haven't been very nice to her, to put it mildly." Marissa shook her head regretfully. "I thought she was having an affair with Paul, so my behavior toward her may have been a bit curt. And suggestive."

"An affair? Are you serious?"

"I didn't know what to think! She just seemed to be all over him from the minute we got here . . ."

"All over him?" Kavena didn't look convinced.

"Well, she was definitely all doting and touchy-feely like he was the greatest thing since sliced bread."

"Did you ever meet the last GM? That man was a lush and constantly hitting on her and anyone else in a skirt. Your husband is a saint compared to him."

Marissa sighed. "Look, I already know I messed up by giving her the cold shoulder. It just doesn't help that she's so gorgeous. I was certain that she was making a move on him and wanted to seduce him."

Kavena looked genuinely shocked. "Malia is one of the

nicest girls I know. Period. I can't believe you'd think that!"
She looked at Marissa in a way that made Marissa wonder if
Kavena was having second thoughts. Here she was, on the
brink of having two tenants, and now on the brink of having none. The thought was depressing beyond words.

"It just seemed to make sense at the time," she said quietly. "But it wasn't her. And it wasn't exactly something I
could apologize about after. *I thought you were having an affair with my husband, but I was wrong. Sorry!*" Marissa headed
back to the kitchen, thoroughly disgusted with herself.

Kavena didn't say anything as she followed Marissa.
"Well, at least it's a relief that your husband's not having an
affair."

"I didn't say that," Marissa said. "I just said that he
wasn't having an affair with Malia. I found out that he's
been spending time with Angela Thompson. She's the VP
of Marketing."

"Ohhh." Kavena made a face. She obviously knew who
Angela was.

Marissa bit her lip. "So. Are you still up for tea? Or are
you going to run off, too?"

Kavena didn't say anything, but sat down next to Marissa
and gave her hand a strong, sympathetic squeeze.

"The irony is, Malia would be the perfect tenant. She's
conscientious. She looks like she'd be a great housemate. I
know she's desperate to find a place to stay, but I guess it
would be too awkward since I'm her boss's soon-to-be ex-
wife. I mean, you were worried about that, too."

"Marissa, that girl left because she thinks you don't like
her. Pure and simple." Kavena blew on her tea to cool it
down. "She's probably more sensitive since she's pregnant,
right?" Kavena stopped and stared at Marissa. "Oh my goddess . . ."

Marissa closed her eyes. "She's probably mortified that we

know. I doubt Paul even knows. Poor girl." She squeezed the tea bag with her spoon. "I know this is a small island, but it's kind of a weird coincidence, don't you think?"

"You think this is a coincidence?" Kavena had an amused look on her face.

"First you, and now my husband's secretary? It's bizarre beyond words. What else could it be?"

"Fate," Kavena said confidently, her eyes lighting up. "And I'm going to get that girl in here. She belongs with us."

True to her word, Kavena got Malia to move in. Marissa had insisted on trying to talk to Malia herself, but Kavena flat-out rejected the idea.

"Forget it," Kavena had said. "You've done enough. Besides, I have a vested interest in this, too. I don't want any whack jobs around Isaiah."

Marissa wanted to argue but knew Kavena was right. Plus she needed to put her energy into finding another tenant in order to be able to make ends meet. So Marissa let Kavena do all the coaxing, and three days later they had a new housemate.

"Don't mention the boyfriend," Kavena warned in a low voice when they watched Malia pull into the driveway later that week. "He was picked up by the cops about a week after he dumped her. DUI, and not the first time, apparently. He has a couple of other kids, too, and it sounds like he has the deadbeat dad role pretty much mastered."

Marissa grimaced. "I suppose this means child support is out of the question."

"Yup, especially since he doesn't think it's his kid. Malia says it's actually a relief. Now that she's rid of him, she doesn't want him back. Shucks, *I'm* relieved. She's a smart girl and deserves better. Come on, let's give her a hand."

From what Marissa could see, Malia only had a couple of suitcases and a few boxes.

"Are the rest of your things in storage?" Marissa asked as they brought everything into Malia's room. She had put Malia in the room facing the pasture in the back of the house, which was spacious and received a lot of early morning light.

"No," said Malia. Her hand fluttered regularly to her stomach, which was just starting to bulge slightly. "This is all I have. Tom loaned me some furniture for my last place, and the rest came from Rent-a-Center."

"Oh," Marissa said. She added brightly, "Well, if you start getting baby gifts, you'll have plenty of room to store them. You could even fit a crib in here . . ."

Malia looked Marissa right in the eye. "I'm not planning on being here that long," she said quietly. "I really appreciate you offering me a place right now, but I'll need to find another place eventually, before the baby comes."

"Oh, well, of course." Marissa glanced briefly at Tom, who was wisely keeping his mouth shut.

Malia looked visibly uncomfortable. She seemed more vulnerable and defensive. It was a huge difference from the vibrant, friendly young woman Marissa had met—and felt threatened by—before. "I haven't told anyone at work that I'm pregnant. I just passed my first trimester but I haven't been able to find the right opportunity to break the news."

"I'm not going to say anything," Marissa assured her. She wanted Malia to know that the past was water under the bridge. "It's not as if I don't have a few things going on that I'd like to keep to myself. Besides, Paul and I hardly talk about anything other than Pansy these days. As far as I'm concerned, what you do here is your business. I'm just glad to have you."

Malia finally seemed to relax. "Thank you, Mrs. Price."

Marissa rolled her eyes. "Malia, please. Call me Marissa."

"I'm starting to feel like an outsider in my own house," Marissa complained to Jane a few days later at Kava Java. "I used to hate driving up to an empty home. Now there's always someone around. And stuff's happening without my knowledge. Like yesterday, for example. The living room curtains were already open when I woke up and went to the kitchen." She had been unprepared for the brilliant, majestic view of Mauna Kea that greeted her. The sun was hitting it from the east, and the morning light cast a purplish hue over the mountain.

"I'm sure it's all for the best," Jane said briskly as she arranged a basket of scones.

"Sure you do," Marissa said, moodily staring into her cup of coffee. "You don't live there."

Jane let out a chuckle. "Funny, that." She fussed with the corner of the basket.

"Funny what?"

"Well, my home is about to go through a remodel and I need a place to stay. Just a short-term rental situation. And if it's in Waimea and close to work, all the better. Scone?"

Marissa reluctantly declined. Jane was always way too generous with the coffee and pastries but Marissa didn't want to get her in trouble. She made a point of always leaving a generous tip, hoping that it would more than help make up for it.

"So what do you think?" Jane asked hopefully.

Marissa played dumb. "What do I think about what?"

"What do you think about me renting that last room of yours?" Jane disappeared into the small kitchen in back and returned with a loaf of banana bread.

Marissa knew both Kavena and Malia made a decent salary at the resort, but she didn't know if Jane would be able to afford the rent. Plus with Kavena paying only a partial rent, Marissa needed the cash. She couldn't afford to offer any more favors but at the same time didn't want to turn Jane away. "Here's the thing, Jane. The rent's kind of high and I can't really budge on it . . ."

"I saw it in the paper, Marissa. It's perfectly reasonable."

"I just . . ." Marissa looked around before leaning in closer. "I mean, no offense, Jane, but are you sure you can afford it? I know this sounds presumptuous, but I wouldn't want all of your barista salary to get eaten up in rent . . ."

Jane slipped off her oven mitts and turned her back on Marissa, and Marissa instantly felt a sense of dread. This was exactly what Marissa had hoped to avoid. Jane's friendship was important to her and she didn't want money to come between them.

Marissa immediately started apologizing. "Jane, I'm so sorry . . ."

Jane turned around and Marissa was startled to see that Jane was laughing. "Marissa, honey, *this* barista is doing just fine."

Marissa reddened. "What, do you have a trust or something?" She thought of Jane's husband. Of course. He must have left Jane some money.

"I sure do. You're sitting in it." Jane was wiping her eyes. "Boy, you made my day. Really." She burst out laughing again.

"I don't get it."

"Marissa, when my husband died he left me a nice chunk of change. Not huge, you understand, but enough. When the coffeehouse I was working at in Kauai wanted to close, I decided to buy it and change the name to Kava Java. It was doing well, so I came to the Big Island to open this one. I also have two on Oahu. The fifth Kava Java opens in Maui next month."

"You *own* this place?"

Jane leaned on the counter toward Marissa and cocked an eyebrow. "I own *all* of them, honey." She said this slowly to make sure Marissa got it.

Marissa did. "Oh, well, then of course I'd be happy to rent you the room." She breathed a happy sigh of relief.

Jane smiled broadly. "I thought so. I'd love it, thank you."

"I just assumed . . ."

"That's the thing, isn't it? Assumptions are a bitch. And they're almost never right." Jane sliced the loaf of banana bread and gave a piece to Marissa. "On the house. And keep those tips coming—the girls love them."

'eiwa | nine

"April showers better bring May flowers." Marissa stared out the window after almost three weeks of consecutive rain. May was right around the corner and Marissa hoped the rain would start to lighten up soon. She was actually starting to miss walking around the property, even if it only was a short walk.

Jane had made coffee for her housemates while it was still dark and had already left for Kava Java. Kavena was at the table feeding breakfast to Isaiah and studying the original blueprints of Marissa's house, anxious to start on some of the repairs.

"We've been in a drought for a while," Kavena said. "So rain is good." Even though Kavena lived in the *ohana* unit, she was in the main house all of the time, enjoying the company of the other women.

Marissa enjoyed it, too. She had never belonged to a sorority or been in a living situation with other women before. Despite the occasional chaos of having so many X chromosomes in one place, it was nice. Pansy especially seemed to revel in so much girl energy. Marissa hadn't counted on how a few short weeks of their new living arrangement could have blossomed Pansy from kid to young girl status, but it had. She was more outgoing and engaged, and laughed a lot. Hearing her daughter laugh made Marissa's heart swell, and confirmed that she had done the right thing.

Malia emerged from the bathroom, still pale from the morning sickness that had continued into her second trimester. She began to pack her lunch for work as well as lunch for the kids. "It's no problem," she had assured Marissa and Kavena, both of whom were feeling a bit guilty. "I'm doing mine anyway."

When Kavena wasn't looking, Malia added juice boxes to the kids' lunch boxes. "Marissa, I'm going to tell everyone in the executive office about my pregnancy today. And I'm going to tell Paul that I'm living here, too. It's been almost a month."

Marissa was learning to let go. "Whatever you think is best," she said, but then felt the familiar tightening in her chest whenever Paul's name came up.

When she had seen him last week, he had stared speechless at the driveway and yard that was littered with toys, both Isaiah's and Pansy's. Marissa had tried initially to get the kids to put their things away, but eventually gave up.

"What's going on here?" Paul had finally asked.

"Childhood," had been Marissa's guarded response. She had refused to give him details about her new housemates and knew that Pansy had deftly, but lovingly, played dumb whenever Paul tried to pry.

To Marissa's surprise, Paul had turned to look at the oak tree Pansy had climbed their first day in the new house. "I could put up a tire swing," he said slowly. "That branch is low and strong enough."

It was so unexpected that Marissa's mouth went completely dry. When she finally found her voice, she simply said, "Pansy would like that."

But there had been no talk after that, and the tire swing never materialized.

Now Malia sat down next to Marissa, staring into a mug of ginger tea Kavena had made for her. The ginger was supposed to help with the nausea.

"I've never shared my personal life with anyone in the office," Malia said. "I'm a little nervous about suddenly having so many people know about what's going on with me."

"Paul will get over it," Marissa said, though she was pretty sure she knew what his first reaction would be.

"I'm not worried about Paul," Malia said. "I'm worried about *her*."

The women rarely talked about Paul and Angela, but when they did, they referred to Angela as *she* or *her,* which suited Marissa just fine. Pansy still had no idea that her father was involved with another woman, and Marissa intended to keep it that way. That was between her and Paul.

"What would she do?" Marissa asked.

"Make my life miserable." Malia looked unhappy. "Which she does anyway. But I know from experience that it can get worse."

"I've heard that, too," said Kavena.

"She's on her third marketing team." Malia looked grim. "Not a single person under her has lasted more than a year and a half. People say that working for the executive office is the surest way to end a hotel career. I'm sure it's no coincidence that every time I apply for an internal transfer or promotion, I get turned down."

"That sucks," Kavena said.

Malia shrugged. "I know. I wish I had more options open to me, but I probably won't as long as Angela is there. If I go to any other resort, it'll be the same thing—I'm pigeon-holed as a secretary. But it helps that I like working for Paul, so that makes it easier."

Marissa frowned. While Marissa could see how Angela could be a formidable person to work for, she couldn't see her yielding that much power. Large organizations usually had checks and balances in place to avoid that kind of abuse. "I'm not understanding how she's able to pull off that kind of intimidation."

"She's best friends with Jackie in HR," Malia said. "How do you think she managed to get all those women before me fired? I think they've had six different executive secretaries in the time that she's been here. Luckily I have the support of enough people in the office that it's difficult for her to get me fired, though I'm sure she would if she could. She acts sweet in public but when it's just her and me?" Malia shook her head. "And the sexual harassment suits? Gone. Mysteriously disappeared. She knows that I know more than anybody at that resort. The only thing that's saved me is that I have wonderful performance reviews. Except from her, of course."

"What sexual harassment suits?" Kavena asked, leaning forward eagerly.

Malia pretended to seal her lips shut. "Nothing. Forget I said anything."

Kavena sat back, disappointed. "I heard they call you 'the vault,' " she said, disgruntled. "Come on, can't you give me a little hint?"

Malia flashed Kavena a mysterious smile before finishing her tea and standing up. "Anyway, I just can't afford for anything to go wrong right now. Not with the baby on the way."

"Tell Paul first, and then HR," Marissa advised after some thought. "He thinks you're great—he'll absorb the heat, if there is any. So long as you have the details of your maternity leave covered, and he knows that there's somebody covering for you while you're out, he'll definitely be on your side." This was the one thing Marissa knew for certain. It was a relief to know that Paul would probably do the right thing by Malia, even if he couldn't do it by Marissa. "Paul just needs to know things will be okay."

Malia nodded. "I noticed that about him." She gave Marissa a grateful smile before gathering her things and waving good-bye.

Marissa knew exactly when Malia told Paul, because just at that moment Marissa's iPhone began to ring. She had replaced Paul's profile picture with an unflattering image of Homer Simpson drooling in his underwear, and it always made her laugh. She decided to ignore Paul's call, and continued to read the newspaper.

Less than a minute later, the house phone rang and, having turned over the last page of the newspaper, Marissa decided to answer it.

"Hello?"

"Marissa, tell me my secretary did not just come in and announce that she's pregnant AND living in my house."

"If you're thinking that I got her pregnant, I can assure you that our relationship is strictly landlord and tenant."

"Very funny. And what about our top masseuse renting the *ohana* unit? You know that's supposed to be my home office."

"Good point. And since this is no longer your home, it is therefore no longer your home office."

"Where are my things?"

"In the garage, growing mildew. So unfortunate, this wet Waimea weather we've been having."

"Marissa, that's not funny!"

Having Paul so agitated was putting Marissa in a good mood. "Paul, there's something else you should know," she said solemnly.

"What?" She could hear the dread in his voice.

"Your CFO, Bob, has the room overlooking the front yard."

"*What?!*"

Marissa cracked a smile. "Oh, take it easy. A woman named Jane Crisp has that room." No sense in telling him that she owned Kava Java. Marissa still liked her weekly updates on whether or not Paul or Angela were going there, despite Jane's reluctance to tell her. "They're all women, except for Kavena's son, Isaiah. Pansy loves it."

Paul let out a heavy breath. "Marissa, I really don't think it's a good idea."

"What? Oh, you mean having two Kohala Bay employees living here?"

"Exactly! I need to have boundaries between me and the people who work for me."

"Wow, Paul, I couldn't agree more. How's Angela?" Her voice wavered slightly, but she knew Paul couldn't hear it.

There was a stunned silence. "Marissa . . ."

Not wanting to hear his lame excuses, Marissa continued. "And if you must know, I had no idea Malia would be renting the room. I did it as a favor for Tom."

"Tom? Who's Tom?"

"Pansy's riding instructor. Malia's a family friend and she needed a temporary place to stay. Tom's been so great with Pansy that it was the least I could do."

Marissa knew Pansy had raved about Tom to Paul. "I don't know about this guy . . ." Paul said darkly.

"Tom's great," Marissa said resolutely. "Pansy is an amazing rider. In fact, you should come watch her someday. Maybe after you come back from Honolulu?"

"How did you . . . That's what I mean, Marissa! *Bound-aries*. Malia shouldn't have told you . . ."

"Told me what?" Marissa asked innocently. "*You* told Pansy yesterday that you would be gone for a few days to Honolulu."

They both knew she was playing him. "Fine," Paul said flatly. "I can't win. I never can. Why is that, Marissa?"

Maybe because we're supposed to be on the same team, Marissa thought. *I'm not winning either.* Instead she said, "I'm thinking of having a garage sale in a couple of weeks and I'd be happy to put your stuff up for sale. You might even get a whole dollar for everything. Island prices, you know how it goes."

"Just leave it!" Paul ordered, incensed. "Do *not* sell my things for a dollar, Marissa. I mean it!"

He hung up the phone, leaving a smiling Marissa on the other end.

"Try this." Jane handed Marissa a cup carved from a coconut shell.

Marissa sniffed it suspiciously. It definitely wasn't coffee. "Is this what you've been doing for the past week? Stinking up my kitchen with this concoction?"

"First, it doesn't stink. It's just taken me a while to get it right, and I haven't had a chance to throw out the batches that didn't work. Second, you've been under stress and need to relax. This will help."

"And this is . . . ?"

"Kava. The great green hope. It's a medicinal herb that Hawaiians and other islanders have used for thousands of years. I'm working on a couple of proprietary blends but I haven't found a recipe I'm excited about yet." Jane handed a cup to Kavena, who accepted it reverently. "Sorry, Malia. I don't know if it's contraindicated for pregnancy but I don't want to find out. So it's still ginger tea for you."

"No complaints here," Malia said. She was starting to show more and her morning sickness had finally abated. Ginger had become a staple in her diet.

It was a Sunday, and all the women were off. Pansy and Isaiah were playing in the backyard.

Kavena drank hers in one gulp and handed the empty cup back to Jane with two hands. "Wow," she said. "I think that's probably the best kava I've ever had. And I've had some pretty good kava."

Jane smiled. "Thanks," she said, and downed her cup as well.

The women turned and looked at Marissa. With all eyes on her, she took a tentative sip. The watery liquid was lukewarm and bitter. Marissa made a face. "It's peppery and bitter."

"Bottoms up," Kavena suggested. "Otherwise you won't receive the full benefits."

"What, is this supposed to make me high or something?"

"Spoken like a woman who has never been high," Kavena said dryly. It was true. "And I can only hope that, with each day that passes, you learn to embrace all that this island has to offer. In the meantime, just drink it."

Marissa shook her head. "I'm going to Kona, remember?" She held up the list of supplies Kavena wanted her to get from Home Depot. The house was low on groceries as well so Marissa was going to restock at the large Safeway and Costco. "I don't want to feel dopey on the drive down."

"You won't feel dopey," Jane promised. She took Marissa's cup and began to search through the cabinets. She found a thermos and began pouring the drink inside. "Just take it down with you. I wouldn't give it to you if I thought it was unsafe."

"This is one time when you can drink and drive," Kavena added. She gave a happy sigh. "Ooh, it's kicking in. I don't think there's anything you can say now that will upset me, Marissa. Go on, try." Kavena grinned.

Marissa stood up, reaching for her purse. "Sorry, but I'm all out. Maybe later." She glanced at the shopping list. "I'll pick up some things for dinner. What about a roast chicken and a salad? I'll pick up a loaf of garlic bread, too."

"I'll pass on the bread," Malia said.

Marissa crossed garlic bread off her list. "I forgot garlic makes you nauseous. What about sweet potatoes? I saw a recipe on the Food Network for mashed sweet potatoes . . ."

"Keep it simple," Jane advised Marissa. "It's just us."

"Really," Kavena said, smiling sweetly. "Don't overdo it. Besides, I haven't seen you cook since I've moved in."

"I cook!" Marissa responded hotly. "It's just that it's been crazy with everyone moving in and all of you are such good cooks and always offering to make dinner . . ."

Kavena was giggling. "Marissa, I don't think a single knife has been used from that thousand dollar Wüsthof knife block until we came along."

Jane was pouring more kava into the thermos but Marissa could see the familiar shake of her shoulders. She was laughing. Even Malia had a small smile tugging at the corners of her mouth.

Marissa fumed. "It was a wedding present!"

Jane handed Marissa the thermos and ushered her out the door. "Give it a few minutes to kick in," she advised. She quickly closed the door but not before Marissa heard the women burst out in laughter.

Okay, so maybe Marissa was still a bit tightly wound these days. She had been working on letting go, and if her housemates knew what she had been like in New York, they'd have to agree that Marissa had come pretty far. She deserved some credit. After all, it was only April. They had moved to Hawaii last December, Paul had moved out in February, and here she was, only two months later. *What did they expect?* Marissa wondered indignantly as she pulled the Audi out of the driveway.

Black lava rock and dry terrain flashed past as she headed down to Kona on Highway 190. From where she was, Marissa could see the variations in color among the different lava flows that had occurred hundreds of years ago. Despite the large expanse of lava rock, new life had found a way through. Bursts of greenery appeared in the oddest of places. From her vantage point on the highway, Marissa could look down the mountain and see the ocean, shimmering turquoise and aqua blues. The water was so clear Marissa could see the coral reefs just below the surface.

Marissa glanced at the thermos next to her. Maybe she had only been on the Big Island for five months, but Kavena's words rang true. There was still so much about Hawaii that Marissa had yet to discover and appreciate. Last weekend, it was Jane and Malia who finally coaxed Marissa to join them at the beach, taking the kids while Kavena was at work. Marissa had stayed on the blanket, watching everyone from under the shade of the palm tree. It wasn't the resort, that was true, but the aquamarine water was just as beautiful and the sand smooth and white. Two turtles were sunbathing on the beach, oblivious to the people around them who were respectfully keeping their distance.

Her life had turned upside down since her arrival, but in truth she could have been anywhere: New York, San Francisco, Seattle. Anywhere other than Hawaii. She had her blinders on, so absorbed in her own problems that she hadn't taken a moment to look around her. She had pretty much ignored the fact that she was living in one of the most beautiful and breathtaking places in the world.

Paradise.

So Paul had been right, she admitted grudgingly to herself. They were living in paradise and Marissa hadn't a clue.

Well, that was going to change.

She spun off the top of the thermos. Taking a deep breath, she took a sip.

Nothing. Just the same bitter aftertaste she'd had at the house. Maybe she needed to drink more.

Keeping one eye on the road, Marissa downed the contents of the thermos and put the lid back on.

Still nothing.

Great, she thought. She felt on the verge of tears. *Of course it wouldn't work for me. In fact,* nothing *works for me. It's a sign, a sign that I'm not supposed to be here. Everyone else gets to have their big Hawaii experience, everyone except . . .*

Marissa's tongue started to tingle. And then the entire inside of her mouth went numb.

Marissa slowly became aware of the music that had been playing in her car, of her driving, of her environment. She felt her shoulders relax without her having to tell them to relax. A wave of well-being overcame her.

In Kona, Marissa took her time walking the aisles of Home Depot, smiling at everyone she passed and feeling a rush of warmth when people smiled back. People *were* friendlier here, there was no doubt about that. Why couldn't people be like this everywhere? She lovingly selected the roof cement, shingles, rust-resistant screws, and chalk line per Kavena's list. *All world leaders should drink kava,* Marissa thought as she blissfully stood in line, waiting to check out. *That would bring about world peace.*

She had so much to be thankful for. Pansy. Even Paul. If it wasn't for him, Marissa wouldn't be experiencing so many new things. Her housemates, for example. If he hadn't moved out, there wouldn't have been a need for her to find tenants. And not just any tenants—these women were amazing and funny, and they put up with Marissa's idiosyncrasies. They all knew she was trying to fix the house so she and Pansy could move back to New York, and they were more than happy to help. With Kavena's do-it-yourself knowledge, Malia's local contacts, and Jane's penchant for negotiation with contractors, the house was transforming before Marissa's very eyes. Jenny wouldn't even recognize the house when she saw it next.

Marissa's next stop was the grocery store in Kona, which was much larger than the one in Waimea. Marissa hummed to herself as she got a shopping cart. She could afford to spend a little extra on dinner tonight. That had been the big eye-opener last night, when she was paying her bills. Now that she was no longer living in New York—no longer living on the mainland, actually—she was away from her normal temptations. In the old days, she had managed stress through retail therapy, but with no place to really shop in Waimea, shopping had no longer been a viable option.

But Marissa found that owning less stuff, as well as spending less, actually worked. Even though she was still doing takeout for some of her and Pansy's meals, it was nothing compared to what she used to spend on a single dinner in the city. She wasn't pulling in the kind of money she had made in New York—far from it!—but she wasn't spending as much either. Marissa found that her anxiety around money had abated—spending less was helping them make the most of the dollars they did have.

Those self-help gurus were onto something after all, she murmured to herself.

And then there was Paul. Paul had returned from Honolulu and shown up unexpectedly the next day, catching Pansy in a bear hug and then opening the trunk of his car to reveal a clean but used rubber tire. With the help of Isaiah,

the three of them hoisted a rope around a branch and suddenly there was a tire swing. But that wasn't all. Paul had
then returned the next day, despite Marissa reminding him
that she would appreciate a phone call first. Kavena had vehemently agreed in the background, until Paul revealed a
second, smaller tire that he hung up on another branch of
the tree.

For Isaiah.

Since then, Kavena had been strangely quiet about voic-
ing her opinions on Paul or Angela, much to Marissa's an-
noyance. Jane was a diplomat, and also the veteran of a
happy marriage, and refused to take sides. Malia was torn,
liking Paul but suspicious of Angela, and still feeling
bruised from her own recent abandonment.

Which left Marissa alone in her ranting.

And, truthfully, she knew Paul hadn't brought the second
tire to butter up Kavena, though that was certainly the result. Marissa knew from the look on his face that it made
Paul happy to see Pansy happy, to see Isaiah happy. He
probably hadn't given it a second thought.

She had been dragging her feet about calling a lawyer.
Surely that meant something. Clearly Marissa didn't want
to put the wheels in motion. Maybe, just maybe, she didn't
want out. Maybe she still loved Paul.

That single thought made Marissa stop in her tracks.
She still loved Paul.

It had to be the kava, she figured. Maybe it had relaxed
her to the point that she was able to see things clearly.
Marissa had been getting in her own way, letting her stub-
bornness rule her heart. *I'm going to call him,* she decided. *I'm
going to call him and tell him that I still love him.*

She heard Paul's laugh and found herself smiling. She
loved the sound of his laugh. She missed it.

This stuff is good, she thought, and started to push her cart again. *It's almost as if he's here with me.*

But when Marissa turned the corner of the canned goods aisle, her sense of peace disappeared and was replaced with disbelief.

It *was* Paul. With Angela and a boy who was obviously her son.

Marissa jerked her cart back, ducking behind a display of Spam luncheon meat, her heart beating furiously in her chest. They were no more than twenty feet away, but they hadn't seen her.

"What about pasta?" Angela was saying. She was casually dressed, her wavy red hair cascading down her back. Full makeup. "We could go to the refrigerated section and pick up some tortellini."

Paul shook his head. "No, no. Linguine and clams is my specialty. I have that recipe *down*." He began to look through the packages of linguine. Marissa knew he was searching for his favorite brand.

Barilla, Marissa thought silently as she watched Paul pull a package of Barilla linguine off the shelf in triumph. It was the only dish he knew how to make, but he was right—he had mastered it, and it was delicious. She couldn't remember the last time Paul had cooked linguine and clams for her. She felt a pang of envy as she watched Paul pull another package off the shelf.

A shopper came up behind Marissa and looked at her impatiently. What happened to birds singing and everyone smiling around her? Marissa began to fill her shopping cart with cans of Spam as she motioned for the shopper to go around her.

"You cook, too?" Angela was teasing. "I thought you were doing the bachelor thing. Pizza and hot dogs for dinner."

"That, too," Paul said with a grin. He gave Angela's son a nudge. What was his name? *Chris.* "I'll leave it to you: linguine and clams or pizza and hot dogs?"

"That's easy," Chris said with a grin. "Pizza and hot dogs."

Paul laughed. "My other specialty. Lucky for you, I happen to have all those things at home already."

"What about a bottle of red wine?" Angela asked coquettishly.

Paul put the linguine back on the shelf. "I'm shocked you even have to ask."

"I still want my pasta dinner," Angela pouted.

Chris rolled his eyes, embarrassed by his mother. Paul just laughed. "Some other time," he said.

Marissa watched as they headed toward the exit, Angela teasing while Paul and Chris laughed.

Marissa felt panic welling up inside of her. What was this? Paul playing family with somebody else's family?

Not wanting to run into them in the parking lot, Marissa went to the checkout lane farthest away from the exit. There was a hard knot in her stomach. She squeezed her eyes shut, willing herself not to cry.

"What in goddess's name happened here?" Kavena stared dumbstruck at the four brown bags full of the Spam luncheon meat. She started pulling out the rectangular tins, one after another. "Regular Spam, Spam Lite, Turkey Spam, Low-Salt Spam, Spam and Garlic, Spam and Cheese, Spam with Bacon . . ."

Marissa's eyes were still red from having cried all the way home. "I didn't know what happened until I got to the checkout lane," she sniffed. "And by then it was too late."

Jane peered into the bag. "You didn't get anything else?"

Marissa shook her head.

Malia hefted a couple of the rectangular tins in her hands like weights. "My uncle would *love* you," she said.

"Is he single? Because it looks like I'm going to be back on the market soon." Wadded-up tissues were in a pile around Marissa's feet. She lowered her voice so the kids, who were playing in Pansy's room, couldn't hear. "You should have seen how happy he looked! It was like they were . . . a family. So where does that leave Pansy and me?"

Malia was the first one to speak, her voice low and apologetic. "Maybe you should just focus on doing what's best for you and Pansy."

"Why? Do you know something?" Marissa looked at her.

Malia looked uncomfortable. Kavena gave her a nudge and Malia said reluctantly, "Well, um, she spends a lot of time in Paul's office, and they go out to lunch pretty regularly."

Jane frowned and quickly added, "But that doesn't necessarily mean anything . . ."

Both Kavena and Malia gave Jane a knowing look. "And he put your picture away," Malia said. She looked uncomfortable, clearly not enjoying this. "The one that he used to keep on his desk? It was there until a couple of weeks ago. It's not there anymore."

Marissa felt faint. He still kept her picture on his desk? She knew the one: it was the black-and-white picture of her from their wedding day. The photographer had snapped it when Marissa was gazing out the window, waiting until it was time to walk down the aisle toward Paul. He always said it was his favorite picture.

Was.

Kavena gave Malia another insistent nudge.

"Okay, okay!" Malia looked at Kavena, exasperated. "Stop pushing the pregnant lady!" She turned to Marissa, her voice apologetic. "I did something. I was caught off guard, and I just responded without thinking. It must be from the hormones; I'm not normally like that."

"What?"

"She was hanging around my desk last week, making all sorts of innuendos about how she hoped you were holding up all right, and how it must be hard for you now that Paul has moved on. I just got so mad that I told her that you were doing just fine, and that you had made a lot of new friends . . ." Malia trailed off, looking suddenly nervous.

"Go on," Kavena said impatiently. Jane threw up her hands and turned to put the groceries away.

". . . a lot of new friends," Malia repeated. "Like Tom." She was instantly apologetic. "I don't get into other people's business, you know that, but I'm pregnant and my hormones are all over the place . . ."

"Nice try," Kavena said, clucking her disapproval. "And, by the way, I *know* you're the one who's been eating all my macadamia nut bars."

"They're not for me, they're for the baby," Malia said. She turned her attention back to Marissa. "Anyway, I could tell it threw her off. I hope this hasn't caused a problem, Marissa." She looked worried.

Marissa looked away, a feeling of helplessness and finality overcoming her. "There was a much bigger problem before you said anything, Malia. And thanks for having my back. I appreciate it. I think at this point I just need to move forward." She gathered all of her used tissues and threw them in the trash.

They could hear Pansy and Isaiah walking down the hall into the living room, probably to play on the GameCube. Not only had Kavena allowed Isaiah to play on occasion, but she had also been caught playing a few rounds of Mario Kart when she thought no one was home.

Jane nodded toward the living room. Whenever the kids were within earshot, the women had made it an unspoken policy not to talk about Paul. "Now, we need to start thinking dinner because I'm starving and looking at a helluva lot of Spam and not much else."

Kavena headed toward the back door. "I can't eat this stuff. You'd think by now they'd come up with a vegan Spam or something . . . I'm going to my place and grabbing some granola. I'll be right back."

"Suit yourself," Jane said mildly, choosing a few cans and walking them to the stove. "I know there's leftover rice and pasta, some black beans, tortilla chips, a couple of tomatoes and a bunch of green onions . . . this could be ugly, but I'm willing to give it a try."

"I thought you women were supposed to be gourmet cooks." Malia walked to the stove and held out her hand. "This is Spam 101. Move over and let me show you how it's done."

Jane handed Malia the spatula. "Be my guest." She settled into a chair next to Marissa and put her feet up. "So has anyone heard the latest news? The volcano is on the move again. All the tourists are coming into the Kava Java and talking about it. It's supposedly pretty spectacular. You don't have to hike very far in to see it."

Kavena returned to the kitchen, a large glass container under her arm. "That's what you need!" she exclaimed. She rummaged in the cupboards for bowls. "A trip to see Madame Pele. Obviously she hasn't thrown you back to the mainland yet, so it's probably relatively safe for you to go."

"I don't know . . ." Marissa thought back with a lurching stomach to the helicopter ride. "Maybe. But it's not like she's welcomed me with open arms, either."

Kavena raised an eyebrow. "Pele doesn't play hostess, Marissa. But if she didn't like you, you'd know. Trust me."

Half an hour later, Malia placed a steaming platter on the table in front of the women. "Spambalaya. With my compliments."

Jane served herself and Pansy while Isaiah made a face at the bowl of granola in front of him. "Sorry, honey," Jane told him as he looked longingly at the Spambalaya.

"Look, Isaiah, yum!" Kavena took a spoonful of her granola and tried to look gleeful. "Delicious!"

Isaiah wasn't fooled until Pansy momentarily pushed her dinner aside, reached for the granola, and began eating a bowl herself. This seemed to do the trick and Isaiah quickly followed suit.

Marissa took a bite of the Spambalaya and was surprised by how good it tasted. She'd been so upset at seeing Paul with Angela that she hadn't had anything to eat since leaving the house that morning.

Jane was chewing her food thoughtfully. "Shoot, I hate to admit it, but this stuff's pretty good."

Malia sat down and helped herself to a small serving of Spambalaya. "Oh, I've forgotten how good this is," she murmured with a sigh. She polished it off and then reluctantly reached for the jar of Kavena's granola. "I need the fiber," she said, then added hesitatingly, "It's for the baby."

"That's what we all say," Kavena said, digging her spoon into her granola with a heavy sigh. "Motherhood's a blessing, but the constipation sucks."

A peel of laughter broke out around the table. Marissa looked at the women, her heart swelling in gratitude for her new friends. To have so much friendship and joy under one roof was a blessing—Marissa knew that, and she could actually feel it in her body. For the first time in a long time she felt genuinely happy.

It was time to stop living in the past and start enjoying the present, maybe even start focusing on her future. But moving forward was going to be difficult if she kept putting her energy into fighting with Paul. He had moved on—it was time she did as well. Maybe they would be one of those couples that got along better as friends.

The table erupted in laughter again, and Marissa made a mental note to call the divorce lawyer in the morning. She wanted to get the paperwork going so she could start living again.

'umi | ten

"Mom, I'm really going to need my own gear soon," Pansy was saying as they walked toward the stables, hand in hand. "At least my own boots and helmet."

Marissa sighed. Back in New York, she wouldn't have given another thought to anything Pansy needed—school supplies, ballet slippers, an expensive costume she'd only wear once. But now Marissa was reluctant to spend her money on something that would probably be gathering dust in a few months. It was unlikely that Pansy would continue riding once they returned to New York.

The divorce lawyer had been polite, asking an hour's worth of questions and promising to have the Third Circuit Family Court send the divorce paperwork for Marissa to look through. "Eighty percent of the people who begin divorce proceedings go through with the divorce," he told her. He was casually dressed in khakis and a short-sleeved aloha shirt, his long gray hair in need of a haircut. "I just like to advise my clients to look at the paperwork carefully before they start checking boxes and filling in blanks."

Even though Marissa was fairly sure it wouldn't be a contestable divorce, she was shocked to learn that both she and Paul would be expected to sit through parenting classes as part of Hawaii's requirements. Her lawyer assured her that it would still be much easier than trying to get a divorce in New York, which would certainly be astronomical in terms of attorney's fees. He said this right before his secretary handed Marissa an invoice and waited expectantly for payment. New York or Hawaii, this wasn't going to be fun.

But Marissa wasn't interested in fun—she was interested in freedom. No more fights, no more games, no more emotional roller-coaster rides. She had Pansy, she had Kate in New York, and she had her housemates here. She didn't need Paul. She didn't need romance, she didn't need men. She didn't need any of it—not anymore.

"Dad!" Pansy released Marissa's hand and shot ahead.

Marissa's eyes followed her daughter as she ran toward a figure leaning against the gate of the corral. *Paul.* Marissa wanted to bolt and head in the opposite direction, but she forced herself to keep moving forward, her stride uninterrupted.

"Are you staying to watch me ride?" Pansy was asking excitedly, catching her father in a hug.

"Do you see me standing here?" Paul planted himself firmly on the ground with a smile, his hands on his hips.

Pansy grinned. "Yes!" Her smile revealed a gap in her mouth. One last tooth had finally made its way out the night before.

"You lost a tooth?" Paul asked, pretending to inspect her mouth.

Pansy kept her mouth open wide. "Laff nigh."

"Tooth Fairy come?"

"I gah high hollers." Pansy closed her mouth. "I got five dollars."

"Five dollars!" Paul looked impressed. Marissa saw him glance at her out of the corner of his eye. "Sounds like the Tooth Fairy's feeling generous."

"I'm going to save it to buy some riding boots and a helmet. And I'd really like some riding pants, too."

"Well, maybe you should write to Santa Claus."

Pansy rolled her eyes. "Dad, I don't believe in Santa Claus anymore. Only the Tooth Fairy is real. And the Easter Bunny."

"Shoot. Now you know." Paul snapped his fingers in disappointment.

Kaui came out from the tack room and waved to Pansy.

"Dad, I have to go to work. Just wait here, okay? Don't go anywhere!"

"Do you see me standing here?" Paul asked again. "I'm not going anywhere. In fact, I think my shoes are stuck in the mud."

Marissa finally found her voice. "That's not mud," she said and followed Pansy into the tack room.

Tom was in the side office, looking through a catalog. He had his reading glasses on, which made him look both serious and scholarly. He looked up and smiled, then reached into his minifridge and pulled out bottled water for both of them, something that was becoming a regular ritual. Marissa knew he didn't offer water to any of the other parents and generally asked students to bring their own.

Marissa unscrewed the lid and took a sip. "Tom, you should know that the man standing outside is Pansy's father. I had no idea he was coming. In fact, I'm not really sure why he's here."

Tom arched an eyebrow as he took a quick look out the door. He pulled off his glasses and stood up. "To see his daughter ride would be my guess."

"Well, yes, I know. I'm just saying that in all the three months we've been taking lessons, this is the first time he's chosen to come down."

"It'll be fine," Tom told her. He touched her shoulder, giving it a reassuring squeeze. "I'll go out and say hi."

Marissa knew better than to try to convince him otherwise. She watched nervously as Tom walked over and introduced himself to Paul. Paul visibly stiffened as they shook hands. Marissa wished she could crawl under a bale of hay and hide until he was gone, but then she saw Tom point to the bench where a horse blanket had already been laid out on the bench for Marissa. To her chagrin, Paul walked over and sat down. In *her* spot. On *her* bench.

Pansy was leading a horse into the riding ring, beaming and waving to Paul then turning to search for Marissa. Knowing that she had little choice, Marissa headed toward the bench, her legs somehow managing to carry her across the yard until she was standing in front of Paul.

"That's my spot," she said, feeling immediately foolish as she said the words.

Absently, Paul moved over to make room, his eyes still on Pansy. "Wow, she's pretty good at handling those horses."

"I know." Marissa saw Tom watching her out of the corner of her eye and knew a hissy fit probably wouldn't become her. Reluctantly, she sat down. "Pansy's a natural. Tom says she has great horse handling skills."

"Does he now?" She could detect a slight edge in his voice.

"He does."

"Well, good for her." Paul kept his eyes on his daughter. "I'm glad she didn't inherit the Holiday Inn gene." He was referring to their failed trail ride in Colorado.

The comment caught Marissa off guard, her resentment replaced by a wry smile. "I think it skips a generation."

There was a long pause before Paul cleared his throat, keeping his eyes on the ring. "So that's Tom," he finally said.

"That's Tom."

"Do you know how long he's been doing this? Did you check his references before she started?"

"Paul, come on. He's great." Marissa took a sip of water as she watched Pansy return with another horse and take instruction from Tom about tapping the horse's knee to offer Pansy its foot. "Pansy is in good hands. You have nothing to worry about."

Paul didn't say anything, silently watching Pansy as she started scraping at a horseshoe, laughing as she talked with Kaui.

During the group lesson, Marissa knew that Tom had given Pansy a chance to show off a bit, allowing her to gallop through the pasture and even master a low jump. She forced herself not to ask Paul why he was here in the middle of an afternoon of a workday. But she let her eyes drop to his left hand, and that's when she noticed that he was no longer wearing his wedding band.

Marissa felt a stab of anguish, and berated herself for looking. Why did it even matter? She had vowed to move forward, and yet here she was, sitting next to Paul, frozen as she stared at his bare ring finger.

Tom walked over as the students dismounted and led their horses back to the stables. Marissa didn't know if he had noticed the stricken look on her face, but she felt Tom slow his pace as he neared them, undoubtedly noticing that Paul was starting to bristle.

"Your daughter did great out there," he said simply to both of them.

Marissa smiled and said, "Thanks," but Paul just made a noncommittal sound, his jaw set.

Tom didn't seem to notice. He turned to Marissa and asked, "Do you have a **moment?**"

"Sure." Marissa knew Paul was watching her as she stood up and met up with Tom a few steps away, just out of earshot.

Tom's cowboy hat was slanted over his eyes, and he pushed it back so Marissa could see his entire face. The day was bright, however, and he squinted as he glanced toward Paul, then looked out at the mountains.

Tom cleared his throat. He actually looked a bit nervous, which Marissa found amusing. It wasn't like Tom to look nervous. "Listen, I know this is probably not a good time, but Malia mentioned to me that you were planning to go to Volcanoes National Park sometime soon."

"Yes," Marissa said. She had decided that Kavena was right: a visit was definitely in order. "I was thinking about going in the next couple of weeks. Just for one night, to see the sights. Malia offered to watch Pansy while I'm gone."

"Well, I've been meaning to go out there myself. It's been a while, and I thought it would be a good time to go since the lava's flowing. I thought maybe we could go together, unless you were thinking that you needed to make the trip on your own, which I would completely understand."

Marissa hesitated, unclear if they were still in friend territory or going someplace new. If it was the latter, it opened up a whole new set of issues, and Marissa wasn't sure she wanted to go there yet. Besides, she was hardly his type and doubted that their harmless flirtations were anything more than that.

But he was good-looking. And nice. And obviously in excellent physical condition, not that it mattered to Marissa. After all, they were just friends.

But then she made the mistake of looking at Paul and her eyes went straight to his bare ring finger. Marissa felt a pang of remorse, and then immediately berated herself. Why was she trying to be the pious wife? Sure, she had taken her ring off first but it had been Paul's idea to separate, not hers.

Paul was pretending to look straight ahead but Marissa could see he was trying to eavesdrop while watching them out of the corner of his eye.

Tom leaned in closer, and Marissa smelled a musky aftershave mixed with sweat and grass—a completely masculine, rugged smell. Her breath caught as he gave her a sly smile, turning on the charm full blast to reveal a sexy, seductive Tom she wasn't aware existed.

And then he winked.

Marissa smiled to herself. So that was it. He wasn't asking her out on a date. He was coming to her rescue, showing Paul that Marissa also had a life.

"That would be great," she said, mustering as much enthusiasm as she could. "I hadn't decided on the weekend yet, but I want to go soon since the flow could go underground again at anytime."

"I'm open," Tom said. "Just tell me when."

"I'll check with Malia to see what will work for her. I know she's trying to get a lot done at work before she goes on maternity leave. But now that I think of it . . ." Marissa turned and looked directly at Paul, who had clearly overhead parts of their conversation and was now glowering. "Paul," Marissa called nonchalantly, "can Pansy stay with you next weekend?"

Paul balked. "I don't know . . . I'd have to check my schedule—it's a busy time at the resort right—"

"Great," Marissa said. She turned back to face Tom, just as he reached over to tuck a lock of stray hair behind Marissa's ear, causing a little shiver to run down her spine. *God, he was good.* "Next weekend would be wonderful. What can I do to help with the plans?"

"Nothing. I'll take care of everything." Tom lingered a moment, his eyes on Marissa, before tipping his hat to her and then to Paul. He turned and strode back to the office.

Paul's face looked red as Pansy bounded toward him, her friend Kaui in tow. "Dad! I want you to meet my friend Kaui. She's the one I keep telling you about."

"Hi, Mr. Price." Kaui held out her hand.

Paul reluctantly turned his attention back to the girls. "Hi, Kaui," Paul said distractedly, shaking her hand. "Do you go to Hawaii Day School with Pansy?"

"No, I'm homeschooled."

"Isn't that cool?" Pansy gushed.

"Very. Well, I should probably get going, Pans." Paul stood up, brushing off his slacks.

Pansy's face fell. "Already?"

"You're going to do a sleepover at Dad's next weekend," Marissa told her, before Paul could protest.

"Really?" Pansy looked ecstatic.

Paul shot Marissa a dirty look that she hoped the girls didn't see, then turned back to Pansy, who was beaming. "Um, really." He turned his back on Marissa, clearly pissed. "I have a few minutes before I need to head back. Do you want to go for a shave ice, Pansy?"

Pansy was bouncing on her toes, unable to contain her happiness. "Can we invite Kaui?"

"Sure. Just ask her parents first," Paul said. The two girls ran off in search of Kaui's mother. He didn't turn around to look at Marissa. "I'll bring her home within the hour," he said flatly.

"Whatever works for you." Marissa headed toward the office.

Tom was reclined in his chair, talking on the phone. "Hold on a second," he said when he saw Marissa. He covered the mouthpiece. "Heading out?"

"My work here is done." Marissa couldn't stop grinning. "Tom, thank you for everything just now. Really. Pansy, the whole volcano thing . . ."

"Anytime."

"Paul was seeing red. He *was* red. You were so convincing, I had to remind myself that you were just acting."

Tom held the phone against his chest and beckoned her to come closer, as if he had a secret.

"What?" Marissa edged toward him.

"Closer."

She leaned toward him until her face was almost next to his. "Okay. What?"

The next few words were whispered in her ear. "It wasn't an act, Marissa."

And then he kissed her.

"You kissed him? *You kissed him?*" Both Kavena and Jane had their hands over their mouths.

"He kissed *me*. I didn't see it coming. And then I realized that he was serious. About everything! I thought we were trying to psych Paul out, but by the time I made it to the car, Tom had already booked two rooms with a crater view and made dinner reservations at eight." Marissa was pacing now, in a mild panic.

"Well, obviously you're going to have to call him back and tell him that there's been a mistake," Jane said briskly.

"Why?" Kavena demanded. "Maybe she *should* go. Send the message that she's moving on!"

"Exactly!" Marissa said. "At first I was mortified, but then I thought, what's the harm? My marriage is over. Paul's moved on. What am I waiting for?"

"Your marriage is *not* over!" Jane said vehemently. "If you want to start dating, at least have the decency to file the paperwork first! It's too soon, Marissa. I don't want you to do something you're going to regret later."

At that moment, Malia flew through the door, cell phone in hand. "I just heard!" she said breathlessly. "This is so great!"

Marissa stared at her. "What are you talking about?"

"*You and Tom.* I knew he was interested, but I thought that maybe you'd get back together with Paul, so I told him to wait a bit, but he just told me that you two are going away for a weekend."

"As friends . . ." Marissa tried to clarify.

"Friends who kiss," Kavena corrected her.

"You *kissed*?!" Malia was beaming. "Marissa, you don't understand how huge this is! The man doesn't even *date*. One of the most eligible bachelors on the island, huge trust fund . . ."

The three women gaped at Malia, who had opened the lid to a container full of Kavena's homemade macadamia nut bars. "Trust fund?" they repeated in unison.

"Come on. Tom Oakes? The Oakes family? Pualani Stables, as in Pualani *Ranch*?" Malia reached in and took a square, closing her eyes as she took a bite. "God, I've been craving this all day. Can I take some extra bars to work tomorrow?"

Kavena waved her hand impatiently in accession. "Stay on topic. Are you talking about *the* Pualani Ranch? As in the one surrounding the town of Waimea and half of the island?"

Jane felt for a chair and sat down heavily. "Mercy," she said.

"None of you knew?" Malia looked from woman to woman, surprised. "He's on the list every year. One of Hawaii's richest men, one of our island's most eligible bachelors . . ."

"Well, we're not exactly in the market so I can see how we would have missed this," Jane said. "Of course, now that you've told us, it's obvious."

"What?" Marissa wanted to know. "What's obvious?"

"Tom," Kavena said, fanning herself and Jane with a newspaper. "The Oakes are an old *kama'aina* ranching family of Hawaii. Which now makes sense why the two of you know each other." Kavena looked at Malia. "I have to say I couldn't quite get how your brother and he were such good friends, but this explains everything."

"They were classmates at Punahou," Malia said. "And then roommates at UH Manoa. Our families have a long history together: our grandfathers used to run cows together. A lot of women are interested, but Tom likes to pretend that he's too busy to get involved. Which is why this is *completely* unprecedented. He really likes you, Marissa." She polished off the rest of the macadamia nut bar, a satisfied look on her face.

Jane gave Marissa a pointed look. "Marissa . . ." she started, a hint of warning in her voice.

Marissa glanced at the clock, then back at the ecstatic face of Malia and the pale faces of Jane and Kavena. Paul would be dropping Pansy off soon and she didn't want Pansy to overhear any of this.

"Look, Tom is an adult, and I am an adult. He knows I'm separated but not divorced. He may be one of the richest men in Hawaii"—Marissa felt a little faint just thinking about it—"but he's also Pansy's riding instructor and I don't want to botch things up for her. I don't see why we just can't be two friends who go to Volcano. He got two rooms, after all."

"I don't think this a good idea," Jane said, shaking her head. "You should call him and cancel."

"No," Marissa said firmly. "I want to go to Volcano, Tom

wants to go to Volcano. We're going to Volcano." She was determined to see the flow this time.

Jane looked at Malia, slightly accusatory. "I thought you said you made a point of not getting into other people's business. What about all that talk about the vault?"

Malia didn't look at all guilty. "Oh, the vault," she said dismissively, as if she had only a vague idea of what Jane was talking about. "It must be the hormones." She turned to look eagerly at Marissa. "So, how was it? How was the kiss?"

How was it? Marissa realized with a shock that she actually couldn't say. "Um . . ."

The women looked at her expectantly. Marissa strained to remember. Stables . . . Paul . .. Volcano . . . Paul . . . telephone . . . Paul . . .

Tom's lips had touched hers—she was sure of that. She would have remembered if it had been a bad kiss, which she was sure it hadn't been. He just didn't look like a bad kisser. No tongue. But beyond that, everything seemed a bit hazy. "I don't really remember," she finally confessed.

The women stared at her, confused. "What?"

Marissa sighed. "I don't remember what it felt like exactly. It happened so fast. I was distracted—Pansy was outside, Paul was there . . ."

There was a sharp intake of breath from her friends.

"Well, that's *not* a good sign," Kavena said, pursing her lips.

Jane looked relieved. "I really want to go on record—*again*—as saying that I think this is a terrible idea. Even if you're serious about this divorce, you need to give yourself some time. A few months. Years, if possible."

Marissa was appalled. "I'm not waiting until I'm fifty to start dating!"

"There is nothing wrong with fifty!" Jane shot back. "Many women reach their sexual peak at fifty!"

Malia was frowning. "I don't want to see Tom get hurt, Marissa. He's the closest thing I have to a brother since Kai died."

Marissa heard Paul's car pull into the driveway. "I know," she said, heading toward the front door. "He knows what I'm going through, and we'll just take things one step at a time. Don't worry."

The weather in Volcano was rainy and misty. At four thousand feet, it was colder than Waimea. A chill swept through the truck and Tom turned on the heat.

"I didn't bring any rain gear," Marissa said, staring out the window of Tom's truck as the windshield wipers cut through the rain and fog. "The last time I was here I was up in the air, looking down only when necessary."

"Yeah, Volcano can get pretty wet," Tom said, adjusting the heat. "It shouldn't be any trouble picking something up. I'm sure you're not the only one to come here and find that it's not quite what you were expecting."

"I'm not expecting anything," Marissa lied, her fingers crossed under the jacket in her lap. *Just a torrent of rushing lava or a message written in the sky. One or the other would do.*

Tom had shown up at the house with his truck washed. In all the time Marissa had known him, she had never seen his truck clean. It was usually caked with mud and red dirt. He had been the perfect gentleman, carrying her bags and opening her door, helping her adjust her seat. He had even taken the liberty of picking up two coffees, which were sitting in the cup holders, still steaming. Marissa suspected that her housemates were lurking behind the curtains, watching and no doubt continuing their debate over whether or not this was a good idea.

The original plan had been to drive to Volcano, check in,

grab some dinner and then head straight down the Chain of Craters road where they would hike out to the lava flow so Marissa could finally have her *National Geographic* moment. The next day they would hike the rim of the crater, where Marissa could slip the offering out of her backpack, some 'olelo berries and a bottle of Gordon's gin, since legend had it that Pele liked her gin. There was some controversy over whether or not to leave an offering, so Marissa had decided to do it discreetly, feeling it both important and necessary.

The drive took almost two and a half hours, but time flew by. Marissa entertained Tom with stories of her old life in New York, in particular her escapades with Kate. Tom returned the favor by pointing out sights along the way, giving Marissa a mini history lesson of the Big Island. He even deviated from his professional, ever-appropriate riding instructor demeanor to share bits of gossip about a few high-maintenance students and their even more high-maintenance parents. Listening to Tom recount their unrealistic and even ridiculous requests made Marissa laugh, in part because the parents were so unbelievably demanding and difficult, but also because she was relieved, for once, not to be one of them.

She was enjoying herself so much that she was surprised when they pulled up to the entrance of Volcanoes National Park. It was still pouring down rain, but there was a line of cars waiting their turn to get into the park. Marissa felt her heart rate quicken. She was finally going to see the lava flow. She was finally going to get some answers.

Or not. When the truck finally pulled up to the guard booth, the guard handed them a map and greeted them with the news that the lava flow had changed direction.

"Changed direction?" Tom asked. "Closer or farther away?"

"Neither," the guard said. "Under."

Marissa tried to hide the dismay in her voice. "Under?"

"Yeah, everyone coming through is disappointed. Blame it on the weather: it cooled the lava faster, so it was quicker to form a lava tube. But it's still easy for visitors to step through the newly formed crust. If you still plan to hike out, you have to be careful that you don't fall through and get hurt or burned, or worse. Temperatures can get up to twenty-two-hundred-degrees Fahrenheit."

Hurt or burned. Marissa shuddered. The lava flow no longer seemed idyllic, but menacing and dangerous.

Tom looked at Marissa. "Well, that's too bad. What do you want to do?"

Marissa shrugged, unable to mask her disappointment.

A line was piling up behind Tom, so he thanked the guard and drove into the park, heading for the hotel. "We don't have to stay," he was saying.

"No, no." Marissa thought about the offering in her backpack. "We can still walk around the crater tomorrow. Maybe the weather will be better. The park is still pretty amazing." She halfheartedly waved the map in her hand to prove her point.

Tom gave her an empathetic look. "I know it's not the main event, but you're right. The park *is* pretty amazing. We'll have a good time."

"Absolutely." Marissa forced a grin.

The rain slowed to a dull drizzle. They checked into their individual rooms and then Marissa went to the gift shop and bought a warm fleece. With the slight reprieve in weather, they borrowed the hotel's umbrellas and spent the afternoon walking through Volcano Village, taking in the quaint art galleries and gift shops. They ended up at the Volcano Winery.

As they stood at the glass-covered koa bar, Marissa felt herself unwind as she sipped a wine made from guava and white grapes.

"Would you believe that in all the time I've lived here, I've never been in here?" Tom asked. He expertly swirled the wine around in his glass.

It hadn't escaped Marissa that beneath Tom's simple cowboy demeanor was a man who had been brought up well. "You're kidding," she said. The wine was sweet on her lips.

Tom brought his glass up to his nose. "No, really. I don't socialize much, as you probably guessed. I've gotten pretty used to keeping my own company."

"Are you saying that you never date?" She thought about Malia's words.

Tom looked off in the distance, a boyish smile on his face. "Rarely," he said.

Marissa sipped her wine. "I find that so hard to believe, Tom. Handsome man, good job, great with kids . . . You're the whole package."

He looked back at her, his blue eyes steady. "You think?"

"Absolutely. I still don't understand why you're not married." Marissa grinned when she saw his cheeks redden slightly from embarrassment.

Tom laughed, rubbing his neck. "Now there's a story that'll take ten seconds to tell. I'm surprised Malia didn't say anything."

"Not a word. Besides, she's got an early onset of baby brain. The other day she actually drove to work without her shoes."

"That's Malia, our island girl. Growing up, she didn't wear shoes unless she absolutely had to."

"Don't change the subject," Marissa reprimanded. "I'm on to you."

Tom grinned before settling comfortably against the bar. "I was married once, a long time ago. It didn't take. I met her when I was on the mainland one summer—we got married in City Hall. No frills. Then we came back here and she couldn't stand it. She went back to Washington and the divorce was final by our one-year anniversary." He seemed to be humored by the memory. "You've probably heard that the Big Island isn't for everyone: she was no exception. Anyways, it was a while back. It's become one of those things that we don't discuss anymore, like when I lost control of a four-wheeler when I was thirteen and decimated my aunt's vegetable patch."

Marissa laughed.

"I was grounded for a month and had to help my aunt replant the garden and do backbreaking chores for my uncle while all the other kids got to ride into town and go to the movies or go surfing—regular kid stuff. But that was the summer I got hooked on horses, so I suppose it's true that all things happen for a reason." Tom finished his wine and put his empty glass on the counter.

Marissa gave a careless shrug, the wine having relaxed her completely. "I know people say that, but I don't know. What would be the reason for my having moved to Hawaii? Everything started to fall apart once we got here. Paul and I were having some problems before, but we always managed to get by. Once we got here, getting by apparently wasn't good enough, and then he had to go and have another midlife crisis. So now I'm getting a divorce and am stuck in a house I can't sell. I've had to rent out rooms. I no longer have a career. And I've gained at least ten pounds." She motioned to her hips in disgust.

Tom raised an eyebrow as his eyes slowly scanned her body, making her blush. "You could have fooled me." His eyes swept her body appreciatively one more time.

Flustered, Marissa tried to play it off. "So tell me what it's like to be on the list of Hawaii's most eligible bachelors . . ."

Tom groaned. "That list is idiotic. I can't imagine anybody would even bother to read that list."

"Are you kidding?" Marissa chided. "We drew straws for the top four bachelors. Jane came in first, then Malia, then Kavena, then me."

"Which, of course, is regrettable seeing how I'm number five on the list."

Marissa gave an exaggerated sigh. "Yes, it was a pity. I think the guy I ended up with has twenty-five patents. *And* he's supposedly a good kisser. It's kind of hard to top that, so don't beat yourself up."

Undaunted, Tom flashed a mischievous grin. "Trust me, if necessary, I can top *anything*." He offered her his hand and, feeling giddy, Marissa accepted. "Now let's go see what kind of food this town has to offer."

Dinner was a satisfying meal of cream of celery soup, followed by medallions of venison with sautéed mushrooms and a fresh salad. Marissa felt comforted by the warmth emanating from the restaurant's fireplace next to them. She gazed into the fire, her mind quiet. When she turned back to look at the dessert menu resting in front of her, she noticed that Tom was looking at her thoughtfully.

"What?" she asked, smiling almost shyly. She picked up the dessert menu and gave it a cursory glance, not wanting him to see how self-conscious she felt.

Tom gave a shrug, giving nothing away. "So . . . what looks good? I'm leaning toward the apple pie . . ."

Marissa gave him a knowing look. "Tom, come on." She felt a sense of trepidation but was curious to hear what he had to say.

Tom put down the menu and looked at her, then leaned back in his chair and laced his fingers together. "Okay—you asked. I was just thinking that this was not exactly how I envisioned our first date."

Despite having had two glasses of red wine, Marissa felt herself snap to attention. There was nothing like relationship talk to sober things up.

"Is this a date?" she asked, forcing herself to keep her voice light. "I thought we were just friends taking a weekend to check out the volcano."

"We are. I was just speaking hypothetically." His gaze was steady and then he looked into the fire and smiled. "Because it's definitely not my style to get involved with a woman who's still married."

Marissa couldn't have agreed more, but she teased him anyway. "You have home-wrecker written all over you."

Tom's brow furrowed, uncertain if she was serious or not.

"I'm just kidding, Tom" Marissa said. "You're the furthest thing from a home-wrecker. That title belongs to somebody else." Angela's smirking face appeared before her eyes, making Marissa grit her teeth. At least she knew that Paul wasn't with that woman tonight since he was on Pansy duty.

"Do you still love him? I mean, I'm sure you do, but do you want to get back together with him? Save your marriage, give it another chance?"

Marissa felt the frustration building up inside of her, as if the decision were up to her. But more important, she was beginning to realize that she was done settling with just getting by. She wanted the whole package now. Love, romance, friendship, partnership, great sex. Was it really too much to ask? She heard Paul and Angela laughing in her head, their playful voices from the grocery store. Marissa felt a longing but pushed it away, focusing her attention on the handsome, kind man sitting across from her. "There's nothing to save," she told Tom firmly. "It's over."

He studied her, unconvinced.

"I don't want to talk about Paul anymore," she said.

"What I want to talk about is how you envisioned our first date. Hypothetically, of course." Marissa touched the rim of her wineglass and looked at him through her lashes. It was a subtle but sensual move that always worked with Paul, and it seemed to be working with Tom as well. He cleared his throat and straightened up.

"Um . . ." He was blushing, her suggestive look having rendered him speechless. Marissa smiled to herself, pleased. She still had the touch. Thank God.

We're two mature adults, she told herself as she watched Tom fumble. *It's ridiculous to think that the only thing holding me back from getting involved with Tom is a piece of paper.*

But as Tom recovered and then launched into a detailed description of how he would court her, equipped with roses and wine and even a scene with them riding off into the sunset, Marissa found herself thinking about her honeymoon in Maui. Paul had surprised her with a simple picnic dinner on the beach, lit tiki torches at every corner of the blanket, holding it down. A beautiful older woman, old enough to be someone's grandmother or even great-grandmother, danced a graceful hula accompanied by a young man on a ukulele. Afterward, Paul and Marissa had taken a long walk along the water, not minding that their feet got wet as they watched the sun set over the horizon. They had made love in their hotel room with the warm night breeze from the open balcony drifting through their room.

Tom had finished talking and was now looking at her patiently. ". . . but, based on the riveted look on your face, I should probably go back to the drawing board. Although, to be honest, I think this day has gone better than any date I could have planned."

"It has gone well," Marissa said, feeling instantly guilty. From seductive to guilty in five minutes or less. She made herself pull out her inner flirt once more. "Today was a great first date. If it *had* been a date, that is."

Tom didn't miss a beat. "Right, because it wasn't, seeing how we're just friends."

"Exactly."

Marissa looked at the dessert menu one more time, then tossed it aside. What was she waiting for? If Paul hadn't been with Pansy tonight, he probably would have been out with Angela. "You know, I'm not feeling much like dessert."

Tom cleared his throat. "Really?" She could tell he was resisting a witty comeback.

"Let's go back to the hotel. We have a big day tomorrow and should probably get some sleep. Or something." She let her voice linger on the last two words.

"Or something?" The look in his eyes was cool but Tom immediately gestured for the check.

Marissa reminded herself again that they were both adults, and that it was time for her life to move on. It would take less than ten minutes to get back to the hotel. She gave him her sexiest voice yet. "I guess you'll have to wait and see."

The car ride back had been quiet, the air loaded with innuendo and possibility. Marissa felt her heart pounding in her chest, unsure if she could really go through with it and, at the same time, resenting the fact that she would even second-guess herself. They walked into the lobby of the Volcano House, the energy between them sizzling.

"Mrs. Price?"

The desk clerk held out a slip of paper. "You have a message."

They walked down the hallway as Marissa unfolded the paper. It was a message from Paul. *Please call right away.*

Marissa checked her phone, wondering why he hadn't tried to call her directly. She swore. No service.

When they reached her room, Marissa fastened on a bright smile, unable to muster anything sexy. Damn Paul for ruining the moment. She'd call him, check on Pansy, then get back in the mood. "I'll just make sure Pansy's all right," she started to say, but then Tom was leaning into her and Marissa felt her back press against the door.

His face was inches away. If even. She could feel the heat radiating from his body, beckoning her. "Marissa?" he murmured.

"Yes?" she said faintly.

And then he was kissing her, hot and heavy, not too urgent but persistent. Promising. Very promising.

When he pulled away, Marissa sighed and thought, *Now* that *was a kiss to remember.* Tom removed his room key from his wallet and started to walk next door, then hesitated. He turned around and strode back to her.

"Marissa, the one thing I'll say about me is that I'm patient," he said. "I'm not in any sort of rush. I've waited this long to meet the right woman, and I can wait a bit longer. Let's say good night and look forward to tomorrow. Are you okay with that for now?"

Still mute from the kiss, Marissa felt she had no choice but to give a disappointed nod. Tom brushed her cheek gently with his hand then turned to go into his room.

Alone in her room, Marissa sat on the edge of the bed, not sure if she was enraged or relieved. She dialed Paul's number and waited impatiently for him to answer. He picked up on the first ring.

"Hey, thanks for calling me back," he said. "I hope I wasn't interrupting anything."

There was a twinge of sarcasm in his voice, which Marissa ignored. "Is Pansy all right?"

"Pansy? Oh, she's fine. She just went to bed." She heard music in the background. John Legend.

"Is that my CD?" she demanded.

"Oh, you mean the CD that I gave you last year on our anniversary? The one that still had the cellophane on it when I took it from the house on Valentine's Day, when you kicked me out? Yeah, I didn't think you'd miss it."

She hadn't, but that wasn't the point. "It's my CD, Paul. Send it back with Pansy."

"Should I try to put the cellophane back on first?"

Marissa bristled. "Just send it back, Paul."

"Whatever you want, Marissa."

"What do you want, Paul?" Her voice was clipped, tired of the back and forth. "Why did you call?"

He cleared his throat. "I just wanted to tell you I'd like to offer Kaui's family a six-month complimentary guest pass to use the pool and beach areas at the resort. Thought you might want to be the one to give it to them since you're really the one who sees them."

"Oh." Marissa felt herself soften. The resort gave pool and beach privileges to VIPs only, and at fifteen hundred dollars a year. "They'll appreciate that."

"Pansy really likes Kaui and her family. I thought it would be a nice way to say thanks for being so good to our daughter."

The emphasis on *our* wasn't missed, but Marissa wasn't sure what he meant. Did Paul mean *our* as in they were still married and had a beautiful daughter together? Or did he mean *our* as in he could meet Pansy's needs as well as Marissa could? She hadn't counted on any resistance from Paul regarding custody, but suddenly she felt apprehensive.

"Is there a reason you had to call and tell me this now? It's almost ten o'clock."

"I didn't want to forget to mention it. Besides, it was six when I called. Where were you?"

"That's none of your business," Marissa retorted.

"Is Tom with you right now?"

"Again, none of your business."

"Because I've given it some thought and I'm seriously thinking about taking some horseback riding lessons. How much does he charge again? I really think I might be a natural. I might even get my own horse."

A smile tugged on the corners of her mouth but she didn't say anything.

Not hearing a response from her, Paul tried to laugh it off. "Fine, don't say anything. I'm just trying to make small talk."

Marissa sighed, a mixture of frustration and regret. "Paul, I think we're past the days of small talk. I'm hanging up now. Good-bye." She replaced the receiver, and all that remained was a lonely silence.

Marissa walked into her house Sunday afternoon and was greeted by three expectant faces in the living room. Her housemates were dressed in coveralls. They were pulling out the frayed carpet and padding, motivated by their success in patching the roof. Kavena had soldered patches in the steel flashing that had developed pinhole leaks.

"Well?" Kavena demanded, dropping her section and brushing her hands on her coveralls.

"Well what?" Marissa eased off her shoes and plopped onto the couch.

Malia tugged on her section. "How did it go?"

"How did it go?" Marissa gazed up at the ceiling as her friends waited impatiently. "We had a great time. Of course, the lava went underground and it was raining worse than Waimea, but we had fun nevertheless. I left my offering for Pele, so let's hope some good things start flowing my way soon. Is Pansy back yet?"

The women shook their heads. "So by 'great time,' you mean as friends, right?" Jane clarified.

Marissa bit her lip and then said, "Yeah. As friends."

"I saw that!" Malia gasped. "You hesitated!"

"She hesitated," Kavena confirmed.

Marissa protested, "I was catching my breath!"

"So you didn't kiss?" Jane's eyes were narrowed.

Ugh. They caught her again. "It happened last night, and it was completely innocent." She corrected herself. "Okay, maybe not completely innocent," she admitted as Malia squealed and Jane groaned. "But that was it. We hiked around the crater today and then it was time to drive back. Nothing else happened."

"He didn't try to cop a feel?" Kavena asked, curious.

"Kavena!" Malia looked offended.

"No, he did not," Marissa said. "Tom was a complete gentleman."

"Well," Jane said briskly, tossing Marissa a pair of coveralls and a linoleum knife. "Since you don't seem to be bothered by tight situations, see if you can jimmy that stretch of carpet from the tackless strip. It seems to be jammed in there pretty good."

Marissa was relieved to be off the subject of Tom and tossed her overnight bag aside. "I'm on it."

Later that night, Marissa tucked Pansy into bed. "Did you have a good weekend with your dad?" she asked. To the best of Pansy's knowledge, Marissa had gone to Volcano on her own.

Pansy nodded. "We collected a bunch of shrimp from the tidepools near his apartment," she said with a yawn. "We put them in a glass jar in the kitchen. They're swimming around, happy."

"So long as your father doesn't cook them by accident," Marissa said.

"Mom!" Pansy laughed. "They're not those kind of shrimp. These are the baby shrimp. Dad'll take care of them during the week and I'll take care of them when I see him on the weekends. They're my pets since you and Dad won't let me get a dog."

"Dad can't keep a dog at his place and I don't want to be cleaning up after one in ours," Marissa reminded her. "Besides, we have the cows out back—they're practically like pets. Just the other day the brown one with the large white spot on its back snorted at me when I told it to keep it down. It was a very touching moment."

Pansy giggled. "That's Jennifer. She's a heifer."

"What, you're naming them now?" Marissa looked fondly at her daughter.

"Just the ones that come closest to the house. Jennifer, Patricia, Nancy, and Becky. Oh, and Luanne. I told Chris he could come and see them sometime. He thought it was neat that we had cows in our backyard."

At the mention of Chris's name, Marissa felt her insides clench. "Who's Chris?" she asked, knowing perfectly well who he was.

"He's Angela's son. Remember her? We met her at the holiday party."

"Oh, right, I remember now." Marissa tucked the blankets around Pansy's body, cocooning her. She tried to keep her voice light. "Where did you see them, anyway?"

"They stopped by Dad's house last night when we were about to barbeque. They stayed for dinner. We played Monopoly after. It was fun." Pansy snuggled deeper under her covers. "Chris also goes to Hawaii Day School, but he said next year he might be going to boarding school. His dad is going to pay for it. Then Angela said there was no way she was going to let him go to boarding school, even though Chris says he really wants to go."

"Really?" Marissa wanted to strangle Paul. Typical that he would bring up Tom in conversation but conveniently leave out any mention of Angela. Marissa smoothed Pansy's blankets, furious that Paul let Angela and her son encroach on his personal time with his daughter. There was that, plus the fact that she didn't want that woman anywhere near Pansy.

Pansy's eyes fastened on her. "Would you let me go to boarding school if I really wanted to go?"

If it doesn't make me look like Angela, yes, Marissa wanted to say, but instead settled for a truthful, "I don't know. It's a big decision and you're too young right now anyway." Marissa turned off the bedroom light and Pansy's nightlight flickered on, casting a soft, soothing glow around the room.

Pansy was silent for so long that Marissa wondered if she had drifted to sleep. "Mom?" Pansy's voice was suddenly serious.

"Yes?"

"I have something I need to ask you. It's important." Pansy sounded nervous, even a little scared.

Marissa smoothed Pansy's hair as it fanned out on her pillow, her heart beating furiously. She could dimly see Pansy's face, covered in part by shadow. "Pansy, it's late, sweetheart. You've had a long day." She was still seething at the thought of Angela with Paul.

"I know, but . . . I talked to Dad, and he said I should talk to you." Pansy's voice faltered, and she gulped.

Marissa's anger quickly dissipated and was replaced by fear. Suddenly, in the dim light of Pansy's room, it dawned on her that perhaps she had misunderstood more than she realized. Maybe Paul wasn't just having a selfish moment, a thoughtless affair.

Maybe he was in love.

It would certainly explain the nonsensical, rambling conversation the night before. And his generous gift to the Nilssons. An attempt to get on Marissa's good side, right before breaking the bad news.

Marissa pulled herself back into the moment, forcing herself to focus on Pansy, to be there for Pansy.

"Mom?"

"Yes, Pansy?" It wasn't a question, but a statement. She steeled herself, willing herself not to cry or get hysterical. If Paul admitted to Pansy that he didn't love Marissa anymore, or wanted a divorce, then Marissa needed to deal with that with as much poise and grace as she could muster. Or at least not break down completely until she got to her own bedroom.

Pansy took a deep breath. "I want to be homeschooled."

'umikūmākahi | eleven

"Why am I the only person who thinks this is a terrible idea?" Marissa complained early the next morning.

"What's so terrible about it?" Jane asked. She was standing indecisively over a colorful array of Crocs lined up by the back door. Jane had small feet so the eight or so pairs of size sixes were hers. Two new pairs were jumbled in the mix but were an obvious size ten. Kavena had sworn off her Birkenstocks since the straps were made of leather.

"Homeschooling is in," Kavena informed Marissa. She was packing the kids' lunches, which meant lots of fruit, sticks of raw vegetables, her macadamia nut bars, and a couple of slices of spelt bread with a hummus spread. Pansy didn't mind it but Isaiah detested it. Malia, whose lunches were more kid-friendly with juice boxes and gummy snacks featuring Disney characters in various fruit "flavors," would probably sneak a couple of packs in when Kavena had her back turned. "It's trendy."

"I don't care," Marissa said stubbornly. "I don't think it's healthy for a child to be cooped up at home with her mother. Plus I'd be a terrible teacher. Look what kind of example I'm setting for her now! No, she's better off in school. The teachers there can give her what she needs."

"Marissa, the girl is bored," Kavena said. "She's smarter than those other kids in her class. If you homeschooled her, you'd be able to come up with something that worked for her."

"They are getting into the good colleges these days," Jane said thoughtfully as she slipped into a pair of pink Crocs. She changed her mind and tried on the light blue ones instead. "Harvard and Yale specifically recruit homeschooled kids. There was an article in *USA Today*. I remember reading it at Kava Java."

"You should ask Pansy's friend Kaui, the one who helps out Tom at the stables," Malia said. She was fastening a safety pin on to the latch of her skirt, hoping to gain another inch or two to accommodate her expanding waistline. "She's homeschooled. Her parents are scientists working at one of the observatories. You could probably ask them how they do it."

"They're scientists?" Marissa thought of the times she had seen them at the stables or at playdates. Despite the frequency that Pansy and Kaui were together, Marissa limited her exchange with Kaui's parents to polite small talk outside Marissa's house or their house, a spacious cedar home at the end of a long private road just outside of town. Marissa had always declined offers for tea, not meaning to be rude but not really in the mood to make new friends. They looked like ordinary people, not scientists, and certainly not like the type that would have time to homeschool their daughter.

"I think Tom said he's in charge of the telescope. The

head honcho. The mom does something with some instru-
mentation or something . . ." Malia shook her head. "You'll
have to ask Tom."

Marissa had assumed Kaui was homeschooled for financial reasons, and now felt foolish about the guest pass Paul
had given them. "I thought she was working at the stables
in exchange for lessons."

"She is," Malia said. "It's an internship."

"An internship? At nine?" The thought had never occurred to Marissa.

Malia shrugged. "Tom says she's great, even better than
some of the older kids he's had in the past. And she loves
horses. Like Pansy. It makes a big difference when you're
doing something you enjoy."

"Well, since we only have a week until school is out for
summer, I've told Pansy we're tabling this discussion until
I know where we'll be in the fall. I'm hoping it's just a passing whim."

"Pansy's never struck me as a whimsical kind of girl,"
Jane said. "She's more focused than that."

"Well, I'm not ready to commit to anything right now,"
Marissa said resolutely. It was her turn to take Pansy to
school and Isaiah to daycare. She peered into the living
room. "I'm going to need some help prying the kids away
from the TV. Who put in that tape of *Pocahontas* this morning? I thought we had a no-TV rule in the morning."

The other women looked pointedly at Malia. "Hormones," the young woman said finally, shaking her head in
mock regret. "I'm forgetting everything these days."

"You only have a few more months to use that excuse!"
Kavena informed her hotly.

"No, I'm planning to play the postpartum card for a
while, too," Malia said mildly. "I didn't realize how good

pregnant women have it. Anyway, what's the big deal? It's educational."

"Native American cultural studies," Jane agreed. "Hey, there's your homeschool curriculum right there. Social studies and history. You could probably make a case for music and art exposure, too." Jane was tying on an apron, which meant she would be cooking up another batch of her kava blends.

"Right, the Disney curriculum. Now why didn't I think of that?" Marissa gave Jane an exasperated look before reaching for her car keys. "Should I make plans to stay out for the rest of the day?"

Jane was pulling out all of the pots and pans, lining up empty bowls side by side. "Whatever floats your boat. You know where I'll be."

"I'll help you load the kids in the car," Kavena told Marissa. "And then I'm coming back for my happy hit."

Marissa let out a yawn as they headed toward the living room. "If this homeschool thing means that I no longer have to worry about dropping off or picking up Pansy from school, maybe I seriously should consider it."

"Yeah," Kavena said, patting Marissa on the back. "Being able to sleep in would be an excellent reason to homeschool."

By the time Marissa returned home, the Kava Java kitchen and tasting lab was in full swing.

The music was blaring, the windows were open, and the sun was streaming into the kitchen. Jane had recruited Kavena to help, and the two women were hovered over the various pots and pans, pouring and measuring.

"Aloha!" Kavena called out, dancing toward Marissa with a coconut shell in hand.

"That one has a hint of chocolate," Jane explained, checking her notes. "I used unsweetened cocoa from the chocolate farm in South Point. Cuts the bitterness a bit. I'm thinking of calling it the Kava Java Sweet Tooth blend."

Marissa took a cautious sip and felt the familiar tingle on her tongue. Jane was experimenting with kava in earnest now, wanting to combine the ancient medicinal herb with new flavors so that it might become more accessible to the general market. "The healing properties alone could help people with a number of ailments," she explained. "Plus it's a natural remedy that promotes a sense of peace and well-being."

After Marissa's disastrous trip to Kona that yielded a month's supply of Spam along with the unwelcome discovery that Angela and Paul were spending more and more time together, Marissa had sworn off kava, blaming it for her blissful state that allowed her to entertain the notion of reconciliation. But after a week of angry days and sleepless nights, Jane had insisted that Marissa try her Kava Java Sleepytime blend, and within an hour Marissa was in a deep sleep. She awoke the next morning refreshed and committed to supporting Jane as she continued to experiment with her kava blends.

Still, it did create a great stink in the kitchen as Jane overcooked, undercooked, chopped up other herbs, and discovered what was complementary and what was not.

"I'm getting all of the medical disclaimers together, and I think I'm going to be ready to trial run some of the blends at the coffeehouse," Jane was saying now. "One plus is that we don't need FDA approval, but the flip side is that I have to include so many disclaimers that most people won't be willing to give it a try."

"What about side effects?" Marissa asked. She could taste the smooth, warming cocoa in her mouth now. It was subtle, but enough to add a bit of flavor. Marissa began to fill out the rating card that Jane had for every blend.

"That's just it. There aren't any proven side effects, especially when taken in moderation." Jane frowned as she tested the consistency of one of the blends.

"If your Kava Java customers like it, you should figure out how to bottle it and sell it to the spa at Kohala Bay," Kavena suggested. "They'll pay you a pittance, of course, but it's how I get my massage oils out there. Or the health food stores. They'd eat this stuff up."

Marissa sipped the Sweet Tooth blend again and continued to write comments. "Oh, I don't know," she said absently. "Word of mouth is incredibly powerful for a product line like this. Personally, I'd bypass the health food stores altogether at this stage. I'd go straight to those natural doctors—naturopaths—and get them to recommend it or prescribe it or whatever it is they do. Give them free samples to start off with, provide a small display and brochures. Focus on making the naturopath your customer, not the end user. I'd try to create a demand at that level. You'd be able to charge more of a premium while building credibility in the product and testing the market, and then let it trickle into the stores for the average consumer."

Jane had turned down the music and was listening intently.

Marissa went on. "Better yet, get a big name from Hollywood to endorse it. Find the latest Oscar winner who suffers from depression or insomnia. Does Britney Spears have insomnia? Or Halle Berry?"

"Hilary Duff," Kavena said slowly. "She's one of my clients when she stays at the Bungalows. And Meg Ryan . . . they both have stress and problems sleeping at night. Oh, and Keanu Reeves."

"Oh, he'd be great," Marissa said. She got up and walked

to the pantry in search of something to eat. "He's part Hawaiian. That adds some local credibility."

"Pierce Brosnan," Kavena added. "And Nicole Kidman. They were both born in Honolulu. And they're really nice. I'm sure Jane's kava blends would address some ailment they have. They're Hollywood, after all—they all have something going on."

Jane was writing frantically.

"Which brings me to another point," Marissa said, turning to Kavena, who looked startled to have the attention turned to her. "Right now you're only distributing your oils through the spa at the resort. If you really want to start building a future for you and Isaiah, you need to think beyond being a masseuse."

"I enjoy my work," Kavena said defensively.

Marissa found a bag of taro chips and opened them up. "But what if you get hurt or sick? You can't do this forever. And you're lucky, you already have a product line. The way I see it, you need to explore two channels: first, grow your distribution."

"Like other spa shops?"

"Possibly. You have good shelf life with the massage oils, so you could even look at catalogs. Go beyond Hawaii. Quite frankly I think you should have an online store—that would be one of the easiest and most effective storefronts for you to manage. Repeat customers would know where to go, they could place orders in the middle of the night. You have so many Japanese clients at the hotel, it would be easy for them to order when they get home as well. It would be a relatively inexpensive way to move your product."

Kavena's mouth was hanging open in astonishment, and she looked at Jane, her eyes wide.

"Don't worry," Jane told her, scribbling away. "I'm taking notes for you, too."

Marissa was staring out in space, munching on the chips. "The second thing to explore would be expanding your product line. You have the three essential oil blends . . . add soaps and lotions into the mix. You don't even have to worry about making them yourself. Just find something you like and private label it under your brand. You can differentiate yourself by including Hawaiian words or chants or prayers on little cards and attach them with raffia around the neck of the bottles—wait, scratch that. Raffia may be too down-market. Maybe use a gold or red silk cord instead. Hey, what about packaging them as incentive gifts for all those corporate groups that hold conferences and sales meetings at the hotel? I'm sure they'd love to put something different in the goody bags—alarm clocks and mag lights and iPods are getting old. Plus it would fit into the whole Hawaii healing and natural market. You'd be branding Hawaii and the whole natural whoosy-whatsits that everyone is getting into these days. You might even be able to get a grant from the state since you're a Hawaii-based product and company."

Marissa stopped talking when she noticed that the women were staring at her. "What?"

"Do you always do that?"

"Do what?"

Jane was laughing and held up the pad of paper that held a full page worth of notes. "It's so second nature to you, you don't even realize you're doing it," she said.

"You were channeling your inner consultant in a very scary, but intriguing way," Kavena said. "That's a compliment, by the way." She fell into a chair. "Whew! I'm tired just from listening to you."

Marissa felt a wave of contentment pass over her and she let out a happy sigh. "I don't know if it's the kava or that I was finally able to use my brain in a creative, constructive way, but I feel great."

"I think you just generated enough brainpower to fuel the neighborhood for a week," Jane said. But then she stared at the pad of paper is dismay. "Playing around with the kava blends is a definite passion of mine," she said. "And I can handle using my customers as my test market and selling the blends through the Kava Java coffeehouses. But really getting it out there? I don't think I've got the time or the energy."

Kavena suddenly blurted, "But I do." She sat up straight in her chair, her eyes bright with excitement. "My schedule is pretty flexible at the resort, and I have time in the evenings after Isaiah's asleep. I'm lucky I've always been able to make enough so I don't need to find a second job, but I need more if I want to save for a house of my own someday. I could look into it. Maybe we could even try an online store with your kava blends and my essential oils and see what happens." She nodded toward the pad in Jane's hands. "Plus take a look at all that other . . . stuff." There was admiration in her eyes as she gave Marissa an approving grin. "You're good."

"At solving other people's problems," Marissa clarified. "Clearly I am unable to use my superpowers in my own life." She said this with a touch of disgust, remembering Arthur's praise only months before.

"Oh, I don't know about that," Jane said. She started to clean up the kitchen and both Marissa and Kavena jumped up to help. "I have a feeling you may be using your superpowers more than you realize."

"You're drafting *what?*" Kate asked, practically shouting into the phone. "You'll have to talk louder. I'm in a taxi, heading to Grand Central Station."

Marissa could make out the sound of the city in the background. "We're draft-proofing the doors and windows," she said again, raising her voice. She handed the caulking gun to Pansy and stepped outside. "This house has so many gaps and cracks we may as well be sleeping outside."

"Haven't you sold that house yet?" Kate sounded exasperated.

"We're not finished fixing it up yet," Marissa said. She wandered into the yard, grateful for the fresh air. "I'll probably be able to have our real estate agent take a look in another month or so. The market's still kind of slow, so we need to do what we can to make it as desirable as possible."

Marissa and her housemates had agreed that, despite the repairs and renovations they had done so far, something still seemed to be missing. "It's the layout," Jane had finally said. "The house probably worked great as a vacation rental and it's certainly serving our purposes now, but it's just too carved up. New carpet and a coat of paint isn't going to change that."

"Maybe you'll find someone as desperate as you were," Kavena said. "Some naïve couple from the mainland might snatch it up."

"Some families have their in-laws living with them," Malia pointed out. She was sitting with her feet elevated, her stomach the size of a basketball. "This layout would work great for them."

"No, Jane's right." Marissa's eyes swept around the house. "The house is too much of a white elephant. There's a lot of room, but it doesn't feel like a single-family home. Jenny said that most of her clients are families, and most families are going to want something that feels cohesive."

The women weren't sure how to accomplish this, but Jane's general contractor had agreed to come and take a look and offer some suggestions.

Now Kate was sounding impatient. "I thought you

wanted to get back to the city as quickly as possible!" Her voice sounded almost accusatory.

"I do, Kate, but it's not that simple. Early fall, if I'm lucky."

"No, I don't think so," Kate said. "I have my money on you coming back sooner."

"Really?" Marissa teased. "What are you, a mind reader?"

"No." Kate paused dramatically before continuing. "I'm a fiancée! I'm engaged! Oliver just proposed and we're going to get married!"

"Oh, my God!" Marissa gasped. "Congratulations, Kate! When did this happen?"

"Last night. We told our parents this morning. My family had pretty much given up hope, so I had to be careful and make sure my dad didn't have a heart attack. Oliver's parents were thrilled, too."

Marissa wished she could give her best friend a hug. "I'm sorry I'm not there to celebrate the good news with you."

"As long as you're here for the wedding. Oliver and I decided an elaborate, fancy wedding doesn't make sense. I mean, I'm forty! Can you honestly see me walking down the aisle in one of those dopey white dresses? Ugh. We're going to do a civil ceremony at City Hall. Then have a small get-together afterward. Keep it elegant and simple."

Marissa was impressed. While "bride" had never been on Kate's list of things to do when she grew up, she had expected Kate to push for something extravagant. "Just tell me when."

Kate didn't hesitate. "July sixteenth, in exactly six weeks."

Marissa almost dropped the phone. "Six weeks!"

"I told you: Oliver and I don't want any fuss. You'll be my maid of honor, right? Or is it matron? What's the term if you're separated but not divorced? Anyway, you're it and I'm going to look at dresses this weekend. I already picked out your dress. Jim Hjelm has this gorgeous lilac sheath; I know it sounds tacky, but I swear, it's not . . ."

Marissa was confident it wouldn't be tacky, but she also knew it wouldn't be cheap. Add in airfare, a gift, meals out, subway tokens, and cab fare . . . Marissa felt nervous at the thought of all the money that would get spent in a seventy-two-hour period.

But it would also give Marissa a chance to finally sit down with Arthur and try to get her job back. She could also pay a visit to L'Ecole Jardinière and begin apartment hunting. It hadn't crossed her mind before, but Marissa began to get excited. A trip back to New York would revive her and remind her of what she had to look forward to. It made perfect sense.

She had to add sealant to three more windows and had a couple of doors that needed excluder strips screwed into their bottoms. Then she would get on the Internet and start searching for the cheapest flights into JFK.

"I'm thinking you, me, a couple of horses, and a picnic somewhere up in the hills of Waimea." Tom was at the house, helping Marissa put together a crib for Malia.

The women were throwing Malia a surprise baby shower later that evening. Kavena and Isaiah had driven Malia to Hilo to look for a new car, bribing Malia with a stop at Big Island Candies. Malia had developed a craving for the dark chocolate bar with crushed potato chips and macadamia nuts. This gave Marissa about five hours to get the house cleaned up and decorated for the shower. Pansy was spending the day at Paul's and would be home right as the other guests would be arriving. "Candlelight optional."

Marissa playfully nudged him and then held out her hand. "Screwdriver, please."

"Or we could fly to Honolulu, act like city slickers for a couple of days." His eyes were on her, watchful and attentive.

Marissa had forgotten what it was like to be so physically close to Tom. It was unnerving. After their weekend in Volcano, Marissa had kept a safe distance, unsure of what to do next. She didn't trust herself to be alone with him again, and even less sure of why it even mattered.

He tried again. "Okay, how about this: you, me, takeout, and a video?"

She tightened a screw then shook the guardrail on one wall of the crib. "Depends on the video."

Tom looked intrigued, arching an eyebrow in interest.

"I didn't mean it like that," Marissa said in mock exasperation.

"I didn't say anything." Tom feigned innocence. "I don't know what *you* were thinking."

Marissa stood up and looked at her masterpiece. "What do you think?" she asked proudly.

"It looks great. Malia will love it." He gave it a little shake, satisfied.

"You think?"

Tom nodded as he ran his hand along the gentle curve of the crib. "It's soft and feminine, much more so than those other ones. It'll suit her."

"That's what I thought, too." Marissa pushed it against the wall near Malia's bed. Jane had sprung the big bucks for a leather glider and ottoman in a creamy beige that matched the crib perfectly. Tom had made a changing station from scratch, and Kavena had sewn several nursing gowns that had identical onesies so mother and baby could match. Pansy had made a small booklet of coupons for babysitting, to be redeemed at any time the new mother felt exhausted.

Tom stepped up behind Marissa as she put the tools back

in the toolbox, his breath warming her neck. "Well, that's done. What's next?" His hands rested on either side of her waist and he pulled her gently toward him. She was wearing a sundress with spaghetti straps. She shivered when his lips brushed against the bare skin of her shoulders.

"Streamers," she croaked, disentangling herself and walking quickly to the living room. The last thing she needed was for someone to walk in and see them, and Jane, of all people, was due back any minute. "And I need you to tie these little plastic booties on to the ribbons of the gift bags."

Tom reluctantly accepted a pair of pink booties and a pair of blue ones. They seemed dwarfed in his hand as he squinted at them. "I'm not sure I have the fine motor skills to pull this off."

"Oh, you'll do great." Marissa handed him a spool of extra ribbon. "I'll put up the streamers." She quickly crossed the room, eager to put a little distance between them.

Tom gave her a pained expression as he looked longingly at the ladder and then back at the small packages of plastic baby booties. "Wouldn't it make sense if *I* did that?"

"It would, but I promised the girls I'd get a picture of the rugged cowboy surrounded by all this baby paraphernalia." Marissa pointed to the camera sitting on the kitchen table. "We thought it would be a definite keeper for the baby book."

Tom shook his head but, always the gentleman, sat down and began the tedious task of slipping the satin ribbon through the tiny loop at the top of the booties and tying it onto the shimmery fabric gift bags. "On a completely unrelated note, I've been meaning to thank you for everything you've done for Malia. I have to admit I've been dragging my feet on helping her find a place—it'll be hard to find a place that will top this. She loves it here."

"The feeling's mutual," Marissa said. She climbed the ladder and taped one end of a streamer on the wall. "She's a huge help with the kids, and I'd forgotten how fun it was to be around a pregnant woman. Did you know that Kavena's her birth coach? They've been doing Lamaze together."

"I get the play-by-play details. I think I could write a book by now." Tom finally finished his first gift bag and held it up. "Not bad, if I do say so myself."

"Hold on . . ." Marissa came down and reached for the camera, snapping a picture. She looked at the digital image on the screen. "The quintessential Kodak moment. If I didn't know better, I'd say you were glowing. Are *you* pregnant, Tom?"

Tom turned a shade of red before putting down the gift bag and starting on another. "Haven't had the pleasure, but I certainly wouldn't mind."

A red flag went up. Marissa put the camera down. "You want kids?" She felt silly asking the question. Tom was great with kids; of course he'd want kids.

"I always thought I'd settle down and have lots of kids. I was always envious of my friends who came from large families. And it would be nice to have permanent help at the stables."

"Ah, slave labor," Marissa said.

"I think I'm one of the few people who has a family business. Having the family around wouldn't be a problem. In fact, my business would probably thrive. That's the irony: it's a great family business but I'm single."

"Which, again, is still a puzzle to me."

He was looking at her steadily now. "Like I said, I'm a patient man."

Marissa turned around to face him. It seemed only seconds before he crossed the room and closed the space between them. His lips were hot on hers and Marissa felt herself melting, wanting desperately to feel sexy and loved again. At that same moment, she heard the side door open and knew that Jane was home, probably laden with food for the baby shower.

Tom heard Jane enter as well, and reluctantly stepped away.

Marissa cleared her throat, still feeling a bit weak in the knees. "Tom, it's just not the right time for me to get involved with anyone. It wouldn't be fair to you or anyone else." Her eyes darted inadvertently to the family picture hanging above the fireplace. Marissa had left it for Pansy's benefit.

Tom didn't notice. "Oh, I have competition now?" They could hear Jane opening and closing the fridge. "I knew I should have made my move when I had the chance."

Marissa smiled, grateful that he could still make a joke. "Can you wait a little longer?" she asked.

"I'm going to go help Jane," Tom said, sidestepping her question. "Are you okay in here?"

She nodded, breathless.

"Okay, then."

"Today, we're sealing the deck," Kavena announced. "It's been almost a week since we power-washed it and I can't stand staring at it anymore. It's nice and sunny, and I want to get started before the clouds roll in and that Waimea rain kicks up again."

"Oh, do we have to?" Pansy groaned. She was lying upside down on the couch, her feet in the air, an open book on her chest. "I was going to meet Kaui at the stables. We're going to clean out the side room. There's a lot of old junk in there."

"I'll take you," Malia offered, pushing herself up from the

floor where she had been stretching. Her belly was nice and round, and the baby was moving a lot. "We'll get the mail, too."

"I swear, if I didn't know better I'd think you were carrying twins," Kavena said, looking critically at Malia's stomach. She was taking her role as birth coach seriously, monitoring Malia's meals and accompanying Malia to doctors' visits, much to the exasperation of the nurses and Malia's ob-gyn. Kavena plagued them with questions and had already provided them with a birth plan of what they wanted once Malia went into labor. Malia loved the mothering and had shown the other women her hospital bag, which was already packed even though her due date was seven weeks away. "Okay, children and pregnant women are off the hook. Go, before I change my mind."

Malia and Pansy made a quick getaway, ushering Isaiah away from the TV and into the car, while Jane and Marissa stared after them enviously. "I wish I were pregnant," Jane muttered. "You'd think Malia's nesting instinct would have kicked in and she'd be single-handedly getting this house in shape. I sort of had this picture of relaxing today with a glass of lemonade."

"If you want hemorrhoids, gas, and high blood pressure, I'm sure she wouldn't mind changing places with you," Kavena said as she led the women out to the deck.

"Malia has hemorrhoids?" Jane wrinkled her nose.

"Do you really want the details? Just trust me on this." Kavena handed each of them a paint brush and can of sealant. "And if you want to make lemonade, be my guest. Let's get going."

With the three of them working and laughing, the time passed quickly as it had for many of the projects they had already completed around the house. By the time Malia and the kids had returned, the deck was drying nicely and the women were enjoying a cold glass of lemonade in the kitchen.

"I'm pooped!" Pansy announced, handing Marissa a bundle of mail. They were all covered with dirt and cobwebs. Marissa would have normally ordered Pansy into the shower right away, but instead she poured her daughter a glass of lemonade and gave her a hug as she plopped down next to her mother.

"That makes two of us," Malia said, sitting down heavily. She looked exhausted, but very pleased. "We're going to have a stable sale next weekend. He's got a lot of stuff he doesn't need anymore, and the girls thought a sale would be fun. They took it a step further and suggested that all of Tom's students be allowed to bring things they want to sell and set up small tables and booths. Make it into a little event."

"And Malia's going to help him start a store!" Pansy exclaimed. "I'm going to be an assistant buyer."

Malia gave Pansy a kind smile. "Now that he's got a free room, we thought it might be great to convert it into a store. Some apparel items, some gift items, even some feed."

Marissa couldn't picture Tom ringing up sales. "Is he going to have time for that?" she asked. "He's got a lot going on."

"Oh, I completely agree," Malia said. She took a long drink of water. "That's why I proposed trying the honor system. Everything will be priced and bar-coded. People can scan in the tags themselves. The computer will calculate tax, and customers can just approve the total and swipe their credit card. He'll be paying the credit card company fees, but also won't have to worry about cash or checks. People can even bag their own merchandise. Tom won't even have to be in there."

"What if people steal stuff since it's not monitored?" Kavena asked.

"Since his customers will primarily be his students and clients, that's not likely, but of course anything is possible. I did some research a couple of years ago for the resort when we were considering an honor system for the media rental service—you know, where guests can borrow music and DVDs—and it turned out that there were lower instances of theft with an honor system than with one that was monitored. Of course, that wasn't enough to convince them to try it, which is probably one reason the media rental service was a complete flop." Malia shook her head. "The Four Seasons does it, and it's very successful for them. Guests *like* being trusted, it makes them more loyal to the resort, which in turn makes them inclined to spend more." She shrugged. "That's my take, anyway."

"I think that's very observant," Marissa said, impressed. Malia definitely had a good head on her shoulders, and she had a future ahead of her if she could break out of the secretarial groove. "You could mention it to Paul again. I know he'd love for the Kohala Bay to be head-to-head with the Four Seasons."

"This falls under Marketing and Guest Services," Malia said with a smirk. "If I go to Paul before going to *her*"—Malia cast a careful glance in Pansy's direction, but Pansy was busy getting a snack for her and Isaiah—"things will be even more difficult than they already are. And I already know what she's going to say, since she was the one who nixed it a couple of years ago when I first brought it up."

"We're going to go play with the hose outside and rinse off," Pansy told Marissa, holding on to Isaiah's hand. His other hand clutched a bag of taro chips. "Is that okay?"

Marissa gave her daughter a nod. "Sure. Just don't use too much water—the island's still having a drought."

"Speaking of *her*," Kavena said once the kids were out of earshot. "Don't you find it interesting that we haven't heard much on that front?" She looked to Malia for confirmation.

Malia drummed her nails on the table. "I know. It's kind of weird, actually. She's keeping it very professional in the office, not flirting or joking with anyone, which is a bit out of character. And you should know that Paul was a little upset that we didn't invite him to the shower last week."

"But you said that Carol did something at the office," Marissa said, surprised that Paul would even care. "Anyway, it was ladies only."

"Well, ladies and Tom," Jane corrected.

"You mean ladies that were all over Tom," Kavena added with a laugh, and all the women smiled. Almost every woman—eligible *and* ineligible—had zeroed in on him the minute they walked through the door.

Malia smiled fondly at the memory. "I think that's what made Paul feel left out. And I guess it's kind of strange since I am living in his house . . ."

Marissa tried to appear indifferent as she shuffled through her mail. "I really don't care anymore," she said. "Besides, it wasn't about him. It was your baby shower, and we only invited your close friends. It would have been awkward if Paul were here."

"Actually, it would have been nice," Malia said wistfully. "He's by far the best person I've ever worked for."

"That's because you make him look smart," Marissa pointed out.

"He *is* smart," Malia insisted.

"It doesn't matter," Marissa said, staring at a large envelope in her hands. "It's over."

Jane sipped her lemonade. "It's not over til it's over," she quipped.

Marissa held up the envelope for all the women to see. The paperwork from the Third Circuit Family Court had arrived. "Well," she said, "then I think we're pretty damn close."

PART III

Paradise Found

E lauhoe mai na waʻa; i ke kā, i ka hoe;
i ka hoe, i ke kā; pae aku i ka ʻāina.

*Everybody paddle together; bail and paddle;
paddle and bail; and the shore is reached.*

'umikūmālua | twelve

Marissa's plane landed with a bump on the runaway of John F. Kennedy Airport.

She hadn't realized it, but she had been holding her breath from the moment the lights and skyscrapers had come into view. She had mentally prepared herself for returning to the city for Kate's wedding, but she wasn't prepared for how her body would react. It had seemed to tense from the moment she stepped through the security machines at the Kona airport, turning for one last time to wave good-bye to Pansy and Malia. Leaving Pansy had never been a problem before, and while Marissa knew her daughter was in good hands since Paul had agreed to do double-duty to cover for the week Marissa would be gone, she suddenly wished they had spent the money for an extra ticket.

But Marissa had a packed seven days ahead of her, and it would have been a lot for Pansy. Kate's original plans for a simple civil ceremony had changed dramatically in the past month. Kate had pulled her own strings to have the ceremony and reception at the Frick Art & Historical Center, and the guest list had swelled from twenty to four hundred.

Marissa also managed to squeeze in a meeting with Arthur, and a headhunter as well. The headhunter was confident that she could place Marissa into a similar position, which buoyed Marissa's spirits considerably. If Arthur didn't want her, someone else most definitely would.

Which is exactly what Marissa told her housemates a few days ago, when the paperwork to begin uncontested divorce proceedings had arrived. It had been Paul's decision to leave, she reminded them. If he wasn't sure he wanted Marissa, fine. There would be someone who did.

She didn't have to say Tom's name, but everyone knew who she was referring to. Out of defiance, she had ripped open the envelope and wrote her name—in pen—on the blank titled, "Plaintiff." She filled Paul's name on the blank titled "Defendant," then had to stop because her hand started shaking. Marissa put the half-inch thick document away, still reeling with the legalese and finality of it, upset that she found it too difficult to continue but still determined to go through with it.

It was in her carry-on bag now, and Marissa intended on completing it and putting it in the mail before her trip to New York was over. Even though there wouldn't be any argument over the division of assets or custody of Pansy, there were still hoops to jump through, and Marissa wasn't looking forward to it. Why did the process have to feel so awful?

Paul hadn't fought with her when she had announced that she wanted to file for divorce. A look of utter defeat, coupled with a look of defiance, maybe even resentment, flashed across his face before he had scowled, "Whatever you want, Marissa. I'm tired of fighting you. Do whatever you want, since you're going to do that anyway."

She wanted to remind him that this was all his fault to

begin with, but as she watched him drive away, it was clear the time of blame had passed. They were both in it now, and life was dragging them forward, like it or not.

"Marissa, you've changed," Kate exclaimed by way of greeting when Marissa emerged from behind the security exit. Kate gave her girlfriend an enthusiastic kiss on both cheeks before stepping back to run a critical eye up and down her friend. "What have you done to your hair?"

"Nothing," Marissa replied, her hand self-consciously touching her long locks.

"That's my point." Kate looped her arm through Marissa's. "That's okay. I have an appointment on Friday with Clio at Vidal, and he can probably squeeze you in as well. Highlights and a cut. At least. God, and your nails— we'll have to do a mani and a pedi, otherwise it'll be obvious in the photos."

Marissa had figured as much. Her nails were short and chipped from doing all the work around the house.

Kate walked briskly toward the exit. "Come on. Oliver's curbside. I can't wait for you to meet him! He'll take us straight to the bridal salon for a fitting."

Marissa was exhausted. "*Now?* But I just landed, Kate."

"So?" Kate was laughing, unconcerned. "Hit the ground running—you were always good at that. Remember? And we have reservations at Spago, right after. Oliver's parents have already flown in, and I want you to meet them. Bridal brunch is Saturday morning at the Russian Tea Room." She scanned the cars and noticed that airport security was waving away passengerless cars. "Shit, he must have had to circle around."

Marissa turned on her iPhone and it immediately beeped with two voice messages. The first was from Pansy, assuring her that everything was fine, which only made Marissa miss her more, and the other was from the headhunter Marissa had signed with.

"Bain is *very* interested and their managing director wants to set something up right away," the woman was gushing. "Call me immediately so I can line it up."

When Marissa told Kate the news, Kate was ecstatic. "You see? They'd be lucky to get you." She said this with a touch of loyal arrogance, making Marissa smile. "When do they want you to come in?"

"I'm scheduling all of my meetings for after the wedding," Marissa told her. She was also planning to visit Pansy's old school and asking the headmistress to informally hold a spot for Pansy, just in case. "Your wedding comes first."

"I'm so happy you're finally here." Kate beamed as she waved down a silver Mercedes. "There's Oliver. You're going to love him, Marissa!"

Marissa did love him. He was the perfect match for Kate. He was ten years Kate's senior, slightly more sophisticated, but clearly enthralled by his fiancée and not the bulldog attorney Marissa had expected.

"He's great," Marissa told Kate later in the dressing room as she straightened her matron-of-honor gown. It was pinching at the waist. Her fault for fibbing slightly on the measurements. "And he's obviously completely taken by you."

"I know. That's one reason I love him—he's absolutely crazy about me." Kate looked regal in her strapless wedding gown, the empire waist flowing dramatically to the floor in a long train behind her. In the end she had opted for a traditional white gown after all, having got caught up in all the wedding hype and hysteria. "Of course, I'm absolutely crazy about him, so that makes us pretty even."

She noticed Marissa struggling in her dress and turned away from the mirror to look at her friend unsympathetically. "You have been a size four for as long as I can remember," she complained. "And then when you went up to a six,

I didn't say a word. But now you've totally let yourself go! If you had flown in a week earlier like I'd asked, we would have had time to get that taken out."

"You're lucky I was able to get away for the week," Marissa retorted. She no longer cared about having gained a few pounds. She knew she still looked good if she wasn't trying to squeeze into a dress the size of a toothpaste container. "Besides, if you hadn't changed your mind about the dress so many times, I could have had it taken care of in Hawaii."

"Right, and probably ended up with a seamstress living in your house as well." Kate scornfully turned back to the mirror. Marissa's regular updates about Kavena, Jane, and Malia annoyed her to the point that Marissa no longer mentioned them. But today Marissa felt mildly defensive.

"The house is really shaping up, thanks to them," she said. "Did you know that we retiled all of the bathroom floors? That's for four and a half bathrooms! It's gorgeous now. Almost makes me wish I didn't have to move."

"Marissa, there are people who do that," Kate said flatly as the headpiece was tucked into her upsweep.

"Yeah, that would be me."

"I meant people who do that for a *living*."

There was no use arguing with Kate. Maybe it was pre-wedding jitters, but it wasn't worth fighting over. Marissa turned back to her own mirror just as the unmistakable sound of silk shantung ripping filled the room.

"Oh, my God," Kate gasped, staring into the mirror at Marissa's open seam.

"Well, better now than during the ceremony," Marissa tried to joke, but Kate just glared.

"Oliver is going to be here in twenty minutes," Kate said. "There's not enough time to get it fixed!"

"Don't worry," Marissa said. "I'm sure we'll figure something out. Add a panel or something. On the bright side, you'll look really good next to me when we're standing up there."

Kate almost smiled, then her face crumpled.

Marissa wanted to kick herself. What was the matter with her? She could have gone on a diet for a couple of weeks—it wouldn't have killed her to make an extra effort for Kate's wedding. "Kate, I'm sorry. I should have lost some weight or told you to go up a size. Or two."

Kate was blinking rapidly, her eyes growing wet. "It's not that," she sniffed. "It's just that I had all these plans about what it would be like when I got married, and you weren't around for any of them."

"I know. I'm sorry. But I'm here now." Marissa gestured for one of the bridal consultants to stop fussing with Marissa's dress and to get a box of tissues. "Don't cry, you're going to mess up your makeup."

Kate fanned her eyes rapidly, looking up at the ceiling. "I mean, I know that you're going through a lot right now with Paul and that damn house . . ."

"It's actually not so bad—" Marissa tried to interject but Kate held up a hand.

"And while I am so mad at him for being such a complete loser, plus the fact that I hate the way he parts his hair, it hit me when I saw you without your ring that you're getting a divorce." Kate burst out crying, tears streaming down her cheeks.

There was no saving Kate's makeup now. "Kate, I think you're a bit emotional with all the wedding plans . . ." The tissues arrived and Marissa handed one to her friend.

Kate shook her head vehemently. "I need to know that two people with issues can stay married! Otherwise Oliver and I don't stand a chance in hell!" She was starting to hiccup. "I don't want to get pregnant and then get divorced ten years down the road!"

Well, neither did she, but what could you do? Marissa took her girlfriend's hands and gave them a squeeze. She swallowed the lump in her throat and said as firmly as she could muster, "You and Oliver are going to have a great marriage." It was a promise Marissa knew had no guarantees, but it was one worthy enough to try.

Kate was about to start blubbering again. "But . . . but . . ."

"I'm in the fifty percent that gets divorced, you'll be in the fifty percent that stays married," Marissa said, her voice thick. She tried to make a joke. "Look at it this way: our divorce will increase your odds of staying together."

Kate managed a smile as she threw her arms around Marissa, still crying. Marissa hugged her back, blinking back her own tears. Kate was right: why couldn't two people with issues stay married?

There was the sound of another seam ripping. The women stepped apart, and Marissa looked down at the two slits that were now running up both sides of her gown.

"You are going to look *so* good next to me," she promised her girlfriend, and they collapsed into each other's arms, crying and laughing.

It had been an exhausting couple of days leading up to the wedding. Marissa definitely felt out of step, craving the lazy days she'd left behind in Hawaii. Of course this wasn't just about being in New York. Weddings were always this way, frenzied and emotional, usually with too many people and too many opinions. For once, Marissa was content to let everybody else argue over where to eat or what to do. It didn't bother her to follow Kate or the group, meeting new people while reconnecting with old friends. Marissa had forgotten the language of New York, and found that her nor-

mal calling card—what she did for a living, where she lived,
where she went to school or where Pansy went to school—
was sparse and outdated.

But she had become somewhat of a celebrity, regarded
with rapt interest when she told people that she now lived
in Hawaii. There were sighs of polite envy before the conversation turned back to the latest restaurant opening or
celebrity spotting.

Desperate for fresh air, Marissa excused herself from the
gaggle of women she had been listening to and quickly
stepped outside. She dialed home.

"Mom!" Pansy sounded delighted to hear from her, and
Marissa instantly missed her daughter even though they had
spoken every day. "We're baking chewy chocolate chip
cookies."

"Vegan!" Kavena shouted from the background. "They're
vegan. We're saving the world one cookie at a time."

Marissa heard a ripple of relaxed laughter and felt envious. "Well, save one for me," she said.

"I will," Pansy promised. "And guess who's . . ."

There was the sound of the phone fumbling, and Marissa
heard a man's voice.

"Hey, Marissa."

It was Paul.

It took Marissa a minute to find her voice. "What . . .
what are you doing there?" she finally managed.

"Just thought I'd stop by and spend some time with my
best girl. Just my luck they were serving lunch, too. Kavena
made sandwiches, Pansy did the potato salad, Jane . . .
What did you make, Jane? Oh, she boiled the water for
the corn. No, no, that's a big job. Somebody had to do
it . . ."

There was laughter in the background. Since he had
moved out, Marissa had never extended an invitation for

Paul to come in beyond the front door. The fact that he was inside—*and having lunch with her housemates; where was the loyalty?*—was very disconcerting.

"The house looks great," he continued. "I can't believe you did all this."

"Well, I had help," she said shortly. She hoped her housemates knew that she was generously sharing the credit. *She* didn't have a problem with loyalty.

"Yeah, they told me about the day you installed the double-pane windows." He chuckled and Marissa heard a faint ripple of laughter in the background, making her scowl. She had been feeling impatient and decided to replace the front windows on her own. It had taken her almost two hours, and then she realized she had installed them upside down.

"So," he said, as if they talked every day. It was clear that he was eating as he talked to her. "How are things with you?"

What was going on? The laughter coming from her home bothered her. Why didn't her housemates kick him out? "What are you doing there, Paul?" she finally asked.

"I dropped Pansy off and then she and Isaiah wanted to play on the tire swings and they needed someone strong and manly to push them." Marissa heard a round of good-natured protests in the background. "Okay, okay. Everyone was busy fixing lunch, so I volunteered to play with the kids outside. Then they invited me to stay for lunch and I was starving so I stayed."

"I don't approve of your using two little kids to finagle your way into my house," she retorted.

"You mean *our* house?" he corrected.

Marissa let out a frustrated sigh. "I have three other women living there, Paul. I don't want them to feel uncomfortable with you there."

There was a peal of laughter in the background, Kavena's distinctive laugh above everyone else's.

"Yeah, they're really concerned," he said mildly. "So, how's New York?"

Marissa thought about hanging up but was surprised to find herself answering his question instead. "Fine. I'd forgotten how busy everyone is. And how tall the buildings are. It seems more crowded than I remember, which is strange. I don't know, maybe it's just me."

"It's not the same anymore, is it?"

Marissa turned the silver Tiffany & Co. bracelet on her wrist that Kate had given her as a matron-of-honor gift. "Some things are. The restaurants are still good, cabbies still yell at you, the city's still awake all hours of the night . . ."

"I wasn't talking about New York, Marissa."

There was a long, awkward pause. "I should probably go," she finally said.

Paul cleared his throat. "Yeah. Well, have a good time and tell Kate congratulations. Hey, what's gluten by the way? It was in the sandwiches."

"I'll let Kavena educate you," Marissa said, knowing that Kavena would launch into a diatribe about "wheat meat." Paul would be lucky to get out of there before midnight.

There was the sound of a large *thud* in the background, and Marissa heard a nervous murmur. "What's going on?" she asked suspiciously.

"What? Nothing. Well, see you when you get back." Paul suddenly seemed to be in a rush to get off the phone.

Marissa started, unsure if that was a statement or a question, but before she could respond Pansy was back on the line, breathless. "Mom, I have to go. Miss you. Wish you were here. Bye." There was a *click*.

Marissa stared at the phone for a moment, wondering what was going on in her house. Kate's cousin, one of the bridesmaids, was gesturing for Marissa to come back inside. With little choice, Marissa tossed her phone into her purse and went back inside to join the festivities.

The noon wedding ceremony went smoothly the next day, with Kate shedding the requisite amount of tears that made everyone sigh and get teary. Marissa felt her eyes water, too. Wild and crazy Kate, who swore to be single forever, was now a happily married woman of five minutes.

It was a welcome relief to finally sit down after having been on her feet all morning, and Marissa was grateful for the plush chairs. She watched as everyone else mixed and mingled, air-kissed one another and raved about the Frick collection. Kate and Oliver made their rounds, greeting everyone and posing for pictures. The waiters started to bring out the food, and Kate found her way back to Marissa at the head table.

"We still need to say hi to everyone seated in the reception hall," she said, her cheeks flushed with exhilaration. "But I have *got* to take a break and get a bite to eat." She nodded toward the front of the room. "They're going to run our slide show during the meal," she said. "It's fantastic! I've only seen parts of it but I swear it's Oscar-worthy."

Plates of Maine lobster salad with rhubarb and daikon were placed in front of them as the lights dimmed slightly. The slide show began; Kate reached over to grasp Marissa's hand, completely taken by the moment. The music cued up and the show began, an MTV-Disney-esque production that took Marissa completely by surprise.

"Why do I think this video cost more than my entire wedding?" Marissa whispered to Kate. Kate giggled and squeezed Marissa's hand.

The first few minutes were dedicated to Kate, highlighting her life, family, and friends. Suddenly Marissa saw herself on the screen, larger than life, at her own wedding where Kate was a stunning bridesmaid. Paul stood next to Marissa, his arm around her waist. They were all laughing. A series of other images followed, no doubt meant to highlight Kate and Marissa's friendship, but Paul was in almost every shot. They were happy images, including some she'd never seen.

Marissa watched, captivated. There was a picture on the Cape, where they had all gone for the Fourth of July one year. It was taken at dusk, the sun having dipped beyond the horizon, and the three of them held sparklers in their hands. Pansy was just a baby, asleep on the blanket next to them. They had stayed up late that night, after the fireworks had ended, nestled in sleeping bags on the beach. Marissa and Paul had zipped theirs together, with Pansy tucked in between them. Marissa felt the warmth of her family as she and Kate talked until the fire was just glowing embers.

Kate was silent next to her. "Marissa, I'm so sorry," she finally whispered. "I just gave my albums to the wedding coordinator. I had no idea which pictures ended up in the slideshow. I should have paid more attention."

"It's fine," Marissa said. "I had almost forgotten about that weekend on the Cape." She gave a small smile. "It's a good memory."

"It's one of my favorites." Kate squeezed her hand again and they turned their attention back to the screen.

As the afternoon wore on, Marissa felt more lonely than she had since Paul had moved out six months ago. She watched her girlfriend dance with her new husband, both aglow. In her heart, she wished them luck. Marissa had never spent much time thinking about marriage—hers or anyone else's—until she was at risk of ending the one she was in. Suddenly it seemed like a precious thing.

All her years with Paul. They hadn't been bad years, just busy years. Too busy, maybe. Too busy to notice the good things. She was guilty of this, she knew. Paul, for example, knew that Marissa liked bagels and cream cheese, but only if her bagel was toasted, a major no-no among New York bagel aficionados. He would fight for her right to have a toasted bagel, even if his request was met with disdain. But Paul was a Midwesterner at heart, not easily intimidated by New Yorkers. Marissa could usually count on getting a bagel just the way she liked it.

In the early years of their courtship and their marriage, Marissa would go to work and always find an e-mail from Paul, even though she had seen him not twenty minutes earlier, wishing her a great day and letting her know how much he missed her. It was sweet at first, but then Marissa got so accustomed to the e-mails that sometimes she would skip reading them altogether. Eventually she told him that he probably had enough to do when he got to work and didn't need to do that, so he stopped. At the time it had been a relief—it had seemed almost like overkill—but now she longed for those e-mails.

He also had an impeccable memory: he never forgot a birthday or holiday. He remembered the date of their first Yankees baseball game; he even remembered what Marissa was wearing (Marissa remembered neither). Marissa, on the other hand, managed to forget their anniversary one year and twice—not once, but twice!—scrambled for a birthday present for Paul from the drugstore on the corner.

But there were other things, too. Like when she was pregnant with Pansy and having a difficult third trimester, uncomfortable and unable to sleep. Paul would come home with an armful of funny movies and a pint of ice cream. He'd give her foot massages and soothe her to sleep. When she had been hurt and disappointed that her mother had little interest in seeing her new granddaughter, it was Paul who found a way to make her smile. Marissa loved Kate like a sister, but in the end it was Paul who had logged the most hours with her.

He had heard it all, seen it all, gone through it all with her. Some of the best moments are saved for friends, but with spouses, it was 24/7 of the good, the bad, and the ugly. And lately there had been a lot of ugly.

And there was Pansy, the bonus. Marissa and Paul had been a good team, the two of them, and then when Pansy came along, they had become a family. It seemed like a lot to be letting go of.

The move to Hawaii hadn't made them separate; it had just brought things to a head. The past few months had revealed things she didn't know about Paul or even about herself, and Marissa didn't know what that meant. More than a decade of familiarity and intimacy suddenly took the backseat as Marissa realized that she didn't recognize the man who was still legally her husband. The difference was insignificant to Pansy—he would always be her father, no matter what. Even if they fought. Even if Pansy chose to stop speaking to him, should she choose to grow into a difficult teenager. None of that would change the fact that Paul was her father. Period.

But a simple piece of paper could suddenly render Marissa single again, her marriage a thing of the past. It was ironic. Pansy was Paul's daughter through a choice Paul and Marissa had made, and that choice could not be undone. But Paul and Marissa had chosen to be together, they had come together of their own free will, and undoing that choice was a matter of a simple signature and a few co-parenting workshops supervised by the Third Circuit Family Court of Hawaii.

There was a chorus of silverware hitting the crystal champagne flutes as Oliver dipped his wife and planted a kiss on her lips. They had a suite at the Ritz, brunch with family in the morning, then a flight to Bali for a three-week honeymoon.

Marissa smiled and laughed as she watched the couple blush and take a bow before they resumed dancing. Suddenly she knew what she needed to do, and she was grateful that she had chosen not to drink.

She needed to keep her wits about her; the night wasn't over yet. Her job here was done, but her daughter and her life were in Hawaii. Marissa didn't feel any remorse as she gathered her things and made her way across the dance floor to give Kate one final hug as she explained that she would be catching the red-eye back to Hawaii that night. There was just enough time to stop by Kate's apartment to get her things, and catch a cab to the airport.

It may have been eight o'clock at night in New York, but in Hawaii the afternoon was just getting started. Marissa had been on standby and the gate attendant had just called her name. Relieved and thrilled, Marissa pulled out her iPhone to make a few calls.

She knew that it was a risk to cancel her meetings with Arthur and the headhunter, but Marissa felt it was necessary. She had been good at what she did, and she was now confident she could find a job if they came back. The trip alone was worth it just to realize that. If she and Pansy were going to be back in New York, Marissa needed to be sure it would be the right move, and ironically that meant leaving New York, *now*.

The next call was answered on the first ring.

"Marissa!" Malia sounded genuinely pleased to hear Marissa's voice. "How's New York?"

Marissa smiled and felt herself relax. "Great. How are you doing?"

"Feeling very pregnant. Tom and I are in Kona, getting some last-minute things for the baby. Do you really think I'll need a diaper pail or can I just throw the diapers in the trash?"

"A diaper pail will be in everybody's best interest," Marissa said, remembering. "Listen, I've moved up my flight and I'm catching the red-eye tonight. Are you able to pick me up at the airport?"

"Sure. What time?"

Marissa gave Malia her flight details. "Thanks, Malia." After a moment's hesitation, she added, "Tell Tom I say hi."

Marissa made one last call to Pansy. No one was home, so she left a message on the machine, telling her that she was on the afternoon United Airlines Kona flight and would see her soon.

As she waited at the gate to board, Marissa looked around at all of the happy honeymooners and tourists, already dressed in anticipation of Hawaii. There was a nervous, excited buzz. Marissa was suddenly struck by the realization that while everyone else was going on vacation, she was going home.

'umikūmākolu | thirteen

The now familiar view of the ropey lava fields put Marissa at ease as her plane came in for a landing. The island was so unassuming, so unpretentious—a wide expanse of land with not much else going on. No skyscrapers, no traffic, no bustle of people with places to go. Just beautiful beaches, majestic mountains, blue water, and blue skies.

She was tired, there was no question about that, but it felt good to be back. She knew there was a smile on her face as she walked through the outdoor terminal toward the gate. The sliding doors parted and Marissa's eyes searched the small crowd for Malia.

Malia wasn't there and, from the looks of things, wouldn't be coming. Instead, there in the bright Hawaiian sunlight stood Tom.

And Paul.

The two men were glaring at each other and hadn't yet noticed Marissa. Paul held a bouquet of flowers while Tom had a flower lei draped over one arm.

Marissa's heart pounded. What were they doing here? Malia must have sent Tom in her place, and perhaps Pansy had let Marissa's flight details slip to Paul. Tom would have his truck, and Paul his BMW. Marissa just wanted to go home, and suddenly that simple desire seemed more complicated than ever.

People pushed past her into the arms of friends and family, others in search of their hotel pickup or tour group leader. Marissa remained there, frozen as she considered her options. At that moment, Paul looked over and spotted her, striding forward and reaching her before Tom could do the same.

"Marissa, hi. Wow, you look . . . great." Paul held out the bouquet of flowers. "I wanted to surprise you, maybe take you out for an early dinner . . ." He gave her a hopeful smile before casting a furtive glance at Tom, who had stepped up next to him.

"Marissa." Tom didn't look at Paul but kept his blue eyes steady on Marissa. "Welcome home. How was your flight?"

"Fine," she finally managed. "Umm . . ."

Tom held the lei toward her. "It's a *haku* lei, a head lei. One of my students has a grandmother who's a famous *kumu hula*, a well-known hula teacher. I asked her to make it for you."

She allowed him to rest the fragrant flower tiara on her head, and saw Paul roll his eyes.

"Let me take your bag," Tom offered, reaching for her carry-on.

"No, I've got it," Paul said, reaching for it as well.

"No, *I've* got it." Marissa held on to the strap firmly and pulled it close to her body.

Both men dropped their arms and stared back at her. Marissa had been dreading this moment, hoping to coast as long as possible before having to make any sort of decision, but it was time to set things straight.

"Look," Marissa said. She slipped the lei off her head and handed it back to Tom. "Tom, I'm sorry. I know I've led you on these past few months. I didn't mean to, but that's no excuse. You know I think you're an amazing man, and you deserve somebody who can give themselves wholly to you. I just can't." The moment she said the words she knew she had spoken the truth.

Tom didn't flinch, but silently accepted the lei. Paul gave him a sympathetic but gleeful look.

Marissa handed the flowers back to Paul. "Paul, I appreciate the gesture, but I'm not sure what to say. And you should know that the divorce paperwork arrived. I need time to figure out what I'm going to do next."

The stricken look on Paul's face told Marissa that he hadn't expected this.

Marissa saw her bags appear on the conveyor belt of the baggage carousel. "Now, if you'll excuse me, I'm going to grab my bags and catch a taxi home."

Marissa stepped out of the cab, glad to be home. Even the sight of the cows grazing in the pasture made her smile, their eyes watching her with bored interest as she paid the taxi driver.

The door of the house flew open. Her housemates, along with Pansy and Isaiah, poured out quickly, closing the door firmly behind them.

Pansy flew into Marissa's arms, giving her mother a tight hug. "I'm so happy you're home!" Marissa hugged Pansy back, loving the feel of her daughter in her arms.

"Welcome home!" Kavena said, catching Marissa in a bear hug. She was dressed in coveralls and had a fine layer of dust in her hair.

Marissa had only been gone for five days, and hadn't

really expected her return to be such a big deal, not that she minded. "Wow, thanks. What's everyone . . ."

"Let's go to Kava Java for some coffee and pie," Jane suggested, dangling her car keys. She was also dressed in coveralls and her hair had slipped out of the ponytail holder. Her face looked dusty.

Malia and Pansy had bright, guilty smiles pasted on their faces. Marissa knew something was up.

That was the trouble with good girls. They couldn't lie worth a damn.

"Okay, what's going on?" Marissa demanded.

Isaiah gave a little whoop. "Boom!" he shouted. Flakes of plaster seemed to be caked in his hair.

"Boom?" Marissa looked beyond him and saw a pile of broken sheetrock at the far end of the driveway. The familiar dated wallpaper lay in strips.

"We thought you would be back on Thursday," Jane said nervously. "My general contractor gave us some great advice on what we could do to improve the floor plan and Kavena and I wanted to surprise you . . ."

"And I'm *really* sorry about sending Tom to the airport," Malia apologized. "He's just been thinking about you a lot and I thought that it would be a nice surprise."

"It was a surprise all right." Marissa glanced at her daughter. "And you told Dad?"

"Actually he was here when we played back the message," Kavena said.

Marissa couldn't believe it. "He was here *again*?"

"He's been here a lot, actually." Kavena wouldn't look her in the eye.

"Great!" Marissa couldn't hide her disgust as she opened the front door and stepped inside. "Next you're going to tell me . . ." She stopped midsentence as she stared at the disaster that was once her living room.

The furniture had been pushed to one side and was draped in plastic. Chunks of plaster and wallpaper were littered over the floor.

"It's not as bad as it looks!" Jane flew in front of her. "We didn't have time to clean up, and then we thought, what was the point? It would just get messy again . . ."

"We're taking out the walls that create the hallway to the guest rooms and getting rid of that extra wall in the living room that separates the other side of the house," Kavena added quickly. "I know it may be hard to visualize now, but you can already see how the light . . ."

"How the light fills up the house," Marissa murmured. Sunlight now filled corners of the house that previously had been blocked by one of the many walls. She looked with admiration at her friends. "It actually feels like . . . a real home."

"No more white elephant?" Kavena asked.

Marissa shook her head. The house finally looked like it fit together. "I can't believe you did all this."

The women glanced at one another awkwardly. "Well, we did have some help . . ."

"Tom?" She could picture him swinging a sledgehammer, the wall crumbling and breaking in two.

Kavena coughed and Malia pretended to study something on the ceiling. It was Pansy's eager face that gave it away.

"You're kidding." Marissa stared at them in disbelief yet somehow not altogether surprised.

"He wanted to help," Jane said. "And we figured that since this was technically his house, we couldn't really say no."

"Plus that sledgehammer's kind of heavy," Kavena added.

Marissa glanced at Pansy, who was beaming, and sighed. It didn't matter. The house *did* look amazing if you could look beyond the debris.

When night came and the house was finally quiet—Pansy and Isaiah asleep in their beds, Malia and Kavena at birthing class, and Jane working at Kava Java until closing—Marissa sat down with a cup of tea and began to look through the stack of mail resting on the dinner table.

The first thing that caught her eye was an issue of *Time* magazine that had been opened and stuck at random in the pile, disguising itself as mail despite the fact that Marissa had cancelled all magazine subscriptions months ago. A smile twisted on Marissa's mouth. The article was entitled "Home (School) Improvement" and there was no doubt as to who had put it there.

Ever since Pansy had first expressed her desire to be homeschooled, Marissa or her housemates would find articles posted on the fridge or quotes from famous homeschooled notables dotting mirrors and doorways. Andrew Carnegie, Thomas Edison, Ben Franklin, C. S. Lewis, Ansel Adams, Claude Monet, Agatha Christie, and no less than nine U.S. presidents and three Supreme Court justices. An oversized poster of tennis champions Venus and Serena Williams, both homeschooled, suddenly appeared on the pantry door one morning. Pansy found a way to casually work the topic into their conversations, stating statistics, SAT scores and Ivy League acceptance rates.

This deluge of information seemed to be working on their housemates, who were coaxing Marissa to at least look into it, but Marissa still wasn't sold. All this information was fine and good, but somebody had to actually teach Pansy, right? And, if she understood it correctly, that somebody would be *her*.

Marissa stood up and crossed the kitchen, adding the article to the box of articles and printouts Pansy had given her, relentless in her efforts to show Marissa the benefits of homeschooling. Marissa would find them in her purse or under her bed pillow, even balled up in her tennis shoes. Pansy would always feign innocence, scratching her head in confusion as to how that might have gotten there. "But," she'd say as Marissa gave her a knowing look, "it probably wouldn't hurt to take a look, right?"

Marissa sat back down and continued to go through her mail. The bills didn't cause the panic they once had. Marissa carefully scanned each one to make sure it was correct. That was another funny thing. In the past, she would skim a bill and then pay it, not really giving it much attention. Now, Marissa tended to look more carefully, even reading the small print, and on more than one occasion, had even caught an error. Not a huge one, but enough to make her look at each bill as thoroughly as she would any due diligence report or client financial statement.

The catalogs went right into the trash. Marissa didn't need the temptation right now. The final piece of mail was a notice from Hawaii Day School, requesting the balance of Marissa's deposit for next year's tuition. The formidable number swam before Marissa's eyes. It was actually less than what they had paid at L'Ecole Jardinière but somehow Marissa found herself musing about what would happen if they didn't spend that money on tuition. And it wasn't just tuition—there were uniforms, books, supplies, field trips, fundraising events that parents were expected to donate to and participate in.

Her eyes glanced at the box on top of the fridge. Not paying tuition meant that Marissa wouldn't be as hard-pressed to come up with so much extra income every month. She knew that public school wasn't a good option for Pansy; in fact, if she was going to be honest she knew that private school wasn't the best option either. In the past, she would have felt despair, but now there was a new option. It held the greatest appeal to her daughter and, in light of their current situation, was starting to grow on Marissa as well.

Marissa pulled down the box of homeschool articles, amazed by the amount of information Pansy had accumulated in such a short time. She poured a fresh cup of tea and, with a sigh, began reading everything that was in front of her.

Malia had taken the kids for hot chocolate at Kava Java while Marissa, Jane, and Kavena donned dual-cartridge respirators and prepared to spray paint the exterior of the house. They had opted to use traditional *paniolo*, or Hawaiian cowboy, colors for the exterior—a pine green with red and white trim. It looked understated yet handsome on the other homes that were painted this way, and Marissa liked the way it looked set against the green pastures behind the house.

Marissa's voice was garbled through the respirator as she complained to Kavena and Jane, who were concentrating on spraying their sections of the exterior in long, even sweeps. "There's just so much information out there. How do I figure out what curriculum to use? What if I screw up? I'll be one of the homeschooling stories you never hear about, the kind that go bad. We'll end up on *Jerry Springer*. Pansy will never get into college."

"Marissa, even if Pansy's homeschooling curriculum consisted of nothing more than watching the National Geographic channel, she'd still be ahead of most kids," Jane said confidently, her voice warbling through the mask. "Don't worry."

"There's got to be some sort of support network out there," Kavena said. She sounded like a breathy Darth Vader. She swung the sprayer, missing a spot. "Shoot. I think my arms are too short for this. I'm better off with the ol' paint brush and roller."

"Just keep your sprayer parallel to your body," Jane advised.

"And testing," Marissa lamented. "*I'm* supposed to administer the tests. And what if I don't understand something? How am I supposed to teach something I don't understand?"

"For the love of—" Kavena turned off her sprayer and pulled off her respirator. She gave Marissa an exasperated look. "You're a consultant, for God's sake! Figure it out!"

"Go visit Kaui's parents," Jane advised, nudging Kavena out of the way as she continued to spray along the side of the house. "No sense in reinventing the wheel if you don't have to."

The house looked remarkably different now that the extra interior walls had been removed. Jane's general contractor had applied for a permit after the fact, much to the displeasure of the county inspector who grudgingly signed off on the work after giving them a sharp reprimand.

"It would have taken months to get approval otherwise," Jane said after he had left. "Besides, it's always easier to ask forgiveness than permission."

"Desperate times call for desperate measures," Kavena had agreed.

Once the paint dried, the final touch would be laying the new carpet and having Jenny and an appraiser come in for a look. The market was still soft, Jenny had warned her, not wanting to get Marissa's hopes up. She needn't have worried. Marissa was nothing but practical these days.

The next time the Nilssons invited Marissa for tea, she decided to accept.

Kaui's father, Josef Nilsson, greeted them at the door. He was fair and had a slight accent. Later Marissa would learn that he had dual citizenship in the United States and Sweden.

"Eventually we want to build a stable so Kaui can house and ride Protheus here, but he's so happy at Tom's that we haven't really made much headway with that project." Kaui's mother, Lauren, was lean and athletic, but had the thoughtful look of an academic. She was giving Marissa a tour of their five-acre property and the girls were getting a good workout, chasing each other and climbing trees.

Lauren watched the girls for a moment, then turned to face Marissa and said earnestly, "Our thanks to you and your husband again for the guest pass to the resort. It was very generous and we've had a lot of fun using it. Kaui loves being able to meet Pansy down there."

"Oh, the feeling's mutual," Marissa said. "The highlight of Pansy's week is being at the resort or at the stables with Kaui."

Lauren waited until the girls were out of earshot before asking Marissa, "Tom seems kind of low lately. Have you noticed?"

Of course she had, but Marissa wasn't about to reveal that she suspected the reason lay with her. "Um, not really, no."

"He's normally in pretty good spirits. I'm a bit worried but I don't want to say anything."

"I bet it has to do with a woman," Josef said, putting his arm around his wife.

"Tom?" Lauren frowned. "I had no idea he was seeing someone. I'd love to see him settled down—he's such a ter-rific guy. And handsome. He deserves someone good." Her face looked thoughtful.

"You're already taken," her husband reminded her firmly.

Lauren gave Marissa a wink. "Yes, I know." She gave her husband a kiss on the cheek.

"Maybe he's got a lot on his mind with the stable expansion," Marissa suggested quickly. Malia had started to stock the sales room, and their inventory was selling out the moment she priced it and put it out on display.

"Maybe." Lauren wasn't convinced but her eyes lit up at the thought of the new store. "I love those lined waterproof jackets, have you seen them? We each got one. They're perfect for Waimea, and of course Kaui loves that it has the stable's logo on it. And I heartily approve of the honor system. It's ingenious. It's good for the kids, too."

"I agree." Marissa had never experienced anything like it before, but there was something thrilling about being trusted to choose your own products and pay without another person watching over you. It actually made you want to come back and buy more so you could experience it again.

Anxious to change the subject, Marissa made a point of glancing appreciatively around the house. "You have a lovely home," she said.

Lauren dismissed the compliment with a wave of the hand. "It's such a hodgepodge of things that Josef and I have picked up over the years. Meaningful to us but probably wouldn't land us in *Architectural Digest* anytime soon."

Maybe not, but Marissa loved the way the home felt both cozy and personable. It seemed to reflect its occupants—intelligent, practical, family-focused. One wall was clearly devoted to Kaui's schooling. A large world map, a poster of algebra equations, and some of Kaui's artwork was neatly taped to the wall. On another wall hung numerous framed photographs of the Nilssons in several different countries.

"Do you travel a lot?" Marissa asked.

"Whenever we can," Lauren said. "Sometimes it's a short trip, a few days at a time. Other times we might take a short leave and travel for a month or two. That's one of the beauties of homeschooling—the opportunity to travel."

"It certainly is nice to have the flexibility," Marissa agreed.

"We like that we can give Kaui a chance to see the world," Josef said. "We actually consider it part of her educational curriculum, to be exposed to other cultures and people."

"Well, I'm not so sure that I've worked that into our . . . curriculum," Marissa said, somewhat nervously. These people were PhDs—of course *they* could homeschool. They were academics at heart; this stuff probably came easily to them.

"Oh, I remember when I first started homeschooling," Lauren said with a laugh. "I'd had several friends who homeschooled their children and Josef and I noticed how great these kids were—not just academically but socially and emotionally. We were convinced it was the thing to do. But I didn't last two weeks."

"Really?" Marissa sat up straighter.

"Kaui didn't want to sit at the table and we would be yelling at each other five minutes into it. Me, arguing with a six-year-old!" Lauren shook her head. "I actually went so far as to call Hawaii Day and beg them to hold a spot for us, even though the school year had begun. But I was too late. Classes were full and there was a wait-list. So I didn't have a choice."

"What did you do?"

"She made a deal with me," Josef said with a smile. "Lauren preferred to go back to work and told me I could take a leave to homeschool Kaui."

"He's much more patient than I am," Lauren explained.

"I told her fine, but it wouldn't be for at least a couple of months because I had to finish up work on a grant we had received. By the time I was ready to request a leave, Lauren and Kaui had found a rhythm and didn't want to give it up."

"I got off the table and onto the floor," Lauren said, her

eyes twinkling at the memory. "I spread out the workbooks and asked Kaui what she wanted to start working on. I was always clear that we would have to cover a certain amount of material every week, but I let her choose the order. Being on the floor was more comfortable for Kaui, too. We worked that way for about a year, sometimes watching educational videos together or playing with math rods or magnetic phonics, then eventually returned to the table. There was a period where we did nothing but games: Clue, Monopoly, Battleship, Scrabble . . ."

"But how did you decide what to teach? There's so much out there, I don't know where to begin."

Lauren nodded. "I was so gung ho when we first started that I spent all this money ordering several different curriculum packages, not sure what would work."

"Which ones worked?" Marissa fumbled in her purse for something to write on.

"None of them. At least not as a complete package. Kaui would like the phonics in one program but hate the math. Or love the math and hate the handwriting exercises. It took a while before I let myself trust Kaui to show me what she liked, how she learned. And, of course, once I figured we finally had a system down, something would change. Every year is different for us. She also takes some classes with other homeschool kids—that also changes for us every year."

Marissa was feeling exhausted already. "I don't know," she said doubtfully. "Pansy's wonderful but I just don't know if I have it in me to homeschool her all day."

"All day?" Josef and Lauren chuckled and Lauren reached over to give Marissa's knee a reassuring pat. "Oh, goodness, no! I'd probably go mad. Working one-on-one with your child goes much faster than in the classroom. We home-school for a couple of hours in the morning and, if we're feeling really ambitious, one more hour in the afternoon. It varies, and we also homeschool year-round so we don't have the pressure of trying to hit certain academic benchmarks in nine months or less. We also have days—weeks, even— where we don't homeschool at all."

"There are lots of different ways to homeschool," Josef added. "We have a list of homeschool families in the community. I'm sure they would be happy to talk to you as well."

"That would be great," Marissa said gratefully. "But—and I hope you don't mind me saying this—it just doesn't seem possible that it's as easy as you're making it seem. Is it?"

"It really is." The Nilssons looked back at her. "You'll be amazed at how simple it really is. Most things are much simpler than we realize."

'umikūmāha | fourteen

"I'm not putting my hair in a bun or wearing a gingham jumper . . ." Marissa started to tell her daughter, but Pansy had thrown her arms around her mother in a grateful hug before she had a chance to finish.

"Mom, thank you, thank you!"

"One semester, Pansy. That's all. We'll try homeschooling for one semester and if it doesn't work, you have to promise me you will not give me a hard time and go back to Hawaii Day School or L'Ecole Jardinière, wherever we end up."

"I promise, I promise." Pansy released her mother and, in a show of good faith, headed to the bedroom even though it was Friday night. "I'm going to get online. The Dome Cam in Chile is going to be up soon and Kaui's astronomy group thinks they may have discovered a comet!"

The women began to clear the table, each of them giving Marissa a supportive smile or thumbs-up.

"Are you going to tell Paul?" Kavena asked once Pansy

was out of earshot. It was her turn to do dishes and she reluctantly tied on an apron.

Marissa shrugged indifferently. "I left a message on his voice mail at work. I don't think he'll care much, one way or another."

"Why is it that you assume that Paul doesn't care?" Jane asked. "In that week that you were gone, the one thing that I learned about Paul is that he *does* care. A lot."

"Yeah, about getting a free meal," Marissa said peevishly. "But not when it comes to other people's feelings. He didn't seem to have a problem leaving us in February, remember?"

"You kicked him out," Kavena reminded her, filling one side of the sink with hot soapy water.

"He already had an apartment, Kavena!"

"Really?" Kavena frowned, looking confused. "I thought you told me that he got the apartment a week or two later."

Marissa paused, trying to remember, then sighed in frustration. Kavena was right: the apartment had happened later, after Marissa had told Paul to move out. But it probably would have happened eventually, wouldn't it? "Well, he knew he wanted a trial separation," she insisted stubbornly. "He initiated this, not me. And now he's had his trial. He got to be a bachelor again, got to date and sleep around . . . I don't know how I could ever take him back." She shook her head.

"Well, Malia did say that Paul doesn't spend time with Angela in the office anymore," Jane ventured.

Malia nodded. "He doesn't, Marissa. And even though they flirted, I never did see them . . . together."

"Well, of course not," Marissa said irritably. The memory from the day in Kona still played fresh in her mind. Her girlfriends weren't in the store, they didn't hear the playful banter, the obvious intimacy. Marissa did. "Look, I'm not saying that Paul is being manipulative, but let's be honest

here. The two of you are on the payroll with Kohala Bay Resort, and you . . ." Marissa looked at Jane, unable to figure
out why Paul would go out of his way to try and win over
Jane. ". . . well, you live with me. All of you do. Being
friends with you is a way to get back at me."

"I really don't think he's trying to get back at you,"
Kavena said. "And I'm not just saying this because I got an
unexpected pay raise last week."

"You did?" Marissa looked at her in surprise.

"I was talking about maybe going out on my own with
the private label idea and I think they got nervous and
thought I was going to take off altogether. The next day,
there was a letter in my box and an extra three hundred dollars in my paycheck."

"Congratulations!" The women crowded around Kavena,
giving her hugs.

Kavena nodded and beamed. "And the irony is, now that
I have a little extra cash, I am going to look into that private label idea you had. Soaps seem like the easiest and
cheapest place to start, and I've already found a company
that has a line of private label skin care products that's actually vegan. I'm going to talk with them next week."
Kavena felt in her pockets and pulled out an envelope,
which she proudly held out to Marissa. "And here. Now
that I'm making more, I can pay my fair share of rent."

Marissa shook her head and pushed it back to Kavena.
"Invest it in your business—you've more than paid your
share."

Kavena pinked with pleasure and embarrassment, the
first time Marissa had ever seen her blush. She tucked the
envelope back into her pocket then straightened up, a determined look on her face. "I think you should give Paul another chance," she said firmly.

"I agree," Jane said, stepping next to Kavena to help with

the dishes. "I don't think he's trying to get back at you. I actually think he's trying to get back *with* you."

Malia let out a small sigh. "As much as I would have liked to see you and Tom together, I have to agree. Paul's been asking about you a lot, really interested in what you're doing and how you're doing. I don't think it's manipulative. I think it's sincere." She gave a yawn. "I have to go to sleep. This baby's been keeping me up nights and I just can't seem to keep my eyes open anymore."

"Your body's gearing up for the big event," Kavena said, nodding. "It'll be any day now."

"Don't say that!" Malia spun around to face her birth coach. "I'm still a good month away from my due date! I'm not ready!"

"You're as ready as you'll ever be," Kavena said calmly.

"No," Malia said, storming off to her room. "I'm really not!" The door slammed closed behind her.

Jane and Marissa looked at the closed door with concern. Kavena wasn't perturbed. "Yep, any day now." She turned her attention back to Marissa. "So if you're not having a change of heart, what's the deal with that paperwork? Are you still planning to go through with it?"

Marissa kept the divorce paperwork in a drawer, not wanting Pansy to see it by accident. The truth was, she didn't like seeing it much, either. Every time she lifted up her pen, the words on the page seemed to blur together. "Yes. No. I don't know. I mean, if what you're saying is true, then why is Paul agreeing to an uncontested divorce? He pretty much told me that he'd go along with whatever I want."

"Maybe because he thinks it's what you want," Jane said. She leaned toward Marissa. "Now I loved my husband more than life itself—you know that, Marissa. But if I didn't tell that man what to do every now and then, I swear I wouldn't have had all the good years that we did."

Marissa knew she was pouting, but she couldn't help it. "I was there for him the first time," she said. "And yet, here we are again. Why is it my responsibility to be the one to keep this marriage together?"

"It's your responsibility to tell Paul what you want," Jane said. "What you *really* want. That thing about men are from Mars and women are from Venus? It's true. Every word of it."

"I disagree. I think a man needs to step up to the plate without having to have a woman prod him," Kavena said, scowling. They knew she was thinking about Isaiah's father. He made Paul look like a saint.

"Oh, Kavena, honey, you're living in a dream world. The only way a man is going to step up to the plate is if you take him by the hand and show him where it is. Even then, you got to line him up, just so." Jane chuckled.

"Well, I don't want to be rushed anymore," Marissa said resolutely. "He's called the shots for the past year; a few more months won't kill him. Anyway, I have someone else on my mind." She stared at Malia's closed door.

"I thought you said it was over with Tom," Jane said disapprovingly.

"It is. Between him and me," Marissa said. "But not between him and Malia." She gave her housemates a knowing look.

"Oh, I can already tell I don't like where this is going," Kavena said, furiously scrubbing a dish as she shook her head.

"No, don't you see? It's perfect. They're good friends, they're compatible, they work well together at the stables. They always have each other's best interest at heart."

"What about the age difference?" Jane asked.

"Come on. Do you really think that matters to either of them? Besides, it's only fifteen years. It's not like he's a lecherous old man robbing the cradle. Oh, I can't believe I didn't see this before. I can't believe *they* haven't seen it before!"

"Maybe there's a reason why," Kavena pointed out. "Like maybe it's a terrible idea."

Marissa couldn't stop grinning. "I have a really good feeling about this, Kavena. Even you can't put me off. And it's not a terrible idea. When Malia's brother died, it sort of froze their relationship in time. They kept things respectful, almost creating a sibling relationship among themselves. He wants a family, she needs a partner . . ."

"You need to have chemistry," Jane said. She wiped down the kitchen table. "It doesn't matter if everything else lines up. No chemistry, no relationship. I don't think either of them is interested in a marriage of convenience."

"This is different," Marissa insisted. "Tom and Malia already have a friendship. They trust each other. They make each other laugh. They help each other out all of the time. Who did she write down as the emergency contact when she preregistered at the hospital?"

"Me," Kavena said stubbornly.

"And?" Marissa already knew, but she wanted to hear Kavena say it.

Kavena's nose wrinkled in irritation. "Fine," she muttered. She glanced at Malia's closed door and lowered her voice. "Look, that girl is finally in a good place. She doesn't think about that loser boyfriend and she's happy about this baby."

"And so is Tom. He built the changing station, after all. And I know for a fact that he's going to set up a small trust for the baby."

Kavena wasn't swayed. "This is a completely harebrained idea."

"Maybe. But it was a harebrained idea that got you a place to live," Marissa said with a confident smile.

"Ooh. Good point." Jane started wiping the counters. "Marissa, I have to say that I think you may be on to something here."

Kavena stared at both of them in disbelief before returning to her dishes. "Holy mother of goddess," she muttered.

"What? No, absolutely not!" Malia was shaking her head, horrified at the thought of dating Tom. She pushed her breakfast away, appetite lost.

Kavena shot Marissa a knowing look and pushed the bowl of granola back at Malia. "Eat up. You need your energy."

Marissa didn't understand why Malia couldn't see it. "But, Malia, it's perfect!"

Malia dug her spoon into the granola. "No. *No way*. He's like a brother, Marissa."

"I know." Marissa reached across the table to catch Malia's hand. "But here's the thing, Malia. *He's not*. And I really think you would be perfect for each other."

Malia shook her head. "It would be too weird. I don't think of him that way. I don't *want* to think of him that way."

Marissa wished Jane was here to back her up. "If you would just give it a try . . ."

"Look, I appreciate your interest in trying to set me up with someone, but I'm fine taking care of this baby on my own. Tom's friendship is really important to me," Malia added. "I'm not going to put that at risk."

"But . . ."

"No," Malia said firmly, pulling back her hand and picking up the bowl of granola. "I don't expect you to understand this, Marissa, but I hope you can respect my wishes. I'm going to finish my breakfast in my room."

After Malia was gone, Kavena said, "Nice job. A few minutes longer, I think you would have induced labor."

"Very funny." Marissa stood up and smoothed her slacks with the air of a woman on a mission. "I'm not giving up yet."

The day was clear and sunny, a perfect day to be fixing the fence behind the house. The women were up early, wanting to finish the job in one day. The cows were keeping their distance, eyeing the women suspiciously as they set the stakes and guide strings along the perimeter of the property, just a couple of inches in front of the old dilapidated post and wire fence. Once the new posts and rails were installed, they'd get rid of the old fence.

Malia and the kids were resting on the porch, dispensing cool drinks and snacks while offering unsolicited feedback. "That post looks crooked," Malia called to Kavena, who was staring at her work critically.

"Don't you need to go into the office and organize your files or something?" Kavena asked.

"Already done." Malia was still working but had trained a temp to cover her when she went into labor.

"You're more than welcome to come down here and do a little work," her birth coach told her. "You're nine months pregnant; not an invalid."

"I'm good, thanks." Malia gave her a gleeful look before reaching for a handful of popcorn.

In the past couple weeks, the sweet, easygoing girl had transformed into a snappier, more sarcastic version of herself. That, and she had become somewhat more argumentative and demanding, suddenly content to let the other women take over her responsibilities in the house.

"Oh, give the pregnant lady a break," Jane said as she braced her fence post with a couple of wooden stakes.

"I agree," Marissa said. She called up to Malia, "Just put your feet up and enjoy the view."

"Yeah, the view of the three of us doing all the work." Kavena tamped the dirt around her post.

Instead, Malia sat straight up, her hand still hovering over the popcorn bowl.

"What's wrong now?" Kavena called out. "Not enough butter on the popcorn?"

"No," Malia said. She looked down between her legs at her chair. "I think something just happened. I think my water just broke." She looked back at the women, a look of panic on her face.

"Okay, okay, you're doing fine. No need to look so worried." Kavena spoke calmly but was ripping off her gloves and tearing toward the house. Marissa and Jane were right behind her.

Malia stood up and the bottom of her dress was wet, a small puddle around her feet. Kavena peered at the puddle and then put her arm around Malia's wide waist.

"The amniotic fluid is clear . . . that's good. Okay, into the house so I can wash up and we'll start timing your contractions."

"But I'm not ready!" Malia doubled over as a contraction overtook her. "Shit!"

It was probably the first time any of the women, much less the kids, had heard Malia swear.

"I'm going to call Paul to come and get Pansy and Isaiah," Marissa said. "And then I'm going to put Malia's hospital bag in the car."

Kavena nodded. "I'll help Malia change into something more comfortable. Jane, if you could make her some miso soup . . ."

"I'm not hungry," Malia moaned.

"You need something in your system to get us through

the next few hours," Kavena said in a firm but soothing voice. "Let's get you changed. Do you want to get in the shower now to calm your nerves or wait until later when the contractions are stronger?"

"I don't want a shower and I don't want any soup!" were the last words Jane and Marissa heard as Kavena led Malia into her bedroom.

"Well," Jane said. She hurried to the sink to wash her hands. "This is going to be interesting. I've never been pregnant but I swear I felt that contraction when she did. She's definitely become . . . emotive."

"First baby," Marissa said, even though she had never been in labor herself. Pansy had been breech and attempts to turn her had failed. Marissa ended up with a scheduled cesarean section. Pansy's birth was enough; Marissa had never felt the pull to have more children. She didn't gaze wistfully at other people's babies or wonder what it would have been like to have had a natural birth. She didn't feel like she had missed anything; she was good.

But now she found herself full of anticipation, her own adrenaline racing, thrilled by the simple act of watching Malia's water break.

As Jane warmed up some miso soup, Marissa went into Malia's bedroom. Her hospital bag was packed and lying next to the crib. Marissa picked it up just as Kavena and Malia emerged from the bathroom.

"Let's get you on the birth ball," Kavena suggested. "That might relax you."

"I'm plenty relaxed!" Malia had changed into loose-fitting sweats and was putting her hair up in a ponytail. She leaned against the wall and heaved a slow breath. "You didn't tell me it would hurt so much!" she said accusingly to Kavena. Her eyes pinched through another contraction.

"It must have escaped me," Kavena said, rolling her eyes

at Marissa. She went to put her hands on Malia's back but the young woman waved her away. After what seemed like forever, her breathing seemed to return to normal.

"Whew. I'm okay now. I think I'm just going to walk around for a bit." She straightened up, appearing normal except for her eyes, which were shiny and bright. "I'll go out on the driveway. Here, Marissa, I can put my own bag in the car. You don't have to do that." She took the bag out of Marissa's hand and went out the side entrance of the house.

"That seemed a bit like the Malia I know," said Marissa, slightly bewildered.

"Ten minutes apart," Kavena said with a sigh. "Expect it to only get weirder. This might take a while."

"What? You're kidding!" Marissa was suddenly nervous. "I know she wanted to labor at home, but maybe we should take her to the hospital right now to get her checked out."

"No, that will just agitate her. At least she's comfortable here." Malia had shared her birth plan with her housemates, explaining that she had an aversion to hospitals ever since her brother had been admitted after his car accident, only to pass away days later from internal injuries. "Her doctor agrees that laboring at home for as long as possible is probably best. Besides, the hospital is only a mile away."

"Well, what should we do in the meantime?"

Kavena peeked out the window where Malia was circling the driveway, her disposition much calmer. "In the meantime we wait. Give her some space. Keep her hydrated."

After circling the driveway a few times, occasionally bending over or squatting to help get through a contraction, Malia returned inside and announced she was hungry. She drank two bowls of the miso soup before she started pacing again, this time inside the house since the weather had turned and it was starting to rain.

The hours passed quickly. It was now late afternoon and Malia had a woman under each arm, propping her up as they slowly walked through the house. Malia's labor pains escalated, so Kavena had bustled her into the shower in an effort to relax her body.

"I think we should think about heading in soon," Kavena called out to the women.

"I'll get the car," Jane said. She opened the front door then froze.

"Do you want me to drive?" Marissa asked.

Jane turned to face her. "I don't think anybody's going to be driving," she said. "Look."

Marissa hurried over to the door, where Jane stepped aside to reveal a driveway full of cows.

"What the hell?"

"They must have broken through the fence," Jane said. "Maybe when they saw us leave, they came over to inspect and realized the fence was a joke."

Marissa went to the back of the house and looked out the window, where the old fence was destroyed and the new materials trampled. More cows milled around in the backyard, and two had discovered Kavena's vegetable garden.

"Okay, we're ready . . ." Kavena and Malia emerged, a tense look on Malia's face. "What?"

"We may have a problem," Jane tried to mouth to Kavena, but it was too late. Malia had spotted the cows.

"Oh, God!" she shrieked, gripping Kavena's arm.

"Just go out there and shoo them to the side," Kavena told Marissa briskly. "Get in your car and honk the horn. They'll move out of the way."

That would require Marissa walking through the cows to get to the car, something she wasn't feeling too confident about. "Are you sure?"

"Well, we have to do something because I can now say unequivocally that this baby is on its way!"

"Okay." Marissa took a deep breath and grabbed her purse, then walked toward the driveway, only to turn around and come right back. "I can't. I'm sorry! There's too many of them and they're huge!"

"I'll try," Jane said, only to retreat back to the house seconds later.

"Should I call 911?" Marissa asked. "The hospital's close by—they can probably get here quickly. Then we'd just have to get her through the cows to the street."

"I'm about to have a baby—I am *not* walking through those cows!" Malia doubled over for another contraction.

Kavena looked at her, startled. "Okay, okay. Call 911. In the meantime, let's get you to the bedroom. Jane, grab my midwifery kit."

Heart pounding, Marissa raced for the phone and dialed. The dispatcher took her information and promised they would be there shortly. Marissa hung up, and found herself staring at the emergency phone list taped to the wall. Before she could give it another thought, she picked up the phone again and dialed Tom's number.

"Hello?"

"Tom, it's Marissa. We're at home and Malia's in labor and cows are blocking the driveway . . ."

"I'll be right there." He hung up before Marissa could say thank you.

"An ambulance is on the way," Marissa said. Malia was leaning on the side of the bed and Jane was stacking towels and bed sheets nearby.

"I am not going to go in an ambulance to the hospital!" Malia was bellowing.

"I also called Tom," Marissa added.

Malia's face crumpled in relief and gratitude, and then she was hit by another contraction.

"Enough talking," Kavena said sharply. She had gloves on and was feeling for the baby. "Malia, are you ready?"

"What, is she going to have the baby *now*?" Marissa felt herself panic.

"Possibly." Kavena didn't seem fazed. "Jane, she's having back labor—can you put some pressure on her back, right there?"

Malia was moaning now, and Marissa watched, helpless, as Kavena eased her to the bed. "Marissa, I need you over here," Kavena snapped. "Jane, you, too."

Malia was panting now, and Marissa saw a tuft of black hair as the baby's head emerged.

"Oh, my God," Marissa said, enthralled.

Jane had tears in her eyes. "Oh, my God," she echoed.

Tom rushed into the room, hat in hand. "I moved the cows. The EMTs are right behind me." He realized what was happening and turned away a second too late. "I'll wait outside."

"No!" Malia held an outstretched arm toward him and Kavena motioned for him to get by her side.

"Take a break and then one more push," Kavena said.

Malia gave a final push and the baby slipped out. Kavena caught the baby and did a quick sweep of the inside of its mouth with her finger. The baby let out a cry and its body started to pink and take on a rosy glow.

"You have a girl," she said proudly, bundling up the newborn. "I'd say she's a good eight, nine pounds. You did a wonderful job just now, honey." Kavena smiled as she gently handed the bundle to Malia.

"A girl." Malia gazed in wonder at her daughter. The pain and distress were suddenly gone.

"She's beautiful," Tom said, equally in awe.

Kavena expertly clamped and cut the umbilical cord. Marissa helped cover Malia and the baby with a warm blanket just as the EMTs rushed in with a stretcher.

"Out," Kavena instructed, pointing.

"Isn't she in labor? Don't you want us to take her to the hospital?" one of the men asked.

"She already had the baby," Kavena said, pointing to the little bundle in Malia's arms. "We're waiting for the placenta now. Once she delivers the placenta, we'll let her rest and then take her in."

The EMTs frowned. Kavena snapped off her gloves and put her hands on her hips. "Have either of you delivered a placenta before?"

The EMTs were young. "No," they admitted.

"Then thank you for coming and please leave."

"But . . ."

"Out." Kavena pointed to the door again, unyielding.

"You're good," Marissa said admiringly. "Scary, but good."

"I've delivered a few babies in my time," Kavena said. "Although I have to admit it's been a while. Still, it's not something you forget. Those bozos, on the other hand . . ." She jerked an exasperated thumb after the EMTs, making both Marissa and Jane grin.

"I'm naming her Kaili," Malia said softly, oblivious to Kavena's short exchange with the EMTs.

Marissa saw that Tom's eyes grew wet. "After Kai," he said. Kai was Malia's brother.

Malia nodded. "She looks like him."

"And like you." Tom gave her a smile and wiped Malia's sweaty forehead with his handkerchief.

Marissa and Jane slipped away, both physically and emotionally exhausted. "How come she's not as tired as us?" Jane asked. "She's been at it for hours."

"Hormones," Marissa said with a smile.

Jane poured them both a tall glass of iced tea. "That was something else, wasn't it? My hands are shaking. I've never seen a live birth before."

"When I had Pansy, it was a C-section," Marissa said. "It looked really different from, well, where I was standing."

Kavena came into the kitchen holding Marissa's salad bowl. "Nice job, ladies," she said. She cast a sidelong glance to Marissa and sighed. "And maybe your harebrained idea wasn't so harebrained after all."

"Which one? Oh . . ." Her voice trailed off as Kavena nodded to the bedroom. She smiled. "I told you so."

"Fine. You were right." Kavena efficiently lifted the placenta from the salad bowl and into a large Tupperware. She snapped on the lid and put it in the freezer.

Startled, Marissa said, "Um, excuse me, but the garbage can is *that* way . . ."

Kavena took off her gloves and washed her hands, a serene smile on her face. "Your house is now blessed, Marissa. Malia wants to bury the placenta later, so we're saving it until she knows what she wants to do with it. Some people place it near the entrance of their home, or plant a tree on top of it."

"That's a lovely gesture," Jane murmured.

"It is," Marissa agreed, reaching for the phone. She wanted to call Paul and Pansy and tell them the good news. "Tell Malia she can keep the salad bowl, too."

'umikūmālima | fifteen

September was a flurry of activity for many families with school-aged children, but not for Marissa and Pansy. Marissa didn't feel confident enough to adopt the Nilsson's more laid-back approach to homeschooling, so she chose a curriculum that included Stanford University's Education Program for Gifted Youth, which would let Pansy receive some computer-based distance learning instruction in addition to some other grade-level workbooks recommended by Kaui's mother. Pansy would continue to help at Pualani Stables, where her internship included helping Malia manage the inventory for the growing business.

"My right-hand girl," Malia said affectionately of Pansy. Malia and Tom were dating now, and the women had secretly placed bets at how long they thought it would take for Malia and Kaili to move in with Tom.

On the house front, Marissa was delighted to discover that the broken fence had been fixed the day after Kaili's birth. Tom had contacted the ranch that owned the cows and told them that their livestock had broken through the fence and wandered onto private property. Marissa had assumed that the fence was her responsibility, but it wasn't—it ran along the property line for the pasture.

Grateful that no one was hurt and that no other damage had occurred, the owner had quickly dispensed six men to repair the fence, taking Tom's suggestion that they reimburse Marissa for the trampled materials *and* build a fence using the same materials Marissa had purchased. In the end, Marissa got a fence that complemented her house and yard—but was not her responsibility to maintain. And while the cows continued to snore, the sound that once kept Marissa awake now lulled her to sleep.

Marissa was feeling good. For the first time in a long time, everything felt right. Her daughter was happy, her housemates were happy, she was happy.

Sort of. Seeing Tom and Malia together made her envious and she felt a deep desire to be in a relationship with someone she loved and who loved her back. She didn't want Tom—it wasn't about that.

She wanted her husband. She wanted Paul.

But Paul, it seemed, was suddenly preoccupied. There were no more hopeful phone calls, no more requests for dinner or even lunch. The exchanges between them were short, almost curt, when they did the drop-off or pick-up with Pansy. He no longer looked Marissa in the eye, and even seemed to be avoiding her housemates.

"Is Paul all right?" Malia asked worriedly after he had come to pick up Pansy for ice cream. She was still on maternity leave and hadn't seen him since Kaili's birth almost three weeks ago. "He doesn't look good."

"I know," Marissa said. Paul looked pale, as if he had given up going to the beach or pool. There were also dark circles under his eyes. For the first time in a long time, Marissa was concerned for him.

When Paul returned to drop Pansy off, Marissa let her daughter into the house before stepping onto the porch and closing the door behind her. "Paul, let's go for a walk."

Paul glanced at his car. "I should really be getting back," he said.

"It'll take a minute. Did you see the fence out back yet?"

Paul shook his head, so Marissa led him down the path that circled the house, telling him the story of how it got fixed. When they reached the backyard, the sun was setting, casting hues of orange and pink into the sky.

"Wow," Paul said as he took in the backyard. "The fence looks great. And there she is, good ol' Mauna Kea. I can see her from my place, of course, but it's not the same. And the house . . . I just can't believe everything you've done. You're amazing, Marissa. I've been meaning to tell you that, but . . ." He was rambling. His voice trailed off.

"Thanks," Marissa said, surprised by the compliment. "It was a lot of work, but it was worth it."

Paul gazed miserably into the pasture. "I know. It's all my fault that we're in this mess in the first place. You've had to rent out rooms, pull Pansy out of school . . ." He looked positively distraught. "I've succeeded in driving everything we've worked so hard for into the ground. Paradise—ha! What was I thinking?"

She didn't know why, but she didn't want to see Paul like this. After months of dreaming about how she could make him suffer, now that he clearly was, Marissa didn't like it one bit. "Paul," she said firmly. "It takes two people to make a marriage. And while you made a pretty good effort to single-handedly unravel everything, you should know that I'm not ready to throw in the towel yet."

A flash of hope crossed Paul's face, then disappeared. "Marissa, there's something you should know."

Marissa felt a sense of dread. "Is it about Angela?" She prayed he would say no.

He looked away. "Yes."

"Are you still seeing her?"

Paul stared at her, dumbstruck. "What? No. I told you, I was never seeing her."

Marissa shook her head, adamant. She needed to get this straight, needed to know for sure. "Paul, come on. I saw you one time in Kona, at the grocery store. Angela was with her son and you were going to cook them dinner." The memory of their banter made her flinch but she continued. "And then there was the time when they came over when you had Pansy for the weekend."

Paul shook his head impatiently. "It wasn't like that. I mean, I can see now how it may have looked, but that's just not how it was. That time in Kona was weird—I bumped into them at the bookstore and she asked if I had plans for dinner. She was with Chris, her son, and it was hard for me to say no. He's a good kid. She was going on about how she wanted to see my place since it's on the beach, so I offered to cook them dinner. The truth is I really didn't like eating alone so the idea of company sounded good. It seemed harmless since she was with her son, you know?"

Marissa gave a noncommittal nod, not sure where this was going.

"The next time they came over you were in Volcano with Pansy's horse guy, which is why she was with me that week-end. Remember?"

Marissa felt her cheeks flush. "Paul, about that . . ."

He held up a hand. "Let me finish. So Pansy and I are hanging out and they drive up. I would have asked them to leave but I have to admit I was still a bit put out that you were in Volcano. I'd met Angela for coffee a few times out of the office and she seemed to be going through something similar with her ex-husband, and she seemed to be a good listener. So when they showed up I invited them to stay. It was strange—we had fun but for some reason it made me start to miss you. I missed us all having dinner together, doing things together. You, me, and Pansy. Even though I knew you were with that horse guy, I made up my mind then and there that I was going to find a way to get us back together." He paused and looked at Marissa, a distraught look on his face.

Confused, Marissa waited.

Paul continued. "So, after dinner the kids watched a movie while we cleaned up in the kitchen, and she tried to kiss me. I was shocked. I told her that I didn't see our friendship in that way, and that I had decided that I wanted to find a way to reconcile with you. Angela stopped talking to me altogether, even started ignoring me in the office. I didn't really care, but it was awkward. It became uncomfortable for everyone. But my focus was on how I could get back together with you, and I wanted to make sure I didn't mess it up this time. I kept waiting for the right opportunity but it never seemed to come up." His voice faltered and he looked way.

Relief washed over her. "But Malia said you took my picture off your desk."

"It broke. I came back from a meeting and it was facedown and the glass had shattered. It took me forever to get it fixed. And then when I did, I didn't know what to do. You wanted to file for divorce. I thought you were with Tom. So I put it on my nightstand at home. I look at it every night."

"You do?" She could feel the tight nugget in her heart that had been so angry, so wounded, so desperate, and so scared these past few months start to dissolve and, in its place, something new started to grow.

Hope.

Paul nodded, still looking miserable. The sun disappeared and the sky had turned a grayish-blue, readying for nightfall. Something was still troubling him.

Marissa touched his arm. "What is it, Paul?"

The despair in his voice ripped through her. "Angela has filed a sexual harassment suit against me."

"That's utter bullshit!" Malia was livid, holding a sleeping Kaili in the cloth baby sling Kavena had given her. Marissa had given the Björn sling to her as well, partially in a friendly act of defiance to Kavena, and it turned out to fit Tom perfectly.

"I don't know what we can do," Marissa said, dejected. Paul had left and Marissa had called an emergency meeting after the kids had gone to bed. "Fallon has put him on leave until they've finished investigating the case. He's going to lose his job no matter what happens."

"I don't believe it," Kavena said, shaking her head.

"Neither do I," Jane agreed. "And I'm an excellent judge of character."

"Well, neither do I, believe it or not, but it's out of our hands. I think we all know how something like this is going to go." Marissa slumped forward and put her head in her hands. "I can't bear to think what Pansy's going to go through when she hears about this. I'm actually relieved that she's not at Hawaii Day School so that nobody can give her a hard time if this gets out. Now I can't wait to get this over with and get back to New York."

"How do you prove or disprove something like this?"

Kavena wanted to know. "Don't you need evidence? Wit-nessses? Something?"

"Paul said Angela made up e-mails from him to her that were . . . amorous. And she cites at least twenty-five examples of impropriety or outright harassment. She's saying she's been in fear of losing her job or being passed over for a raise if she didn't succumb to his advances."

"Give me a break!" Malia looked positively rabid. "That was never the case! If anything, it was the other way around!" She shook her head, adjusting Kaili in the sling so she could continue her rant. Pregnancy and birth had definitely brought out a fiery side of Malia. "If there was a sexual harassment suit in the works, I would've known about it. That sort of thing is rarely subtle. But I didn't hear *anything* about this before I left. Trust me, I would be the first to know!"

"You're on maternity leave," Marissa said, dismayed. "Talk about timing, huh?"

Malia froze, then smacked the table with the open side of her hand, making the women jump and Kaili cry. "Oh, my God, that's it! Don't you see?"

The women, still startled, shook their heads.

"*She waited until I was on maternity leave to file the complaint,* because she knew if she did it while I was there, I'd counter immediately and the whole thing would go nowhere." Malia was getting excited as she bounced Kaili back to sleep. "Who'd she file it with? Jackie, her friend in HR. She's backing Angela on this one, I guarantee it."

"Why would she put her career at risk?" Marissa shook her head. "It doesn't make sense."

Malia smiled mischievously. "Not to the naked eye. I'm the vault, remember? I know things that would make your head spin."

"Like *The Exorcist?*" Kavena asked.

Malia picked up her cell phone and began to dial. "Better."

Malia needed a couple of days to get things together, and in the meantime swore the women to secrecy. "You can't even tell Paul," she told Marissa. "We can't risk a run-in with Angela and him spilling the beans."

"I just can't believe how deceptive women can be," Jane complained. "Women like Angela make it hard for the rest of us."

"Stop grumbling," Kavena ordered. "And get back to work." They were assembling small woven *lauhala* baskets filled with soaps, candles, and Kavena's signature essential oils for a corporate meeting the following week.

"I'll be right back," Marissa said, checking her watch. "I told Pansy I'd drop her off at the stables. Can I get anybody anything while I'm out?"

"Drop these off at Kava Java, if you wouldn't mind," Jane said, nodding to a box by the door.

Marissa collected the box and she and Pansy headed to the stables. Tom waved as Marissa drove up. He was wearing Kaili in the Björn as Malia had gone in stealth to the resort for the morning.

"She's sleeping," he said, nodding toward Kaili. "Something about being outdoors and near the horses seems to put her to sleep."

"Well, she looks very cozy and happy," Marissa said. "As do you."

He kissed the top of Kaili's head. "I am. And what about you?"

Marissa took a deep breath and smiled. "I think I'm getting there, too."

*   *   *

"Great, I was wondering where those were." The assistant manager of Kava Java accepted the box from Marissa. "Do you mind delivering a fax to her? It just came in. Hold on— I'll get it for you."

Marissa helped herself to a free sample of macadamia nut chocolate shortbread, and took a moment to look around the coffeehouse. It was always crowded with regulars and tourists, but despite her success Jane was careful not to grow too fast. "I don't want to bite off more than I can chew," she liked to say.

The familiar cluster of PTA moms and strollers were gathered around the fireplace, and Marissa noted that a number of customers had their laptops out, taking advantage of Kava Java's wireless Internet. But it was a woman with fiery red hair that caught Marissa's attention. She was typing efficiently on her laptop, pausing to take a sip of her coffee before going back to what she was doing. She was casually dressed in jeans and a low-cut V-neck sweater. Her hair was down and she wore silver hoops in her ears. A smug smile was on her face. Sensing that somebody was watching her, Angela looked up and darkened when she saw Marissa cross the room toward her.

Every voice inside Marissa's head was telling her to turn and leave, but she couldn't. Paul's job was at risk. Even though Marissa knew that she couldn't trust anything Angela said, she had to know, had to ask.

Angela's mouth twisted into a smirk as Marissa neared. *You manipulative skank!* was what she wanted to say, but instead Marissa simply asked, "Why?"

The question seemed to catch Angela off guard, but she quickly regained her composure and looked Marissa defiantly in the eye, closing the lid of her laptop with a snap. "Why what?"

"Why did you go through all the trouble to be nice to me if you were going to go after my husband?" Marissa kept her voice low, not interested in making a scene and yet, at the same time, needing to know. "At the holiday party? I *liked* you!"

Angela pursed her lips. "I didn't go after him," she retorted. "He went after me. That's why I had to file a sexual harassment claim. I'm taking a couple of vacation days because I'm suffering from post-traumatic stress disorder."

Marissa struggled to keep her cool. "Are you kidding? Nobody's going to believe that!"

"Really? Well I have e-mails dating back to December that prove otherwise."

Marissa crossed her arms. She knew she should keep her mouth shut but she couldn't. "Why do I have a feeling that they're fake?"

"I don't know." Angela looked back at her innocently. "HR has known about this for some time. Are you saying that I'm making this up?"

"Gosh, let me think . . . Yes."

Angela started to gather her things. "I don't have to take this. I'm going to file this meeting under the sexual harassment claim as well."

"Be my guest." Marissa glanced at Angela's bare ring finger as she slipped her laptop into its case. "You're no longer wearing your wedding ring, I see."

"My divorce was final in January," Angela said shortly. "Turned out the details came together all at once, and then it was over." Her chin lifted defiantly but Marissa saw the shadow cross her face.

"Oh. I'm sorry." Marissa didn't know why she said that, but she did.

Angela seemed to soften for a moment but then she

straightened up and glared at Marissa. "Look, I'm sorry if this is getting personal for you, but that's just the way it is." Her attitude was flippant.

"You're damn right this is personal for me," Marissa retorted. "You're playing the revenge card."

"And why would I do that?" Angela smirked. "Why would I need to do that?"

"Because my husband decided that he wanted to stay married. To *me*."

Angela seemed to wince. "You're the one who wanted a divorce," she said accusingly.

"That's right, I did. But that's between me and Paul. You're upset about what didn't happen between you and Paul, and now you're looking for a way to get even." What was her ex-husband's name? Rich. "You can't get back at Rich, but Paul's the next best target."

Angela snorted. "Nice theory. What else?"

"You have your friend in HR helping you out, and you timed it so the heat would happen while Malia was on maternity leave. You're going to lose your job, Angela, for filing a fraudulent sexual harassment claim." Marissa felt a twinge of regret—she knew she'd said too much.

Angela didn't seem to care. "Really? Because last I checked, an individual filing a discrimination or sexual harassment charge is protected from retaliatory action by an employer, even if the claim is factually baseless or even false. Not that mine is." Angela tossed her sleek hair over her shoulders and stood up. "This conversation is over. And for the record, Marissa, since you were the one blazing the trail to Family Court, I guess the thought of Paul being with another woman was enough to make you change your mind." She gave Marissa a haughty look.

Marissa stared at her rival. "And which woman would that be?" she asked mildly. "Since we know it wasn't you?"

Angela swept past her without another word just as Kava Java's assistant manager came up to her, holding out the fax for Jane.

"Here you go," he said. His eyes followed Marissa as she watched Angela's retreating back. "Is she off to another hot date?"

Marissa spun around to look at him. "What did you say?"

He instantly reddened and looked uncomfortable. "Nothing. Is she your friend?"

"Not at all."

"Oh. Whew." He gave Marissa a nervous smile.

"Do you guys have a sexual harassment policy?" Marissa suddenly asked. She knew she could ask Jane when she got home, but she was curious how much the assistant manager knew.

"Yes. No. I actually don't know. Am I in trouble?" He looked alarmed.

"No, no," Marissa assured him. "I was just wondering."

Relieved, he tried to think. "We probably do. There are some posters in the break room. Should I look?"

"No, that's okay." Paradigm must have had one as well, Marissa was sure, but she hadn't known anything about it either. You never knew until you needed it.

"No, she's right," Malia said. "The resort can't fire her just because she filed a false claim. They have to extend absolute protection to individuals who file a charge so they won't fear retaliation if their charge is later determined not to have merit."

"And, of course, now that she knows that we know . . ." Marissa sighed. "I was just so taken aback by seeing her that I spoke before I thought."

"Don't worry," Malia said briskly. "I'm prepared for all

inevitabilities, which is why I didn't tell you more than you needed to know." She grinned as Marissa looked hurt. "Trust me, you'll thank me later. Anyway, as Jane likes to say, it's not over til it's over, and it's far from over."

"What are you going to do?"

"Jackie concludes the HR investigation tomorrow. Angela might be able to get away with filing a false claim, but she won't be able to get away with lying during the investigation."

"So you're going to be there?"

Malia shook her head. "Sexual harassment investigations are confidential and only involve the two parties involved, plus Human Resources. Technically nobody's supposed to know what's going on, but of course everybody does."

"It's amazing that you know all this," Marissa said. "You could easily do Jackie's job."

"I could easily do a lot of people's jobs. But they don't like to hire from within, at least not locally. They'd much rather bring someone in from the mainland."

"That's a shame. You'd be great."

Malia shrugged. "It's the way things are."

Things were looking bleak. "So how are you going to do this?" Marissa asked.

"The purpose of an internal investigation is to protect the best interests of the company. And since I happen to know that this is not the first time a complaint has been filed, I thought it was my duty to bring it to the attention of the head office. The head of HR for Fallon Resort Properties will be here tomorrow." Malia looked pleased with herself. "I got her a nice room and scheduled a massage with our top masseuse. She'll need it after she gets through the pile of previous sexual harassment claims that have been sitting in a drawer somewhere in Jackie's office."

"Previous claims? Angela has filed previous claims

against other men in the office?" Marissa couldn't believe it. "How many bogus claims has she made?"

"Oh, these aren't bogus claims," Malia said with a smile. "These are the real deal. And Angela didn't file them."

Marissa looked at her, not comprehending.

"These were filed *against* Angela."

epilogue

E lei kau, e lei hoʻoilo i ke aloha.

*Love is worn like a wreath through the
summers and the winters.*

 "Anthuriums or orchids?" Paul held up two
bunches of flowers and looked at Marissa ques-
tioningly.

Marissa pointed to the mixed spray of white and purple
dendrobium orchids. "Definitely the orchids. And go for
the largest arrangements."

They were standing inside the nursery at Akatsuka Orchid Gardens in Volcano, the largest tropical florist on the
island. Marissa knew that they had the best orchids, and she
was determined that her housemates get the best, even if it
meant driving two hours to get them. Without them,
Marissa doubted she would have come as far as she had.
She'd probably still be hiding in her closet, eating chocolate
by the boxful, her divorce en route to becoming a reality. No
matter how you looked at it, a selection of the best orchids
was still far cheaper than any therapy Marissa could have
paid for. Marissa had also placed an order to be sent to Kate,
who had her own news.

She was pregnant. With twins.

Marissa had called with the update that she and Paul were back together again, and Kate had surprised her by sounding genuinely happy for them. "Marissa, that's terrific! I'm really happy for you. And I know Pansy must be thrilled."

Marissa had waited for a witty endnote, but there was none, and then Kate broke the news about her unexpected pregnancy.

"We may have been a little overzealous on our honeymoon," Kate admitted. She and Oliver had gone to Bali for three weeks. "The time difference screwed me up and then I was so excited to see everything. We ate, drank, slept, had amazing sex . . . It wasn't until a couple of days later that I realized I had forgotten to take my pill."

Despite having sworn that she would never have children, Kate seemed excited, albeit a little nervous, about becoming a mother. "I don't know what I'm more scared about, getting fat or giving birth," she said. "But Oliver is over the moon and I am, too. Just goes to show that I don't really know what I want."

"Don't I know it," Marissa had agreed.

Now Marissa watched as Paul reached for three bunches and then, on second thought, added two more to their cart.

"Paul, why are you getting more?" Marissa asked.

Paul patted the flowers fondly. "These are for you and Pansy." He gave Marissa a kiss, then reached down to ruffle his daughter's hair.

"Dad," Pansy said, pleasantly embarrassed. She gave him a hug, her arms holding him tight. When she released him, her face was shining with happiness. She gave her parents a broad smile, then ran up the path in front of them.

"Wow, she's not a little girl anymore," Paul said, watching Pansy as she examined the large pink Cattleya orchids. "I think I missed out on more than I realized."

"She's always been her own person," Marissa reminded him. "Even back in New York."

"That's true." Paul smiled, his hand caressing the curve of Marissa's back. It was a small, innocent gesture, but Marissa felt herself warm to his touch, felt herself drawn toward him. She glanced at Paul, wondering if he had noticed, and saw that he was looking at her, too. When he slipped his hand into hers and they laced their fingers together, she felt her heart give a little flutter of joy. They continued to walk down the aisles of the nursery, hand in hand, their eyes on their daughter.

They had decided to make the drive to the nursery after news had come back to them about the findings of the sexual harassment claim. Both Jackie and Angela had been fired. A new HR director would be brought over from one of Fallon's properties in Florida. But that wasn't all: Malia was offered a new position in HR as a training manager, which not only meant more pay but an opportunity to develop an executive career with lots of opportunity for advancement.

Paul had received a formal apology, but not much else. Cases like these were downplayed, which suited him just fine. He wanted things to get back to normal as soon as possible, and that included reuniting with his family.

When Malia had called them with the news, Marissa threw her arms around her husband and felt him put his arms around her. They held each other this way for a long time, long enough for Marissa to know that the only place the divorce paperwork would be going was in the trash.

But she wasn't ready to have him move back home yet. There were her housemates to think of, and Marissa wanted

to make sure she and Paul were ready to move forward together. At this rate, another month or two wouldn't matter,
and she suspected he would be back home sooner, rather
than later.

They had taken a walk around the perimeter of the
property, elated and also immensely grateful, as Paul
promised to do whatever was necessary to make things
right again.

"I know you want to go back to New York," Paul said.
"And I don't blame you. This whole year has been a disaster. And I want Pansy to get a good education. I feel terrible that we've had to pull her out of school. You were right:
giving Pansy a good education is one of the best things we
can do for her."

"Paul—"

He held up his hand, wanting to finish. "I've talked to
Sam, and I told him that the house has depreciated in value
since we purchased it. After all that's happened, he's willing
to transfer us back, at Fallon's expense. They'll try to cover
the difference or might even buy the house from us at our
original sale price." He looked at Marissa, expecting her to
nod in agreement.

Instead, Marissa shook her head. "I don't know, Paul."

"What do you mean?" The earnest look on his face faded.

"The appraiser valued the house *over* our original pur-
chase price. If we were to sell it now, we'd have an eight percent gain. Which means we'll be able to move back to New
York." She shrugged. "If that's what we want." It was starting to rain, and Marissa looked up at the sky.

Paul seemed oblivious of the rain. "What do *you* want,
Marissa?" he asked quietly.

She had her answer ready. "Well, Jane's house will be
ready soon, so she'll move back home. And Malia's going to

move in with Tom." Marissa resisted the urge to reveal the news that Tom was planning to propose. She was under oath not to breathe a word to anyone but knew some of the details, which included a stable full of plumerias and tea lights strung along the rafters. The diamond was remarkable, an Oakes family heirloom. Marissa knew that Malia suspected something and was abuzz with nervous energy, primping a little more than usual, subtly trying to glean whatever information she could from her housemates. Only Marissa knew what was in store for Malia, and she was wisely avoiding the young woman until Tom popped the question, which would happen later tonight.

Paul was waiting, his eyes intent on Marissa.

"And Kavena . . ." Marissa paused to let this sink in. ". . . Kavena is going to stay here with us and continue renting the *ohana* unit."

Paul nodded solemnly. "That all sounds good."

"We'll have the rental income, but more important, it's been a huge help to Kavena to have us as a backup, and vice versa. Also, Isaiah hates preschool so we're going to let him hang with Pansy and me and then decide what to do when he's ready for grade school."

Paul looked like he was about to protest but then nodded. "Okay, I trust you on this." He gave her what she used to call one of his deep, soulful looks, a look that used to annoy her to no end. But now it seemed different. The look wasn't needy or touchy-feely—it was the look of a man who loved and acknowledged the woman standing in front of him.

Marissa continued. "There's another thing, too: I'm glad you understand how important it is for Pansy to get a good education. Which is why I'm going to keep homeschooling." She was starting to get seriously wet and brushed the

water from her arm. *Rain is good luck in Hawaii.* Marissa
smiled to herself.

Paul seemed to be holding his breath. "So what does this
mean? That we're staying?"

Marissa turned to face him. "I want another shot at paradise, Paul." And for the first time in months, she kissed her
husband.

Now, with the car loaded with the orchids, Paul pulled out
of the parking lot and was about to head back toward
Waimea. But he hesitated.

"What?" asked Marissa, looking back. "Did we forget
something?"

"You know, we're just so close to Volcanoes National
Park that it seems like a shame not to go in and take a look.
Pay our respects."

"I did that a few months ago. Even brought an offering.
Nothing happened."

"Really?" Paul gave her a thoughtful glance. "It seems in
my estimation that quite a lot has happened."

Marissa hadn't considered this. "Maybe," she conceded.
"But with my track record, it would be a wasted trip. The
lava isn't flowing aboveground anymore and it's going to be
dark soon."

"It's still pretty amazing," Paul said. "And it's only a few
minutes away."

"Mom, can we go? Please?" Pansy had only seen the volcano from the air, when they had gone up in the helicopter
almost a year ago.

"Fine, sure." Marissa settled back comfortably in the car,
content just to be in the company of her family. The idea of
spending more time together felt good.

She had called her mother in Chile with the news that she

and Paul were back together again and committed to making it work. Her mother had murmured, "That sounds like a very good choice, dear," and continued on about a new art instructor that was visiting from England. She remained placid and unruffled even when Marissa told her that they were thinking about doing a homeschool astronomy trip to visit an observatory in Chile and, if it wasn't too much trouble, her as well.

Paul's parents had been overjoyed by the news and then proceeded to floor them by announcing that they had booked tickets to Hawaii over Christmas. "We want to make sure we catch Pansy over the holiday break," they said.

"Pansy's homeschooled now, so she doesn't keep the same kind of school schedule," Marissa tried to explain for the umpteenth time. "You can come anytime."

"Of course," Paul's mother replied exuberantly. "Homeschooling is wonderful, we hear so many good things about it."

"So right," his father agreed, then asked, "When are you planning to put her back in regular school again?"

Marissa just sighed and didn't say anything. "They'll see it with their own eyes when they get here," Paul whispered in her ear. They would be staying for two weeks in Malia's old room.

Now, instead of taking a right, Paul took a left out of the parking lot and headed toward Volcanoes National Park.

The sun was setting when they pulled up to the guard's booth. "Is it too late for us to go in?" Paul asked. "We can drive around the crater rim before it gets too dark, right?"

"The park is open twenty-four hours a day," the ranger informed them, handing them a map. "But if you drive down the Chain of Craters road, you'll get a surprise. There's an outbreak of new lava coming down the hillside into the ocean."

Marissa couldn't believe it. "Really?" she asked. "Would we be able to see it?"

The ranger smiled. "I think so."

"Oh, let's go!" Pansy was excited. She read the sign in front of them and pointed. "Go straight, Dad. Go straight!"

They drove southwest around the Kilauea Caldera, taking in the smoky basin full of steam vents, the smell of sulphur in the air.

"Wow, it's a clear night," Paul noted, glancing up at the sky. The moon was large and round, a bright disk in a cloudless sky. "It looks like we have a new moon tonight."

Pansy had turned on the interior car light so she could study the park map in detail. "Actually, Dad," she said, not looking up, "it's a full moon. You can't see a new moon. When it's a new moon, the moon isn't visible from earth, because the side of the moon facing us isn't lit by the sun."

"I am really starting to love this homeschool thing," Marissa whispered to Paul as he looked in the rearview mirror in amazement.

They drove down the Chain of Craters road for twenty minutes, silent as they watched the moonlight shimmer off the Pacific Ocean in front of them. It was a comfortable silence, and Marissa relished it. It had taken them a long time to get to this place.

When they reached the bottom, Paul drove to the end of the road and parked the car. "We're here," he announced jubilantly, but Marissa put her fingers to her lips and nodded behind her. Pansy had fallen asleep, a content smile on her face, the map a makeshift blanket covering her.

They slipped quietly out of the car. They would wake Pansy in a little bit, but for now they'd give her a few more minutes of sleep. It was cool, and a small breeze made

Marissa shiver. Paul wrapped his arms around his wife, planting a kiss on her neck. She snuggled against him, sighing happily, and then something caught her eye. She turned to see the first red glow of the lava flow, slowly coursing its way down the mountain and into the ocean, on its way to creating new land.

The Recipes

E ʻai i ka mea i loaʻa.

What you have, eat.

Guava Grilled Steaks with Tasty Asparagus

Serves 2

The meal that gave them a taste of Hawaii and would change their life (and their marriage) forever. Recipes courtesy of Volcano Winery (volcanowinery.com).

Guava Grilled Steaks

4–5 pounds rib eye steak
1 bottle of Hawaiian Guava wine
½ cup minced onion
10 cloves garlic, minced

1. Tenderize the steak using a fork.
2. In a large bowl, place wine, onion, garlic, and steaks. Marinate for at least 3 hours.
3. Place on grill and cook as desired.

Tasty Asparagus

1 bunch fresh asparagus, woody bottoms removed
¼ cup minced onion
4 cloves garlic, minced
1 teaspoon sesame seeds
1 pinch dried basil
1 pinch dried thyme

1. Boil asparagus in 1 inch of salted water in a wide skillet for 3 to 5 minutes. Immediately rinse under cool water to stop the cooking and preserve the bright green color.
2. Remove any remaining water from skillet. Add seasonings.
3. Simmer on low for 15 minutes. Serve immediately.

STORING FRESH ASPARAGUS

Stand the spears in a sturdy glass or jar, in a mixture of water and dry white wine, which will enhance the flavor of the asparagus. Store in the refrigerator up to 2 days before using.

WARM CHOCOLATE LAVA CAKE
Serves 6

Chocolate doesn't get any better than this, and the name of this delectable dessert heralds what's to come. Recipe courtesy of Chef Keoni Chang, Foodland Super Market, Ltd.

> *5 ounces bittersweet (not unsweetened) or semisweet chocolate, chopped*
> *10 tablespoons unsalted butter (about 1¼ sticks)*
> *3 large eggs*
> *3 large egg yolks*
> *1½ cups powdered sugar*
> *½ cup all-purpose flour*

1. Preheat oven to 450° F. Butter six ¾-cup soufflé dishes or custard cups.
2. Stir chocolate and butter in heavy medium saucepan over low heat until melted. Cool slightly.
3. Whisk eggs and egg yolks in large bowl to blend. Whisk in sugar, then chocolate mixture and flour.
4. Pour batter into dishes, dividing equally. (This recipe can be made one day ahead. Just cover and refrigerate.)
5. Bake cakes until sides are set but center remains soft and runny, about 11 minutes (14 minutes for batter that was refrigerated). Run a small knife around the cakes to loosen.
6. Immediately turn cakes out onto plates. Serve with ice cream and fresh raspberries.

HAWAIIAN-STYLE CRISPY DUMPLINGS WITH GINGER-CHILI SAUCE

Makes 25

Marissa and Pansy are poolside and going *kau kau*—eating and snacking Hawaiian style. It's almost winter and yet the temperature is a balmy 86 degrees: even Marissa has to admit that living in Hawaii might be a pretty sweet deal. Will these flavors of the Pacific get Marissa in the mood to say yes to the move? Recipe courtesy of Chef Mark Vann, Huli Sue's Barbecue and Grill (hulisues.com).

Crispy Dumplings

25 round wonton wrappers
½ pound ground pork
½ teaspoon minced ginger
1 clove garlic, minced
½ tablespoon thinly sliced green onions (about 1 stalk)
2 tablespoons sesame oil
1 ¼ cups finely shredded Chinese cabbage
1 ½ cups oil, for frying

1. Combine all ingredients (except for wonton wrappers and oil) in a large bowl and stir until well mixed.
2. Place 1 heaping teaspoon of pork filling mixture into each wonton wrapper.
3. Moisten edges with water and fold edges over to form a half-moon shape. Roll edges slightly to seal in filling. Set

dumplings aside on a lightly floured surface until ready to cook.

4. Set a 12-inch wok or 10-inch skillet over high heat and pour enough frying oil to cover the wontons. Heat the oil to 375° F and deep-fry the wontons, no more than 10 at a time, for about 2 minutes or until crisp and golden.
5. Transfer to paper towels and drain excess oil.
6. Serve with Ginger-Chili Sauce (see below).

Ginger-Chili Sauce

1 ½ tablespoons chili sambal
2 ½ teaspoons soy sauce
2 ½ tablespoons sushi vinegar
4 garlic cloves, minced (about 1 ½ tablespoons)
3 slices ginger, minced (about 3 teaspoons)
1 ½ teaspoons sesame oil

1. Mix all ingredients together and reserve.

LEMONGRASS, MINT, AND GINGER ICED TEA

Serves 4

There's iced tea and then there's lemongrass, mint, and ginger iced tea . . . there's really no comparison! This refreshing beverage helps keep Marissa cool when she's feeling a little steamed about the resort's sexy executive secretary and (unbeknownst to her at the time) her future friend and housemate, Malia Fox.

1 stalk fresh lemongrass
¼ cup sugar
8 thin slices fresh ginger
4 rounded teaspoons loose green tea (or 5 single-serve green tea bags)
4 mint sprigs

1. Cut lemongrass into 2-inch lengths, then crush with the flat side of a large knife.
2. In a 2-quart pan, bring 4 cups water, sugar, ginger, and lemongrass to a boil. Remove from heat and add tea leaves; let steep about 4 minutes or until desired flavor and color are achieved. Let cool, about 30 minutes.
3. Pour through a fine strainer into a glass pitcher. Cover and chill until cold, at least 2 hours. Pour into tall glasses filled with ice and garnish with a sprig of mint.

TIP

Opt for glass as opposed to plastic or metal containers, which often impart flavors that interfere with the taste of the tea.

MARISSA'S "WINGING-IT" CHICKEN WITH SPINACH AND MACADAMIA NUT PESTO

Serves 4

So she's not much of a cook, but you can't blame a girl for trying. This is one dish that Marissa was able to perfect, adapting what was available and making it work. Of course, don't be so preoccupied leaving the store that you hit another car, even if it ends up getting you a free cup of coffee and a new best friend.

2 boneless chicken breasts, split
2 cups lightly packed baby spinach leaves (about 2 ounces)
½ cup macadamia nuts, lightly toasted and coarsely chopped
2 tablespoons lemon juice
1 teaspoon grated lemon peel
⅓ cup plus 2 teaspoons extra-virgin olive oil
⅓ cup freshly grated Parmesan cheese
salt and freshly ground black pepper to taste

1. Heat a grill or lightly oiled grill pan on medium-high heat. Sprinkle the chicken with salt and pepper. Grill the chicken until cooked through, about 5 minutes per side.
2. Combine the spinach, macadamia nuts, lemon juice, and lemon peel in a food processor, pulsing lightly. Slowly add the oil, blending until the mixture is creamy. Add salt and continue to pulse.
3. You will only need half of the pesto for this recipe. Put

the other half into ice cube trays and store in the freezer for future use.

4. Transfer the rest of the pesto to a medium bowl. Stir in the cheese. Season with salt and pepper, to taste.

5. Spread the pesto over each piece of chicken and serve.

WOK-CHARRED AHI

Serves 2

Ah, the memories. Valentine's Day is usually one of those holidays you don't forget, and in Marissa's case, there's no question about that—this one is definitely unforgettable. Recipe courtesy of Chef Peter Merriman, Merriman's Restaurants (merrimans-hawaii.com).

Wok-Charred Ahi

2 (6–8 ounces each) ahi tuna steaks (¾-inch thick)

For the marinade

½ cup vegetable oil
2 teaspoons chopped shallots
2 teaspoons grated fresh ginger
2 teaspoons crushed garlic
1 teaspoon dried thyme
1 teaspoon dried marjoram
2 teaspoons crushed dried chilies
½ teaspoon cayenne pepper
½ teaspoon salt
juice from ½ lemon

1. Mix all marinade ingredients together.
2. Dip the tuna steaks in marinade, and sear in a hot wok or hot skillet for 30 seconds per side. Slice and serve with Dipping Sauce and Slaw (see below).

Dipping Sauce for Wok-Charred Ahi

2 tablespoons wasabi powder
2 tablespoons water
1 cup soy sauce
⅓ cup fresh lemon juice
⅓ cup mirin (Japanese sweet cooking wine)

Make a thick paste with the water and wasabi powder. Add the soy sauce, lemon juice, and mirin. Mix well and reserve.

Slaw for Wok-Charred Ahi

1½ cups thinly sliced Chinese cabbage
½ cup mung bean sprouts
½ cup thinly sliced Bermuda onion
¼ cup chopped cilantro

Mix all ingredients together. Chill until ready to serve. Divide into portions. Top with seared, sliced ahi.

KAVA JAVA'S KONA MOCHA MAC NUT BISCOTTI

Makes 2 dozen

Random acts of kindness, like a freshly baked biscotti tucked next to her cup of coffee, soothed Marissa when she thought her life was falling apart. This Kava Java favorite keeps Jane busy, but it doesn't feel like work if you're doing something you love. Eat it plain or dip it into your coffee. Recipe courtesy of Debbie Davis, Kamuela Coffee N' Cones.

1 package chocolate cake mix
½ cup whole wheat flour
¼ cup instant Kona espresso powder
2 eggs
½ cup butter, melted
½ cup macadamia nuts, coarsely chopped

1. Preheat oven to 350° F. Cut parchment paper to fit a large cookie sheet.
2. In a large bowl, blend dry ingredients for biscotti. Add eggs and blend just to mix.
3. Add melted butter to biscotti mixture. Blend until thoroughly mixed.
4. Add the macadamia nuts. Continue to blend until thoroughly mixed.
5. Using your hands, shape the dough into a log and lay it on the parchment paper. Roll it out to approximately 5-inch wide and ½-inch thick.
6. Shape into a rectangle.
7. Bake for 25 minutes.

8. Remove pan from oven and cool for 20 minutes.
9. Cut biscotti into even horizontal strips, approximately 1-inch wide. Lay each biscotti on its side on the cookie sheet, leaving space between each one.
10. Bake at 350° F for another 10 minutes, then lower the oven heat to 200° F and continue baking for another 40 minutes. Cool on wire rack, then glaze (recipe follows).

Glaze

½ cup powdered confectioners' sugar
2 tablespoons Kona coffee, cooled

1. Mix confectioners' sugar with 1 tablespoon of cooled Kona coffee. Stir until consistency is a little thicker than maple syrup, adding the remaining coffee as necessary.
2. Place glaze in a plastic sandwich bag and squeeze the glaze to one end. Cut off the tip of the corner of the bag.
3. Glaze top of biscotti in a zigzag pattern. Let the glaze cool completely before serving. Store any remaining glazed biscotti in an airtight container.

COFFEE PICK-ME-UP

Freeze leftover coffee in ice cube trays. Once frozen, place cubes into a freezer bag until needed. The frozen cubes make great iced coffee when you want a refreshing pick-me-up drink. Just fill your glass with the coffee cubes, add some hot coffee, and enjoy!

JANE'S TROPICAL MEDLEY MUFFIN
Makes 12

Visitors and *kama'aina* alike love the fresh tropical taste that can be found in these muffins. Each bite is bursting with flavor, and tastes great at any time of the day.

> 2 *cups flour*
> 1 *cup sugar*
> 1 *tablespoon baking powder*
> 1 *teaspoon salt*
> ¼ *cup butter*
> ½ *cup milk*
> ¼ *cup oil*
> ¼ *cup crushed pineapple, drained well (reserve ¼ cup of pineapple juice)*
> 2 *eggs*
> 1 *teaspoon vanilla extract*
> ½ *cup flaked coconut, toasted*
> ¼ *cup dried tropical fruit (opt for a brand that keeps the dried fruit moist and juicy)*
> 1 *tablespoon fresh orange rind*
> ⅛ *cup crystallized ginger, chopped (optional)*

Topping

> ½ *cup flaked coconut, untoasted*
> 2 *tablespoons flour*
> ½ *cup macadamia nuts, chopped*
> 2 *tablespoons butter*

1. Heat oven to 350° F.
2. In a large bowl, combine flour, sugar, baking powder, and salt. In a small bowl, melt butter in microwave. Add milk, oil, pineapple juice, eggs, and vanilla. Stir into flour mixture just until moistened—do not overmix. Fold in the toasted coconut, pineapple, dried fruit, orange rind, and ginger.
3. In a small bowl, combine topping ingredients.
4. Fill 12 nonstick muffin pans ⅔ full. Sprinkle topping over unbaked muffins.
5. Bake for 25 to 30 minutes; cool in pan on a wire rack.

MALIA'S PREGNANCY GINGER TEA
Serves 2

Malia battles her morning sickness with the help of Kavena's special ginger tea. Malia can pour it into a thermos and let it sit all day, adding hot water when needed. She adds a touch of honey for sweetness, and sometimes a slice of lemon if she's really feeling adventurous. You don't have to be pregnant to enjoy it: it takes the edge off a cold day while strengthening the immune system. It's also helpful for motion sickness.

½ cup fresh ginger root, peeled and thinly sliced
3 cups water
honey (optional)
lemon (optional)

1. In a small saucepan, combine the ginger root and water.
2. Bring to a boil and simmer for 15 minutes. Simmer to desired strength.
3. Strain and add honey and lemon to taste.

SPAMBALAYA

Serves 6

It wasn't one of Marissa's finer moments, lurking behind a Spam display at the grocery store while spying on her husband. But what she saw was so upsetting that it wasn't until she got home before she realized she had more Spam than she knew what to do with. Fortunately, Malia found a way to get food on the table for everyone. Serve this with fresh green beans or a salad for a complete meal. Recipe courtesy of Hormel Foods (Spam.com).

¾ cup chopped onion
1 clove garlic, chopped
2 tablespoons butter or margarine
1 28-ounce can crushed tomatoes
1 13¾-ounce can chicken broth
1 cup water
1 teaspoon chili powder
½ teaspoon thyme
½ teaspoon salt
½ teaspoon sugar
1 bay leaf
1 cup long-grain rice
1 (12-ounce) SPAM® Classic can, cubed
½ pound cooked shrimp, shelled, and deveined
1 large green pepper, seeded, and cut into thin rings
¼ cup pitted black olives, halved

1. In a large pot, sauté onion and garlic in butter until tender, about 3 minutes.
2. Add tomatoes, broth, water, chili powder, thyme, salt, sugar, and bay leaf and bring to a boil.

3. Stir in rice and Spam cubes, then cover and reduce heat. Simmer for 15 minutes or until rice is tender.
4. Add shrimp, peppers, and olives. Cover and simmer for 5 more minutes.
5. Remove bay leaf before serving.

KAVENA'S VEGAN MACADAMIA NUT BARS

Makes 2 dozen

Who says vegan can't taste good? Kavena makes these delicious energy bars for her and Isaiah, but Malia eats through most of her supply. Fortunately, this is an easy recipe to double, even triple, so Kavena always has plenty on hand . . .

1 cup flour
½ teaspoon salt
½ teaspoon baking powder
¼ cup margarine or vegan butter substitute (you can also use ⅕ cup canola oil)
½ cup brown sugar or vegan sugar substitute
1 teaspoon vanilla
egg substitute equivalent to one egg
1 cup macadamia nuts, chopped
½ cup dried fruits (dates, raisins, cranberries, coconut), chopped

1. Preheat oven to 350° F.
2. Sift flour, salt, and baking powder together.
3. Cream butter and brown sugar together. Add vanilla and egg substitute.
4. Beat well. Stir in flour mixture, macadamia nuts, and dried fruits (if using coconut, reserve some for topping).
5. Spread mixture in greased 9 x 4½-inch pan. Sprinkle with remaining coconut if desired.
6. Bake 25 to 30 minutes. Cool completely before cutting into rectangles or squares.

COCONUT CREAM OF CELERY SOUP
Serves 4

Marissa's not sure if it's the crackling fire or Tom's steady gaze that keeps things hot on that rainy day in Volcano. The hearty soup helps her keep her head straight and her heart focused. Recipe courtesy of Chef Albert Jeyte, Kilauea Lodge (kilauealodge.com).

10 cups chicken broth
3 pounds celery stalk, cubed
2 pounds Russet potatoes, peeled and cubed
17 ounces of milk
½ cup heavy cream
½ cup coconut syrup
1½ teaspoons celery salt
1 teaspoon white pepper
8 ounces unsalted butter
parsley, finely chopped (for garnish)

1. Add chicken stock to a 4-quart pot. Bring to a boil.
2. Purée celery and potato in food processor until very fine. Add purée into boiling chicken broth and beat with a whisk for 2 minutes.
3. Add milk, heavy cream, and coconut syrup. Stir.
4. Bring to a fast boil, then reduce the heat to low and let simmer.
5. Add celery salt and white pepper. Stir.
6. Cover the pot and continue to simmer for 40 minutes. Stir frequently.
7. Remove pot from heat. With a 2-ounce ladle, force liq-

uid through a fine sieve into 4 bowls. Discard the heavy purée in sieve.

8. Cut the butter into ½-inch cubes and add to soup bowls. Stir with a small whisk until butter has dissolved.

9. Sprinkle parsley for garnish and serve.

KAVENA'S FOREST GREEN GODDESS DRESSING

Yields 1½ cups

Paul certainly knows when to crash a meal—right before it's being served! He stumbles onto this homemade fare at the house while Marissa is in New York and finds a way to win over Marissa's housemates. This dressing has a fresh, clean flavor and tastes great as a dressing on salads or as a dip or sandwich spread. Recipe courtesy of Ira Ono, Volcano Garden Arts Café (volcanogardenarts.com).

¼ cup raw tahini
¼ cup lemon juice
¼ cup canola oil
¼ cup chopped green onion (bottoms and stems)
½ cup green pepper, chopped
2 tablespoons parsley, chopped
1 teaspoon salt
1 teaspoon honey (optional)

1. Blend all ingredients until smooth.
2. Chill for 1 to 2 hours, shake and serve.

JANE'S MANGO CRISP
Serves 8

Hawaii's mangos are the most luscious of fruit: juicy, sweet, and creamy. Jane makes this during the summer months when mangos are plentiful, but you can substitute with ripe peaches, nectarines or plums. The housemates love the crisp topping, and it's a hit with Paul as well. Recipe courtesy of Hawaii foodie Joan Namkoong (foodie@hawaii.rr.com).

5–6 cups firm, ripe mango, sliced
juice from 1 lemon
2 tablespoons raw white or turbinado sugar

Topping

1½ cups flour
1½ cups quick cooking oatmeal
2 cups raw white or turbinado sugar
1 teaspoon ground cinnamon
1 teaspoon freshly grated nutmeg
1 cup unsalted butter, frozen for 10 minutes

1. Preheat oven to 350° F.
2. Place fruit in a 9 x 13-inch baking dish or deep pie dish. Sprinkle with lemon juice and sugar; mix together.
3. Mix flour, oatmeal, sugar, cinnamon, and nutmeg together in a bowl.
4. Quickly and carefully grate butter by hand or in a food processor. Toss grated butter with flour mixture using two table knives (or cut cold butter sticks into 8 to 10

pieces and blend into dry ingredients with a pastry blender) until mixture resembles coarse crumbs.

5. Once butter is evenly incorporated, place mixture on top of fruit. Bake for 45 to 60 minutes or until top is browned and crisp. Remove from oven and cool.

6. Serve warm with whipped cream or ice cream.

Hearts of Palm, Avocado, and Jicama Salad

Serves 6

There's no place like home . . . It takes Marissa a while to get it, but when she does, she does. Not only is she grateful to be living in paradise, but she's grateful for the small cow town that's chock-full of farm-fresh produce. For a woman who can't cook, Marissa's discovering that some of the best recipes aren't so difficult after all. Recipe courtesy of Chef Bev Gannon, Hali'imaile General Store (bevgannonrestaurants.com).

1 cup jicama, peeled and sliced thin
1 cup fresh hearts of palm, peeled and cut into ¼-inch-thick rounds
1 avocado, peeled and chopped
1 teaspoon fresh lemon juice

Dressing

3 tablespoons extra-virgin olive oil
2 tablespoons fresh lime juice
2 tablespoons fresh orange juice
1 tablespoon fresh cilantro
1 teaspoon salt
½ teaspoon freshly ground pepper
¼ teaspoon freshly ground ginger
¼ teaspoon grated orange peel

1. In a sauté pan over medium-high heat, sauté hearts of palm for one minute. Add 1 teaspoon lemon juice and sauté for another minute. Allow to cool.

2. In a mixing bowl, whisk together all dressing ingredients.
3. In a separate mixing bowl, combine jicama, hearts of palm, and avocado. Toss with 3 tablespoons of dressing and refrigerate. Refrigerate unused dressing as well. Chill up to 4 hours.
4. Serve on a bed of lettuce. Drizzle remaining dressing over salad and serve.

TIP

If fresh hearts of palm are not available, you can use canned hearts of palm but skip step 1. Canned hearts of palm are soaked in water and usually much softer, and would fall apart if sautéed. Jicama can be substituted with water chestnuts or crisp white turnips.

MARISSA AND PAUL'S
MIDLIFE MAI TAI

Serves 2

Mai tai for one is fine, but two is better. Reunited, Paul and
Marissa want to toast the moment as they sit on the deck of their
house, watching the sun set over the ocean. But champagne
doesn't seem right (been there, done that), and then it hits
them—what better way to celebrate how far they've come than
with a couple of mai tais? And boy, have they earned them. Bottoms up!

> *2 ounces dark rum*
> *2 ounces light rum*
> *2 ounces orange Curaçao*
> *4 ounces orange juice*
> *juice from 1 lime*
> *dash of French orgeat*
> *dash of simple syrup (bar syrup) or rock candy syrup*

Combine all ingredients and shake well, then strain into
two old-fashioned glasses filled with shaved or crushed
ice. Garnish with a sprig of fresh mint, a slice of pineapple, or an orchid blossom for a splash of color.

credits

Pele description and quote on page 53 reprinted with permission from Mardie Lane, Park Ranger, Hawaii Volcanoes National Park (nps.gov/havo).

Hawaiian quotes and translations by Aunty Mary Kawena Pukui (1895–1986), adapted from her book *'Ōlelo No'eau: Hawaiian Proverbs and Poetical Sayings* (Bishop Museum Press, 1983).

SPAM® and SPAM® derived terms are trademarks of Hormel Food and used here with permission.

Recipes used by permission unless otherwise noted.